Throne of Dusk

LOST FAE QUEEN TRILOGY

E. R. JENSEN

TRIGGER WARNINGS

Imprisonment
Torture
Forced proximity
Suicidal thoughts
Graphic fight scenes

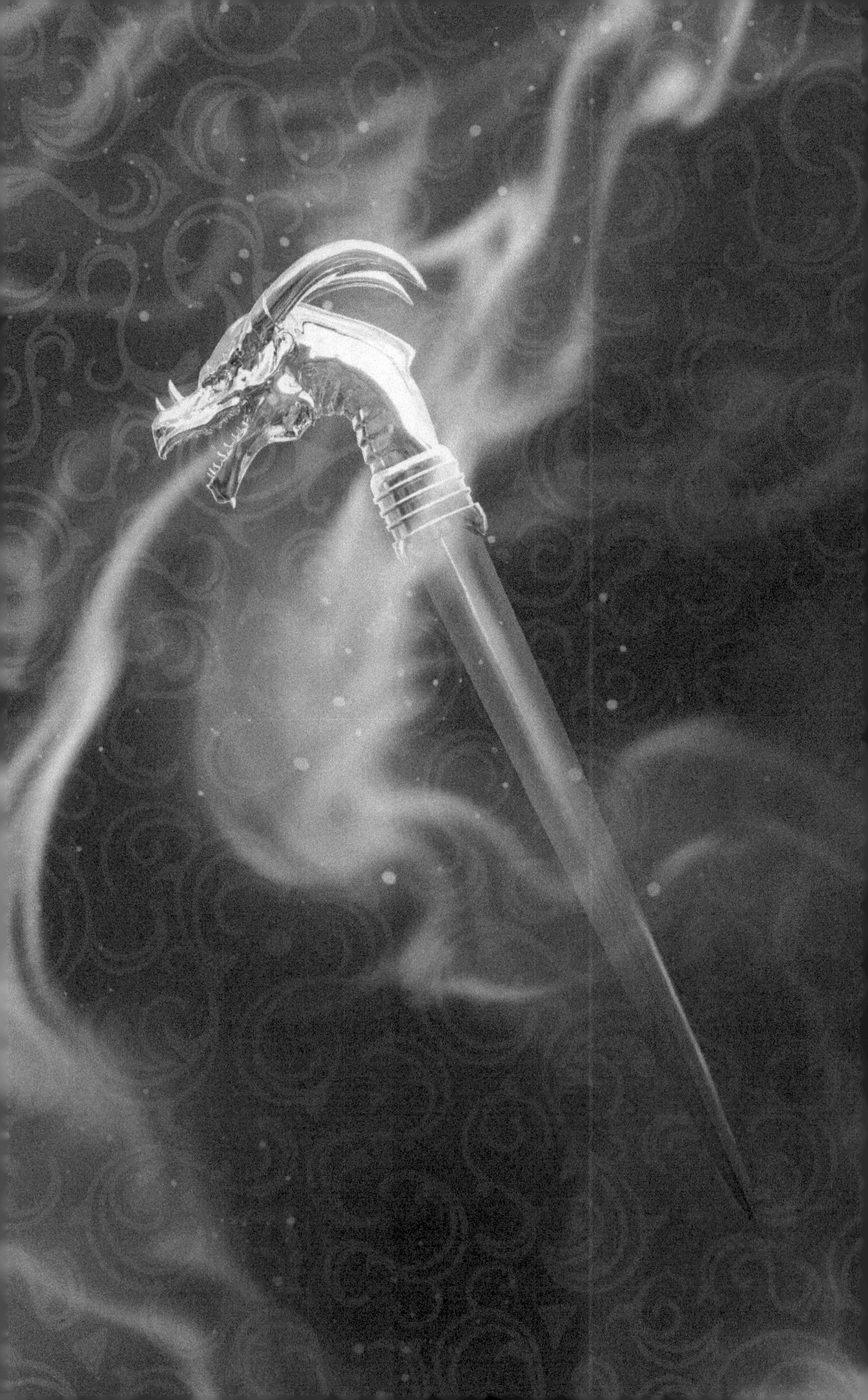

OTHER BOOKS

The Lost Fae Queen Trilogy
Throne of Dusk
Heir of Blood (*coming late 2025*)
Crown of Emeralds (*coming 2026*)

Twisted Talent Series
Hoodwinked in Hotlanta
Spellbound in Spud City

JADE WILDS
COURT O
LOCHAN SGÁILE
WHISP
EMBERGATE
WEST IRON
EMBER MOUNTAIN
COURT OF DUSK
COUR
GLASS OASIS

MOON
HICKET
EMERALD
MINES
EMERALD VALLEY
EAST
SILVER
COURT OF DAWN
THE SUN
N
W
E
S
RT

Part One

One

I sprinted through the vibrant emerald grass, hand curled tightly around my sword, russet braid swinging across my back. It was only a matter of time before the Fae male chasing me caught up. I was faster than a human, but slower than a trained full-blood Fae warrior. My legs were getting tired, but I pushed forward. *I cannot give up.* Up ahead, I spied a rock outcropping and chose it as the spot I would make my stand—my best chance at survival. With a slight course alteration, I felt I could make it in time. A few strides from the target, my toe hit a rock hard, and I lurched forward, arms spread to regain my balance, barely avoiding hitting my head on the large boulder. I took a few deep breaths when a sword kissed my neck.

"I just wanted to talk. Why did you have to run?" asked the cold male voice. "Turn around so we can have a proper conversation."

I slowly turned. The sword stayed at my throat, just far enough away to allow me to face the male. He was tall, taller than any I had seen before. He had teal skin and blue-black hair. A large antler crown sat on top of his head.

"If you wanted to talk, chasing me was not the best way to get my attention," I said. It was a struggle to keep fear out of my voice. The only Fae who wore crowns were the four rulers of the courts. None of them had any reason to pay attention to a nobody like me, unless it was to take my life, whether for sport or some other ill-intentioned purpose.

I saw a flash of gray behind the prince's shoulder. I blinked, assuming I was imagining things. There weren't any wild animals in these woods that would risk getting this close to us. The prince touched the tip of the sword to my throat, applying just enough pressure to draw blood.

"Who are you?" the prince demanded.

I opened my mouth to speak and then realized I didn't know my name. My throat tightened. *Why don't I know my name?*

"Who are you?" the prince demanded again, pressing the sword sharply against my skin. I sucked in a breath, as it was more than just a prick this time. A loud snarl erupted from behind the prince, interrupting my reply, as a huge cat with light gray fur and black spots lunged at him.

Gasping, I sat up in bed. My night shirt clung damply to me underneath the entangled sheet. I peered around the room; the dim light of dawn was starting to creep through my tent flap. Freeing myself from the tangled sheet, I rose and walked to the table for some water. Sometimes my dreams featured a snow leopard in the forest, but never a prince or the snow leopard attacking anyone.

I wasn't sure what to make of it. My lack of magic meant my dreams were just that, *dreams*. Rather than trying to go back to sleep for a short amount of time, I chose to run early and enjoy some time alone. I didn't want to let a bad dream set the tone for the rest of my day.

The dead leaves crunched under my feet as I ran through the bright green forest, weaving through the familiar path in the trees. Almost every morning since I had arrived at the Fae training camp, Jade Wilds, I went on a run.

My heartbeat was a steady thump in my chest. As I entered my fourth lap, I heard the snap of twigs, a telltale sign that I was no longer alone.

"Serafina!" called Fiera. I slowed my speed to allow my close friend, Fiera, to catch up to me.

"Good morning," I said as Fiera reached my side. I resumed my previous pace, and she matched me stride for stride.

We ran in companionable silence for a while. Fiera cocked her head to the side as though listening for something. As a full-blood Fae, Fiera had superior hearing, though my half-Fae hearing was better than a human's. I took a deep breath and held it, focusing on the sounds of the forest. Except there were no sounds of the forest—the birds and squirrels had gone quiet.

I flicked my gaze to Fiera, and she shook her head, giving me the hand signal to keep running. The solid weight of my dagger tucked in my belt was reassuring, though my sword, I thought wistfully, was back in my tent. Fiera had a dagger too, *and* magic. All full-blooded Fae had magic, though their abilities varied. All trainees, except for me, had twice weekly magic training. Instead of magic training, I received lessons in Fae history and law.

Out of the corner of my eye, I saw a glimmer of movement. I leaned backward, and a cloth-tipped arrow sailed just a hair over my chest and thudded into the tree behind me. I yanked the dagger out of my belt and dashed toward a large fallen tree, hoping it would provide cover while Fiera and I devised a plan. Arrows whizzed through the air. To avoid being hit, I executed a low slide and slammed into the tree with an *umph*.

Fiera chuckled from the shadows. "I don't think you needed to be quite that fast."

I rolled my eyes, knowing she was right, but now wasn't the time to dwell on should-haves. Commander Meriel Leoydark, the Fae warrior in charge of the Jade Wilds training camp, took exercises like this seriously.

"Do you still have your dagger?" Fiera asked.

I waved it in the air.

"Well, I lost mine. We're down to one dagger and magic," Fiera said.

"I'm assuming there's at least two trainees out there. Too many arrows for it to just be one archer," I replied.

"My thoughts exactly. If we can pinpoint them, then I can bind them with my magic," Fiera explained.

Binding foes with magic was the strategy we frequently practiced, since it didn't require a huge well of power to temporarily bind someone. In battle, a few seconds could turn the tide.

Growing up in the human kingdom of Gaskal, my parents told me tales of Fae magic and winged horses. I believed they were fantastical stories until eleven years ago, when I ended up at Jade Wilds and discovered that magic was real—and winged horses, too. Upon learning of my half-Fae heritage, I had prayed religiously for magic. Unfortunately, my prayers hadn't been answered.

Assuming the archer would have a high perch, I scanned the trees around us. "There, to the left, on the second branch of the oak tree," I said, pointing, but careful to keep my arm low so as not to make it a target.

Fiera nodded. "On the count of three. One...two...three!"

Bright red magic with orange threads filled Fiera's hands, then disappeared. It reappeared as a rope around the archer in the oak tree. The archer gasped, and I heard a hiss of frustration from who I suspected was the other archer behind me. I spun around and stood up, holding my dagger by the blade, ready to throw. Just as I released the dagger at the archer, who was almost invisible against the trunk of a large maple, Fiera's red-and-orange ropes appeared, forcing the archer to drop his bow and nocked arrow.

The archer scooted sideways, and my dagger hit the maple and fell to the ground. I ground my teeth together, slightly annoyed that Fiera had done all the work.

I hopped over our fallen tree hideout and sprinted toward the bound archer. A stride away, Fiera's ropes disappeared. The archer, a tall, broad-shouldered male Fae with pale blond hair and brown eyes, smirked and threw a punch at my stomach. I ducked and rolled, snagging my dagger out of the leaves before popping up behind him.

I pressed the dagger into his back. "Got ya," I said confidently.

He threw his elbow back, catching me in the stomach. I doubled over and nearly lost my grip on my dagger. Instead of throwing another punch or trying to take my dagger, he merely stood there. "I don't think we've formally met before. I'm Edrym."

As I straightened, I eyed him warily. "Serafina."

Commander Meriel appeared a few strides away. She had long white hair in a ponytail and piercing gray eyes. I preferred to avoid meeting her gaze often because it felt like she could see into my soul, a place I didn't want anyone but me to see.

"Fiera and Serafina. Your response this morning was appropriate. However, Serafina, your timing could improve. By not coordinating with Fiera to bind Edrym, you lost your only weapon and gave Edrym an opening. You could have avoided these events if you still had the dagger. You also failed to find your third foe," Commander Meriel explained.

My eyes widened; we had tried and apparently failed to identify the third. The leaves behind the commander shifted. I tightened my grip on my dagger, when the figure stood up and shook, revealing Ghilanna, my other close friend. Dried leaves and twigs peppered her dark hair.

Ghilanna gave Fiera and I appraising looks. "There were a few times I thought you were going to step on me. My assignment was to wait until you both were close to Edrym and then attack if you subdued him."

At Ghilanna's explanation of her task, I immediately understood the mistake Fiera and I had made—assuming that the foes would not be using camouflage other than blending in with the trees.

Commander Meriel clapped her hands once to get our attention. "Now that you're all warmed up, we will head back to the training yard and begin the morning drills."

I bowed my head in acknowledgement and fell into a single-file line with Edrym in the lead, Ghilanna, then me, and Fiera at the back.

Two

TRISTAN
360 AQ

My fur rippled in the slight breeze as I panted. My back stung where my father, Elre Gilvrye, had struck with a dagger. I hadn't been quick enough to dodge entirely out of the way, but I knew I should count myself lucky. It was just a scrape. To my right, Gantar, in his bear form, was bleeding from a gash on his stomach. To my left, Drannor's right front wolf's paw was dangling uselessly.

I flexed my light gray paws, revealing my deadly claws. I kept my eyes forward, but I could just barely discern motion behind me. Keeping my movements as subtle as possible, I bunched my muscles and leaped forward, spinning to face Elre. A snarl escaped before I could squash it. Elre's eyes darkened in anger, and he charged.

It was against the rules of Glass Oasis to shapeshift into animal form during a Fae-form fight. The same rule applied to shifting to Fae form during an animal-form fight. Once a warrior chose a shape, they had to commit to it. Though annoying, the ancient rule ensured fair fights in Glass Oasis. It also ensured that any of us who were shapeshifters were equally comfortable in combat with either form. Not using one or the other as a crutch.

At the last moment, Elre pulled up. My father was skilled at training us and was not willing to go easy on me because I was his son. I had never figured out if that was because he hated me, or because he wanted me to be better. What I knew was that in my father's eyes, nothing I ever did was the right thing. Whether it was in training or household chores, Elre always found a flaw and punished me for it. More time chopping wood or running additional laps around the village were his favorites.

"Get cleaned up. The lot of you have earned a chance to go to the Glass Fair," Elre announced.

I rocked back on my haunches, eyes wide, tip of my tail flicking the dirt. *Is this a trick?* I glanced over at Gantar and Drannor. They were not hesitating to see if Elre would change his mind. They had already shifted back to Fae form and were sprinting toward their homes.

"Well, what are you waiting for, Tristan? Go get cleaned up. You know very well you can't go into the Glass Fair as a snow leopard. You'd terrify the humans," Elre said.

I closed my eyes and shifted to my Fae form. The graze on my back was barely noticeable, as it had nearly healed. I bowed to my father and then headed quickly to our cottage before he could give me more orders.

Taking a deep breath, I savored the smells of herbs and cooking meat wafting down the path from the Glass Fair. Once a year, the humans from Gaskal would travel to the Fae village, Glass Oasis, for a weeklong market. Gaskal was home to the human-run gold mines. This was our best opportunity to trade for gold and the humans' superior silver-iron weapons. Especially if humans also came from Quetzal, the human territory with iron mines.

8

Glass Oasis was home to the highest concentration of Fae shapeshifters of any Fae territory. Many of the humans came for the opportunity to see a Fae shapeshift in person. Which meant there usually were at least one or two Fae who had market stalls where the humans could pay to watch a Fae shapeshift. Despite our leaders' disapproval of shapeshifting for money, they did not prevent it. Likely because it generated the highest profit when compared to all the other commodities being sold at the Glass Fair.

There was a rumor going around that Prince Rhangil Fenmyar of the Court of the Sun was visiting, but I hadn't laid eyes on him or any of his entourage, so I assumed it was just a rumor. My father had not indicated the prince was indeed coming. I decided that whether the prince was at Glass Oasis would change nothing for me and I shouldn't waste time worrying about it.

The Glass Fair was set up in the park at the center of the village. Row after row of colorful vendor stalls squeezed into every available space. The yellow tents were from Gaskal, dark gray from Quetzal, and the bright blue belonged to the Fae residents of Glass Oasis and the surrounding areas. Though each tent had its primary color, the owners could decorate the fronts however they pleased.

The wares ranged from prepared food and fresh fruits and vegetables to weapons, clothing, and more. I had a few coins my mother had given me to buy a snack. I sped by the Quetzal weapon tent, not wanting to tempt myself by looking at the silver-iron weapons. My father had one, as did several of our most highly trained warriors, but they were expensive. Until I had completed my warrior training at a training camp, I could not earn money to afford such superior weapons.

As I paid for a meat pie from a Gaskal tent, out of the corner of my eye I saw Gantar and Drannor at the Quetzal weapon tent. I walked in the other direction, not wanting to be a part of whatever they were doing. Gantar's shout rang out. *I should just ignore whatever they're doing,* I told myself. Unable to ignore my instincts to help, I turned toward the weapon tent. Gantar had a sword in his hand and the human who ran the tent was angrily motioning for Gantar to put down the sword. Drannor was rigid like a statue, his hand on his sword hilt, but he had not drawn it yet.

I reached for my sword and grimaced when I realized I had left it at the cottage. "Gantar, what's going on?" I called, trying to keep my voice conversational.

"None of your business, Tristan," Gantar said, keeping his eyes on the vendor.

Edging closer, I grabbed Gantar's arm. "Did you pay for the sword?"

The vendor shook his head, confirming what I had thought—that Gantar was trying to bully the vendor into giving him the sword. "It is my right to have this sword," snarled Gantar.

"No, it's not. You know as well as I do that the Glass Fair happens so we can purchase or do an equal trade for any items that we want. You cannot steal," I chided, keeping my grip on Gantar's arm.

"The blade is mine," Gantar repeated and shook my hand off. He turned to face me, his back now to the weapon vendor. The sword was between us; I glanced at it, then back at Gantar's eyes.

"Stealing is forbidden," I warned, tension spread through me. *Diffusing the situation is not working.*

"It was a gift," Drannor said, finally chiming in.

"I don't believe you," I replied, trying to keep the edge out of my voice.

Gantar jabbed at me with the tip of the sword, and I jumped back, raising my fists. He jabbed again. I blocked it with my arm and the blade sliced down my forearm, splitting the skin from wrist to elbow. I sucked my lip as pain welled up. *Those silver-iron blades sure are sharp.*

Gantar swung again, and I danced out of the way, droplets of blood spraying around me. I snapped my foot out in a kick and Drannor chopped down at my leg. I recoiled my leg to keep from having it cut off. Shooting glances around me, it looked like no one else noticed or cared that the three of us were fighting.

Gantar and Drannor came at me, much like in our two-on-one training exercises, except I didn't have a weapon. *I can shift*, I reminded myself. Yet I hesitated. If I shifted, I would break a major rule—by taking an "unfair advantage." I snorted. To shift would be to protect myself against Gantar and Drannor taking an unfair advantage over *me*.

Drannor's blade sliced across my bicep. I snarled in pain. Blood dripped down my arm as I backed up a step, but they kept pressing forward. I inhaled, nostrils flaring. The wound on my forearm was already starting to heal, yet if this kept going, it would only be a matter of time before they did severe damage to me. They were giving me no choice. In the blink of an eye, I shifted from Fae to snow leopard, falling forward onto light gray paws. I snarled again, louder, and bounded forward, slashing with my razor-sharp claws, aiming for Drannor's legs. Ribbons of blood bloomed on his pants in the wake of my claws. I did my best to not go as deep as I could. As much trouble as I would be in for shifting, it would be even greater if I were to kill either of them.

Out of the corner of my eye, I saw Gantar sweep his sword down toward my head. I sidestepped out of the way, considering my next move, when a big, booming voice rang out over the fair. "What is the meaning of this?"

Gantar lowered his sword and took a few steps back. I gave him a wary look and shifted, wanting to face whomever it was when I could talk and they could read my expression. My father and Prince Rhangil were walking toward us. My father was furious, but I couldn't tell what the prince was thinking.

Magic spilled from the prince's fingers, yanking the sword from Gantar's hand and floating it to the prince. The prince confiscated Drannor's weapon as well.

Without an explanation, my father stepped over to me and held his sword to my throat. Blood trickled where the sword pierced my skin. I wasn't worried because I healed quickly, as did all Fae—if he didn't decide to behead me.

"You are a disgrace to the Gilvrye name," my father growled. I kept my eyes focused on the floor. I knew no words that came out of my mouth would do me any good; instead I pressed my lips together and prayed that he wouldn't kill me.

Prince Rhangil stepped forward, his eyes going over all three of us in distaste. "The three of you know better than to brawl in the middle of the village, let alone during the Glass Fair." The prince paused, letting his words settle on us. "However, that is the least of my concerns. *You*, Tristan Gilvrye, broke one of the most important rules of Glass Oasis. Tell me, which rule did you break?"

I swallowed hard and my father's sword nicked my skin again, a warning of what would come if I failed to answer. "I shapeshifted in a fight in Glass Oasis when my opponents were in Fae form."

"Good, you are aware of your transgression. I could punish you by death," Prince Rhangil said.

I licked my lips; my throat had gone dry. I had not expected the prince to be here, and I did not know whether he would order my execution or offer an alternative punishment.

"You have two choices. I will be nice and let you decide. Embergate or execution," Prince Rhangil announced.

I blanched. Embergate was the Fae training camp ruled by Prince Tanyth Neriwraek, who hated shapeshifters to the point he actively had them hunted and killed. *How do they expect me to survive Embergate?*

"Decide now. You will leave within the week," ordered Prince Rhangil.

I took a shaky breath. I had only one option, because I did not want to die. "I choose Embergate."

Three

SERAFINA

411 AQ

Commander Meriel ordered us to gather our gear for drills. I was wearing a tan tunic and a thin pair of pants, but my training armor was missing. With Commander Meriel's approval, Fiera, whose magic gave her extraordinary skills in weapon and armor crafting, had created heavy leather pants imbued with magic for me. The heavy leather did not have the longevity of plate armor but was an excellent substitute for training.

I put first one foot, then the other in the legs of the leathers, before tugging on the material to get it to slide all the way up. When they were almost up, I started bouncing and yanking. "There!" I gasped. They were finally up to my waist.

I sat down and quickly pulled on my boots, then grabbed a weighted leather vest from the rack and my belt, which had a sword scabbard on my left hip and a long knife on my right. After one more check of my gear, satisfied everything seemed in order, I tucked a strand of loose hair behind my ear, then headed out of my tent and toward the training ring.

Commander Meriel was waiting for us. Fiera approached from the other side of the village, her pale skin and fiery red hair in two braids down her back, a dark blue tunic peeking out from the gaps in her armor. Ghilanna had just stepped into the training ring, her dark midnight skin and hair a stark contrast to Fiera. Ghilanna had a bright purple tunic under her armor. *If she had been wearing that tunic earlier, I would have noticed her under the leaves.*

I wondered if Commander Meriel would comment on it, but instead she said, "Are you ready for our last training session?"

The words caught me off guard. "How can you be so sure it will be our last?"

Commander Meriel shrugged. "Because the next time you are in a training session, I will not be the one leading it."

I raised my eyebrow, but decided it wasn't my place to press. The commander had clearly decided she would no longer be training us. I didn't need to know anything else.

Ghilanna didn't have the same reservations as I did. She took a deep breath then spoke. "What did you *see*, Commander?"

The commander ran a hand lightly over her face, sweeping stray strands of her white hair away. "What I *saw* is none of your concern."

My mouth twitched in amusement. Ghilanna's choice to press the matter hadn't worked. I had learned over the years that the commander only revealed visions she had if they were pertinent to our training. I could count less than a handful of times she had mentioned having a vision. Commander Meriel was the only seer I encountered in the past eleven years. My training included little information about seers, only the basics. A seer could see the future or speak prophecy.

Commander Meriel raised her hand and beckoned. I took half a step forward, but then I realized that she wasn't signaling me. Edrym and a handful of other trainees, who had been waiting to be included, were the ones Commander Meriel was beckoning. Throwing a glance over my shoulder, I realized the two closest to Edrym were brothers. They both had pitch-black hair, olive skin, and brown eyes with flecks of green.

"Now, trainees, if you would begin," Commander Meriel ordered.

Fiera, Ghilanna, and I were in front with Edrym and the other trainees in lines behind us. I was itching to ask why Edrym was here. He wasn't part of Jade Wilds that I was aware of, and I found his inclusion in our training this morning puzzling.

"One," Meriel shouted. All of us brought the swords up in a middle block.

"Two," Commander Meriel shouted. We thrust to the right. The counting continued, and we worked our way through all ten moves before she began with combinations. I could feel the sweat trickling down my back. The sweat plastered the escaped strands of hair to my face.

"Nine, ten, one," shouted Meriel. As I began the prescribed combination, the skies opened and dumped absurd amounts of icy rain on us. We were drenched instantly, and the rain was coming down so hard I could barely see.

To my surprise, Commander Meriel signaled for us to halt. "We are going to end the training session for now and resume if the rain lets up later. Go seek shelter in your tents." Without waiting for a response, the commander turned on her heel and disappeared into her tent.

Mouth gaping, I stared in confusion at Ghilanna. "I'm not complaining," my friend said, then headed toward the tent she shared with Fiera.

I dashed for my tent and stopped just inside, not wanting to drench all my belongings in the cascade of water coming off me. The rain was unusually cold, and I was shivering, my teeth clattering together. I wiped off as much of the water as I could, then retrieved a towel from my trunk.

A bead of water fell from my forehead onto my nose. I lifted my finger and flicked it off. I wondered who Edrym had arrived at Jade Wilds with and if the visitor was why the commander had uncharacteristically ended practice because of the rain. I glanced around my tent, trying to figure out what I should do while we waited for the storm to let up, when my tent flap opened and Fiera entered with Ghilanna hot on her heels.

They both looked drier than I was, courtesy of their magic, I reasoned. Ghilanna smiled at me. "You still look like a drowned rat. I can dry you off," she offered, wiggling her fingers, which glowed with soft white magic.

"I'd appreciate it," I replied.

The white magic covered me from head to toe and then disappeared, and I was dry.

"Much better," said Ghilanna.

Fiera said, "Edrym mentioned the upcoming Rose Fair and expressed concerns that it might be canceled."

I tapped my fingers on my thigh. I had been really looking forward to this year's Rose Fair, the annual market on the outskirts of Jade Wilds where human and Fae trade workers would set up temporary shops for a full week. Over the course of the past eleven years, I had only made it to one Rose Fair, and that was when I was twelve. Whether by design or just an unlucky coincidence, the other years I had missed it I was scheduled for an intense two-week training session outside of the training camp or healing from injuries and indisposed.

"I really hope it's not canceled. I can go this year," I replied.

Ghilanna frowned. "I thought you went last year."

I shook my head. "No. I made it back from training for the last day, but that was when the horse stepped on my foot and bruised it. Commander Meriel told me to spend the whole day in bed and forbade me from going to the market."

"Last year is when Ghilanna tried kissing the human male," Fiera said.

I raised my eyebrows. I hadn't heard this story before. "Really?"

Ghilanna groaned and covered her face. Fiera snickered. "Yes! The male, he bargained with her for a kiss. A silver-iron sword for a kiss. You know how hard it is to get a silver-iron sword, right?"

I nodded in confirmation. The human silver-iron weapons were superior to the Fae-made iron blades, both in weight and ability to hold an edge. It was one of the primary commodities that the Fae traded with humans to acquire, other than the raw metal.

Fiera continued, "Well. Ghilanna took him up on the offer. Little did she know he intended to kiss her with his tongue, and his teeth were all rotten!"

I cringed and could almost smell the rotting teeth in the tent. I shuddered, hoping it would go away. I couldn't imagine kissing a male, let alone one with rotten teeth.

"It was disgusting," Ghilanna replied. "But he gave me the silver-iron sword. I guess I met whatever his expectations were. Or maybe it was just the ability to brag that he'd kissed a Fae. The worst part about the whole thing was that Commander Meriel made me turn over the sword. She said she'll give it back after I graduate."

Inhaling deeply, I noticed the heavy thud of rain on the tent had decreased to an occasional patter. "Maybe we should prep to train again?" I suggested.

Ghilanna nodded, taking the hint that I wanted a bit of time for myself. "See you shortly."

Fiera gave me a hug, then they both left. I peered out of the tent and the rain was just the barest drizzle. Though no one was walking around, large puddles riddled the hard-packed dirt, some too big to go around and deep. *Maybe we won't resume training.*

Once I was certain Fiera and Ghilanna had returned to their tent and no one else was around, I stepped out of my tent and, as stealthily as possible, made my way over to Commander Meriel's. My friends might be content to wait to see who our visitor was. I was not. I found a spot to crouch between stacks of supplies near the back of the commander's tent.

I immediately recognized the commander's voice when she spoke, but it took a while before I could identify her visitor by voice: Prince Almar Vacaryn. Before I could stop it, I felt my lip curling in distaste. *Of course, he would have to be the visitor.* He had made it abundantly clear the first time we met on my second day at Jade Wilds that he thought I should not exist and had even then tried to pressure Commander Meriel into having me executed, citing my existence as a half-blood was an abomination and that the unspoken agreement among Fae was that any known half-bloods were executed upon identification. This agreement was the primary reason—according to Ghilanna—that there weren't any half-bloods, other than me.

As ruler of the Court of the Moon, Prince Almar theoretically had the authority to issue the order. However, he answered to King Pharaan, who not only ruled the Court of Dawn but all Fae, and after eleven years I knew enough of the Fae politics and history to know that such a move on Prince Almar's part would draw the king's unwanted attention. I avoided Prince Almar as much as possible, making sure I was busy whenever he visited the encampment.

"She doesn't belong on the battlefield. Her human half makes her too weak compared to a full-blooded Fae. The risk is too great. King Pharaan will blame me if she were to die, even if it is not my fault, but hers for being mediocre," Prince Almar said in a whiney voice.

His viewpoint was not new to me. Every few days I would hear similar words whispered behind my back: that I am weak, like all humans, incapable of training to the level of "perfection" that the Fae could and therefore unable to hold my own in a sword fight, whether it was one-on-one or in a full-scale battle. Besides the perceived human weaknesses with sword fighting, there was also the factor that, unlike Fae, humans did not possess magic. However, a human could wield a Fae-made magic object and they had silver-iron weapons. It was the silver-iron weapons and sheer quantity of humans above all else that made the Fae wary of them.

Meriel clicked her tongue in disproval. I could only imagine the look of annoyance Meriel usually gave when she clicked her tongue like that. I felt a smile creeping up my lips. "If she doesn't fight, the lost Fae queen prophecy won't be fulfilled," she declared. The smile faded when she said "prophecy." From everything I had gleaned from Fiera and Ghilanna over the years, most of the prophecies were like the human stories of Fae: make-believe to teach the young a valuable lesson. *But didn't I find out when I arrived at Jade Wilds that Fae* do *have magic and winged horses* are *real?*

"The lost Fae queen prophecy isn't even real. It's just a story for young Fae," Prince Almar scoffed, confirming my original thought.

The commander clicked her tongue again. "You're naïve if you really don't believe that prophecies are real, especially when you have witnessed firsthand one being fulfilled. Your great-grandmother was a seer herself. The prophecy being real isn't my point, though. Serafina has proven herself repeatedly in training that she has mastered the Fae sword fighting techniques. Even without possessing magic, she is far more capable than a mere human would be. Why is it so difficult for you and the others to believe that a half-Fae is worthy of our acceptance? Serafina has put in just as much time training all these years as the other full-blood Fae trainees have. Do we not owe her the opportunity to prove herself?"

A heavy pause. I reminded myself I needed to keep breathing and stay hidden.

"I suppose if she were to die at Emerald Valley, that would prove that she should have been executed years ago," said Prince Almar.

I wished I could see Commander Meriel's face to know what she was thinking. "Have you ever spent the time to see Serafina? I mean, really *see* her, and what she is capable of?" A light pause. "'Look closely or you might be blinded, for when the Fae queen returns, not all will know her. People of all races will follow her.'"

Prince Almar let out a throaty growl. "I fail to see how, if perchance the prophecy is *real,* anyone with human blood running through their veins could possibly be qualified for such a role."

I sneezed twice and then winced, hoping no one heard me. I knew Prince Almar didn't like, and possibly hated, me, but I had never thought that should the opportunity to fight as a Fae present itself, I would be barred from doing so. I had put in hard work over the past eleven years and was worthy of their respect in combat, at the very least. Maybe when I had first arrived their comments of a silly, worthless human had been justified, but it had not taken me long to learn how to hold a sword properly.

Commander Meriel began speaking again. "You need to leave this tent, Prince, before I give in to my urge to challenge you to a duel. Your opinions are noted. Now I would like to resume training since the rain has ceased," she said tersely.

I kept still behind the crates; my legs were protesting the position I had chosen. I waited until I heard Prince Almar's footsteps departing and then cautiously stood up. I jumped when Commander Meriel appeared in front of me. "How much did you hear?"

I gasped, my lips parting, wondering how she knew I was listening. "All of it," I said meekly.

"Good," Meriel said and gave my arm a squeeze. I gazed at her curiously, surprised that she approved of eavesdropping. "You know I am a seer." I nodded in confirmation, then she continued. "Because there are so few prophecies that come to fruition, many Fae forget they can be *real*. I suppose it's easier to believe that you have control over your own life and that there isn't a higher power who has the reins."

Meriel said softly, "Now, go grab your sword. We're going to resume practice."

I bowed and then went to my tent to retrieve my sword. An old memory bubbled to the surface of my mind. The day I turned sixteen.

Commander Meriel handed me a small, wrapped package. I opened it eagerly; I rarely got presents. I ripped off the brown wrapping and found in my hands a stack of letters. The writing on them looked familiar. I looked up. "Who are these from?"

Meriel gave me a sad smile. "Your mother."

A sob escaped my lips, and I ran a finger over the words. "She wrote to me?"

Meriel sighed. "She wrote these a long time ago and said if the time was ever right, I should give them to you."

I walked into my tent and went for the top drawer in the desk and retrieved the letters. I opened the letter on top and began reading.

DEAREST SERAFINA,

I WAS GRATEFUL WHEN YOU WERE BORN WITH NO OBVIOUS FAE CHARACTERISTICS, BECAUSE I KNEW HOW HARD IT WOULD BE FOR YOU TO FIT INTO THE HUMAN SOCIETY OF GASKAL WITH THEM. YOUR FATHER AND I RAISED YOU AS A HUMAN AND OUT OF THE PALACE. IT WAS THE BEST WAY TO GIVE YOU A

NORMAL UPBRINGING. YOUR GRANDFATHER, KING LEONARD HELIAS, DID NOT APPROVE OF A MIXED MARRIAGE AND MADE IT ABUNDANTLY CLEAR TO YOUR FATHER THAT IF HE WENT THROUGH WITH IT, NEITHER GARETH NOR ANY OF HIS CHILDREN WOULD EVER BE IN LINE TO RULE.

YOUR FATHER DID NOT CARE ABOUT THE CONSEQUENCES. AS THE THIRD SON, HE KNEW THE ODDS OF EVER BEING MORE THAN A SPARE WERE INCREDIBLY SLIM. ESPECIALLY SINCE HIS OLDEST BROTHER ALREADY HAD TWO CHILDREN.

SERAFINA, WE BELIEVE YOU WILL CHOOSE THE BEST PATH FOR YOURSELF. NO MATTER WHERE IT LEADS. YOU ARE LOVED, MY DEAREST. NEVER FORGET THAT.

YOURS ALWAYS & FOREVER,
SOLANA

I wiped away the tear trickling down my cheek, wishing that I could see her one last time. I had so many questions. Since I came to Jade Wilds, I knew that human-Fae relationships were discouraged, though no one had ever explained why. I carefully folded the letter up and returned the stack to my desk drawer.

I clasped my sword belt around my waist and headed out to the training yard, where I was certain everyone was waiting on me.

Four

I blinked in the bright sunlight. There was no evidence in the sky of the huge thunderclouds that had been there just a few hours before. However, puddles and mud spotted the ground. Fiera and Ghilanna were waiting for me. I was secretly hoping Edrym would not be at this training.

As we made our way to the training yard, Fiera asked, "What do you think about us going to battle?"

"I wish we knew more. Not just 'You're going to Emerald Valley to fight humans,'" I replied.

"We could always ask. They might give us more information," Fiera pointed out.

"Or we will be told it's none of our business," I muttered.

Fiera gave me a sad smile. "The Fae have never trusted humans, nor humans Fae. Our history is littered with skirmishes and small-scale battles. Usually the humans back down, but once or twice it has turned into an all-out war. With the Fae magic and the human silver-iron weapons, the outcome of the two wars was much closer than many care to admit. *We* almost lost."

I searched her face. "Do you think that real peace would ever be possible?"

Ghilanna laughed. I was confused. What I had said wasn't funny. She caught my expression and stopped laughing. "Sorry. I forgot that although you have history lessons, there is so much more to Fae than what you can find in a few textbooks. There was always tension between humans and Fae. The four human kings—Lord of the North, Lord of the South, Lord of the East, and Lord of the West—each have access to metal mines."

I nodded; this was something I had grown up knowing.

Fiera continued, "Fae do not have metal mines in our territories, but each of the four Fae territories could craft different magical objects. Throughout our history, there have been a variety of trade agreements, including the establishment of annual markets, allowing for the exchange of metal ore for magical objects. But there is little trust between Fae and humans, and often things go awry."

"If tension is always high between humans and Fae, why do I exist?" I blurted out.

Fiera gave me a sly smile. "Because your parents had sex, and your mother got pregnant."

I rolled my eyes. "Yes, I'm aware of how babies are made, thanks. What I was saying is that if nothing ever works out between humans and Fae, why would my mother have wanted to become involved with a human?"

"Since I never knew your mother and I know nothing about your Fae family, I am definitely not the one you should be directing that question to," Fiera said. "Now if you don't mind, I'd like to arrive at the training yard before Commander Meriel decides we need to clean the latrines because we're late."

I nodded, and we broke into a jog. None of us wanted the dreaded latrine duty.

Commander Meriel was waiting for us. To my surprise, none of the other trainees were here—not Edrym, nor any of the other residents of Jade Wilds.

"Where is everyone?" Ghilanna asked.

Commander Meriel spoke, and I could hear the frustration in her voice. "Prince Almar has requested that everyone except Serafina participate in a drill he is running in the forest."

I frowned at being excluded. "Commander, what am I supposed to do?"

The commander replied, "You can practice in the western training area if you would like. I know it is empty right now."

I nodded. When my friends and commander had departed, I headed for the western training area. For reasons unknown to me, it was the one that the younger Fae in training avoided. Whenever I had used it, usually on my own, no one else had been there.

I slowed my brisk walk as I approached the western training area. As I expected, it was empty. Wood rail ran around the perimeter, preventing any sparring from spilling out and those walking around the camp from being unexpectedly in the middle of a training session. I hopped over the fence and stepped into the center of the space. I worked my way through the warmup stretches and exercises. The first time was slow and the second I increased my speed. By the time I finished the last exercise, I could feel sweat beading on my brow and was regretting my decision to not dress in layers.

I gave myself a mental shrug. In less than two days, we'd be making our way to Emerald Valley to fight in a battle against a human king. While I knew I could decide when I wanted to practice, I could not dictate when I would fight in a battle. The conditions might be favorable with perfect weather, or we could slog through heavy mud. Which meant the more I trained in suboptimal conditions, the easier it would be for me to handle myself when it mattered on the battlefield.

Our overarching training aim was to be as prepared as possible and able to get out of any situation that would arise. It was one of the key reasons that the Fae supplemented their sessions in the camp training areas with practice scenarios outside of camp. When I first arrived here eleven years ago, I had resisted when they told us we had to train in the forest when it was pouring rain. Now I understood how much it had helped hone my skills. What options were available if my hand was too slippery to keep a secure grip on my sword and how to take advantage of an opponent who had dropped his sword before he or she could recover it. How to use my surroundings to give myself an advantage over my opponents.

The western training yard comprised a low fence bordering the space and compacted dirt. There was a white circle painted in the dirt for those who wished to practice with a penalty for going out of bounds. Since I was alone, I stood within the circle, wanting to use it to keep my drills tight.

Outside of the fence, on the north side, was a small shed with equipment for archery, an assortment of wooden practice weapons, and various targets. The sword I had strapped to my side was iron. It was heavy, but I had gotten used to its weight. None of the trainees had silver-iron weapons, or at least not that I knew of.

I smiled to myself. Here at Jade Wilds, in the company of Fiera and Ghilanna, who were like an adoptive family, I had carved out a small piece of home. I hoped after the time I spent at Emerald Valley for the battle, I would still be welcome here.

Finished with my warmup, I began working through each of the ten maneuvers, keeping my motions smooth and precise. Once I completed a set, I increased my speed and repeated the process, increasing speed by about ten percent per set. I did the final round at full speed twice and finished with a spin.

I saw someone moving out of the corner of my eye and turned, my sword pointed in their direction. It was Edrym. Given

Commander Meriel had said everyone except me was training with Prince Almar, I had not expected company. I lowered my sword, realizing to him I must seem ridiculous, expecting a threat from within the safety of camp.

"You're pretty good," he said and stepped over the fence, heading toward me.

I stared at him, trying to make my mind work. It was rare that outsiders paid me any heed. Hell, it was rare that I got a compliment from anyone at Jade Wilds other than Commander Meriel, Fiera, or Ghilanna. No one else cared how the half-blood did in training. Which suited me just fine. "Uh, thanks," I said lamely.

Edrym didn't seem to notice my reaction to his presence. "Care if I join you?"

I shrugged. "Sure. I just finished my drills."

Edrym smiled. "I know." His response made me wonder how long he had been standing there watching me. I should have been able to detect him as soon as he got nearby. It was a skill I had spent lots of time learning.

Since we were standing in the center, I took several steps back to give Edrym space. He was wearing practical training clothing: a blue short-sleeved tunic and light brown pants. He unsheathed his sword, which I noted was plain iron and utilitarian. I watched him swing a few times and then step to the center, feet spread, sword barely touching the ground.

"I'm ready," Edrym declared.

I raised my eyebrows in disbelief. "You don't want to warm up?" I asked.

"Thank you for your concern. I appreciate it. I did warm up; I was taking part in Prince Almar's training when someone mentioned that you were here and might be interested in a partner," Edrym explained. I waited for him to say who it had been, but he did not divulge any names. It was a little odd, but maybe Fiera or Ghilanna had sent him my way since he had joined us for practice this morning.

"Okay. Ready, one, two, three." We crossed swords and on three he swept wide and slow and brought it back in a fast high strike. I blocked it and then parried it with a slow two-three combination as a lead-in to a low six-nine combination. Edrym easily blocked both of my combinations. I was trying to figure out what his tells were; he didn't appear to shift his weight or do anything obvious to indicate his next move.

Edrym stepped to the left and did a backhanded swing, then swapped hands and pivoted, entering a six-eight combination with a middle then a high strike. I blocked the backhand, but his move caught me off balance and my sword skidded off his when I blocked the middle. The high strike sliced through my tunic and left a line of blood. I clenched my teeth, trying to hide my wince. It was just a scratch, but it stung.

He used the momentum he gained and spun, feinting with another backhand swing, then switched his sword back to his right hand and dove for a low three-three. I jumped over the first and skipped out of its way on the second. I had to force myself into a roll to get my balance back. The way Edrym was throwing his strikes was causing me to tip forward instead of staying centered. With the tipped position, I struggled to stay upright when I executed my own strikes.

I darted away from him, trying to regroup, but he followed as though he enjoyed the chase and was taking pleasure in my frustration. Licking my dry lips, I considered my options to demonstrate I was competent with a sword. Decision made, I leaped to the right and then to the left, and a moment before I reached him, pivoted and swung my sword in an arc. As Edrym raised his sword to block, I chopped upward, hitting his sword hard and forcing him to give up a step. I pursued Edrym with a five-one middle combination and parried his retaliatory strike with a six. To my relief I found I was no longer tipping forward.

There was a flash in the corner of my eye, and I turned my head to see what it was. Edrym used my distraction to his advantage, stomping hard on my foot, startling me. He did a middle-low strike combination. My attempts at blocking were weak and unbalanced. I lost my footing and stumbled forward before tripping over his outstretched foot and falling flat on my face. Edrym's sword tip caressed the back of my neck. "Yield," he ordered.

Flat on my stomach, face in the dirt, I only had one option. I sighed and turned my head so he could hear my words. "I yield."

Dragging myself off the ground, I kept a firm grip on my sword. Edrym's eyes bored into me, assessing every move I made. When I peered up at him through my lashes, to my surprise, his face was full of unmasked anger. A harsh contrast to the polite male I had been dealing with until mere minutes ago.

"You are a fool to think you stand a chance of doing anything but dying when you go to Emerald Valley," he said coldly.

My eyes widened before I could school my face into a neutral expression. "My orders are to report at Emerald Valley. I presume you must have orders too. Who am I to question my superiors?"

"You are an abomination!" he shouted and charged.

I hesitated, wondering what the hell he was doing, when I realized Edrym was not pretending. He was intending to fight again. I twirled out of the way, and he blew past me. Neither one of us had any sort of armor on, which meant we could do significant harm or even kill one another. Our training taught us to try to de-escalate situations like this when they arose.

"Let's talk," I said, offering Edrym a smile. Ignoring me, he charged again, sweeping his sword from side to side. I stepped out of the way, tapping his sword lightly with mine, hoping to jar him out of whatever mood he was in that was causing this behavior.

Footsteps crunched on loose gravel, followed by a thump as someone jumped over the rail. Shooting a glance over my shoulder, I recognized the brothers from the training session entering the ring. They spread out behind me on either side, with Edrym in the center.

In a low voice, Edrym greeted them. "Jassin. Alassin."

I rolled my shoulders back, making sure I was loose and ready. The Fae had strict rules for training, which was, if you're being very loose in the definition, what Edrym and I were doing. If Jassin and Alassin attacked, they'd be breaking the rules, allowing me to use any fighting style I wanted.

Out of the corner of my eye I saw movement as Jassin came at me. I stepped to the left and turned, parrying his strike and continuing the swing to strike at Edrym on my other side. I was certain Alassin had gone around behind me. I watched Edrym the closest because Jassin kept throwing him looks as though he wasn't sure what to do and was hoping Edrym would give him orders.

Keeping my face expressionless, I took a short step forward and then dropped into a roll. As I rolled past Jassin, I snapped my leg out, aiming for his calf. My kick connected, and he staggered sideways. I jumped up and spun, blocking Edrym's strike and ducking under Alassin's. I started a one-two combination and at the last moment, instead of striking with my sword, I did a left hook kick, which connected hard with Alassin's stomach, earning a loud string of curses. *Maybe someone will hear us and put an end to this madness.* I knew, though, that if I didn't end it myself, they would just attack me again, whether here or when we were at Emerald Valley.

Jassin had recovered and was crouched, swinging his sword loosely from left to right. I wasn't entirely sure what he was intending to do other than look stupid. I focused my attention on Alassin; he was trying to sneak up behind me again. Bouncing on the balls of my feet, I took two steps to the right, then two to the left. Alassin shifted his weight and swung, anticipating that I would follow the pattern I had started and take two more steps to the right. Except I went straight, aiming for his calves with a low strike combination. He blocked the first one, but I pivoted and came up behind him, slashing at his unprotected calf. The sword sliced through flesh and hit bone. I yanked on it, but it stuck. Muttering to myself, I gripped my sword with both hands and pulled. Alassin let out a high-pitched shriek of pain and I stumbled backward from the momentum. Jassin's sword made a shallow cut across my left arm. Blood trickled down and onto the ground.

I did my best to ignore the wound. Edrym lunged, and I blocked. Our swords locked. Putting my weight into it wasn't enough compared to Edrym's larger stature. I narrowly missed tripping over Alassin's curled-up form.

I twisted my wrist and my sword slid free. Shuffling backward, I kept Edrym and Jassin in front of me. Of the three of us, I was the most injured, though I was determined not to give up.

Edrym and Jassin shared not-so-subtle glances. Both shifted their shoulders and rocked back on their heels before they sprinted forward at the same time. Except they made a mistake, leaving a gap in the middle. At the last moment, I tucked into a roll right through the gap. Their swords whistled over my head and slammed together, while I popped up to my feet behind them and slashed at their unprotected backs. I made many small slices across both before they untangled themselves and Jassin turned around. I easily blocked his wild swing to the left but didn't see Edrym's jab from the right. His sword tip stabbed my right thigh. I threw an elbow out, popping Jassin in the ribs when he stepped in close. Edrym yanked his sword out of my thigh, sending a bright red spray over both of us. I wobbled but held my feet firm.

Edrym smiled viciously at me. "You do not belong here. Your mother was a whore."

The jibe at my mother hit a nerve. Anger filled me and I screamed in first rage and pain as the ache in my thigh intensified. I leveled my sword at him and charged forward. My sprint was not nimble; my leg hurt too much, and I wanted to save the last bit of energy for one ultimate move. His eyes got wide, and he brought his sword up to block as I leaped upward. Instead of meeting his sword with mine, I aimed my foot for his face. I heard a crunch as my boot connected with his nose. My momentum propelled me over the top of him, and I tucked into an awkward roll to soften my landing.

Edrym began screaming as I lay panting on the ground. I knew I had to get up. Jassin was still somewhere. The cold tip of his sword caressed the back of my neck. He pressed down, and I felt the trickle of blood as it pierced my skin.

I could feel the stomp of booted feet vibrating through the ground before I could hear anything. Someone removed the sword tip from my neck, and I sat up.

Prince Almar, Commander Meriel, and someone I didn't recognize were standing at the head of a group of twenty Fae warriors in full armor, weapons drawn. "What is the meaning of this?" demanded Prince Almar. His eyes locked with mine I tried to hold his gaze, but everything was fading around me. I wasn't sure why.

I felt cool hands on my face and blinked a few times. Commander Meriel was frowning at me. "You've lost a lot of blood." I stayed silent, not sure what to say when her statement was likely true.

I heard sobbing somewhere behind me, but the commander's face was fading again.

"Serafina," she said, snapped her fingers in front of my face.

"What?" I mumbled, not even sure if my words were coherent.

"Why were you fighting?" Meriel said.

"I didn't start it," I protested weakly. "I was practicing by myself." Then I could feel it, the wounds knitting themselves back together. I was being healed with Fae magic.

"Edrym asked to join me. He was polite at training earlier, so I thought it would be fine," I whispered, my thoughts becoming clearer.

"Edrym was domineering, but the session could still be considered a training session. When Alassin and Jassin joined in, I knew it was no longer training. I changed tactics," I said, face flushed, expecting to get reprimanded for my choice.

Commander Meriel smiled. "You have been training for situations like this and the ability to adapt when circumstances of a fight change. I don't have any issue with what you did in your own defense."

I glanced down at my arm and then leg. Though my wounds had healed, I was covered in blood, but feeling more normal. "Prince Almar will not like it."

Meriel shook her head. "If they had acted honorably, and you were the one who turned it from practice into a proper fight, then yes, he would punish you. But these are his warriors who crossed the line. He does not take situations like this lightly." Meriel waved her hand, motioning for someone.

Fiera and Ghilanna hopped over the fence and offered me hands to stand up. I smiled gratefully. Meriel looked at us. "They will help you get cleaned up and find new clothes."

"Thank you," I said.

"You're welcome, but I did not do anything. Today, this was all you," Meriel replied.

Fiera and Ghilanna led me away.

I lay in bed with my eyes closed, running through the meditation exercise.

A rock wall pressed against my back. Sharp stones pierced the skin.

A tall Fae male with teal skin and braided blue-black hair faced me, sword raised, his expression an icy mask. On top of his head was a crown of antlers. He also had a necklace of some sort of animal teeth or claws on a bright gold chain.

"Little warrior, why did you run?" asked the Fae prince, for I was sure he was a prince and was a ruler of one of the four Fae courts.

"I rarely stand around and wait for someone to stab me," I retorted. To my chagrin, my voice wavered.

I saw a flash of gray and black spots behind the prince's shoulder. A beast is coming to my aid? I wondered.

"Little warrior, what is your name?" the prince demanded.

I opened my mouth to speak and then realized I didn't know my name. My throat tightened. Why don't I know my name?

"Who are you?" the prince demanded again, pressing the sword against my ribs.

I opened my mouth to reply when the beast, a huge snow cat with light gray fur and black spots, leaped toward the prince.

I screamed and woke up thrashing, then realized I was in bed and must have fallen asleep. Hand to my chest, I tried to calm myself when I heard a commotion outside. I quickly checked my appearance in the mirror and then stepped out of my tent.

There was a male Fae wrapped in a gray cloak with the hood pulled up, making it difficult to discern any identifiable features. I could tell he had teal skin and blue-black hair and was wearing some sort of crown that was fashioned in the shape of branches or horns. A chill ran through me, and I rubbed my arms. *Teal skin.* My chest tightened as my dream of a teal-skinned prince flickered into my thoughts.

Commander Meriel strode boldly forward, almost as though she were challenging the male. I stayed in front of my tent, apprehension growing as I noticed all eyes were on the guest.

"Why are you here?" Commander Meriel demanded, marching right up into the male's personal space.

They must know each other well for her to do that, I surmised.

"Hello to you too, Meriel," replied a smooth male voice. He kissed her. Gasping in surprise, I took a few steps backward and almost fell into my tent as my heel hit the threshold. Lightning-quick, Meriel slapped him. The male recoiled and his hood fell back, though being able to see his face did nothing to help me identify him, aside from confirming he was indeed wearing a crown and must be one of the ruling princes.

"How dare you come here and then behave as though no time has passed and that our relationship is as it once was," Meriel said, voice carrying across the camp.

A vicious grin crossed the male's face for a moment before his mask dropped back in place along with a relaxed smile. "Is that any way to greet an old friend?"

I could hear footsteps approaching from beyond the training area where we were standing and relief washed through me; we would have backup if whomever this male was attacked. Prince Almar, sword held loosely in his hand, headed for Meriel. Across the way I caught Fiera's eye. She was making some sort of motion with her hands, but I did not know what she was trying to tell me, though I assumed it had to do with the newcomer's identity.

"You are not welcome here, Prince Tanyth," Prince Almar said loudly. The other Fae who had escorted Prince Tanyth visibly bristled at the words. If I had thought Prince Tanyth was difficult to identify, his escort was impossible, because he was wearing a scarf or mask of some sort to obscure his face.

"I haven't done anything wrong or made a move against you, Almar. Why the hostility?" Prince Tanyth asked.

Meriel and Prince Almar exchanged glances. I wondered what the history was among these three.

Meriel replied, "You know why."

Prince Tanyth did not react. "I will leave, but only if you agree to my request to see the half-blood."

"Or what?" demanded Meriel. I thought I saw a brief sparkle of Meriel's blue magic before it vanished from sight.

"I will annihilate you and this camp," Prince Tanyth announced.

My jaw dropped in surprise. *How could one Fae prince possess that much power? Maybe he's bluffing.* I knew Fae had varying levels of magic ability and that princes held their position in part because their magic abilities are significant. But there were many Fae here in the camp, and Prince Tanyth only had himself and his masked attendant. It seemed far-fetched to me he would be capable of following through with his threat.

I could hear the snarl that came from Prince Almar, but no one contested Prince Tanyth's request. Meriel stepped to the side and turned slightly, so her back was not to Prince Tanyth, but she could see both of us. "Serafina is there. I will give you two minutes and then you must leave."

Prince Tanyth nodded and walked toward me. I stepped away from the tent, wanting room to maneuver if he was stupid enough to try something, even with the witnesses. He halted in front of me and took his time inspecting.

I shook when I realized he was the teal-skinned and antler-crowned Fae prince I had dreamed about. But I had never met him before, so I couldn't understand why I was dreaming about him. He was even more terrifying in person than in my dream. The surrounding air hummed with his magic. *Deadly predator.* I clamped my tongue between my teeth, trying to maintain my composure while he boldly stared.

I expected him to say something, especially since I was certain he could tell I was afraid of him. Instead, at the end of his two minutes, he turned on his heel and retreated. When they reached the edge of the tents, Prince Tanyth and his escort disappeared.

I gasped for air, not having realized that I had been holding my breath. Meriel rushed over. "Are you okay?"

I nodded, trying to take slow breaths. "Yes, he just...well, he just stared at me. I don't understand what was going on."

Commander Meriel frowned. "Of the three Fae princes, Tanyth has the most extreme views on what the human-Fae relationship should be and often reacts without thinking everything through. There is nothing he won't do to achieve his personal goals, other than perhaps protecting his son."

My eyes widened at the commander's explanation and that my fear was justified. *I must pray I never encounter him again.*

Five

TRISTAN
360 AQ

I sat on a rock at the base of a large oak tree just off the narrow trail that was hardly more than a deer track and took a sip of water from my canteen. If I was being honest, I didn't need the break. Although the trail to the summit of Ember Mountain and Embergate was challenging, at twenty I was physically fit enough to manage easily.

Staring up at the summit, the highest peak of Ember Mountain glistening with snow in the distance, I wanted to finally come to terms with my decision to train at Embergate—not that I really had had a choice in the matter. Thankfully Prince Rhangil had assured me he had said nothing to Prince Tanyth about who I was or my magic, only that I chose to train at Embergate, which was a small blessing and meant I could hide the fact that I am a shapeshifter. I would have to embrace my shadow magic and suppress my true nature. Apprehension wound through me at the prospect of never shifting again. *Prince Tanyth is known to hunt Fae shapeshifters.* Lifting my hand, I summoned my shadow magic and dark gray threads wound around my hands and arms.

I wanted to live; of that I was certain. *Whatever it takes.*

I stood up and returned my canteen to my pack and slung it over my shoulder. New trainees at Embergate were not permitted to bring weapons. I adjusted the straps on the pack slightly and then took off at a brisk walk up the path.

When I was about two-thirds of the way to the summit of the mountain, I could see the two sentinel rocks marking the threshold to the training camp. I kept my eyes trained on the rocks and continued my trek.

Blinking as the sunlight reflecting on the snow blinded me, I discovered I was at the top of the summit standing in between the two sentinel stones. A few more steps and the small valley holding Embergate became visible. All the stone buildings were in pristine rows. It almost seemed abandoned for how well kept it was, no sign of movement anywhere within its walls.

Inhaling deeply, I began my descent. The path down was not nearly as steep as it had been going up, likely because the valley was not at the base of Ember Mountain but nestled between its highest peaks. Halfway down was a watchtower. As I neared, I realized just how tall the tower was; it soared toward the sky, and I was certain that anyone inside at the top could see out of the valley and over the edge of the mountains.

As I passed the watchtower, I could see small shapes on the wall surrounding Embergate. *I guess the camp isn't empty after all.* The closer I got, the more details I could make out of the armed Fae on top of the wall. All of them were wearing tunics of red. I recalled trainees were assigned into three different training groups based on their type of magic and that red was one of those groups. *I wonder if each group rotates through keeping watch on the wall, or if only the reds are allowed the privilege.*

When I reached the open gate, one guard on the wall waved to me and I walked inside without hesitation. I had no other choice. If I returned home, my father would execute me; if he found out that I did not report to Embergate within the next few days, then he would send out a search party with a kill order. By entering Embergate, I was choosing life over death. No matter how hard it was going to be, I did not want to die.

A Fae was approaching in a red tunic that clashed with his blue-black hair and light teal-colored skin. He halted and gave me a salute. "Greetings, I'm Travaran Neriwraek. I have orders to get you settled when you arrive."

The name rang a bell. *Court of Dusk.* I mimicked his salute, sure I was doing it wrong. "Greetings, I'm Tristan Gilvrye." Travaran didn't comment, he simply turned on his heel, apparently expecting me to follow him. I hurried to catch up. I knew it would be bad if I got lost on my first day. He led me to a smaller building in the shadows of the wall. We went up a short flight of stairs and through the open door.

"This is where new recruits stay. Once you receive your color group, then you will move into the group barracks. Until then you are stuck here," Travaran explained.

I couldn't tell from his tone or facial expression if it was a good or a bad thing to not have a color group. "How long does it usually take to get a color group?"

Travaran shrugged. "I don't know. I knew which group I was going to be in before I got here. My father told me."

That tidbit of information confirmed that Travaran was the son of Prince Tanyth Neriwraek, ruler of the Court of Dusk. A tremor of fear ran through me. *Does the son hate shapeshifters as much as his father?* Trying to act normal, I settled on a simple question. "How long have you been here?"

"Two days," replied Travaran.

Relief went through me. We were having a normal conversation for new recruits; maybe Travaran was just like me and was an entirely different Fae than his father too. It crossed my mind that most of the trainees came from his court. *Maybe he'll introduce me.*

Inside the barracks were a row of four beds on each wall. Next to each bed was a chair, and that was it. If I could rely on the lack of furniture as any sign, I thought it would be safe to assume that most new recruits did not spend long without a group.

"You can pick whichever bed you like since you're the first to arrive today," Travaran said.

I walked down the row and decided that I would rather have a bed at the end away from the door. That way, anyone coming or going wouldn't disturb me. I set my pack on the bed and then turned to Travaran to see if there was anything else he wanted to tell me. "What do I do now?"

Travaran shrugged. "You get to just wait here. I must go back to my post on the wall. See you around!" He waved and then left.

Plopping down on the bed, I wasn't sure what to do. *This is my home now.* A thread of excitement coursed through me. Whether Embergate was the camp I had wanted to attend, being here in a training camp meant that I had earned my place in Fae society as an adult. When I graduated from Embergate, I would have a new title—warrior, maybe even *elite* warrior if I was lucky. Embergate had one of the highest occurrences of graduates departing with the designation of elite. Fae who were elite warriors could find positions within any court they chose, and often were given the opportunity to climb quickly through the warrior ranks and lead their own groups.

As a trainee I would finally have the chance to go to a genuine party, with females who will have sex even with inexperienced trainees. I stretched out on the bed and closed my eyes, then drifted off into a light sleep.

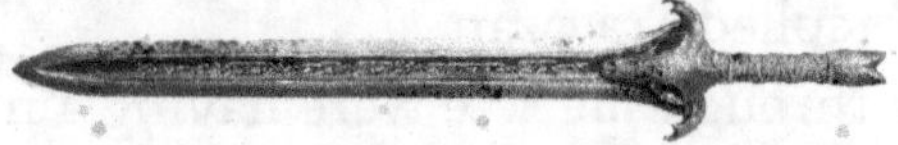

My assumption about how long I would be without a group was grossly incorrect. Three days had passed, and no other recruits had arrived. I was the only trainee who didn't have a group, and it was grating on me. For the most part all the trainees ignored me. Travaran had come by once and given me a training schedule. I joined the red group for sword work, the green group for archery, and the black group for hand-to-hand combat and strength training.

Even without a group I was not idle, but as I watched Fae within groups interact, I saw the camaraderie they had and wished that I could have that for myself. After my shapeshifting magic had manifested at Glass Oasis, I lost all my friends, and my father went from grudgingly accepting me to hating me. Few shapeshifters were blessed with the ability to turn into a large cat, and the ones who had been born in Glass Oasis had a history of being volatile individuals. Shorim, a tiger shifter, had slaughtered half the younglings fifteen years ago. Gora, a black panther shifter, had run wild through the Glass Fair targeting both Fae and human vendors almost one hundred years ago.

I was certain their feelings toward me had to do with me being a snow leopard shapeshifter; that was the only thing that I was aware of changing.

Just as I had looked forward to attending training camp because it meant I was an adult, I also wanted to take advantage of the opportunity it presented to make new friends. Friends who did not know who I was at Glass Oasis and would not judge me based on being a snow leopard shifter.

As the black group wrapped up its hand-to-hand combat training, Lord Zhorlon, the elite warrior in charge of the black group trainees, raised his hand and silence fell. I stood at the back of the group, in formation but separate.

"Beltane is in a few days and we will of course have our annual celebration. As long as you perform appropriately during the upcoming training sessions, all trainees will attend if they wish," announced Lord Zhorlon, then he dismissed us.

The next morning Travaran met me just before I entered the dining hall for breakfast. Once our trays had food, we sat down. Usually we would talk some, but I was too hungry, so I shoveled food into my mouth as fast as possible. I felt like I hadn't eaten in over a week. The last thing I wanted to do was pass out during any of the sessions we had today. I was sure that doing so would not bode well.

"Have you heard anything about when they will tell me what group I'm in?" I asked, hope in my voice.

"Maybe," replied Travaran. "I overheard my father saying that he would announce it the morning after Beltane."

I took a large gulp of water before asking, "Your father is here?"

Travaran nodded. "Yes, he comes by from time to time to see how the training is going. If we're lucky, he will lead some of our sword fighting sessions." I could hear the admiration in his voice, which piqued my curiosity. I knew very little about Prince Tanyth.

"I guess we will see how this week goes then," I murmured.

Six

SERAFINA

411 AQ

I woke up early, still fuming over what had happened yesterday with Edrym, Jassin, and Alassin. Dressed, I pulled the hood on my cloak up and headed toward the dining hall to get breakfast. It was too hot for the cloak, but I was hoping it would allow me to blend in and deter anyone from bothering me.

I let out a sigh of relief as I made it to the dining hall without running into anyone. I tugged on the door and opened it and walked straight into Jassin. "Watch it, rat," he hissed.

I flinched and hastily backed up. My back connected with a solid body. *Shit.* I bit my lip hard, drawing blood, praying it wasn't Alassin. A warm hand gripped my elbow, steadying me. "Good morning, Jassin," said the owner of the warm hand. I sagged in relief. It was Fiera.

Jassin snapped his mouth shut and shoved past us.

"Are you okay?" Fiera said, coming around to face me.

I nodded. "Yes."

"Why are you wearing this ridiculous cloak? I can see you're already sweating," Fiera teased.

I rolled my eyes. "I was trying to not draw attention. But you're right, it is ridiculously hot." I threw the hood back and unclasped the hook, yanking the cloak off. My tunic was damp with sweat; it was a relief to not have the added layer on any longer.

"You were planning to eat, right?" asked Fiera.

I nodded. "Yes. Did you want to eat together?"

"Sure," Fiera said, then we linked arms and headed into the dining hall.

To my relief no one else was in the dining hall. There was a table at the back loaded with food, stacks of plates, and a basket with silverware. I chose a piece of ham, fruit, and some eggs, then sat at the end of the table closest to the food, just in case I wanted seconds.

Fiera sat down, but instead of digging into her food as I was doing, she spoke. "How are you holding up after yesterday?"

I put my fork back down on the plate and wiped my mouth with the napkin. "I've recovered, so the injuries aren't an issue."

Fiera rolled her eyes at me. "That's not what I meant. I've heard whispers around camp. I'm sure you have too."

I grimaced. "I'm trying to just tune everything out. We're leaving shortly for Emerald Valley to fight. I need to stay focused on that. *Fighting humans*."

"Right...you grew up in Gaskal," Fiera said.

"I know we're not going up against humans from Gaskal. Since I've lived here at Jade Wilds, all my interactions with humans at the Rose Fair have been peaceful. I think I just got comfortable with those interactions and forgot that just like there are four Fae courts, there are four human kingdoms, and each is very different. Not all humans will try to keep human-Fae relations peaceful," I replied.

Fiera took a bite of her sausage, and we ate in companionable silence. When Fiera's plate was empty, she sat back in her chair, gazing at me. "When I was six years old, I lived on a farm near the border of the Court of the Moon and Mirim."

My eyes widened. I hadn't realized when Fiera had spoken of growing up on a farm before that she was that close to the border of the Lord of the North's lands.

Fiera continued, "I was out tending the goats, and a group of humans snuck onto the farm. They were loud and had enormous weapons. I hid behind the hay bales in front of the shed. I was too far from the house to go unseen. They got the goats in a tight group; I thought the humans were going to steal them. Instead, they slaughtered them. Blood sprayed everywhere, and they just stood there laughing. Then they left. I stayed hidden for hours, praying my mother would come. When it was getting dark, my father came out, using his magic to illuminate the area so he could find me."

I placed my hand over Fiera's and gave it a squeeze. "That's a terrible thing to witness. I'm glad they didn't harm you."

Fiera swiped at a tear trickling down her cheek. "Thanks. My father was angry and devastated. The goats were our family's pride and joy for centuries. To have them all wiped out at once was hard to swallow. What's more is there was no reason for the humans to have come to our farm. They were just doing it for sport."

"Like Edrym attacked me for sport," I muttered. Fiera's hand twitched at my comment.

"I know what happened to your goats is terrible, but Fae are not above committing acts of violence for no apparent reason. That is human *and* Fae nature," I said.

"You're right," Fiera admitted, then stood up and took her plate to the cart marked Dirty. "I'm going to finish packing. Let me know if you need any help."

I had just taken a huge mouthful of eggs; I nodded, afraid if I spoke the eggs would fall out. Fiera giggled and walked away. I chewed slowly, mulling over our conversation. *Maybe humans and Fae can never truly be at peace because there are too many differences to overcome.* Though as those words came to me, I had to question them. *If that was the case, wouldn't I have no friends here? I look like a full-blooded human. Yet Fiera and Ghilanna and I have found common ground.* I paused. *Or perhaps most humans and Fae are too lazy to put in the work required.* I took a bite of the ham and almost spit it back out; it was rubbery and had way too much salt. I glanced around, confirmed I was alone, and then put it into my napkin, grateful I didn't have to swallow it.

I finished the eggs and fruit on my plate and cleaned up my seat at the table, putting all the dirty dishes on the cart with Fiera's. "I need to finish packing," I said aloud, hoping speaking the words would energize me.

When I reached the tent, I took stock of how much I had left to pack and was pleased there was only the fur blanket on my bed, and I needed to shut the trunk. Otherwise, I was ready.

I sat down on my bed and ran my fingers through the soft brown furs. The past three days had been a whirlwind, and it felt like I hadn't slowed down and processed everything. As I scanned the room my eyes caught on a small book sitting on my desk. *Bedtime Tails.* It was the book of stories that the Fae told their young. I also realized it was the book that Prince Almar had referenced in his conversation with Commander Meriel—the stories were Fae prophecies. I retrieved the book and then snuggled into the furs. I traced the title with my finger; the S was a gray tail with black spots on it.

The book had illustrations with each story. I flipped to the first story, "The Lost Fae Queen."

The illustrations themselves were masterpieces. The title page featured an illustration of the Fae queen in full plate armor and a helmet adorned with a crown. In her left hand was a book and in her right hand a gigantic sword. A cloud of darkness rose behind her. As I started reading the story, I flipped to the next page, which was covered in the likeness of a snow cat. *Like the* one in my dream. I gasped. *My dreams must have been recalling this image.* At the end of the story was the final illustration of the Fae queen side by side with the snow cat and swirls of green and gray magic surrounding both of them.

> *When tension rises and war with the humans has come, the*
> *lost Fae queen will return.*
> *First, she will prove her battle prowess.*
> *Look closely or you might be blinded, for when the Fae queen*
> *returns, not all will know her, yet everyone will follow her.*
> *Be warned, the Fae queen must stay pure until the Great Cat*
> *finds her and their souls unite.*
> *With their souls bound, the heir will be found.*
> *The Fae queen's magic will return and together they will*
> *defend the Fae from the end of time.*
> *Time is of the essence, or the Fae will fall to the darkness.*

I quickly flipped to the next page. A story about a dark green dragon named Rethys, who fiercely protected his treasure hoard. Until one day a young Fae boy entered his cave, not because he wanted to steal the treasure, but because he wanted to be the dragon's friend.

"Dragons aren't real, and if they were…that would just be terrifying. Why would anyone want to befriend something that scary?" I whispered to the book, before flipping the page.

I became engrossed in the stories and the illustrations, and I lost track of time. When I was at the last story, I heard voices outside and knew I should take my trunk to the loading area.

I started to shut the book when the title of the last story caught my attention. The illustrations were gruesome. A sword was peeling the skin from a human's face, revealing the skull beneath. Unlike the other drawings, this one had captions. *Fleshrender.*

Become one with flesh
Summon the dragon with his fang
Bloodsong sang with glee
The one who can tame the three
Can maim all foes against thee.

I wasn't entirely sure this was even a story—more like a poem that made little sense without the illustrations. The second illustration was of a beautiful dagger with a handle in the shape of a dragon's head with green eyes. *Dragonfang.* Behind the dagger was a drawing of a dark green dragon, shockingly like the one that was in the story of Rethys. I paused my study of the drawing and flipped back to Rethys's story to compare them. It took several minutes of close studying, but I was confident that they were the same dragon.

The third drawing was of a worn book with heavy gold decoration on it and what looked like blood seeping from the pages. *Bloodsong Grimoire.* I bit my lip. The name was fitting, I supposed, for a book that had blood coming out of it.

"Serafina!" came Ghilanna's voice. I snapped the book shut and slid off the bed, hastily rolling up the fur blanket and stuffing it into the trunk.

"Coming!" I shouted and headed out to my friend.

On day two of our ride to Emerald Valley we came across a supply train. At the time I was taking a break from riding my horse and was running as a scout near the front of the column. Upon spotting the supply train, I sprinted for Prince Almar.

Breathing heavily, I bowed trying to catch my breath. "Prince Almar, there is a supply train. I believe it is humans, though I could not determine which kingdom it came from."

Prince Almar turned in his saddle and shouted orders for additional scouts. "Good choice, trainee, to report. If they are hostile, the earlier the warning, the better."

I bowed and retreated to where Ghilanna had my horse. "What's going on?" she asked.

"There's a human supply train ahead," I replied, then mounted. "Prince Almar sent more scouts."

We didn't have to wait long before someone shouted orders down the column to continue onward. I presumed this meant the human supply wagon was heading to Emerald Valley to support King Pharaan. Otherwise, I doubted Prince Almar would have allowed them to continue. Allowing the enemy to have more supplies would be a poor tactical decision.

Within half an hour we were riding alongside the supply train. Half the wagons were brimming with silver-iron weapons, while the other half had food. I had mistakenly assumed that all the Fae fighting under King Pharaan would supply their own weapons, but this wagon indicated otherwise, an enormous expense. *Though I suppose if your Fae territory is home to huge emerald mines, maybe it wasn't that expensive of a trade versus if it had been weapons for gold bars.* The presence of the weapons also led me to believe that the other kingdoms either didn't support the Lord of the East's decision to oppose King Pharaan or that money could buy anything.

Glancing up I realized the column had gotten a significant distance ahead. I kissed to my horse, urging it into a canter. I didn't want to get left behind!

My horse stopped moving, and the lack of motion drew my attention back to the group I was traveling with. I was expecting another night in Whispering Thicket. But just ahead, I saw neat rows of gray-green tents blending in with the grass. There were several larger tents scattered throughout the encampment. *For the king and his sons*, I mused.

"Follow me," announced Prince Almar.

Obediently, we fell into a single-file line, and rode slowly into the camp. We passed small groups of Fae sitting around camp-fires. Some were talking, while others were cleaning weapons or armor. They all seemed so relaxed for having been at this camp for over a month, as though this was no big deal.

Finally, Prince Almar halted in front of a large fenced-off enclosure that already held a couple of other horses. "This is where the horses will stay until we need them. Make sure you remove all your gear."

I hastily dismounted and began removing my belongings. When all my bags were in a tidy pile, I waited for instructions. Glancing to my left I saw that Fiera and Ghilanna were tying their horses to a wood railing, so I followed suit.

Picking up my bags, I awkwardly made my way to where my friends were now standing. "Where to?" I asked.

Mere seconds later Prince Almar clapped his hands together to get the attention of all the Jade Wilds trainees. "There are several large communal tents that have been set up for the majority of you, with ten to a tent."

Everyone groaned behind me. Communal tents meant no privacy. Since I was always alone, I was hoping to share a tent with someone and prayed Fiera or Ghilanna would be assigned to the same tent.

"This way." Prince Almar began walking down the wide aisle between the tents. He stopped when we crossed a four-way intersection. "Here we are," he said.

Sure enough, at each of the four corners was a large commu-nal tent that looked as though it could fit at least ten Fae, possi-bly more. I liked the idea of being kept close together, especially since I knew no one except the Fae I had traveled with. I reached for the tent flap, Fiera and Ghilanna at my back.

"Not you," said Prince Almar.

I dropped the tent flap and looked over my shoulder at him. "Is that directed at me?"

He nodded. "Yes. The three of you will share a tent."

Confusion flooded me. *Why are the three of us getting treated differently?* I decided it was wiser to not voice my question and just take the assignment. *More privacy is not a bad thing,* I reminded myself.

Prince Almar led us deeper into the tent camp, pointing out where the kitchen was set up and options for our meals, armorer, and some areas to work on training drills if we wanted. The area hummed with activity. The prince reiterated the need for us to stay within the camp and not wander out on our own. We were facing the Lord of the East soon and could not risk that he might take us hostage or kill us to send a message. I wasn't entirely sure if he was truly worried for the well-being of all three of us. Regardless of his intentions, I would follow the orders to the letter and stay within the camp boundary unless I received an order stating otherwise.

Prince Almar halted abruptly, and I almost ran into him. Fiera didn't stop in time and bumped me; I threw myself sideways and landed in a heap. *At least I didn't knock Prince Almar down.* Fiera offered me a hand, her expression apologetic.

"This is your tent." Prince Almar indicated a tent that I could have sworn was almost as big as the communal ones. "Don't forget to eat," he said, then left.

I eyed the tent, then glanced over at Fiera and Ghilanna. "I guess we should go inside and see our temporary home."

They nodded eagerly, and I led the way into the tent. It was immediately apparent that I was not skilled at judging the size of tents or buildings from their exteriors. Our tent was definitely *not* large enough for ten Fae. In the center of the room were two stuffed chairs and a couch with a table in the middle. Making a semi-circle around the sitting area were three beds, each with a chest of drawers and a small side table. To my surprise, the beds were the same size as the beds at Jade Wilds—large enough for two Fae.

My stomach rumbled. I selected the bed on the left side, deciding to let Fiera and Ghilanna be next to each other as they were used to it and that they could sort out who would be next to me. I set down my packs and my stomach made another noise. "I'm going to go find some food. Do you want to come?"

Fiera nodded and Ghilanna shook her head no.

"Okay, we will see you in a bit."

Ghilanna nodded, though she seemed slightly distracted. Fiera linked arms with me, and we headed for the kitchen. "What was that about?" I asked, assuming Fiera would have some idea.

She shook her head. "I'm not sure. Though if it was important to us, she would share, I'm sure of it."

"Okay," I replied.

After Fiera and I ate, she said she wanted to explore more. I just wanted to lie down and rest for a bit. We agreed to catch up with each other later and parted ways. As I approached the tent, I heard moans and whimpers coming from inside. Hand on my sword hilt, I cautiously opened the tent flap.

Ghilanna was entangled with a blue-haired Fae male on the couch. Jaw dropped, I struggled to make my mouth shut, when Ghilanna shot me an apologetic look before returning her attention to the male. I beat a hasty retreat. I knew my friends had sexual partners, I just had never stumbled in on one of their couplings.

Walking briskly away, embarrassment flooded me. I knew I shouldn't be embarrassed—Ghilanna most certainly wouldn't be if our roles were reversed—but I just couldn't unsee it. Chewing on my lower lip, I kept my eyes up and aware of my surroundings. As I wandered through the camp, the scent of cooking meat and smoke was the most prevalent. I could hear the strike of metal on metal, likely someone getting one last training session in. Voices with mixed pitches and tones occasionally carried a few words to my ears.

A sound caught my attention, and I glanced to the left, heading for the gap between two tents. When I saw two male Fae kissing, I hastily retreated, not wanting to interrupt them. At Jade Wilds the trainees had been more discreet about their partners. Though at the right time of night you could certainly hear coupling, I rarely came across anyone doing so much as a chaste kiss out in the open, where anyone could see.

I lost track of time as I wandered around when a hand touched me. I jumped straight up in the air and shrieked. A familiar laugh came from beside me. *Fiera.* "What was that for?" I demanded.

"I didn't expect you to jump," said Fiera, still trying to control her laughter. She moved so she was standing in front of me and must have seen my expression. "What's wrong?"

My tongue felt like sandpaper as I debated if I should tell her, then decided why not. "I walked in on Ghilanna and a male with blue hair."

Fiera hid her mouth with her hands, trying to stifle her laughter again. I frowned, not thinking it was very funny. She held up her hands. "Sorry. I know you want to wait until you're married to have sex, which I can respect, even if I don't understand it."

I rolled my eyes. "Maybe the only reason you have physical needs you want to sate is because you awakened that part of you. If I wait as I intend, then I will avoid teaching my body about the physical satisfaction you feel sex provides until I am married."

Fiera shrugged. "I can't wait to see the outcome of your experiment."

Seven

TRISTAN

360 AQ

The morning of the day of Beltane I was practicing sword work with the red group. Prince Tanyth had overseen the sword work today and I experienced firsthand why Travaran was so impressed with his father's skills. We were in columns with enough room to maneuver as we ran through individual drills. The training swords were dull, so they couldn't pierce skin in case we accidentally hurt someone.

"One," Prince Tanyth shouted. The group of us brought the swords up in a middle block.

"Two," Prince Tanyth shouted. We thrust to the right. This marked my sixth day at Embergate and I was finally getting a handle on what maneuver each number meant. The combinations were trickier, and I compensated for my uncertainty with slower swings. Which was fine until we were told to increase our speed; then I began making mistakes.

The expectation was that trainees made mistakes. However, it was embarrassing when I was the one making the mistake and I accidentally whacked my neighbor with my sword. The second time I hit him, he turned toward me, face bright red with anger. Instead of shouting at me, he swung his sword at me. I had no choice but to block and step back as he forced me out of line. He swung again; I tried to parry but was too slow and barely got my fingers out of the way before the sword smashed them.

"I'm sorry," I said, hoping he would accept my apology and get back in line before we both got into trouble.

Instead, he ignored me and jumped forward. I blocked, but my grip was incorrect, causing the sword to slip. He lurched forward, slamming into my sword. Blood sprayed everywhere and he began screaming. I let go of the sword and backed up, hands raised. Prince Tanyth barked orders, but my vision was fading to black, and I did not know what he was saying.

When I opened my eyes, I felt the hard edge of a bench digging into my shoulder blades, and I could hear the clash of swords, which meant I was near the training grounds. Prince Tanyth's teal face filled my vision. "You're awake."

I didn't reply, not sure what to say. I had seriously injured another trainee and the prince who ruled this place had only said, "You're awake." I was really confused. I sat up slowly, trying to ensure I wouldn't black out again.

Prince Tanyth smiled at me. "Bravo, Tristan," he said, clapping me on the shoulder.

"What did I do, sir?" I asked.

"You made your first kill, with a dull weapon no less. Very impressive," Prince Tanyth said.

I felt the bile rising in my throat and pivoted on the bench, leaning over just in time to puke between my legs and not on the prince. I wasn't sure if I was throwing up in reaction to making my first kill or the fact that I was being congratulated for killing another trainee.

Someone thrust a canteen in front of my face. I took it gratefully and took a long sip, swishing it around my mouth and then spitting it out. The second sip I swallowed and then allowed myself to sit up all the way. "The trainee is dead?" I asked, wanting confirmation.

Prince Tanyth nodded. "Yes. I will admit when I saw you floundering back there, I was not expecting him to be the one to die when he attacked you. Your instincts are good though. With time, I am sure you will be able to best even me with the sword."

I pressed my lips together. Receiving such high praise from Prince Tanyth on my *sixth* day of training was unreal. My whole body tightened with nerves. I wasn't sure having the prince focused on me was in my best interest, though I was flattered he thought I would one day be better than him with a sword. If I could live up to his expectations, I knew that it meant I could even lead the Fae in a war. Big dreams were not a bad thing to have, but I had to remind myself that I was still only on my sixth day of what would be years of training before I could graduate. A lot could happen. *Look what happened to the trainee, and he was only here for a month.*

I finally mustered some words. "Thank you, sir."

Prince Tanyth clapped me on the shoulder again. "Now, Tristan. I think you have earned the afternoon off and a chance to prepare for your first Beltane. Oh, and just so you know, you are in the red group. Since you have shadow magic, you will fit in just fine there."

I stood up with a half-smile on my face at the praise, my knees wobbling a little bit, a sure sign I wasn't entirely well. I considered maybe using my afternoon off to just go take a nap to recover. I took a step in that direction when Prince Tanyth spoke again. "I had a tub set up for you in the stone cottage by the kitchen garden. There is also an outfit. Since you're new here, I know you don't have any yet. I thought you would like to dress properly."

Before I could reply, Prince Tanyth vanished. I shut my mouth and slowly made my way behind the buildings to the shed where he had told me to go.

I opened the door and my jaw dropped when I saw the interior. The room I entered was a stone bathhouse. There was a massive tub that was sunken into the ground. A pile of folded towels sat on the edge. There was a table with a chair and on the chair, there was a set of clothing draped over it. I decided I really didn't care what the clothes looked like. I wanted to soak in the bath for hours.

A few hours later when I stepped out of the stone cottage, I caught myself on the doorframe in shock. Embergate had been transformed. Gone were the stone buildings and in their place was a luxurious grass field with a huge bonfire with bright orange-and-red flames crackling in the middle, and around the edges were poles and tents decorated in fairy lights and ribbons. The sounds of laughter and music hit my ears. I found myself grinning. My parents had never allowed me to participate in Beltane, citing I was too young.

There was a quartet playing off to the side of the fire. I had to admit they were quite skilled, far more so than the musicians who played at Glass Oasis. I could already feel the thrum of the music in my blood and the closer I walked to the fire, the stronger it became. It was difficult to identify the trainees, because as Prince Tanyth had suggested earlier, everyone was dressed up. I was in a gray sleeveless silk tunic with black pants. My slate-gray hair was held back with a silver clip.

A flash of dark purple caught my eye. As I followed it, I passed by a low table, and snagged a glass of wine. I took a sip and followed the female in the purple dress.

She was hard to track down. But I felt like I needed to meet her, and I wasn't sure why. *Maybe it's the wine.* It was a logical explanation.

I was about to set down my empty cup on a bench when someone bumped into me. I dropped the cup and reached out; my hand gripped an arm. The owner of the arm tugged, but I refused to let go, pulling the Fae toward me.

"Let go," she hissed.

I gave her a lazy smile as I realized that she was the female in the purple dress. "I'm Tristan."

"Callyn," she said tartly. "Now are you going to let me go?"

"Dance with me?" I countered.

"Fine, one dance," she replied. I loosened my grip on her arm and slid my hand into hers. She led me away from the table and into an open space. We began to dance. I am not entirely sure how many dances we had, but the longer we danced the more frequently our bodies touched. When she twirled into my arms again, I dipped her down over my knee, and hesitantly kissed her. To my surprise, she kissed me back, her tongue pressing lightly on my lips. I parted them and she deepened the kiss. I stopped kissing Callyn and swept her upright. Her eyes met mine.

"Would you like to find a tent?" she asked.

A shiver of anticipation went through me; a female was inviting me to have sex during a Beltane party. I could hardly believe it. I gave her a smile and a nod. "Yes." Then she took my hand and led me into one of the tents.

As soon as the flap closed behind me, she unlaced my pants, sliding her hand around my cock and stroking. I moaned in pleasure, frozen in place. I had no idea what she was going to do next, and the anticipation was almost unbearable. When she drew my cock into her mouth my breath hitched in my chest. Callyn wrapped her hands around my hips and tugged; my cock bumped the back of her throat. A ragged breath escaped my lips. I set my hands lightly on her shoulders.

She drew me deep, lightly grazing my shaft with her teeth, and I lost control, body spasming with the release. Instead of letting go, she swallowed my seed and began teasing me with her tongue. I could feel myself hardening again and as amazing as it felt, I desperately wanted to know how it would feel to be inside of her. Regretfully, I took a step back, sliding my cock out of her mouth. Kneeling in front of her, I kissed her, running my hand down the back of her dress, tugging at the laces. The front started sliding down and she stood, allowing me to pull the dress the rest of the way off. As I stood up, I stared openly at her breasts, not sure what to do. She placed her hand over mine and guided it to her breast. It was firm, yet soft. I began massaging it, and a moan escaped her lips. An idea occurred to me, and I dipped down, taking her breast in my mouth and sucking on it. I teased with my tongue and teeth until the nipple got tight and hard, then I switched to the other side. My mouth kept busy with her breasts, I let my fingers blaze a trail down her abdomen and into her wet folds. I wasn't expecting her to be so ready for me. I withdrew my fingers and in one smooth motion thrust inside of her. Standing for this was far more awkward than I had anticipated.

"Pick me up," she murmured in my ear.

My eyes widened; I didn't realize that was something you could do. Fingers shaking slightly, I set my hands around her waist and simply lifted her up. She was lighter than I expected, making it easy to continue a steady rhythm. She tightened against me, moaning in pleasure, and just as I sent her over the edge, she bit my neck hard.

Unable to control my reaction I growled deep in my throat and slammed my cock into her, and my release cascaded through me. Keeping her legs around my hips, I gently kneeled, and then laid Callyn on her back. I pulled out and lay down on the blanket next to her, breathing deeply. We both remained still for a while and then she began trailing her fingers down the muscles on my chest. I did not bite my tongue fast enough to keep the moan from escaping my lips. Her hand slid farther down.

"Are you sure?" I murmured even as her hand encircled my cock and it hardened again. Some small part of me was marveling at the stamina I had, and the other part didn't care. I finally understood why, aside from fighting techniques, the only other thing males talked about was sex.

Eight

SERAFINA
411 AQ

I agreed to join the morning practice session with Fiera and Ghilanna that was overseen by Prince Rhangil, ruler of the Court of the Sun. The name was familiar; I had heard it a few times over the years I spent in Gaskal due to the trade between the territories.

The three of us arrived and found spots among the other Fae. My eyes were drawn to Prince Rhangil, though I wasn't entirely sure why. He had long white hair that pulled severely back at the nape of his neck and tan skin, with piercing golden eyes. At his throat was a large gold pendant. I was about to ask Fiera what she knew about Prince Rhangil when the prince spoke. "Welcome. If you are here for the battle, then you are already in top fighting shape. This practice session is not going to be easy. If you want something easy, go practice with the humans." His comment was met with laughter.

"I will start the exercise. I will run through the combinations slowly twice so you can see what you are supposed to be doing, and then I will speed up," Prince Rhangil explained, then started his demonstration. Two sets of middle jabs alternating left and right, followed by a low left hook and a low right hook. Then he did a one hundred eighty degree turn and repeated. As he returned to his starting position, he added in a sharp kick with each leg.

The Fae around me spread out more. We would need extra room if everyone was going to practice the kicks and punches without accidentally hitting a neighbor. It only took a full set before I found the rhythm of the exercises Prince Rhangil had chosen. It felt good to practice without a sword. At the end of the session, I had worked up a light sweat, but my mind was miraculously clear and focused on the battle that lay ahead.

The group disbanded when Prince Rhangil indicated the session was over. Fiera and Ghilanna went off somewhere. After yesterday, I didn't want to know what they were up to.

I decided to continue my cooldown and take a walk around the camp. As I meandered down one of the narrower paths between tents, I heard what I thought could be a fight to the right. I headed in that direction and sure enough there was a Fae male with braided light brown hair hitting a disheveled Fae male with blue hair, who was being restrained by a blonde Fae female.

I knew I should probably retreat and let whatever was going on run its course, but it wasn't in my nature to stand idly by while another being was attacked and prevented from defending themselves. This was a battle camp, a new experience for me. I wasn't sure what the official rules were on conduct, but I was confident they didn't permit torture.

I sprinted, aiming for the back of the Fae male who was attacking. At the last moment, I leaped into the air and kicked, aiming for his kidneys. My momentum sent me over him as he staggered forward from my unexpected attack. Not wasting a second, I pivoted and whipped out another kick. This time he was ready. He grabbed my ankle, anger and recognition plain in his face, and twisted, flipping me into the air. *Edrym Kealeth*. I bucked and snapped my foot out at his knee as I fell toward the ground. He stumbled backward and released my ankle. I hopped to my feet.

"You little bitch didn't learn your lesson last time," Edrym fumed. The Fae female restraining the blue-haired male had not made a move to help.

I didn't respond. Taunting was a game that I had never found productive. Fists up, I lightly bounced from foot to foot.

Edrym flicked his wrist, and a dagger slid into his hand. He slashed; I raised my arm to block, and was rewarded with a slice that went from my wrist to my elbow. *Stupid mistake*, I chided. Edrym attacked, dagger flashing. I spun and wove out of his way, landing punches when I could.

I was so focused on what Edrym was doing that I did not notice the arrival of more Fae.

"What is the meaning of this?" demanded a deep male voice.

My eyes widened in recognition; it was Prince Rhangil. I kept my fists up, ready to strike again, but stopped trying to hit Edrym.

"Warrior Edrym, what is going on?" Prince Rhangil asked harshly.

Edrym lowered his dagger and bowed. "We were having a minor disagreement is all, Prince Rhangil."

I felt the prince's gaze boring into me. "Trainee Serafina, is that true?"

I was surprised he knew my name. I debated how to answer. Edrym already hated me; I knew lying to protect him would not gain me any of his favor. "I was walking to cool out when I heard noises and decided to investigate. I found Edrym beating this restrained male and thought I should confront him."

"Did you verbally confront him or just attack?" Prince Rhangil inquired.

I drew in a sharp breath. "I attacked."

Prince Rhangil gazed at me and then at Edrym in silence. Moments ticked by while we waited for him to weigh in. "Given that Trainee Serafina did not verbally confront Warrior Edrym before she attacked but was doing so to protect another Fae being wrongfully tortured, I will refrain from punishing either one of you. Next time you feel the need to fight, you must issue a formal challenge. None of this hiding in dark corners nonsense."

"Yes, Prince," we replied in unison.

"Now both of you will return to your tents," Prince Rhangil ordered. I departed, heading toward my tent and as far away from Edrym as possible.

Nine

TRISTAN

FALL 360 AQ

There were thirty of us in the red group at Embergate. We stood in six columns of five, hands loosely around our swords, awaiting the next command. We had been running drills all day every day for weeks. Tension between trainees was running high with the training exercises that pitted the groups against one another, and there were brawls every night within the groups and between them. I had tried to keep my distance, but the others were taking notice that I was not as eager as they were to jump into the fray. I had a feeling that soon I would have no choice but to fight. I also found it strange that the instructors here did nothing to discourage our behavior. Back at home when fights broke out, those involved were severely punished.

A few moments later Lord Zhorlon dismissed us. Over the past three months I had learned that almost everyone in my group headed straight for the dining hall after we were dismissed. If I took my shower first, there was no one around, permitting me a few moments of peace and quiet. I hung back, waiting till everyone had started the trek up to the dining hall. I followed behind until we got to the edge of the buildings and then turned to the right, heading for the red barracks.

The barracks were empty as I had expected. I hung up my leather training armor and took out a clean tunic, breeches, and a towel. I made my way to the bathhouse, a small building with a few shower stalls set up for the trainees to use. Part of me wished we had tubs to use, because most days a soak would be better than just a shower, but I knew that was a privilege I would have to earn in the distant future.

I undressed and put my dirty clothes in a neat pile. My towel was hanging on a hook, and I stepped into the shower. The water was hot. I took my time washing my dark gray hair and getting all of the grime out from under my fingernails. When all the soap was rinsed off, I shut off the water and reached for my towel. But it wasn't there. I peered around, looking for it, but it hadn't fallen, and I was certain I had brought one with me. My clean clothes were also gone.

Annoyance rolled through me. I could hear snickers on the other side of the wall partitioning the showers from the latrines. "Who is there?" I called.

A tall Fae with light brown skin stepped around the partition. "What makes you think that you deserve the right to shower now, before everyone else?"

I raised an eyebrow. "Of all the things you want to get mad at me for, Greyson, this is the thing you choose?"

Greyson bared his teeth at me. I rolled my eyes. With my attention on Greyson, I was startled when a fist landed just over my kidney. I flinched, keeping my eyes on Greyson.

"You're pathetic," he growled, then waved his hand. I assumed it was a signal for whoever was behind me. I snapped my right foot behind me and it connected with someone's leg. I jabbed my elbow straight back and then spun, delivering a crescent kick. I missed but was now facing my opponents. There were two of them, three if I counted Greyson.

Valor threw a few quick punches, but I dodged it. Drolon tried a kick, but I caught his foot with my hand and twisted, slamming him into the wall of the shower stall. I let go and threw punches of my own at Valor. Then Greyson struck from behind. I growled, trying to figure out how to get out of the bathhouse. *I could blast a hole in the wall.* I dismissed the idea; destroying the bathhouse would certainly get me in trouble. There wasn't enough space to maneuver, which was likely why they had chosen it.

I turned and bent at the waist, charging straight at Greyson. I barreled into him and wrapped my arms around his waist and kept going. We burst through the door and tumbled down the steps. I let go of Greyson and backed up a few steps. I had the space I wanted now. Greyson was slowly pulling himself up; he seemed dazed from the tumble down the steps. Just as he sat up, I kicked him in the head, knocking him out.

Valor and Drolon spilled out of the bathhouse. "You'll pay for what you did to Greyson!" Valor yelled. I could hear footsteps approaching and wasn't sure who was going to appear, more trainees or instructors.

I shrugged; it didn't matter. Clearly these three had wanted a fight, so I was going to give them one. Valor took a flying leap toward me and feinted to the left at the last moment. I slammed a fist into his rib cage and Drolon's foot landed on my thigh. I bit my cheek, trying not to react, but I had to admit it hurt. Valor darted in again, aiming for my stomach. I blocked his punches and barely turned in time to dodge Drolon's well-placed kick to the groin.

I rolled my shoulders and changed tactics. The longer I let this drag on, the more likely I was to lose. So, I sped up my attacks. Right-left-right jabs followed by a high kick. Spin to the left and kick, connecting solidly with the side of Drolon's knee. He stumbled sideways, screaming in pain. I couldn't help myself, I grinned—which seemed to anger Valor even more. He started cursing at me. Valor tried high and low punches, but I blocked every time. Sweat trickled down my back, dirt covered my arms and legs. There was a circle of trainees around us, but thankfully none were stepping in.

I stepped to the right, then did a roll to come quite close to Valor's feet. As I passed, I unfolded myself and grabbed his ankle and yanked. He started to fall, and I swept my legs up in a scissor kick and clipped the side of his jaw. He collapsed in a heap beside me. I lay on the ground panting for a few moments before I stood up. Everyone was staring at me in silence.

Minutes ticked by no one spoke or made a move to leave. Finally, one trainee stepped forward, hand outstretched. "I'm Bane. Well met," he said. I took his hand and shook it; he clapped me on the shoulder. "Now, why don't you shower again, and if you're fast, there might still be food left for you in the dining hall."

I nodded and headed back into the shower, trying to wrap my mind around everything that had just happened and that someone other than Travaran was willing to talk me. By now I knew who almost everyone was in the red group by name—from the commander giving orders to individuals. Bane followed and set a clean towel and clothing out for me, then took up a post by the door. It was my first big fight, but far from the last. It had also marked the day when I was finally accepted as one of the red trainees.

A rumor was circulating that there would be another party soon. I wasn't sure I wanted to go to another party, not after the entire red group spent the past few evenings recounting in vivid detail their sexual prowess with various partners from Beltane.

After dinner Travaran approached me. "You should come to the party."

I rolled my eyes. "Why?"

"So you can find a female and let loose for a few hours," Travaran replied. "I know you enjoyed Callyn last time. She was invited again."

Despite myself I perked up at the mention of Callyn. Travaran was right, I had enjoyed her company. Though what I wanted now wasn't so much as sex as just someone to talk to. *Would Callyn want to listen?* I wondered. I sighed. "Fine, I will attend. If you promise to leave me alone."

Travaran grinned and slapped me on the back. "Excellent. Now, hurry up, they're arriving momentarily."

Before I could respond, Travaran strode away. I shook my head. Before dinner I washed my face and changed tunics. I spent several minutes searching unsuccessfully for the gray shirt I wore during Beltane, but came up empty handed, leaving me with no choice but to wear a red tunic and dark colored pants. *Hopefully Callyn won't mind.*

The sounds of music and laughter guided me to the center of Embergate, where the party was. Though not as fancy as the Beltane setup had been there were still several tables laden with snacks and wine. I hovered at the edge, searching the crowd for Callyn. Finally, I spotted her on the other side of the group and waved, hoping she would notice me. Thankfully her eyes met mine within a few moments and I headed toward her.

She was wearing a navy dress with a dagger tucked into the brown belt around her waist. I approached, eying the dagger. "Do you even know how to use that?" I asked, genuinely curious.

Callyn playfully smacked my arm with the flat of the dagger. "Of course I do, why else would I wear it?"

"For decoration?" I replied.

Callyn rolled her eyes. "That seems to be what all males here think—that females only wear weapons for decoration. I am *not* helpless. While I may not have trained at Embergate, I most certainly graduated as a Fae warrior."

I gazed at her with newfound appreciation. "I'm sorry, I didn't realize that you were a warrior."

Callyn gave me a slight smile. "You're lucky I believe you. Now, how about we find a bite to eat and somewhere to talk and get to know each other better?"

I nodded enthusiastically. "Sounds wonderful." I linked my arm in hers and we made our way to the snack table.

Ten

SERAFINA
411 AQ

Fiera stepped out of the tent just as it came into view. She had a longbow slung over her shoulder and a quiver of arrows on her back. *She must be going hunting.* I quickened my steps, hoping I could join her. I wanted breathing room after the run-in with Edrym and wasn't convinced alone time in the tent would suffice.

Fiera waved. "Want to come with us?"

I sprinted the last few steps. "Absolutely!"

Ghilanna emerged from the tent. "Great, grab whatever you need. We've been given permission to take some horses. I believe they hope we get an elk; the cooks go through an absurd amount of meat with the number of Fae here."

Smiling, I ducked into the tent and snagged my short bow off its stand and a quiver. I had never gotten comfortable with the longbow.

"Let's go," Fiera said and led the way toward the pen with the horses.

To my surprise the three horses were tacked up and tethered to a post. I made a beeline for the gray one with beautiful silver-to-charcoal dapples and a black mane and tail. A quick check confirmed it was a he. "Hello beautiful," I murmured and offered him my hand to sniff. His scratchy whiskers were a stark contrast to the velvet of his muzzle as he tickled the palm of my hand. I untied the reins from the post and mounted. Fiera and Ghilanna were already up and waiting for me.

We ambled out of the camp at a slow walk, and I ran my fingers over his neck. *You need a name.* Though I was certain he had a name already, I didn't want to spend the next few hours referring to him as "boy" or "horse." "Dubhar," I said stroking his neck. It was the Fae word for shadows and fitting for a horse of his color.

When we reached the edge of the camp, the wide grassy plain of Emerald Valley sprawling before us, we paused. Fiera looked at us. "The cook said they have had good luck at the edge of Whispering Thicket where the ground starts to rise. I figured we could start there."

Ghilanna and I nod in agreement. The three of us kicked our horses and we burst into a gallop. I bent low over Dubhar's withers, and his hooves dug in deeper, lengthening his strides and pulling ahead of the other two horses. All too soon we had to slow down, lest we scared the very elk we were supposed to be hunting.

The thrill of the hunt was still thrumming through my veins as we began our slow trek back to the camp. All three horses were laden with meat.

Ghilanna scooted her horse closer to Dubhar. "Are you worried about fighting the Lord of the East?"

My lips twitched. "Only in the sense that it is my first real battle. But if your question is directed at fighting humans, no. I grew up in a quiet part of the city surrounding the Lord of the South's castle. My mother taught me herself instead of sending me to one of the schools and honestly it was just the three of us most of the time. I never had many human friends, and the king—I doubt he knew I even existed."

"I thought your father was the king's third son," Fiera chimed in from my other side.

I shrugged. "Yeah, that's right. But we weren't treated any differently than the rest of the city-folk."

"Do you ever wish you had grown up in the castle?" Ghilanna asked.

I considered the question, petting Dubhar's silky neck. "I never really thought about it. The few times I met my grandfather he made it very clear he wanted nothing to do with me. I overheard his steward saying some awful things about my mother too."

"I'm sorry," said Fiera.

"It's in the past. I don't have any intentions of returning to Gaskal," I replied, and as I spoke the words, I knew in my heart that what I said was true. The Lord of the South had no use for his unwanted granddaughter, nor me for him.

We fell into a thoughtful silence for the remainder of the ride.

Eleven

TRISTAN

365 AQ

At dinner we were given notice that the red group would be sent out on our first winter assignment. There was a group of humans—Larks—who had made the rash decision to explore the lower Ember Mountains far from any of the human lands. Our orders were to take them out with any means necessary. We had an hour to pack and then would depart.

Commander Zhorlon was leading us, though he made it clear that Valor was in charge and that he would only step in if we were epically failing. I was not surprised by his choice. Valor, when he wasn't getting into brawls after our training sessions, was quite skilled at getting the males into a functioning group that would follow his orders. I knew it remained to be seen if that was the case outside of Embergate, but I felt optimistic it would be.

As we marched toward our destination, Travaran came up beside me in a chatty mood. "Have you heard about the prophecy about Dragonfang?"

I shook my head; I could not specifically recall one about anything called Dragonfang. "I don't think so."

Travaran smiled. "Then I will tell you.

> *Become one with flesh*
> *Summon the dragon with his fang*
> *Bloodsong sang with glee*
> *The one who can tame the three*
> *Can maim all foes against thee.*"

I listened while keeping my eyes trained on the ground we were on; I didn't want to trip on a rock or tree branch.

"You mentioned it has to do with the Dragonfang, but the words you just recited don't fully name any magic objects," I pointed out, thinking it sounded more like a random poem than a prophecy.

Travaran shrugged. "Not all the Fae prophecies spell everything out to the letter and many of them just read like a story. I will explain it. 'Tame the three' refers to three objects. The first is Fleshrender, a longsword; the second is Dragonfang, a dagger; and the third is the *Bloodsong Grimoire*, a spell book."

"Why is this important to our current assignment?" I asked. The timing was puzzling.

"It's not. My father told me that he is close to finding Fleshrender. So, the prophecy is on my mind," Travaran explained.

"Ah," I said, not sure how else to respond. I expected that if the other two objects did exist—indicating this was one of the *real* Fae prophecies that wasn't just a story—that Prince Tanyth was hoping to acquire them to complete the trio and control their combined power. I knew if such objects really did exist, they would give him significant leverage over the other three Fae courts, especially when it came to determining how to treat the humans and negotiating versus fighting over the metal mines at the center of the human territories.

Travaran apparently didn't have anything else to talk about, because he increased his speed and pulled ahead. I didn't follow suit, not believing that running faster would accomplish much since the slowest male was still quite a ways behind me.

Eventually the signal to halt made its way up the line. Valor waited for everyone to surround him in a semicircle before speaking. "The Larks are just past the ridge. I know we should probably approach from both sides, but I am concerned that if we take the time to do that, they will realize we are here."

Commander Zhorlon nodded in agreement at Valor's assessment. Valor continued, "We will form two lines. Those of you who will be attacking on foot, and the rest who will be using magic."

Greyson started speaking, cutting Valor off. I pressed my lips together, suppressing the urge to reprimand Greyson for his rudeness. "Why waste time sending some of us in with swords for close combat instead of just annihilating them with magic?"

Valor rolled his eyes. "Because, while Larks don't have magic, they do have access to magic objects, and we have no way of knowing if this group possesses any and what they are, or if they have plain or silver-iron weapons. For example, if they have a magic shield up, then the only way of attacking the Larks is with close quarter combat techniques."

Valor assigned me a position in the close combat line. I unsheathed my sword and waited for the signal to approach the Larks. Travaran was on the other end of the line next to Valor. Commander Zhorlon gave the signal for us to start forward once the magic-wielding group was in position.

We moved forward, working our way down the slope of the ravine. It was only a matter of time before one of the Larks looked up and saw us. I was almost on top of my target when a shout went up through the Lark camp. A few Larks grabbed bows and made some wild shots. Just as I was swinging my sword, a ball of dark blue magic sailed by and knocked over my Lark. More balls and bolts of magic sizzled through the camp, taking out the Larks faster than most of the close combat group could react. *I guess they didn't have a magic object after all.* I raised my sword to strike the Lark charging toward me when a ball of bright red magic hit the Lark in the chest and he caught fire. I leaped forward, jabbing my sword into his stomach and yanking it out before the Lark could run through the camp and catch more things on fire.

A sharp whistle came from above, Commander Zhorlon's announcement for all clear.

Valor walked over to me. "I want you to check to make sure they're all dead."

"Okay," I replied and began my task. I checked the pulse on all the Larks, just in case they were using magic objects and a death had been an illusion. As I traversed the camp, I did not find much of interest. Tents, cook fires, everything was just basic. There was no evidence of anything of high value.

I walked into the last tent toward the end of the ravine. I could still hear Valor and Travaran talking amicably, although it sounded like they were heading back up the hill to Commander Zhorlon. *I know these are Larks, but how can they just blindly kill and then behave as though it was merely a training exercise?* I peered around the tent and bent over to lift the bedroll. When I heard the skitter of gravel. I snapped upright, hand on my sword hilt, and stepped outside of the tent.

A group of Larks poured out of the rocks, or what we had assumed were rocks. *A cave.* In one smooth motion I unsheathed my sword. The first Lark was armed with an axe and swung it like he knew what he was doing.

I feinted to the right and did a backhand sweep to the left with a low-strike, middle-strike combination. The Lark brought his axe up to block at the very last minute. I flicked my wrist and made it past his guard, stabbing him in the side. A small stream of blood shot out of the wound and hit me in the arm. Instead of falling over like I had hoped, the Lark's face got bright red, and his axe whirled through the air straight for my head. Scooting sideways, I created enough room to maneuver and slashed at the Lark's unprotected middle. My sword met its mark and dark red bloomed across the Lark's tan tunic. He doubled over, blood dribbling out of his mouth.

The next Lark had a sword but stumbled over the prone form of the first one and I was able to dispatch him before he had a chance to strike at all.

They kept coming. I switched my sword to my left hand and wiped my sweaty palm on my leathers. I was mildly surprised that none of the Fae had noticed what was going on down here. The Larks were quite noisy. I shot a glance up the hill and saw Travaran standing there watching. Anger heated my face. Instead of notifying anyone there was an ambush, he was observing.

This time two Larks rushed out of the cave. I admired their attempt at strategizing and smiled at them. Whether it was my smile or that they weren't expecting to exit the cave and be face-to-face with a Fae warrior, their steps faltered. I leaped toward them with an uppercut followed by a ten-seven combination. I kept the one on my left as the primary target. The Lark on my right tried to jab his sword into my stomach, but his movements were too slow to be effective; I either blocked or simply moved.

I sped up my attacks, wanting to end the fight. The clash of our swords echoed in the ravine. The Lark on the left got a lucky strike in—I felt a burn across my shoulder and a dribble of blood. I did a two-four combination, followed by a low strike aimed at their legs. The Lark on the left jumped out of the way, but the one on the right toppled over as I sliced down to the bone on both of his legs.

"You'll pay for that, you fucking Fae!" shouted the Lark on the left.

I cocked my eyebrow, wondering if he really thought shouting at me would change the outcome of our fight. I wasn't going to waste my breath replying. I heard the slide of gravel behind me—*Maybe someone is coming to help?*—which was enough of a distraction for the Lark. He momentarily took his gaze from me and I stepped in close and slid my sword into his stomach. The Lark gasped, wide-eyed, and then died. I yanked my sword out.

A clap started behind me; I whirled, sword ready.

"Excellent work," said Commander Zhorlon.

I lowered my sword and took a deep breath. I was tired and filthy. I could feel flecks of blood on my face and see it on my arms, chest, and legs. ."Thank you, Commander."

"Now. Let's go back to Embergate. How many Larks was that?" he asked.

My lips twitched; I was surprised he cared. "Around twenty, Commander."

"Enough to have done some serious damage if they had come up behind us unawares," Commander Zhorlon replied.

I nodded in agreement. I was tempted to tell the commander that Travaran had known I needed help and kept it to himself. *But we're friends, and if I ratted him out, then he would be punished. I am still in one piece. It doesn't matter.* I couldn't help wondering what would happen next time if Travaran didn't call for help until it was too late. I bit my lip, deciding just this once I would let it slide. I knew the cave had been well-hidden in the rocks and unnoticed by all of us. Travaran beckoned to me and together we headed to the rest of the group.

Twelve

SERAFINA

411 AQ

Before arriving at Emerald Valley I was familiar with fighting strategies, battle lineups, and things like adapting to particular terrain. But it had never been explained that involved parties could, well, *schedule* a battle. It sounded quite ridiculous to me, and yet here I was in the gray pre-dawn light on the day of the battle between King Pharaan and the Lord of the East.

I was grateful for the silence in our tent as Fiera, Ghilanna, and I put our armor on. We were to wear plate armor for maximum protection against human weapons. Mine was plain iron unadorned with a silvery hue. There were deep scratches, but I knew it would hold up; it didn't have to be pretty to fulfill its function. I had my primary sword, which I wore at my left hip, with a dagger next to it and a short sword on my right hip in case something happened and I needed a backup.

When the three of us were finished arming ourselves we did a quick inspection, ensuring all the buckles were tight and that nothing was missing that could make a critical difference on the battlefield.

Satisfied, we made our way to our designated muster location. Unfortunately, Prince Almar was waiting for us with Edrym clinging to his side. It quickly became apparent that there were four muster locations, one for each of the four Fae courts—Sun, Moon, Dawn, and Dusk. My hands shook slightly thinking about the Court of Dusk and its terrifying prince, Tanyth. Thankfully I hadn't had any dreams about him since being at Emerald Valley. *As long as I don't run into him here.*

"You will form into three lines," Prince Almar explained, his voice pulling me out of my thoughts. "The least experienced warriors will be in the middle line. Stay in formation, obey any orders called by myself or any of the other commanders. Don't do anything heroic."

My eyebrows shot upward in surprise when he said not to do anything heroic. *What does that mean?* I glanced at Fiera, but she didn't seem to have any better idea than I did. There was a high-pitched whistle.

"That is our cue. Move out," announced Prince Almar.

I pinched my lips together as I realized that I was walking out onto a real battlefield. I had participated in skirmishes before where Fae got hurt, but I had never been put into a situation where my intent was to kill. *Not just kill. Kill humans.* I began to shake slightly. *Kill my people.* I glanced over at Fiera and shook my head, trying to rein in my feelings. Fiera and Ghilanna were my people. I did not know the Lord of the East, nor was I acquainted with any of his subjects. *If we were facing my grandfather, then I could justify these feelings, maybe. But we're not.*

I took a deep breath and exhaled slowly. My feet were cooperating and following the Fae in front of me. I could see the hill ahead and as we continued our march, I began to make out a dark line on the hill. *The Lord of the East.*

There were so many of them. The lines of the knights belonging to the Lord of the East kept cresting the top of the hill and advancing down the front toward us. We were given the signal to halt. I unsheathed my sword and held it loosely in my hand. I knew it was likely a premature move, but the feel of the hilt in my hand aided the process of settling my nerves. When the humans stopped advancing, I realized by doing a rough estimate that we were outnumbered twenty to one.

A whistle pierced through the air; I could barely hear it. It was part of King Pharaan's plan to use a sound that was out of the range of human hearing to give signals to the Fae. To give us an edge. Behind our three rows was a fourth. I hadn't known there was going to be a fourth, and when the volley of magic arced over our heads and into the ranks of the enemy, I saw how naïve I had been to not consider the magic Fae possessed.

The front of the human lines began to fall. A distant horn blast sounded, and a big *boom* resounded.. Ten fiery balls sailed over the humans, and I gasped. They had been precisely placed and were hurtling toward our lines—until flashes of blue and purple magic lit up the sky and each fiery ball disappeared. Another volley of magic followed, then the signal I was waiting for—three sharp whistles.

The Fae in front of me began to sprint. I calculated my stride so I would not run into the Fae in front of me or hinder the one behind me. Ahead, the knights charged. I adjusted my grip on my sword. In mere moments we were through their line. Hooves throwing clumps of dirt, swords flashing, and small bursts of magic. It was chaotic, and I quickly became disoriented. I forced myself to slow my breathing and focus on what was in front of me instead of trying to keep an eye on the entire battle.

Behind the mounted knights were an assortment of armed men. With all the training exercises I've done over the past ten years, I had expected my first battle to be a challenge. Instead, I found the opposite. I was using a few basic moves, mostly a well-placed thrust, and the humans fell to the ground in a bloody heap. *Clearly they don't use the silver-iron on their armor.* To say I was disappointed was an understatement. If the Lord of the East only had these poorly trained men at his disposal, then why would King Pharaan have sent for warriors from all four courts?

I looked around and saw a flash of teal skin. Terror gripped me that I might be seen by Prince Tanyth, and a sword came whistling by my face. I leaped backward and hastily brought my sword up, making quick work of the knight who had thought I would be an easy mark. *But I was distracted, and I was an easy mark*, I chided myself. *I am going to die if I don't pay attention to the battle.* Growling under my breath, I looked around, assessing the battlefield as I had been trained. I could see Fiera and Ghilanna about twenty paces to my left. In between, bodies of knights were strewn. Many looked as though they could be sleeping, if you ignored the gaping holes in their armor that blood was seeping out of. Ahead of me, a ragged line of mounted knights approached, although it didn't seem as if anything was beyond them. I could see other Fae scattered in groups.

A horn sounded and the knights coming toward us picked up their pace, mustering again for a full charge. A high whistle came from somewhere behind me. I reached over my shoulder with my right arm and unhooked my glaive. I picked a target: a small knight on a big red horse. Carefully I lined myself up, glaive in my left hand, sword in my right. When the knight was a stride away, I shifted my body, bracing as I sliced the glaive at the horse's chest. Blood sprayed, covering my face and arms. I ducked, missing the swing the knight made with his shield, before doing a backhand sweep across the horse's hind legs as the knight galloped past me. The horse stumbled and then collapsed.

I whirled to face the knight, who was trying to untangle himself from the saddle. I hefted the glaive in my hand, debating if I should throw it at him. I shook my head. *No reason to waste a good glaive on that.* I closed the distance between us and right as he got free of the saddle, an arrow went squarely through his throat. I gasped and peered around, wondering who had shot the arrow.

The whistle sounded twice this time, recalling Fae from the battlefield. I gazed around; none of the mounted knights seemed to have survived. The only movement I could discern was that of the Fae obeying the order to return to camp. There was no other choice than to follow everyone in.

As I picked my way through the bodies, Fiera and Ghilanna caught up to me.

"I had to save Fiera," Ghilanna murmured.

I glanced sharply between my friends. "What happened?"

"A group of knights surrounded me, cutting me off from everyone else," Fiera said softly. "If it wasn't for Ghilanna's perfect arrival, they would have skewered me."

"Other than the one time you were surrounded, how did you feel it went?" I asked, genuinely curious.

I could hear Ghilanna take a deep breath before she responded. "It was close. Twenty to one is insane."

How odd. Almost as though we were on two different battlefields. I moistened my dry lips with the tip of my tongue. . "Were others having similar trouble?"

Ghilanna and Fiera both nodded. I bit the inside of my lip, not sure what to think. *Why did it feel so effortless to me, and not for them? I wasn't doing anything different that I'm aware of. We all had the same training.*

We crossed the invisible line marking the beginning of the camp. To my dismay Prince Almar walked over to the three of us. "A word, Serafina." He gave my friends a pointed glance. They lowered their eyes and quickly departed.

"Yes, Prince?" I asked, meeting his gaze. I was surprised he had sought me out.

"Are you aware that you are responsible for single-handedly killing approximately one quarter of the Lord of the East's knights?" Prince Almar asked in a neutral tone.

"What?" I gasped, eyes wide.

"You heard me," Prince Almar said.

"How is that possible?" I asked and wondered, *How did I not know I killed that many?*

Prince Almar let out a breath. "Some Fae can enter a trance when they are in battle. Time moves differently for them. Since you don't have magic and are half-human, no one ever explained this to you because, well, without magic, it shouldn't be possible."

I stood there gaping at him. "But Fiera and Ghilanna have magic. Why can't they enter the trance?"

"The battle trance is not that simple. Historically magic has always been a requirement, but not a guarantee a Fae can enter the trance. Very few of us are blessed with that ability," Prince Almar explained.

"Then why did King Pharaan not have more of us here, to balance the fight?" I demanded.

"I suppose I can tell you, since he did order me to come talk to you," Prince Almar said. "The king had a vision in which he discovered that the key to winning this battle—and the rest of the upcoming ones against the Lord of the East—is not dependent upon how many Fae we have present, but whether or not *you* are here."

I ran a hand over my face. Nothing he was saying really made sense. *How can the outcome of this war with the Lord of the East depend on me, a nobody?* The prince was looking at me, waiting for a response. "In order for us to win I only have to be present?" I asked, confused. It made no sense why the fate of a battle between Fae and humans, in favor of the Fae, relied on me, a half-blood. Prince Almar's words to Commander Meriel came back to me, when he was saying that I wasn't good enough to fight. *How wrong he was.*

Prince Almar nodded. "Yes, according to King Pharaan's vision. It is always possible there is more required. We can only act upon what we know."

I was debating what to say, when from behind us someone called for the prince. Prince Almar glanced over his shoulder. A brief frown flickered over his face, then was gone when he returned his attention to me. "There is a matter I must attend to. You are dismissed."

I was grateful to whoever it was for their unknowing rescue. "Yes, Prince," I replied before walking away quickly.

I took a long, meandering path to my tent. Anytime someone noticed me I would abruptly change directions to avoid them. My tactic was successful, and I made it to my tent without having to speak to anyone else.

I pushed the flap aside and as it slapped shut behind me, I finally let myself relax. I quickly removed my armor and set it on the stand along with my sword, then went to work cleaning everything. I craved a bath, but I didn't want to risk being stopped on the way. Instead, I washed what I could of the blood and dirt away with a soft rag and then put on some soft deer hide pants and a tunic.

Fiera stopped by to see how I was doing and brought a plate of meat and vegetables and to drop off her gear, which she must have cleaned somewhere else. Thankfully my friend realized I wanted to have time to myself to reflect on the events of the day in solitude. I felt a little bad at wanting time alone when we shared our tent, but she did not comment.

Thirteen

TRISTAN
379 AQ

Talk was spreading around Embergate about graduation, how now that there were almost twenty trainees close to being skilled enough, a date would be set. Once rumors of the impending graduation started, so did discussions of where everyone would end up.

Travaran pulled me aside during breakfast one morning. Instead of sitting at one of the large tables with the red group as we usually did, we were at one of the tiny tables in the far corner. I took a sip of water and Travaran spoke. "The lord commander at Court of Dusk is getting old. When my father and I were discussing possible replacements, your name came up."

I gulped and started coughing as the water went down the wrong tube in my throat. Eyes watering, I coughed until I recovered. Travaran was staring at me. "Are you okay?"

I nodded, uncertain if I was able to speak. I took a cautious sip of water, soothing my sore throat. "Yes." I hesitated. "Why would you think I am a good choice to be a lord commander? I'm just a trainee. Sure, I've led other trainees in some exercises, but to be responsible for all of the warriors within a court…I am not qualified."

Travaran tapped his fingers on the table. "It's the perfect position for you. Everything is provided by my father. You will have access to anything you can dream of."

My eyes widened. It sounded good—at least the way he was pitching it. "I've heard Bane and Greyson talking about court positions offered as a contract with set terms. Is that something Court of Dusk does also?"

"Yes. In fact, I have an example of the contract right here," Travaran said. With a wave of his hand a scroll appeared in a puff of turquoise magic. I took the proffered scroll and carefully unrolled it, then began reading.

I, _______, agree to protect and defend Prince Tanyth Terinrack, his heir, and all possessions against any who seek him harm. I will obey all orders, regardless of their nature, given by the Prince and his heir. Should I disagree with the orders I am permitted to present my reasons for dissent, but their word is final.

Should I disobey any orders or interfere with another Fae who is also under contract with or a prisoner of the court, the severity of punishment is at the discretion of the Prince, including but not limited to removal of a body part, fighting in the arena, or death.

Successes in training, combat, and other milestones chosen by the Prince will be immensely rewarded.

I shall serve until my death or release from the contract by the Prince of the Court of Dusk.

When I was done, I pushed it away from me. "Sounds more like slavery than a leadership position," I said.

Travaran frowned. "That's not how it is there, I swear."

I was skeptical. *Maybe to Travaran and his encounters with Fae at his father's court, they are not treated like slaves. But is that how it really is?* I said, "I have time to decide. Besides, until Prince Tanyth gives me a formal offer, all we can do is speculate."

I watched Travaran closely, worried he might overreact, but instead he just gave me a friendly smile. "Of course, you're right. But wouldn't it be wonderful if you were at my side at Dorcha Palace too?"

I swallowed hard. While I was friends with Travaran, there were times when he didn't have my best interests at the forefront of his mind. Who knew what it would be like once we were officially warriors and not trainees.

Fourteen

I stood on the large grassy lawn outside of Embergate, Travaran at my side, along with the twenty other trainees who had been deemed ready to graduate. We had to wait until our names were called to find out if we had made warrior or *elite*. Travaran was cocky and confident as usual and felt certain he would receive the coveted title of elite.

I kept my emotions masked even though inside they were roiling. Prince Tanyth had offered me a position that was not dependent upon whether I received the title of elite. I still had difficulty believing my luck. He not only wanted me to be in his court as leader of his personal guards, but he also was demanding that I train all Fae warriors within his court. My official title would be lord commander, though it was unclear whether the prince would require that my subordinates—everyone but him—use the title or if it would just be something they would throw around when they had interactions with other courts.

A personal request the prince had also made as a requirement of my position was that I keep his son and heir, Travaran, out of trouble. I of course agreed, but at the back of my mind I wondered if that would ultimately be my downfall. After spending so many years side by side with Travaran and either getting into trouble with him or keeping him out of harm's way, I knew how much of a challenge it would be to protect him.

Commander Zhorlon played a short tune on a horn, which was supposed to alert everyone that the ceremony was beginning. Prince Tanyth himself was going to present the medals after the commander made his speech about how wonderful it was to have everyone in training. *Yeah right, who are you kidding?* I thought.

Then Prince Tanyth stepped forward. "The moment you all have been waiting for is finally here. I want to personally congratulate each and every one of you on your successes and wish you well in your future endeavors. Now I will call you up here, one by one."

The prince began reading through the list. I was surprised that Travaran did not receive the *elite* designation. When he returned to my side his face was flushed and his fists were clenched so hard his knuckles were white. "Calm down," I whispered. Then Tanyth called my name. I gave Travaran's arm a light squeeze, hoping he would chill out and not do anything stupid while I went to receive my medal.

"Tristan Gilvrye, warrior elite!" I stumbled and almost fell to my knees as he announced my title. Today had been unusual for Embergate—so far, I was the first trainee to be awarded elite. I wasn't sure what it meant and at that precise moment I didn't care. Because *I* had gotten the title and had done so without shapeshifting, relying only on the combat skills they had taught me and the use of my shadow magic.

Prince Tanyth put the medal around my neck—it was much heavier than I expected—and then he shook my hand. "I'll see you tonight," he said, pulling me close before releasing my hand and allowing me to return to my seat.

I wasn't entirely sure what he meant by seeing me tonight. But I thought maybe Travaran would know. As I reached my friend he gave me a forced smile that didn't reach his eyes. "Congratulations."

"Thanks," I replied carefully. Travaran wasn't going to take the slight by his father well, especially if I was going to be working for Prince Tanyth. "Do you know what's happening tonight?"

Travaran frowned. "Yeah...the party he hosts every year after this ceremony. I would skip it if I could, but as heir of the court it is my duty to attend the Embergate graduations, since one day I will be overseeing them."

"Ah," I said.

"Once you're there you can't leave," Travaran said, though I wasn't sure if he was talking to me or talking to himself since his voice was so soft.

"What was that?" I asked, hoping to clarify if the words had been directed at me. It seemed like an odd thing to say, that I wouldn't be able to leave.

"The contract with my father. You won't be able to leave unless he orders you to do so. It also has provisions staying that the Court of Dusk is responsible for providing you with anything necessary to live and perform your required duties. Which means you don't have to concern yourself with packing, you will get new things when you get to Lochan Sgàile. Just be at the barracks in an hour," Travaran explained.

I was going to have to review the contract again. Travaran's words about not being able to leave nagged at me. I hadn't signed it yet since it was dependent upon my graduation from Embergate. I anticipated I would be asked to sign it tomorrow, before my first official day began.

Precisely an hour after the graduation ceremony, Travaran and I went through a star portal—one of the Fae's rapid transportation methods. As soon as the star portal opened I assumed it was going to take us to the palace of the Court of Dusk at Lochan Sgàile. I had been right.

Travaran smiled at me when the portal deposited us at the gates to the palace. I was not expecting the palace to be built into the base of Ember Mountain. There was a high wall with several watchtowers and a gate at the center. Beyond the gate I could see the entryway.

"Welcome to Dorcha Palace," Travaran said, pausing momentarily in front of the gate.

He then led me on a winding path through the palace. I noticed that after we passed through the first hallway, the ground sloped downward, giving me the impression that most of Dorcha Palace was subterranean. He stopped in front of a large set of double doors, which opened as he approached. "This is your suite. I'm only down the hall three doors." Travaran waved his hand to indicate which direction.

"Okay, I'll be sure to find you if I need something," I replied.

"Good. Now, there should be some snacks. There will be food at the party tonight. You have about two hours to do whatever you want and then we have to show up at the party. Someone will take you there. Be ready in two hours sharp!" Before I could ask any more questions, Travaran wandered down the hallway and into his room.

Prince Tanyth was waiting for me in the room. I took half a step back so I didn't collide with him and instead jammed my spine into the edge of the door. I awkwardly bowed. "Prince Tanyth."

Prince Tanyth waved his hand for me to come farther into the room. "I brought the contract. I wanted you to sign it now so that you can enjoy the party without worrying about it." The prince offered me a scroll. I took it, unrolling it as I walked over to a chair and sat down. I popped back up when I realized the prince was still here.

"Make sure you sign it before the party. It must be signed in blood," he explained. Emotion swelled at the back of my tongue with the instruction to sign it in blood. That meant I wouldn't be able to break the contract unless I was dead or he released me. *This is what I want—to be the lord commander for a prince!*

"I will do that. Should I bring it to you at the party?" I asked.

The prince shook his head. "No need. I will get it as soon as you've signed it."

"Okay," I said. The prince vanished. I was expecting him to say something else, but I guess he had more important things to attend to. I sat down in the chair and opened the scroll all the way.

The contract was short and to the point, but it left a lot of gray areas that meant if I did anything wrong, the prince could punish me at his discretion—though it also referred to immense rewards. If the luxurious room I had been appointed gave any indication of the nature of those rewards, they would be beyond my dreams, exactly as Travaran had said. I would be able to buy any silver-iron weapons or armor I wanted. Still, I hesitated. Even though at this point my life, I didn't have a reason to say no, part of me was worried that my intuition about the slavery was correct. *If only I had someone I could ask.* Closing my eyes, I took a deep breath, weighing my options. Travaran's pleading expression surfaced; the last time we discussed the contract he had even gotten on his knees and begged me. *I trust Travaran.* Decision made, I removed my knife from its sheath and pricked my finger. Then setting the scroll on the table, I awkwardly signed it with my finger. As soon as I completed my signature, the scroll flared with teal magic and then disappeared.

Precisely two hours after Travaran left me at my new set of rooms, I stepped into the hallway to figure out how to get to the party. A male waved only a few strides away.

"I'm Fallon," the male said. I did a quick examination of him. Fallon was a tad shorter than me, with loose brown hair and dark tan skin. He was wearing a deep teal tunic and pants that were a shade lighter.

"Tristan," I replied, deliberately omitting the title. *I want the Fae here to want to obey my orders, not to feel like they are forced into it.*

"Let's go," Fallon said. I had thought he might offer his hand to shake, but he didn't. I wasn't sure if that was because of my new title or what. While Fallon escorted me to the party, he told me a little about what to expect in the days ahead. As lord commander I was responsible for all of the warriors within the entire Court of Dusk territory. The majority of them called Dorcha Palace home and tomorrow I would assess their skills and establish a training schedule.

Music and the hum of voices filtered through the doors into the hallway. The guards bowed to me, saying "Lord Commander," and then swung open the doors.

My face flushed in embarrassment. *How did they already know?* "Warrior," I responded, my tone flatter than I had intended. Opening my mouth to apologize, I realized Fallon was already through the doors. I rushed after him, pausing only to take in the number of Fae. The guests favored dark gowns and robes tonight. The columns in the throne room had sheer black fabric draped between them, allowing little bits of light to filter through. The quartet of musicians was on a raised platform near the throne. Even though I had attended the parties at Embergate and the Glass Fair back at home, nothing could have prepared me for the hundreds of Fae crammed into this amount of space.

Fallon finally stopped walking when he found a gap between the guests and two chairs. "Sit and relax for a moment," Fallon suggested. "I know this can be overwhelming, especially for someone who hasn't spent much time in a Fae court. I promise you will adjust."

I gave Fallon a wavering smile and sat down, taking deep breaths and trying to let myself relax. It was a struggle. Every time a Fae got close I fought the need to grab a weapon. *They're not going to attack*, I chided myself.

I was not sure how long I sat there when a familiar hand slid itself into mine. A hint of a smile started on my lips. "Callyn," I said softly. It had been several years since she had attended any of the parties at Embergate and I had worried that something bad had happened. Finding her here at Prince Tanyth's court was a welcome surprise.

"Perhaps a drink will help you?" Callyn said, proffering a glass full of a dark wine.

I took the glass and with one long gulp drank the whole thing. She arched an eyebrow at me. "I didn't mean you had to drink it all in one go."

I sighed. "How do you get used to being in such a tight space with so many people?"

Callyn chuckled. "You will in time, Lord Commander."

"You heard too?" I asked.

"Of course. Word travels like wildfire in Dorcha Palace," Callyn replied.

Nibbling on my lip, it occurred to me that she must work here too. "Did you sign a contract with the Court of Dusk?"

Callyn's smile fell. "Yes, many years ago. Honestly, I was surprised that you took the position."

"Travaran begged me to," I said softly. Callyn had made it crystal clear over the years that she did not like Travaran.

"I need a glass of wine," she replied, and, taking my hand, marched over to the table full of brimming wine glasses. As she sipped her wine, we moved into a dark corner. "You shouldn't have come," she said softly.

"Why?" I asked, gut clenching in anticipation of her answer.

"Once you're here, there is no way out," she replied.

Digging my fingers into my palm, I stared at Callyn. *What does she mean no way out?* Eyes widening, I realized that my initial understanding of the contract—*slavery*—had to be what she was referring to. Drawing a shaky breath, mustering my shredded confidence, I replied, "There must be a way. Together we can find it."

Callyn drained her glass and set it down on a ledge and stepped close. Kissing me on the lips, then along my jaw, till her breath tickled my ear. "I believe in you."

"Then dance with me," I said and offered her my hand. We made our way onto the dance floor. Callyn set my hand on her waist and gripped my other hand with hers, and we inserted ourselves into the dancers effortlessly. I was in awe of Callyn's dance step knowledge as the musicians switched from one melody to another. With her guidance I didn't mess up too badly. The close proximity and occasional brushes of her thigh against my cock were distracting. Since this was my first night here, I had no idea how long I was supposed to be present at one of the parties.

Everything was going well until the last dance. I kissed her during the pause between songs. "Not yet," she murmured. A soft growl escaped my lips, earning me a wicked smile. Before I could speak, the music started. I twirled her outward and then when she spun back toward, me I missed the grip switch, and she sailed past me and into another couple. They started shouting and then more joined in until the noise was deafening. Callyn ran back over to me and dragged me behind a curtain. I was going to protest when I realized there was a hallway on the other side.

She led me confidently down the stone corridor illuminated with Fae light wall sconces. We stopped at a worn wooden door on the left. As she dug in a pocket for the key, I ran my hands down her side, cupping her breasts through her dress. She arched against me momentarily before inserting a key into the black lock. There was a brief glimmer of magic, a soft click, and then the door swung open. Callyn ushered me inside, then kicked the door shut and used her magic to reset the lock.

Peering around the room, which had almost the same dark wood furniture as mine, I wondered what her position was at the

Court of Dusk. My cock ached with need, but we didn't always rush. Before I could speak, Callyn shoved me hard backward. My legs hit the edge of the bed and I fell onto it.

Callyn gave me a wicked smile and she stroked me through my pants. "I want to ride you till you're begging me to stop," she declared.

"Absolutely," I replied.

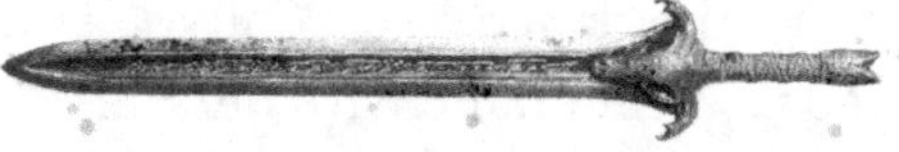

In the wee hours of the morning I made my way back to my rooms, with what I hoped were a few hours left of sleep before I would need to start my duties.

Sleeping in my own bed was not as restful as I had hoped. When I woke up I was still tired. *It could also be due to having sex and talking to Callyn instead of spending quality time sleeping.* I ran a hand over my face and sat up. *I am supposed to inspect my subordinates today. I need to get dressed and figure out where I must go.* Decision made, I stood up and tried to get my bearings in the room. It was dark. I had determined yesterday that there were no windows within my room or anywhere else I had been so far in this part of Dorcha Palace, adding to my theory that the palace was below ground.

I summoned balls of Fae light and sent them to various parts of the room so I could see. I opened the short dresser; inside was a selection of casual attire, tunics and pants in earth colors. Next, I inspected the wardrobes. One contained fancy clothes in silk, velvet, and a heavier jacquard, all in dark colors, intended for more formal occasions, such as the party last night. The other wardrobe held what I considered light training gear. Leather pants, vests, assortments of arm guards of varying lengths, as well as belts, scabbards, and various types of weapon holders. Beyond the wardrobes were several stands and racks. These held chain mail, plate armor, two swords, an axe, and a flail.

As Travaran had said, the prince was providing everything I could ever need or want. *Other than freedom.* Callyn's words that I had made the wrong choice and should have followed my gut still ate at me. But I had signed a blood contract; there was no going back now.

Gaze flitting around the room, I considered my clothing choices. *I am ready to protect Dorcha Palace and its residents.* I returned to the dresser and pulled out a black sleeveless tunic and thin shorts to prevent the leather pants from chafing. I slipped the tunic over my head and then donned the shorts. Next came a pair of thick leather pants. *Ready at a moment's notice, but not hindered by bulky plate mail.* I selected a wide belt that already had a scabbard and knife sheath on it and buckled it around my waist before choosing a sword and long knife.

I ran a brush through my slate-gray hair to smooth it out and then braided tightly. I caught a glimpse of myself in the mirror and was surprised to find everything I had chosen to wear was black. It was a stark contrast to the red I had worn for years at Embergate.

My plan for today consisted of an introduction, inspection of their gear, and a skills test. I knew that I had to earn the respect of my men quickly or I would never be able to successfully lead them. Prince Tanyth demanded loyalty without question. I knew that he expected me to do the same.

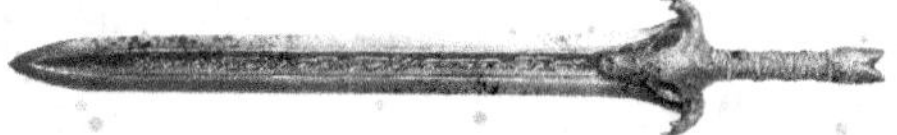

After I left my rooms, I spent about ten minutes wandering the hallways—each one looked the same and I quickly got turned around. Rounding a corner, I caught a flash of light brown hair and a familiar face. "Hey, Fallon!" I shouted while waving my arms. Fallon turned around and waited for me to approach. "Can you give me directions for how to get to, well, to wherever it is that I am supposed to be conducting my inspection?"

Fallon nodded. "Of course. Maybe later today I will have some time and can give you a tour so you will be able to find your way around here without help."

"Thanks," I said. I wanted to be self-sufficient, so the sooner I could figure out how the palace was laid out, the quicker I could accomplish my goal.

We walked in silence, our footsteps echoing when the stone changed from smooth and flat to individual cobblestones. The air was damp and chilly, the way subterranean caves felt, lending proof to my theory that Dorcha Palace was underground.

Fallon halted in front of a large double wooden door reinforced with four metal straps almost as wide as my hands. Excitement filled me—unlike the party last night, training grounds were where I was most comfortable. Fallon raised his hand; I could see a faint glow emitting from it, and both doors opened outward. The ceiling rose high above us, a flicker of brightness near the very center. *Sunlight? Maybe we're not as far underground as I thought.*

Gazing around, I conducted a quick survey of the room. Racks lining the walls boasted an impressive variety of weapons: swords of all shapes and sizes, axes, maces, even an assortment of polearms. On the opposite side of the weapons, male warriors occupied a row of benches. *My new subordinates.*

I strode to the center of the room and stopped, feet spread, hands loose at my side. "Greetings, warriors." I started with the formal introduction we were taught at Embergate. They immediately stopped talking among themselves and focused on me.

"As you know by now, I am Lord Commander Tristan Gilvrye, and from this day forward you and all other warriors under contract with Prince Tanyth will report to me directly. I did not have the pleasure of knowing the former lord commander." A few hastily suppressed snorts circulated along the bench. I kept speaking. "As of today you will start with a clean slate. Ranks, rewards, or punishments that were previously assigned to you are no longer in place." I scanned their faces, noting who was eager and who was angry. "All of you present and those who are not have the same rank—warrior—and you will have equal opportunities to receive a promotion."

One of the males started to speak, but I stepped forward, hand raised. "While I do welcome your feedback, please wait until I am done speaking." I met the eyes of each warrior. "Prove to me you are worthy of a higher position, do the work, and don't shirk your responsibilities. Now, we will begin with a skills test. Each of you will spar with me. Any individual who can disarm me, here today, in our first session will be immediately promoted," I announced. I heard eager whispers, including a few boasts that it would be no problem to disarm me, since I was merely a "wet behind the ears trainee."

I pointed to the male with bright purple hair and olive skin who was closest to me at the end of the first bench. "You are first. State your name and then we will square off. This is a sword fight only. We will test the other skills another time."

The purple-haired male stood up and swaggered over to me. From his swagger I could tell he thought this would be a cakewalk. "My name is Laeroth Daefir."

I motioned for him to draw his sword and stepped a few paces back so we could center ourselves in the painted circle. We crossed blades. "Begin!"

Laeroth twisted his wrist, trying for his first maneuver to disarm me. Unfortunately for him, by the time he completed the movement I had changed positions and taken a large step to the right. As Laeroth was trying to adjust his position to accommodate for what I had done, he turned his back on me for a split second. I spun, sword flashing, and hit him hard from behind on the shoulder. He dropped his sword and gasped in pain.

"Sorry, I underestimated how hard I hit," I apologized. Laeroth peered at me in bewilderment, then went to sit on the bench. *Did the old lord commander never apologize?*

"Next!" I called, and so it went. I disarmed the next four warriors with four strikes or less. Disappointment and concern warred within me. *They are afraid of being punished and out of practice.* I was determined to treat them as respected members of the court. Even if I could not leave, there had been nothing in the contract dictating *how* to perform my job as lord commander.

When the sixth Fae male approached, I could tell he was different from the others. He oozed confidence, back straight, a correct grip on his sword, and his face was calm. "My name is Elashor Daran."

We crossed swords. "Ready, begin!" *Maybe there is hope and I started with the most nervous of the group.*

I started with the same opening move I'd been using and took a large step, this time to the left, then spun, and Elashor met my sword. Sparks went flying as they connected. I parried and began working my way through the ten basic movements. Each movement Elashor made was precise. Hope soared within me, and I eased into combinations. Elashor met every strike with the appropriate parry or block. He even succeeded in taking the offensive advantage a few times. Though Elashor was confident and skilled, he still could not disarm me, nor had he made an attempt.

I spun to give myself space and Elashor took the opportunity. He sprinted toward me, sword raised. As he began to initiate a three-four combination, I swapped my sword into my left hand and chopped down with it across his wrist, pulling up slightly at the last moment. *I don't want to injure Elashor.* He dropped his sword with a hiss, glaring at me. "What was that for?"

I shrugged. "You did very well, but enough time had passed that you should have been able to identify an opening and disarm me. Given you did not, I chose to demonstrate a method of disarming an opponent. Now if you would please go sit on the bench, I have more males to test."

The back of my tunic clung to me, damp with sweat, while I paced in front of the benches where the warriors sat, waiting for me to speak. I struggled to find the appropriate words.

"We will begin the hand-to-hand combat test shortly. For now I want you to take a brief recess," I said. The recess would at least give me time to figure out what to say that would not be too harsh. Often I found sparring helped clear my head, but none of the warriors had come anywhere close to being a good match. Just then, the doors opened. I spun, sword raised, more out of habit than anything. My jaw dropped and eyes widened when I saw Callyn standing there. She wore brown leather pants and vest over a green tunic, with a sword and an axe hooked into her belt. A smile broke out across my face as I eyed her weapons. *Just the partner I need.*

"Are you done here?" she asked, walking forward into the painted circle.

I stepped toward her, ignoring the muttering coming from the bench. "That depends. Did you want to spar?"

I heard a gasp behind me, followed by a yelp. *They're acting like a female isn't allowed to spar with a male.* Rolling my eyes, I tuned them out; their opinions were not important. Callyn was a worthy sparring partner.

"If you think you're up to the task," she said with a glance at my crotch.

I smirked. "For you, always." I stepped into position in the circle opposite her and took several deep breaths to center myself. "Ready when you are," I said, raising my sword.

Callyn crossed her sword with mine, the blades lightly touching.

"Begin!"

Instead of shifting, I parried. We did a quick series of strikes and parries with very minimal movement. As she rocked back slightly, I took a step forward and began a high strike, aiming for her collarbone. Hoping to catch her off guard, I changed angles halfway through the strike and went low. Callyn shifted her stance and blocked, easily. *I'll have to try harder.* I pivoted to my left, trying to get behind her. But she anticipated the move and turned precisely in time to meet my middle strike with a parry. She put her weight behind the sword, forcing me to take a few steps backward, before she skipped to the side.

My lips twitched. Callyn was making me work far more than the warriors on the bench had. *Eventually they can be this skilled too.* Sweat beaded on my forehead, and droplets dripped from Callyn's hairline down to her chin. She took advantage of my momentary distraction and lunged forward, trying to stab me in the stomach, much like the move I had made that had resulted in my first kill at Embergate so many years ago. Gritting my teeth and pushing away the memory, I hastily blocked and retreated a few steps, being careful to not step over the line that would automatically give her the win.

Callyn charged me. I twisted out of the way, and she shot past, over the painted line. A cheer went up from the warriors on the bench. "Tristan! Tristan!"

I growled under my breath, straightening my shoulders and turning toward them. "While I appreciate your praise, Callyn accidentally went over the line. Hardly a reason to celebrate."

The warriors whispered among themselves, but none of them spoke loud enough for me to address whatever it was they were discussing.

Shrugging, I turned back toward Callyn; she was smiling at me in amusement. "I didn't realize you were that close to the line."

It was an easy mistake, nothing more. "Maybe we can have a rematch tomorrow," I suggested.

"Maybe," she replied, then glanced at my crotch and met my gaze again. "Or tonight." And with that, Callyn departed.

I sheathed my sword and turned to face the males on the bench.

Laeroth spoke. "I will look forward to when you and Callyn face off in the arena."

My eyes narrowed and confusion flooded me. "Arena?" As soon as I spoke, I remembered that Travaran had mentioned arena fights.

"Yeah...Prince Tanyth has an arena, and *everyone* is required to fight at some point," Laeroth explained. "There are beasts in the dungeons that are kept for the express purpose of fighting in the arena." I almost didn't suppress my shudder in time. *I have kept my shapeshifting a secret for many years. It would suck if I slipped up now on my first day at Dorcha Palace.*

Trying to hide my reaction, I tapped my lip with my finger. "If I get an order from Prince Tanyth to fight in the arena, then I will obey, same as you."

I cleared my throat. "Going forward, we will spend the next two weeks in what I suppose you could call boot camp. My goal is that by the end of the two weeks, you will be able to successfully disarm an opponent of equal skill to yourselves. When you prove that is the case, we will decrease the time spent on swords to one hour a day and focus on hand-to-hand combat next.

"You will train daily, unless we are out on assignment. It is critical to continue to hone your skills. You are all capable of reaching the same level I am at, it's just a matter of practicing. Am I clear?"

"Yes, Lord Commander!" they all shouted in sync.

"Very well. Lunch will be brought in and then we will do the hand-to-hand combat test," I announced.

Fifteen

SERAFINA

411 AQ

I sprinted through the vibrant emerald grass, fists pumping at my sides, russet braid swinging across my back. The bushes rustled behind me and I was sure the Fae male was hot on my heels. A rock outcropping loomed ahead of me, and I knew if I could just get to it in time, I had a shot at surviving. A movement out of the corner of my eye distracted me and next thing I knew I was falling.

Rocks skittered behind me and I pivoted on my knees, arms raised protectively. A snow leopard with bright blue eyes was staring at me a few strides away. A laugh bubbled up from within me and before I could stop myself it escaped my lips. Hastily I covered my mouth with my hands. *What is wrong with me?*

The snow leopard stood still as a statue. Only the movement of its ribcage confirmed it was indeed a living, breathing, huge cat. *Can I touch it? Curiosity* getting the better of me, I slowly reached my outstretched hand toward the snow leopard.

Sighing, I opened my eyes. *Just a dream.* Part of me really wanted to know if the snow leopard would have allowed me to touch it. *Maybe I'll find out tonight, if I have the same dream.* Satisfied with the possibility of having the same dream tonight,

"

I rolled out of the pile of furs on my bed and stood up, my hair cascading down my back in a tangled mess. The dream coupled with the looming battle had made it almost impossible to sleep. I decided it wasn't worth it to go back to sleep—if my mind was awake I might as well see if I could get breakfast this morning before everyone else.

When I stepped out of the tent there was barely enough light to see my way to the kitchen tent. Food was available around the clock, so I wasn't concerned with not being able to eat. There was a Fae sitting at one of the many tables near the kitchen tent. As I approached the table, I thought the Fae looked familiar, but I couldn't pinpoint why. I snagged a plate of food and decided to sit down at the table and introduce myself. He wasn't behaving in a manner that led me to believe he didn't want company.

I slid onto the bench and gave the Fae male in front of me a smile. He had black hair and green eyes. He was wearing a green tunic and leather armguards, as though he either had been practicing archery or intended to after breakfast.

"Solana?" the Fae male said in almost a whisper.

I blinked in confusion, wondering why this stranger would say my mother's name. "Excuse me?"

The Fae male's eyes widened as he realized what he said. "My apologies, Trainee Serafina, for a moment I thought Solana had returned to me."

"Who are you?" I asked.

The Fae male chuckled and glanced down at what he was wearing. "I suppose you wouldn't know who I am. I'm Pharaan. Solana was my daughter."

My eyes widened. He didn't use his title, but I was confident there was only one Fae who went by Pharaan and that was the *king* of all the Fae. Here, casually eating breakfast alone. I attempted to stand and knocked the bench over instead. I was trying to remember the protocol I had been taught for meeting the king but was drawing a blank for what I should do.

"Serafina," he said in a calm voice. "Relax, sit down, eat your breakfast. There is no need to be formal. We're merely two Fae in a battle camp enjoying a meal."

I pressed my lips together and righted the bench, then sat back down, not convinced there wasn't more to this, especially since he had just referred to me as a Fae. "Is there something you want?"

He shook his head. "No. Simply breakfast before everyone else, same as you."

I took a deep breath and stabbed a piece of sausage with my fork. It was delicious. The two of us ate in silence. It was strange that I had been worried about meeting King Pharaan and now I was here with him, and we were casually eating breakfast like old friends. *How odd*.

As I chewed my food, I ran his words over in my mind. He had revealed something unexpected. *Solana was my daughter*. My jaw dropped, and I had to shut it before my food fell out. *He must mean a different Solana, not my mother*.

"Is Solana a common name for Fae?" I asked.

King Pharaan sighed. "No. It's not. But your question makes me think your mother never told you about your Fae family."

"That is correct. She left me letters, but they spoke of our time together in Gaskal and my father, Gareth. There was never any mention of her Fae relatives," I replied warily.

The king blew out his breath. "Battle camp is not the best time to dive into who your family is, but that is my mistake, not determining the extent of your knowledge before I spoke to you." He steepled his hands together and rested his chin on them. "Solana Wyantha was my daughter. Which makes you my granddaughter."

I gasped and leaned back, wanting to get some space between us. I leaned too far and toppled off the bench and onto my back, knocking the wind out of my lungs. I lay there coughing, waiting for my body to recover. As the pain in my chest eased, I tried to comprehend what King Pharaan said. *I am the king of the Fae's granddaughter.*

Anger flooded me—anger at Commander Meriel, who had known who I was related to, but had kept it a secret for eleven years, and anger at my mother for not feeling it was important for me to know all my heritage, or that I had family still living. I stood up, fists clenched at my side. I bit the inside of my cheek to prevent me from saying something that I would regret to the king.

King Pharaan spoke. "You're angry and I understand. Your mother requested before you were born that you be raised as a human and not pulled into the politics of Fae. I have honored her request, as has Commander Meriel, and the few others who are aware of your Fae bloodline. However, you are twenty-one and about to graduate from Fae warrior training. It is time for you to know your entire family. What you choose to do with that information is entirely up to you. I acknowledge you are my granddaughter and have a right to a place at the Court of Dawn.

"However, I also know of the struggles you have faced at Jade Wilds and here at the battle camp and I do not want to pressure you to come to court. You can choose where you wish to end up and who you want to be. I know that you might fancy finding a husband who is a love match. Common in Fae, due to the mating bond. But should you wish, it is within your options to return to one of the human territories and find a human husband."

I exhaled, following his words and what they meant. *The king, my grandfather, is telling me I can choose who and what I want to be. The new knowledge of who I am, though sudden, does not need to change anything, or it can change everything. I must decide what future I want.* "Should I decide that I want to live in a human territory, will you support this decision?"

King Pharaan nodded. "Yes. You could find a house in a town and figure out a service or trade to offer. Or you could inquire with King Leonard Helias about living in his court as a princess.

I can ensure you have the money necessary to establish the life you desire."

"What if I want to live as part of the court?" I asked.

A faint smile crossed King Pharaan's lips. "Then you will have rooms within my palace, as well as be assigned to duties. Together you and I will figure out what duties are most suitable and appealing to you."

I ate a few more bites of food. "I need time."

"Of course, you can take as much time as necessary," King Pharaan generously replied.

I departed, desperate for room to think without King Pharaan sharing the same space. When I was at the edge of the camp, I ran, thoughts churning.

I hadn't known what to expect when I met King Pharaan, but it absolutely wasn't how our initial meeting had gone. With the king trying to be incognito at an early breakfast. Or to receive his unyielding support for how I wanted to live my life after graduating from Jade Wilds. After spending the first half of my life among the humans and the second half among the Fae in a warrior training camp, it hadn't occurred to me that I could return to the humans and live a *human* life if I wanted. What I needed to determine was, now that I knew it was an option, whether it was one I wanted to take—or if I wanted to stay with the Fae. I remembered the conversation I had had with Fiera before we left Jade Wilds about wanting to go to the Court of Dawn.

Is living in a Fae court going to be like it was here in the battle camp? Training, fucking, and preparing for an inevitable war. *Or is there more to life as a Fae than what I have experienced in Jade Wilds and now here at the battle camp at Emerald Valley?* I would have to get more information if I wanted the answers to those questions. I had to figure out who I should ask. King

Pharaan had behaved as though he genuinely was interested in my well-being, which was a stark contrast to my interactions with Prince Almar. I had no good memories of my human grandfather, no way to know if King Pharaan's behavior was "normal" for a grandfather or not.

My thoughts dwindled until I was lost in the rhythm of running, focusing on the environment around me and not worrying about anything other than how fast I was going and not tripping.

Ghilanna caught up to me when I was making my third lap. "Did you already eat?" she asked, running beside me.

I chuckled. "Yes, I was up insanely early, though I could probably use a second breakfast soon."

"Word has gone out that the Lord of the East is not willing to surrender. Your second breakfast is going to have to wait. Final preparations are underway now for another attack," Ghilanna informed me.

"I have snacks back in the tent. Sounds like we should go get ready," I said and turned to the left. Weaving our way through the camp, we made our way to our tent.

Sixteen

TRISTAN
385 AQ

After five years as lord commander of the Court of Dusk, my operations within Dorcha Palace felt like a well-oiled machine. There had been some bumps along the way, but overall the level of improvement had been tenfold. Though my original assumption that they could all fight at my level with enough practice had been somewhat misplaced. Bane, Elashor, Valor, and a few others were close to my level. If I was being honest, Bane was almost equal. If I didn't pay attention when we sparred, he won.

Practices had been reduced to once a week. I wanted to ensure their skills stayed sharp without being obnoxious about it. Occasionally I would add extra practice time to run mock battles. For those we would use wooden weapons that had been magicked to mark the Fae it hit. If the marks were in a vital area, the warrior would be deemed dead.

Every morning, I woke up early and went for a run. Sometimes Travaran would join me. I enjoyed those mornings when we could hang out like we had in training. *When neither one of us had responsibilities other than following orders.* Since living under his father's command, Travaran had begun to behave more like a spoiled prince than a capable warrior and it was causing a rift between us.

When I arrived in the large training room, Elashor was waiting for me with a scroll in his hand. "Lord Commander," he said with a bow and offered the scroll. I arched my eyebrows in surprise at his formality and took the scroll.

I have been notified of an intruder in the southern part of the territory. Take a squad and eliminate the problem.

I recognized the writing immediately as Prince Tanyth's. The note made it seem as though there was only one intruder not multiple; a full squad seemed overkill.

Travaran walked over and snatched the note from my hand. I bristled. *He could have asked.*

When he finished reading the note, he crumpled it up. "No reason to take a full squad," Travaran said as though he had read my thoughts.

"The orders say full squad, so I will be taking a full squad," I countered. *Why does he want to change the orders? What does he have to gain?*

Travaran smirked. "No. You will only be taking me."

My nostrils flared and I bit my tongue. It would not help if I shouted at him, especially not with an audience. Per the contract I had with Prince Tanyth, I was required to take orders from Travaran too. Given this was not a life-or-death situation, I decided to let this slide. "Fine, but we need to work together. You can't just blunder into things without discussing it first."

Travaran grinned at me. "Absolutely."

"Let me give Elashor my instructions for while we are gone and then I will go pack. Plan for one night," I told Travaran.

He nodded and disappeared; I hoped he was heading to pack. I ran a hand over my face and turned toward Elashor. I wasn't worried about leaving; I was confident Elashor and Bane could handle everything in my absence. "I want you to take over the schedule while I'm gone. There is a list on the wall." I pointed to the board above the weapons. "Run the drills we have been doing and don't worry about changing anything."

"Yes, Lord Commander," replied Elashor. I pressed my lips together into a thin line. *He's using the title because of Travaran,* I reminded myself. Once the warriors and I had become accustomed to each other I encouraged them to simply call me Tristan.

I clapped him on the shoulder and then left.

Travaran and I traveled south. The note had not provided any insight to who or what the intruder might be. Without knowing a precise location, a star portal was not an option. Prince Tanyth disliked horses, which suited me just fine. I had found that horses were not fans of shapeshifters and I always had difficulty when I was around them. Unicorns were a different matter—not that if the prince had a unicorn, he would allow anyone to ride it.

I assumed the individual we pursued was Fae but knew I could be wrong. Either way, the order was the same: elimination. *A harsh punishment for trespassing.* I hoped I would be able to question the trespasser before Travaran took matters into his own hands.

"Might end up close to Glass Oasis," Travaran commented as we ran side by side.

"We don't have time to make a stop," I replied, praying that we would not end up there. I had been well known because of my snow leopard shapeshifting and my father's position on the council, which meant the odds of my shapeshifting staying secret were essentially zero if we went there. Aside from the way I departed over twenty years ago, I knew I was not welcome. Thankfully Glass Oasis didn't come up again.

I held up my hand, signaling for a halt. I sniffed the air and caught a whiff of smoke and an unfamiliar animal.

Travaran's eyes lit up in recognition as he caught the scent as well. Using hand signals, I told him to take the right, I'd take the left, and we'd surround whoever it was. I unsheathed my sword, but Travaran left his in his scabbard. I could see hints of his magic beginning to swirl around his fingers.

I went to the left, keeping my footsteps light so as not to give away my position. *Please follow our plan.* The sharp tang of smoke was stronger the closer I got. Now I could see the edge of the fire ring with bright orange-and-red flames dancing in the small pile of logs. On the other side was a large animal. There was a sharp snap from where Travaran should be, and the animal's head shot upward. *Bear!* I gasped in surprise. The snarling bear focused on Travaran's position.

Fear coursing through me, I sprinted, intending to attack from behind while the bear was distracted by Travaran. But Travaran struck first. There was a sizzle and the smell of burning flesh as turquoise magic hurtled through the air, pelting the bear. In the moments it took me to reach them, Travaran had killed the bear.

Gulping air, throat burning from being so close to the fire, I stood gazing at Travaran with the bear in between us. Then I noticed the bear was changing. My eyes got wide when in place of the bear was a female Fae—Chalia, if I remembered correctly. She had been about ten years younger than I was and she hadn't known what she could shift into when I left Glass Oasis.

I bit my cheek, ordering myself to focus. *This was an assignment, we took out an intruder, there is nothing else to it.* I let out a deep breath and used my sword to poke the female. She didn't move. "Definitely dead."

Travaran smiled, and I smiled back, afraid to let him see my disgust at killing a shapeshifter. "Do you think this was the intruder?"

"Likely, though we should check the area and make sure there aren't any others around before we head back," I replied.

We found no evidence of Fae or humans within an hour in any direction. Satisfied that the bear shifter had been the intruder indicated in the note, we headed back to the palace. I had been expecting Travaran to boast about claiming the kill, but he didn't. We ran in silence, which gave me a chance to think about what had happened. *We killed a bear shifter. Is this what I do now? Kill my own?*

No matter how much I hated that I had participated in killing a shifter, I could not alter the past, only do better in the future. Unfortunately, my options were limited for what I could do to help shapeshifters I came across in the future, especially if I was under explicit orders. Disobeying could be punishable by death if the prince wanted to go to extreme measures. I had to let this go.

We stopped for a few hours to rest before continuing to the palace. I thought Travaran would insist on giving the report to Prince Tanyth with me, but he disappeared as soon as we entered the palace.

I went to the throne room, not sure if the prince would be there. If he wasn't, then I would report in a few hours, when I knew he would be awake.

Prince Tanyth was sitting on the throne with a piece of paper in his hand. He set it down and stood up when I entered the room. "Did you eliminate the intruder?"

"Yes, the intruder was eliminated," I replied.

"Give me more details," the prince ordered eagerly.

I nodded. "Travaran and I found a bear shifter. She attacked, and we killed her."

Prince Tanyth smiled wickedly. "Wonderful. One less shifter to worry about."

I kept my expression blank. To my surprise, the prince set his hand on my shoulder. "You do know why I kill shifters, right?"

I frowned, not sure we'd ever had this discussion before. "No, I don't believe so." I knew I had to tread carefully and not give away the sympathy I felt for shifters, since I was one.

"Since you will continue to follow my orders to eliminate shifters, I will honor you with an explanation," Tanyth said. "You see, the lost Fae queen prophecy speaks about the Great

Cat, a shapeshifting Fae male." I shifted my eyes around the room; I should've known it had to do with another prophecy. Travaran had told me long ago about the prophecy his father believed was real regarding Fleshrender, Dragonfang, and the *Bloodsong Grimoire*. It should not have been a surprise that there was *another* prophecy guiding Prince Tanyth's actions.

I yanked myself out of my thoughts to focus on the prince again, hoping he didn't notice my inattentiveness. "I am sure you are aware how finicky Fae prophecies are. Well, if there are no large shapeshifters—cat or other species—in existence, then it would be impossible for the prophecy to come true."

"I understand," I said, keeping my voice harsh, while inwardly cringing. *A Fae hunt for shapeshifters like me. This is a dangerous line to walk.*

"This will now be your primary task. To either hunt for shapeshifters, or to eliminate them if I get word of their whereabouts," Tanyth said. "If I had known the Fae you went after today was a shifter, then I would have sent you with one of the collars. A bear would have been an entertaining addition to the arena."

"Collar, Prince?" I questioned, struggling to keep the tremor out of my voice.

He nodded. "Yes, I have collars that can prevent a shapeshifter from using their magic. It forces them to stay in animal form."

Clenching my fists, I forced out a reply. "I see. Do you need anything else?"

The prince shook his head. "No. You can have the morning off if you would like. I am sure Elashor can handle your duties for a few more hours."

"Thank you," I replied, relief coursing through me as I departed.

As soon as I stepped into my room, my shoulders slumped as the weight of the prince's words hammered at me and the position I had allowed myself to be forced into. Prince Tanyth was going to use me to hunt shapeshifters. If I protested, as I was permitted to by the contract, then he would demand to know my reasoning, forcing me to reveal that I could shapeshift. I was certain any move I made that wasn't to explicitly obey his orders to kill or capture a shapeshifter would surely reveal my secret. The only choice I had was to follow the orders.

I took a deep breath and filled the tub for a bath. Since he had given me a few hours to myself, I decided I could at least get clean and relax.

When the tub was full, I discarded my clothing in a heap, and then proceeded to submerge myself. The hot water immediately loosened my tight muscles. I closed my eyes.

A shuffle of footsteps had me leaping to my feet with a snarl, sending a huge splash of water everywhere. Fallon, now sopping wet, gave me a droll stare. "I have another assignment for you."

I frowned. "More orders? The prince told me a moment ago to go relax for a few hours."

Fallon shrugged. "You will have to take that up with the prince, if you wish. However, these orders are fairly time sensitive."

"Well, then what are they?" I demanded.

Fallon rubbed his finger over the bridge of his nose, then responded. "Prince Tanyth's scouts have had several disturbing reports of the human, King Lionel Helias of Gaskal, Lord of the South, rapidly approaching our shared border with over one thousand knights."

My frown deepened. *A human king has launched an attack on our shared border.* "I should report to the prince." I stepped out of the tub and reached for a towel.

Fallon stepped to the side to give me room. "The prince has given me all your orders. He is personally riding out to our other borders to ensure this is not a coordinated attack by multiple human kings. You will annihilate the human king and take all the warriors except two squads, which will stay behind for the defense of Dorcha Palace."

My eyes lit up in anticipation of getting another chance to leave Dorcha Palace and to put my warriors to the test against a human king. *A chance to verify their skills are up to par.* Especially the king whose lands controlled the gold mines. Though the gold was too soft to make functional magic weapons, it was the most valuable of the metals that the humans had control over.

I wrapped the towel around my hips and went into the bedroom. Fallon trailed me. I threw my words over my shoulder. "I will take the warriors and send news of the outcome."

"Excellent," replied Fallon. "I will inform the prince and pass along the word to the warriors that they need to make preparations."

The battle against the humans was bloody, with steep losses for both sides. The humans had numerous magic objects at their disposal, allowing them to successfully block many of our magic attacks, along with a large quantity of their superior silver-iron swords. The Fae and humans were closely matched, and I knew I had to find a way to end it.

In the distance I could see King Lionel. I slashed my way through the humans until I reached him. My plate armor was slick with blood, but I kept my grip firm on my sword as I faced King Lionel Helias. There was an odd silence around us, even though I was aware there were still small pockets of humans resisting. The king stared at me before he charged. I met his sword with mine and sparks flew. Parry and strike, strike and parry. I could see that he believed we were truly evenly matched. Snarling at him, I rushed forward in a high strike–low strike combination. Carving a deep gash in King Lionel's armor, I let my momentum carry me into a spin, and with precision I snapped my leg out, aiming for his throat. My boot connected, and the king flew backward at the impact. I leaped toward him, sword raised.

King Lionel was breathing heavily. He pulled up the visor on his helmet and I could see blood trickling out of his nose and mouth. "Negotiate with me," King Lionel whispered.

Doubt flickered momentarily in my mind at his words and then it was gone. I knew my duty. Swallowing hard, I yanked my helmet off and tossed it on the ground, wanting him to see my face. "I do not negotiate with humans. You invaded the territory of Prince Tanyth of the Court of Dusk." I raised my sword and in a smooth motion beheaded him. The head rolled a few feet away. I picked it up in my left hand, keeping my sword ready in my right.

I raised the dripping head and shouted, "King Lionel is dead!" Bile rose in my throat. There were too many eyes on me to do anything other than follow my orders. Prince Tanyth would get many reports, I had no doubt. Including whether I followed the directive of killing the human king and delivering his head to the new Lord of the South.

Carefully, I cloaked myself in shadow magic and hid within a wagon returning to Gaskal. Once I was through the gates of Gaskal, I ditched the wagon, anticipating it would not be heading toward the palace but to the barracks to care for the wounded. Keeping to the shadows and alleyways, I was able to stay hidden under a brown hooded cloak. I was not visibly armed; I did not want to cause alarm before I had completed my task. The city around the palace was quite disorganized in design and left me wondering how the humans ever accomplished anything if they couldn't even make a straight road.

I walked around the base of the palace wall and when I found a suitable location, I strengthened the magic hiding me and scaled the wall. I followed one of the servants through a side entrance and then with some good guesses made my way to the throne room.

It was obvious the new Lord of the South was not aware the old one had died. I was mildly surprised since the wagon I had hitched a ride in had come from the battle and *should* have carried the news. *Maybe their messengers are truly that slow.* Taking a deep breath and preparing myself for what was next, I stopped about five strides from where the heir was standing near the throne, threw back my hood, and dropped my magic. He gasped in shock.

"Greetings, King Leonard, Lord of the South," I said and tossed him the bag I had been holding.

He caught it, eyes wide. "Who are you and what is this?"

"I am Lord Commander Tristan Gilvrye from the Court of Dusk," I replied. I had deliberately braided my hair back so that my pointed ears were quite visible. I wanted him to know it was the Fae who were responsible for the king's death.

Instead of asking more questions, Leonard opened the bag and then promptly dropped it, sending the head rolling down the aisle. "What the hell! Is this some kind of trick?"

I shrugged, continuing my performance. "King Lionel decided to attack the Court of Dusk unprovoked and has paid the price."

Anger flashed in the king's eyes. "You had to kill him?"

I narrowed my eyes in annoyance. "Death is the nature of war."

"The fact that he was beheaded implies that this was personal," replied the king.

"Then perhaps he should have had you fight instead, and the outcome would have been different," I responded.

"Leave. Fae are not welcome here in Gaskal," King Leonard ordered.

"Good day," I said. I concentrated on the spot where we had found the bear shifter and summoned a star portal. As I stepped through, the last thing I saw was the bloodthirsty expression on King Leonard's face.

A quick glance showed I had made a good choice. No one else was here. I bent over as my stomach clenched and I heaved up what little remained of my breakfast. Tears dribbled down my chin as my stomach kept clenching. Every moment with the king I hated what I was doing, wishing there was an alternative. *His life or mine*, I reminded myself.

Seventeen

SERAFINA
411 AQ

Waves of green grass stretched out before us. The dead bodies had been moved—using magic, I surmised—leaving the battlefield surprisingly unblemished from the battle yesterday. I found the lack of evidence of the battle disturbing. *Wouldn't it encourage the Lord of the East to surrender if the evidence of lives lost was still strewn around?* I bit my lip. *Or it would cause everyone to get sick from the stench of rotting flesh?* My stomach rolled at the thought. I glanced to my right, where Fiera was. A little way behind her I caught a glimpse of a teal-skinned male Fae. His eyes bored into mine. Shuddering I looked away. *Teal skin, like my dream again—and Prince Tanyth.*

The call of the battle horn sent ripples down the three lines of Fae. I adjusted my grip on my sword. *Focus*, I chided myself. *Thud, thud.* I gazed upon the sloping hill in front of us as the human knights became visible. Their lines were more ragged today, with larger gaps. *Their losses must have been much more than we believed.* Moments later, a barely audible whistle came from behind me, the same as yesterday.

The fourth row of Fae sent a volley of magic over our heads, arching through the air. Streamers of blue, purple, and silver lit up the sky and fell upon the human knights. The strides of the horses faltered under the magical onslaught. A horn sounded from the other side of the hill, and a hundred balls of fire sailed into the air. *Where did they get so many catapults overnight?* A bead of sweat rolled down my nose; I swiped at it with my free hand.

Once again blue, purple, and silver magic shot into the air and collided with the fireballs, but only half of them went out. The rest continued their trajectory, heading straight for the first line of Fae. Moments before the first one would have collided with the warriors in its wake, a wave of deep green magic swept the remaining fireballs away, and they landed a safe distance away in the grass, flames extinguished.

Finally, then, the signal I was waiting for—three sharp whistles. The warriors in front of me began sprinting and I followed suit. Turquoise flickered in the corner of my eye and then was gone. I shook my head. *Now is not the time for a distraction.* Adrenaline coursed through me and we slammed into the line of knights.

Eighteen

TRISTAN
400 AQ

Over the years I had occasionally been ordered to fight in the arena. For the most part the fights were the prince's way of showing off my skills to his guests. As much as I despised being used as a pawn, at least he wasn't constantly trying to have me killed—like the beasts in his dungeon. The fights varied; sometimes they were solo and others I was teamed up with warriors under my command. The opponents varied as well. Beasts from the dungeon or prisoners. I tried to stay away from the dungeon as much as possible. The prisoners' captivity struck too close to home.

Except for today. This morning, I had woken up with a burning desire to go into the dungeon that I couldn't shake. Every hallway housing the beasts was the same—dark, damp, and reeking of rotting meat and decay, with cells too small to comfortably hold them. By the time I finished my tour, I was shaking and unable to suppress the fear that Prince Tanyth would learn my secret and I would be trapped down here too.

Blinking, I made myself pay attention to my current objective: the impending arena fight and defeating my foe, whoever it was, using weapons, without magic. Prince Tanyth enjoyed battles in his arena that involved non-magical types of combat. His preference suited me just fine. If I was honest, I was more comfortable with a sword in my hand than wielding the shadow magic. The prince's expectation was that I would win again, and I did not intend to disappoint him.

Tonight, I was given an iron breastplate and a fauld to protect my waist, plus my longsword. While I was warming up in the antechamber, the gate opened behind me.

"Tristan," called Travaran. I whirled in surprise, keeping my sword point low.

"What are you doing here?" I demanded, noting Travaran was wearing the same armor as I was.

Travaran shrugged. "My father wants us to team up tonight."

I arched my eyebrows in surprise. The arena was dangerous and not a place that I would willingly send my heir. *Another example of how little I really know Prince Tanyth.* Taking a deep breath, I resumed my warmup, not wanting to appear shaken by the new development. Concern welled up within me. Though I was confident in my ability to stay safe within the arena, I knew the prince would expect that I protect his son at all costs. I prayed that Travaran was able to stay focused in the arena.

"Travaran and Tristan, you're up," announced the guard.

I adjusted my grip on my sword and took the shield the guard offered me. Travaran was also offered a shield. Every arena battle was different, which meant the weapons, armor, and layout of the arena would change, too, and sometimes there was even a theme. We followed the guard up the ramp and the heavy bars of the gate rattled as it was cranked open. We jogged forward into the arena. Walls of pale stone, the height of four Fae standing on each other's shoulders at least, rose above us. Together, we raised our swords in the air and the crowd went wild. Even from their seats far above us, the sound was deafening.

The arena was full of beige sand and wide open. The walls that could be moved into place from underground, raised and lowered at Prince Tanyth's whim, were not currently visible for the impending fight. My heartbeat was a steady thump in my chest. I felt primed and ready, my grip solid on my hilt. Embracing years of training, I kept my focus only on the arena.

Clink, clink. Telltale sound of chains moving, followed by a harsh scraping of metal, and then an earthshaking roar. *Oh shit!* I spun at the same time as Travaran and we bumped shoulders. I growled under my breath in annoyance and scooted to the side to give myself more room. My friend didn't seem to even notice that he had invaded my space. He was too enthralled by the beast.

Wind rushed toward us as a small dark green dragon with a chain around its leg began flapping its wings. The dragon seemed familiar, but I didn't have time to determine why, not if I wanted to stay alive. It roared again, sending hot flames rolling across the sand toward us. The flames were so hot that I could see some of the sand turning to glass in its wake. I glanced over at Travaran. As far as I knew, neither one of us had ever faced a dragon. He would have boasted about it, and I'd only read about them in books. *The* Bedtime Tails *book has a story about a green dragon.* My eyes widened. *There's no way this is Rethys from the story.*

"Breathe fire, thick skin, poor eyesight," Travaran mumbled. I assumed those were traits that dragons typically had. I wondered how *poor* the eyesight of a dragon was. Was it as bad as a human's? Or worse?

"What is the plan?" I asked, deferring to Travaran. He was too mesmerized by the dragon; I didn't think he would follow any orders I gave while we were in here.

"You go to the left, I go to the right, and we take it out," Travaran said. "Or at least incapacitate him to the point the crowd will think he's dead."

My jaw dropped open. *We aren't supposed to kill the dragon?* I snapped it shut, stemming my anger and focusing on the rest of what Travaran had said. His plan to conquer the dragon. The plan was simple, *too* simple. I waited hoping he would add to it. To my dismay he never did.

Concerned every second we delayed the dragon would catch us off guard, I agreed with him. "Okay." Then I carefully moved to the left, keeping my steps slow so as not to attract the dragon's attention. Out of the corner of my eye I saw Travaran move to the right, mirroring my steps.

Wisps of smoke curled out of the dragon's mouth as it waited. I sniffed the air and immediately regretted doing so—it smelled strongly of rotten eggs. The way the dragon moved, I wasn't convinced it couldn't see us. *Slow and steady.* We crept closer, and it struck, snaking its head toward me, close enough that I could make out a pattern of scales on its neck and see an iridescent sheen to the scales on its top ridge. The dragon let out a stream of fire. I dodged to the right and rolled. The heat was intense, I could feel my skin burning and blisters beginning to form as sweat dripped down my back. Rolling took me closer than I had expected to the dragon, which had turned its attention to Travaran.

I sprinted for its stomach, knowing that the black underside was likely not as well armored as the rest of the dragon. Travaran ran into me. *What the hell!* I stumbled and tucked into a roll to recover, fuming. I popped back up to my feet, barely in time to see Travaran swinging at the dragon's clawed foot. My face was hot, though from anger or the dragon's fire I wasn't sure.

To my surprise the dragon balanced on three legs like most other animals could. Travaran's back was turned, intent on his target, as the dragon swiped at him with claws extended. *Get your head in the game!* I was afraid to shout to him anything other than basic suggestions, lest the prince overhear and get angry. Travaran was not under my command here.

"Move!" I shouted, praying he would hear and heed my warning. I sprinted, shield raised, intent on getting between Travaran and the dragon. There was a momentary stinging sensation on my calf as I ran but I thought nothing of it. Pushing forward, I was almost there. Travaran brought his sword down on the dragon's foot and chaos ensued.

An ear-piercing roar blasted across the arena as the dragon bellowed its fury, then snapped its pearly white teeth dangerously close to my face; I could feel the hot, smelly breath on my neck. Wings, tooth, and claw were a flurry of movement. I raised my shield and struck with my sword, but it was impossible to tell if I was even doing any damage at all to the dragon. It was moving too quickly, sending up clouds of sand that obscured my vision and stuck to my sweat-slicked skin. Tears rolled down my face, my body's natural defense against the sand in my eyes.

Swiping my hand across my face, I heard Travaran shouting. In the nick of time, I swept my sword in front of me, sending a spray of bright blue blood into the air as it connected with the dragon. A loud screech echoed across the arena and the dragon retreated.

Breathing deeply, I thought of calm water and my racing heartbeat slowed down. As the dust settled, we had some time to evaluate ourselves. Travaran had a long slice down his teal forearm. *Armguards would have prevented that.* The wound was bleeding slowly but he seemed otherwise unscathed. The pain from the scratch on my calf from earlier intensified. I peered down at it and was surprised to see through the flaps of flesh the stark white of my bones. Shuddering, I hastily looked away, knowing the more I dwelled on the wound, the more it would hurt. I ripped a strip off the bottom of my tunic and wrapped it around my calf, then tied it to help stanch the bleeding.

"You okay?" Travaran asked.

I shrugged. "I'll live. We need to be smart about our next move."

There was a trail of bright blue blood from where we had fought to where the dragon was in the opposite corner of the arena. Splashes of red dotted the arena too. The dragon's black eyes tracked every movement we made, but it did not approach or indicate it was going to attack. I gazed at it warily. The stalemate was not entertaining to the crowd above us; boos rang across the arena. I prayed Prince Tanyth wouldn't add anything else to liven things up.

"It's wounded," I said softly to Travaran.

"In several places," he agreed, waving his hand at the blood trail.

"We're not entirely whole either," I replied. It would be a race to who could finish the other off before the blood loss was too great. "How about we—" I started, when a few feet away from us an opening appeared in the sand, and we could see the top of a metal helmet rising. The golden armor shone brightly, making it difficult to see the exact details of the newcomer. I gritted my teeth. *Just what we need, another opponent.* Before the platform finished rising, the golden warrior leaped into the air and landed in the arena with a resounding thud. He was holding a double-headed battle-axe and hefted it as though it weighed nothing. I did a double take when I realized the blade was silver-iron, which meant it *did* weigh less.

I was barely able to raise my iron shield as the axe came down in a blur of motion. The impact made my arm throb. I twisted out of the way as Travaran darted in, but his sword slid off the golden armor with an earsplitting screech. I kept moving, afraid to stay still and make myself an easy target. At the back of my mind, worry for what the dragon was doing was growing. I shook my head, sending droplets of sweat into the sand. *I must focus on the opponent in front of me.* Hunting for an opening or a weakness, I found one at the neck. The rest of the golden armor seemed to be one continuous piece of metal with no gaps. *Magic. Hopefully it doesn't have other magic properties or abilities too.*

Travaran caught my eye and, using hand signals, told me to sprint on his signal and attack. I nodded, biting the inside of my cheek. The coppery tang of blood flooded my mouth. Sprinting was going to hurt. Clenching my jaw, I ignored the pain and charged toward the golden warrior. Sword raised, I leaped at the last moment, chopping down hard toward his collar bone. Travaran went low. The golden warrior blocked Travaran's sword with his axe, and mine connected with the armor, a loud clang reverberating across the arena. My arm was vibrating from the impact. I almost had to switch to swinging my longsword two-handed to steady it.

The crowd cheered, "Travaran! Travaran!" I landed with all my weight on my wounded right leg, and it buckled. I fell forward into the sand, gasping as pain shot through me. *Get up*, I ordered myself. I don't recall how long it took me to get up, but I did. The golden warrior sent a fast sweeping blow toward Travaran. He blocked it with the shield but went flying backward upon impact and landed hard in the sand, sending up a cloud of dust.

I dragged my gaze back to the golden warrior. Travaran was out of the battle at least for the moment. My movements were slow. I took a deep breath, trying to tune out the pain. The double axe came down, and I blocked high with my sword.

There was a flicker of movement in the corner of my eye. A slight breeze stirred the sand. *The dragon*. I inhaled, my nostrils flaring at the suddenly suffocating smell of rotten eggs, and sped up my attack. Subtly I shifted my position until the golden warrior was between me and the dragon. Speed was my friend—the faster I was able to strike at the golden warrior, the more its own attacks slowed down, almost as if it was confused by my speed. Thankfully my arms were working well, even if I was barely able to put any weight on my right leg. As I pressed forward it was forced to take steps backward, seemingly unaware that it was nearing the dragon.

I was too slow in blocking, and the axe sliced along the side of my left bicep. I dropped the shield, blood running down my arm. I took a shaky step forward, determined not to let the golden warrior win. I began a strike aimed at his neck when the dragon ran toward us, opened its mouth, and chomped down on the golden warrior.

I swayed on my feet, breath ragged, sweat trickling into my eyes. Travaran was frozen on the other side of the arena. I focused on him, trying to use hand signals to get his attention. From here I was certain he had not been further injured, which meant he should be coming to help me. Travaran did not move or reply with hand signals.

I growled under my breath. *So much for teamwork.* The dragon was distracted by its meal of the golden warrior and was slowly stripping it of armor and taking bites. Bile rose in my stomach, and I kept my gaze averted as much as possible as I shuffled across the sand as fast as I could manage to get to Travaran. It felt like it took me ages to get over there. Then the dragon moved, sweeping its tail across the sand toward me. I made a split-second decision and, gripping the sword in both hands, swung downward toward the tail. Blue blood sprayed, and the sword got stuck. I yanked and it would not budge.

The dragon sent a column of fire toward me. I abandoned my sword and rolled out of the way, between its legs. The dragon danced around, trying to figure out where I went. I struggled keeping up with its movements, hoping it wouldn't step on me and kill me.

Travaran is not going to help, I informed myself. I knew I was in bad shape, and it would not be long before I lost too much blood and passed out. We were not supposed to use magic or kill the dragon, but the prince had not specified if that meant we could not use magic to call in another weapon. I knew it was my last option.

The handle was wrapped in plain leather, but the blade itself was jagged. I gripped the dagger and moments before the dragon stepped out of reach, I stabbed it upward, blade piercing the flesh. I yanked, dragging the dagger in a long line across the soft black belly scales, making a cut deep enough to inflict a severe injury, but hopefully not enough to kill the dragon. *What do I know of dragon health though?* The dragon roared, rearing up on its hind legs. I let go of the dagger and rolled, trying to get out from underneath it.

The ground trembled beneath me as the dragon stomped unsteadily, bright blue blood streaming out from the wound I had opened. Pain gnawed at me and black clouded my vision. I blinked rapidly, trying to keep myself from passing out.

With one last roar of defiance, the dragon collapsed on the sand.

The dark green dragon opened its jaws and lunged. Heart pounding, I gasped and opened my eyes when I realized it wasn't arena sand underneath me, but a bed, and the dragon was nowhere to be seen. At the foot of my bed was one of Prince Tanyth's healers. "Good, you're awake."

I stayed silent. *I'm alive, the dragon is gone. Where is Travaran?* Anger wound through me as I recalled how Travaran had not helped me at the end of the fight. None of the words that came to mind would have been wise to speak aloud, not to someone who reported directly to the prince. When the healer didn't say anything else, I sat up. Rough bandages wrapped around my abdomen. I flexed my fingers and curled my toes, mildly surprised at the lack of pain. I healed fast, but not this fast. The healer must have been ordered to repair any damage I had sustained in the arena with magic.

I felt eyes on me and looked up. The healer was staring. "Yes?"

"Prince Tanyth has ordered you attend the party tonight. To celebrate Travaran's win in the arena," the healer said.

I arched an eyebrow. "Travaran fought again?"

The healer frowned. "No, he defeated the dragon."

With an iron will, I kept myself from punching the healer, clenching my fists in the sheet on the bed so hard my nails dug hard into my skin. I took a deep breath, nostrils flaring as I tried to clamp down on my fury. "I see. When is the party?"

"You have thirty minutes before you are expected to be there," the healer replied.

My lips curled in annoyance, and I swung my legs over the bed. The sheet fell to the floor as I stood up, but the healer hadn't moved out of my way. "Are you going to move on your own or do I need to use force?"

The healer licked his lips and his gaze traveled from my face down to my feet and back up, lingering far too long on my cock. I took a step forward, annoyance flaring. "Get out of my way," I growled. The healer was an idiot. He had told me I was expected in thirty minutes and was now blocking my exit.

I stared at him, knowing full well we would both get in trouble if I was late. Finally, the healer broke my stare and stepped out of the way. "See you soon."

I turned on my heel, snagging a robe off the hook and putting it on as I walked out. Once I got my bearings for which part of the palace I was in, I headed to my suite.

By the time I arrived at my suite, I was running out of time. I could have simply called appropriate clothing in and went directly to the party, but I wanted a moment to settle. It was unnerving to lose hours and have no way of knowing what had happened.

I peered at myself in the floor-length mirror, inspecting my whole body, but it appeared as though all my arena injuries were gone, as if I had never even fought a dragon or a golden-armored opponent. I ran a hand over my face. *I can't forget that Travaran hid in the corner instead of helping.* I clenched my fist and then forced my fingers to relax.

As I looked in the mirror, I called in the clothing I wanted to wear tonight. A long-sleeved white silk tunic, a black dinner jacket, and a deep blue sash that tied at the waist and was the same color as my eyes. I brushed my slate-gray hair and tied it with a fresh leather thong at the nape of my neck, then departed.

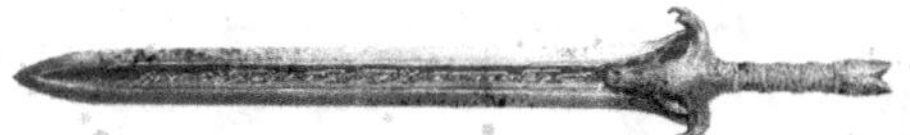

The press of bodies in the throne room was annoying. I felt my grip on my anger at Travaran slipping as I bumped into several Fae who refused to move out of my way like normal. I skirted around the back of the room as much as I could and eventually made it over to the throng surrounding the throne.

I cleared my throat and the female in front of me gave me a look of annoyance before recognizing me and dipping into a curtsey. "Lord Commander." Instead of responding I took advantage of the gap she had created for me and found myself in front of the throne.

I bowed and when I looked up Prince Tanyth was giving me a strange look. "Tristan," Prince Tanyth said.

"Prince," I replied with a curt nod, hoping that tonight would end up like all of Prince Tanyth's other parties.

"I trust you feel well?" Prince Tanyth inquired.

"Yes, thank you," I replied. At the edge of my vision, I could see Travaran working his way toward us. He wore his ceremonial armor with the crest of the Court of Dusk engraved on it.

"Ah, Travaran, the new champion," Prince Tanyth said with a broad smile. He stood up, beckoning for Travaran to climb the two steps of the dais to stand next to him. Prince Tanyth clapped his hands and silence descended upon the room.

"Guests, may I present to you my heir, Travaran the dragon-slayer!" Prince Tanyth announced.

I bit my tongue, coppery blood flowing into my mouth. *I cannot react,* I reminded myself. I kept my expression neutral and joined the guests in clapping. Callyn stepped forward; I hadn't noticed her hiding in the shadows on the other side of the throne.

"The dragonslayer needs an appropriate dance partner. Tonight, I have bestowed that honor upon my most treasured female warrior, Callyn," Prince Tanyth announced.

I kept my eyes on Travaran, wanting to see his reaction, as Callyn stepped out of the shadows and beside me. At first he was surprised, and then I could see his interest in Callyn quickly increasing. I didn't want to know what she was wearing. It hurt enough to know that Tanyth was not only rewarding Travaran for an achievement he did not accomplish, but Callyn was willingly going along with it.

Travaran stepped off the dais and bowed to Callyn, then offered her his arm, which she took. I was staring at the bottom step of the dais, running through breathing exercises as a distraction, when Tanyth crouched in front of me. "What is on your mind?" he asked, and I knew I was required to answer.

"Training drills I want to run tomorrow," I replied.

Tanyth stood up. I kept my gaze on him. "I don't believe you. I won't punish you for lying this time...but if you lie to me again, there will be severe consequences."

I blinked, wishing I hadn't blacked out in the arena so I could be one hundred percent certain about what had happened at the end. Even though the prince was claiming Travaran was now a dragonslayer, I didn't buy it. Prince Tanyth only had one dragon in his possession, and I doubted he would have allowed us to kill his most prized beast. Either way, I knew that when I was interacting with the prince, I had to be careful with how much anger I allowed to show. I licked my dry lips, then replied, "The healer had said you needed me here at the party. Is there anything else you require me for, or may I retire?"

Prince Tanyth frowned. "If you really are too tired to be here, then by all means leave."

I waited, expecting him to say something else. However, Tanyth was no longer even looking at me. Something else in the throne room had drawn his attention. I sighed and decided to leave.

Nineteen

SERAFINA
411 AQ

At the end of the second battle, the Lord of the East had officially surrendered by raising a white flag and then withdrawing all of his troops. My friends were gazing at me in adoration. I wished I could wipe those expressions off their faces. I couldn't bear it if my best friends began treating me differently because I could suddenly go into a trance and kill hundreds of people on my own. I also had a deepening concern that my ability to go into a trance wasn't real at all but was someone else performing magic on me. A shudder rippled through me at the idea of being controlled like that, without my knowledge or consent.

As we walked back toward our tent, Fiera was smiling at me. I finally took the bait. "What?"

Fiera shrugged. "You know you could likely have your pick of the Fae males now."

I snorted. "Is that all you can think about? I would gladly give you any males who come my way. In fact, that's what I will do—tell them *you* are interested."

Just then a big drop of gore rolled down my forehead, along the bridge of my nose and fell with an audible plop on the floor.

Shuddering in revulsion, I wiped my hands on my face, then stared at them. "Is this how I look? Covered in...blood and guts?"

Fiera giggled. "Yes, but I imagine I look the same. I have an easy solution though."

I raised my eyebrows, wondering what Fiera was going to do. Fiera raised her hands and they began glowing white, then a large metal tub appeared between us and slowly filled. Steam rose from the water. "Who goes first?" I asked. As much as I wanted to jump in, Fiera had used her magic; it was her right to go first.

Fiera grinned. "You can. I'll make another one."

"Thanks!" I said with a smile and began unbuckling my armor. I knew I would have to wash it too, but right now I desperately wanted to get rid of the feeling of goo stuck everywhere before it made me puke.

Fiera replaced the water in both of our tubs mid-bath to remove the blood and other bits floating in the water. Inhaling deeply, I slipped underneath the water for one last rinse. When I emerged, Ghilanna was peering at both of us. To my surprise she was perfectly clean, as though she'd never gone to battle at all. Even her armor was pristine.

"How?" I asked.

Ghilanna smiled. "Same as you two. I just didn't take a bath in here."

She offered me a towel and I reluctantly got out of the bath and wrapped myself in it. "Thank you," I said.

When I was clear of the tub, it vanished. I made my way to my dresser and selected a pair of dark brown pants and a tunic that was a few shades lighter. Using the towel, I dried off my hair as best I could.

"Now what?" I asked, since we were all clean and dressed. I had no idea what you did after the battle was over. *Does everyone just pack up and go home?*

Fiera opened her mouth to reply when I heard footsteps crunching on the gravel outside.

I exchanged a confused look with Fiera, then pivoted so I was facing the tent flap. King Pharaan stepped in. "Good morning, Serafina."

I bit my lip to keep my jaw from dropping open. I gave him a bow before replying, "Good morning, King Pharaan."

He tsked in disapproval. "Please, just call me Pharaan. Or 'Grandfather,' if you're comfortable with that."

I gulped. I wasn't sure I really liked the way either would roll off my tongue, since both indicated we were far more comfortable with our relationship than I actually was, given this was only the second time he'd ever spoken to me in my entire life. He also told my best friend that I was his granddaughter before I had come to terms with my new family member and told her myself. "Grandfather," I finally squeaked, deciding at least I could still make that feel like it was respectful.

He smiled. "Granddaughter, I was hoping to take you to see the emerald mines."

"I would like that," I replied, not sure what else to say. At some point I had been told the Court of Dawn had emerald mines within its territory, but I had no idea where they were.

"I have two unicorns waiting for us," he replied.

Excitement welled up inside of me. *A real unicorn!* I was intrigued that he would prefer to ride over running. "Sounds wonderful," I replied. "When are we leaving?"

"Now. Grab your sword. The unicorns are outside," he said.

I gave Fiera an apologetic look. She shrugged, though I could tell she was brimming with questions and would bombard me upon my return. I belted on my sword and followed the king outside. Sure enough there were two unicorns—one black with a silver mane and the other white with a gold mane—being held by his attendants. We mounted. I waited expectantly, assuming that we would have an escort.

"Let's go," King Pharaan said, bumping his unicorn with his legs, and we departed at a brisk trot. When we reached the edge of the camp on the side where the battle had taken place, he urged the unicorn into a canter.

As we both adjusted to the smooth gait, he glanced over at me, smiling. I was surprised at how at ease he was—with me and with not having an escort. "Why don't we have an escort?"

He chuckled. "I don't need one. I am not the king of the Fae because I look pretty. While it is a title that is handed down based on bloodline, it is also tightly tied to skills."

I took the bait. "What kind of skills?"

"Magic, but also ability with weapons. I would know if anyone was approaching, and if for any reason it was a threat I couldn't handle, then help would come. However, not only am I king, I am also ruler of the Court of Dawn, and we are in my territory. Those things combined make us almost untouchable," he explained.

I gave him a perplexed look. "I don't understand. Commander Meriel has taught me a little bit about the Fae, but since I don't have magic, we have never gotten into an in-depth explanation."

"I see," he replied. "Let me help you understand. All Fae are born with magic. Though type and potential maximum skill level vary, we are all capable of doing something with magic. The Fae courts also have magic and the ruler of a particular court's magic is enhanced when they take the role of ruler. I guess the best way to explain would be by percentages. Becoming prince of a court increases a Fae male's magic by about twenty percent over what he was capable of before he was granted the title. When a prince is in their own territory, their magic then increases another twenty percent. So you see, by simply being ruler and in the territory I rule, I am forty percent stronger. However, since the other three courts also serve me, I theoretically gain even more power from that."

I was surprised that the king was talking as though Fae are only able to be ruled by males. Afraid that question would be inappropriate, I vowed to ask Fiera or Ghilanna when we returned. Instead I asked the other question nagging at me. "You mentioned that not all Fae have the same amount of magic or skill. Wouldn't that mean that there could be a prince with significantly less magic than the others, if he had less magic before he took on the title?"

"Yes. You are very perceptive. Without conducting a trial by combat, which we do very rarely, it is impossible to know exactly how powerful a Fae is," he said.

"Then how do you know you are the strongest?" I blurted.

"Because before I was king, I was in a trial by combat, and I beat the other Fae who are currently ruling the other territories. Unless they have somehow altered their magic, they would still be weaker than I am," he replied.

"Does age change that?" I asked.

Minutes ticked by. I wondered if I had offended him by asking about age, even though I hadn't asked how old he was or said anything that would imply he was old.

"I don't really know the answer. Typically, when a Fae nears his or her time, they simply walk into the forest and are never seen again," King Pharaan said with a frown.

I decided to let the subject drop. He had given me more than enough to ponder and I didn't want to anger him by asking too many questions—or the wrong question. Ahead I could see a steep hill, though I hesitated to label it a mountain, starting to become visible. It was covered in thick green foliage. As we approached, the mine itself was revealed. At the base of the hill, layers had been cut away from the hill and deeper into the ground as well. I could see shimmering in the air around it and decided that it must be a magic shield. There was no wall or physical barrier to protect the mine from intruders, at least not that I could see.

Grandfather slowed his unicorn to a walk, and mine eagerly followed suit. Just as I thought he was going to ride through the barrier, a small archway appeared, barely large enough for us to pass through. I cast a glance over my shoulder and watched the archway close.

A female Fae was waiting for us. I dismounted, and she took the reins of my unicorn. Grandfather beckoned me to come closer. "Welcome to the emerald mine. Let me show you around."

The ground sloped down gently at first and then it got steep. The path wound its way around the edge before the ground leveled out and we were at the bottom of the mine. There were bins full of chunks of rock. In some bins I could easily see the emeralds, green flashes in the sunlight; others, nothing more than random pieces of rock. There were about ten Fae down here with us, each busy doing a task. Most appeared to involve magic. I did not see anyone using a pick and smashing at the rock, yet there were bins slowly filling up with rocks.

"Is this why we fought the Lord of the East?" I asked.

Grandfather nodded. "Yes, or sort of. I made the mistake of inviting him to see the mine and he got greedy and decided he wanted to wrest control of the mine from me. It started with a small force that he sent, and when that failed...well, you were on the battlefield."

"Will you continue to pursue him?" I asked.

Grandfather shook his head. "No. Though there are Fae who believe I should. Enough lives were lost that I believe the Lord of the East learned his lesson. When he recovers and decides he wants to trade again, I will of course double the price and make fewer emeralds available. But I would not halt trade or take his life. The give and take, shifts of power, between Fae and humans has been going on for hundreds of years. Without the humans, Fae would lose access to the metal mines. We still rely too heavily on the metal ore to be able to lose access to it entirely."

"Can't you just use magic to create metal?" I questioned.

Grandfather smiled. "You are quite astute. We do sometimes use magic to create metal. Depending on the application, it works fine. However, crafting magical objects requires real metal ore. Weapons hold up better if they are crafted with it as well."

My grandfather's words reiterated what I already knew: humans and Fae relied on each other for resources.

"There is one other thing I want to show you," he said and hooked our arms together companionably.

"Okay," I replied curiously.

We climbed the path to the top of the mine and then went through an elaborate stone archway into the hill. Inside was a room carved from the stone; here and there I could see evidence of emeralds embedded in the walls. In the middle were two giant natural emeralds. They were taller than my grandfather, and had a table between them. The table was also emerald, but it had been carved and was exquisite. I couldn't imagine the amount of effort that had been put into crafting something that large out of one emerald.

"This is where the Court of Dawn creates magical objects," Grandfather said.

"It is?" I said, eyes open wide.

"Yes. You can touch the table if you would like. It is safe," he offered.

I stepped closer and ran my hand over the table. It was cool to the touch and incredibly smooth. "What kind of magic objects do you make here?"

"Mostly jewelry. Though over the course of Fae history, there have been a few other non-jewelry items," he said.

I ran my hand over the table again, and then an odd thing happened. It began to glow green. I hastily stepped back, but it kept glowing. I glanced at my grandfather, but he had retreated as well. I couldn't read his expression.

An image appeared within the glowing table. A silver dagger with a handle in the shape of a dragon and two emeralds for eyes. The image was visible for a few seconds before it disappeared, and the table stopped glowing. I gasped as it dawned on

146

me—I had seen that image before. It was one of the illustrations in the book of *Bedtime Tails*. *Why would I see that dagger here? It doesn't make any sense.*

Grandfather was snarling. His hand was on his sword hilt.

"What's wrong?" I asked. I didn't know anything about magic objects or their creation. I had no way of knowing if the dagger we had seen was one or not.

"We need to go," he said sharply and turned on his heel, his steps carrying him away. I hurried after him, afraid to be left alone in the cave.

I followed him back to the unicorns, but once we were mounted, I wanted a better answer. "Please tell me what's going on."

The king looked at me. "I'll tell you once we have departed from the mines, outside of the barrier."

"Very well," I said agreeably.

True to his word, when we cleared the barrier he began his explanation. "The dagger that we saw within the table was Dragonfang. It is one of three magic objects that are in a particular prophecy, where whoever wields all three will have a significant amount of power at their disposal. The problem isn't that the dagger exists, it's that it has been lost for centuries. What happened at the emerald table means it is no longer lost."

I opened my mouth to reply when something cold coiled around my throat. I gasped, dropping my reins and clawing at my throat, but there was nothing physically there. *Magic!* I struggled to breathe; the only sounds I was making were weird squeaks. King Pharaan had looked away from me as he was talking and I wasn't sure I could get his attention. *I have to try.* I flailed my arms in the air, which didn't get the king's attention, but it did spook my unicorn. It shot forward, bucking. With my hands still at my throat trying to yank off the invisible magic, I was unable to regain control of the unicorn. With one massive buck it launched me into the air. I curled into a tight ball as I had been taught and prepared for impact. I blacked out.

Twenty

TRISTAN
411 AQ

The clang of the two swords echoed loudly in the empty arena, accompanied by the occasional fizzle of magic hitting a shield. Prince Tanyth observed from a bench a healthy distance away.

Striking high with my longsword in my right hand, I threw a ball of dark gray shadow magic at Travaran. He ducked under the magic and blocked my strike with his shield. The impact left my hand vibrating. Taking a few steps back, I inhaled deeply. The gritty feel of sand on my bare chest was a nuisance I tuned out. Travaran was panting, sweat gleaming on his teal skin. I decided it would be a good time to take a water break.

Travaran and I approached Prince Tanyth's bench and retrieved our canteens. Travaran sat down next to his father, and I opted to stay standing.

"King Pharaan is announcing a call to arms to fight against the Lord of the East, who tried to take the emerald mine by force," Prince Tanyth said.

I swallowed. *Is he going to obey the call to arms?* I knew if the prince didn't, the rift between the Court of Dusk and the king of the Fae would grow. *Not that Prince Tanyth cares.*

The prince continued, "When the news first came to me, I was already considering a visit to the Court of the Moon to learn more about the half-blood at the Jade Wilds training camp." Prince Tanyth gave me a pointed look. "From what I know she is from Gaskal."

The memory of my battle with the Lord of the South and delivering his head to his son, King Leonard, flashed into my thoughts. Shame washed over me; it was one of the orders I still regretted following through with.

"Well?" Prince Tanyth pressed.

I blinked, realizing that I hadn't heard his question as I had been lost in memories. "Sorry, can you repeat that?"

The prince glared at me, then spoke. "Prepare the legion."

I flexed my grip on my sword hilt. "To travel to Emerald Valley or Jade Wilds?"

Prince Tanyth's gaze seared into me. "I want you to prepare the legion to go to Emerald Valley. However, Travaran will be leading it. You will remain here."

I bowed. "As you wish, Prince." I was puzzled by the order to stay in Dorcha Palace. *Why is he sending his heir into danger?* I set down my canteen and Travaran and I continued sparring.

When the sparring session ended, I found Fallon and together we sent runners with orders to various Fae within the palace. Armor and weapons were to be inspected and repaired; food prepared; and any last-minute tasks seen to. Once the messages were sent, I made myself available in the training room for anyone who wanted to ask a question or needed a gear inspection. During the hours I had to myself, I worked out a modified schedule for the two squads that I would be commanding to protect Dorcha Palace in Prince Tanyth and Travaran's absence. I decided to put them on an eight-hour schedule with Bane's squad starting on duty and Elashor's squad starting with the rest period.

After Prince Tanyth and Travaran departed, a strange silence fell upon the palace. I thought the staff would be eager for the prince to leave since we were all held here under contract. Instead I discovered they were deeply concerned about what I was going to do. I ignored them, dividing my time so that I was accessible to both squads.

While I did not particularly care about the outcome at Emerald Valley, I was concerned about what would happen if Prince Tanyth or Travaran were to die, or, fates forbid, if they both perished in battle. A thought flickered across my mind. *Then I'd be free. The contract would no longer bind me.*

Callyn was part of the legion fighting at Emerald Valley, so I threw myself into a rigorous training schedule, just like at Embergate. Even the time I spent in the throne room in case a courtier showed up needing something was not idle; I practiced hand-to-hand combat. The days blurred together as I lived at eight-hour intervals.

Twenty-One

The snow leopard prowled toward me, its bright blue eyes locked with my blue-green ones. Just before it reached me, it reared up on its hind legs and moved as though to set its great paws on my shoulders. Except then in the snow leopard's place was a male. He had light gray skin with long pewter hair and bright blue eyes, like the cat's. Mesmerized, I could not make myself look away.

I woke up with a start. *Why am I dreaming about the snow leopard changing into a Fae male of all things?* It took a moment for me to realize what had woken me up wasn't the dream, but the sharp point of something at my throat. My eyes snapped open.

A sharp, harsh laugh, then footsteps as the owner of the sword stepped into my line of sight. The Fae male had blue-black hair and light teal-colored skin. A longbow was strapped to his back and he had a large sword in his scabbard. He looked a lot like Prince Tanyth Teriwraek.

"I'm Travaran," he introduced himself.

I slowly sat up. My hands were bound in front of me with rough rope, and I could feel and see the red welts forming underneath it. My neck throbbed where the magic had choked me.

How long was I unconscious for? I wondered. I peered around but all I could tell was that we were in a forest. There was forest surrounding the edge of Emerald Valley and across many Fae territories, so I had no way of knowing if we were close to the battle camp or many miles away. What I did know was that they had captured me, not the king. But the king must know I was captured. *Someone will look for me.*

"Why did you want to capture me?" I asked.

Travaran smirked. "You really don't have any idea, do you?" He paused for a long moment, clearly enjoying having the upper hand with whatever information he seemed to think was important. "Your existence is an abomination, and your mother should have been executed before she gave birth to you. My court has ordered me to eliminate you."

I pinched my lips together. King Pharaan had made it sound like not many Fae knew I existed or that my mother had married a human. Yet this Fae male whom I'd had no other interactions with knew enough to be able to specifically target me in a camp of several thousand Fae. *Unless he was targeting King Pharaan while he was out at the emerald mines and I happened to get in the way.*

Travaran kicked my boot. "Cat got your tongue?"

I flinched before gathering myself and responding, "Then what are you waiting for?"

"Very well. Kneel," Travaran ordered.

I raised myself onto my knees from the forest floor, taking a moment to subtly scan the area to ensure there really wasn't any help. Travaran took up a position at my side. Out of the corner of my eye I could see him raising his sword.

Suddenly a sword punched through him as someone stabbed him from behind. Travaran staggered to the side and fell over. I gasped when I saw Fiera grinning at me with the bloodied sword in her hand.

"How?" I asked. I tried to stand and almost fell onto my face. Fiera hastily grabbed my elbow and hauled me upright. When I was standing firmly on my own two feet, Fiera pulled out a knife and made quick work of the rope binding my wrists.

"We need to go. I'll explain everything later," Fiera said. I dug my fingers into my palm to prevent myself from voicing the cascade of questions threatening to come out. With one glance at Travaran's body, Fiera took off at a run. I sluggishly followed. My body was stiff, and it became obvious that I was not going to be able to keep up with her.

I heard voices behind us. *They must have found the body. But who are they?* I took a shaky breath, willing my legs to run faster. My toe hit a rock, and I flew through the air, arms windmilling as I tried unsuccessfully to right myself. "Oof." I landed with a poof in a pile of dried leaves, sending them fluttering around me.

I was almost standing when Fiera came jogging back, exasperated. "What are you doing?"

I rolled my eyes. "I tripped. I don't know how long it's been since I was captured, but my legs are super stiff. I'm trying to be fast, it's simply not going as you'd planned."

Fiera huffed, but she snapped her head up at a sharp crack behind me. "We'll split up. I'll buy you some time."

"Are you sure? You don't need to risk your neck for me, I'll manage," I said, afraid my friend would sacrifice herself for me and that I'd get captured anyway. A quick self-assessment left me with the brutal truth that I wasn't going to get away, unless I could hide well enough until they gave up.

Fiera nodded and gave me a hug. "Yes, I'm sure. Promise me you will do everything you can to keep from getting captured."

I hugged her back. "I promise to try."

Reluctantly, Fiera let go of me. I watched as she sprinted away. Instead of moving silently, she was altering her steps to make as much noise as possible in the dead leaves. I took a deep breath and began my slow run in the opposite direction of Fiera, scanning the area for any possible hiding spot.

As I continued my trek, the ground began to slope upward and my pace slowed to barely a crawl. My muscles burned. I hadn't heard any sounds behind me for a while. *I lost them.* The forest was silent. There were no birds or squirrels chattering among the leaves. I ran a hand over my face. *I must keep going.* As I focused ahead of me, I saw a cluster of rocks. *Maybe a hiding place—finally.* Energized at the thought of hiding and being able to take a break, I let myself narrow my focus to the rocks ahead.

Suddenly, there was a brief shadow in front of me and a heavy rope net fell over me. I threw myself forward, trying to disentangle myself, but the net merely tightened. "Well, well, well, what do we have here," came an ice-cold voice that sent a shiver of fear down my spine.

I tipped my head up and gasped. The Fae in front of me was tall, taller than any I had seen before. He had teal skin. His blue-black hair, the same shade as Travaran's, was in hundreds of tiny braids, with small beads at the ends. On top of his head was a large crown that had been formed from antlers. On his shoulders, holding his white cape in place, were large pale gray paws with huge claws, almost as though a cat were resting his paws there. A chain connected the two paws and had large teeth strung along it. My eyes widened in recognition. *Prince Tanyth.*

"You *murdered* my son," Prince Tanyth said.

I bit my tongue hard, hoping it would help me stay grounded and not say anything I would regret later.

"As I am sure you are aware, when you murder a Fae, the family of the fallen is allowed to execute or enslave the individual at fault," he explained. "I have not yet decided what I want to do with you." Prince Tanyth motioned with his hand and four Fae appeared and came forward.

"Wait!" I said.

The prince gave me a cruel glare. "What?"

"I didn't kill your son!" I replied.

Prince Tanyth laughed harshly. "Then how did he die in the forest? I know he captured you and now he's dead. There isn't anyone else to blame but you."

I opened my mouth to protest, but found the words would not come out. I began coughing, unable to get a proper breath.

"Take her to Dorcha Palace," Prince Tanyth ordered.

The four male Fae bowed to the prince, then approached me. I thought they were going to remove the net to get my gear and weapons away from me. Instead, the blond one put his hand on my forehead, and I passed out.

I was sitting in a meadow and the snow leopard was approaching from the other side. I watched warily. I still did not fully understand these dreams or why this beautiful animal would have an interest in me. As it neared, its steps slowed, almost as though it were afraid. When it was within arm's length, it stopped and we stared at each other. I wasn't sure what to say. I had never been this close to a large cat before. He lifted a paw as though to touch me, when suddenly a net was thrown over me and I was dragged away. I struggled, but nothing I did would free me from the net. The snow leopard tried to follow but kept hitting some sort of invisible wall.

Part Two

411 AQ

Twenty-Two

TRISTAN

Punching left, right, left, I worked through the hand-to-hand combat exercises, losing myself in the rhythm. A cough to my right had me skidding to a halt midway through a crescent kick.

Fallon emerged from the shadows. "Prince Tanyth is on his way."

I ran a hand through my disheveled gray hair and straightened my tunic. *I don't have time to change; this must suffice.* "Thanks for the heads up."

Fallon walked closer to me, gaze holding mine. "Rumors are traveling ahead of him that someone died."

I sucked in a sharp breath, wrapping my arms around myself. "Who?" My voice wavered.

Fallon shook his head. "I don't know. But they will be here momentarily."

I nodded in understanding. My chest felt tight and I swallowed, wishing for a drink of water. The doors swung outward and I was out of time.

Prince Tanyth strode in, and I could feel waves of anger rolling off him even from my position by the throne. Peering behind him, I waited for the warriors who had accompanied him, or at least Travaran, to enter the throne room. Yet no one came.

Tucking my hands behind my back and clasping them together, I prayed the prince would not notice I was shaking. My expression was schooled into an emotionless mask.

Prince Tanyth brushed by me and threw himself on his throne. "Fuck," he growled.

I turned to face him so I could try to anticipate what he would do, but I stayed silent, waiting for the prince to give some indication of what had happened. No matter how badly I wanted to know who died, I was afraid to ask.

"I gave Travaran the order to kill the half-blood," Prince Tanyth announced. My eyes widened in surprise. These were not the first words I was expecting the prince to say. I ground my teeth together, waiting, still anticipating Travaran waltzing through the doors any moment.

Prince Tanyth wasn't looking at me; he was staring at the wall or column, I wasn't sure which. "I have no idea how, but Travaran fucked it up, and since you weren't there to protect him, he's the one who died—at the hands of the half-blood."

A strangled gasp escaped my lips as the news crashed over me. *Travaran dead?* Devastation washed over me. Regardless of our differences, Travaran had still been my first friend at Embergate. I inhaled slowly and realized that the prince had also said something else: "You weren't there to protect him." I gave him a wary glance. *Is he going to blame me for his son's death when it was his own orders that had me here at Dorcha Palace instead of protecting Travaran?* My skin heated as anger ran through me at the accusation that I was at fault.

I glanced under my lashes at Prince Tanyth and discovered he was studying me. "Good, you're angry. I want to harness that anger and channel it into your next task."

My fists clenched, part of me hoped he would allow me to kill the bitch half-blood. *Make her pay.*

"You will fight in the arena tonight. Go prepare yourself," he ordered. I bowed eagerly and departed.

Twenty-Three

SERAFINA

I was sitting in a small glade in a forest full of oaks in their fall splendor. A snow leopard approached from the other side. The sunlight filtered through the leaves, casting dappled shadows on its light gray coat with black spots. When it was within arm's length, it stopped, and the air around it shimmered. When the shimmering stopped, there was a Fae male crouched in place of the cat. He had no tunic, revealing his well-muscled chest. His skin was light gray, and I could almost see the faint spot pattern of the snow leopard.

We stared at each other. I wasn't sure what to say. I had never seen a Fae who could shapeshift. He opened his mouth to speak, but arms wrapped around me and I was yanked sharply backward.

My eyes flew open. I was curled up in the fetal position underneath a rough brown wool blanket inside of a small cage. I couldn't stand or stretch out fully without hitting my head on the heavy dark metal bars. I sat up and the blanket slipped off. I gasped as the cold air hit my chest and yanked the blanket up. I peeked underneath the blanket; I was completely naked. *I suppose I should be grateful they even gave me a blanket.* I closed my eyes and took a deep breath to steady my mind and focus. It kept drifting back to my dream of the snow leopard turning into a Fae male with gray skin. While interesting, neither the dream nor my nakedness was going to help me get out of the situation I was currently in. When I opened my eyes, I surveyed what was beyond the cage.

I was near the back of what seemed to be a large hall. There was another cage next to mine, but it was empty, with no traces of its last inhabitant. For the time being I was alone. I could hear voices coming from the other end of the hall, but there were several chairs on a raised platform that blocked my view. Most of the area surrounding me was cast in heavy shadows, making it difficult to discern anything noteworthy. I inhaled slowly through my nose; I could smell smoke from a fire and cooked meat.

A sharp pain in my stomach made me wonder how long I had been asleep if I was this hungry. A building pressure in my abdomen informed me that I would need to either find a chamber pot or an escort to the facilities.

Taking a breath to steady myself, I opened my mouth and spoke loudly enough to draw someone's attention. "Hello, hello! Is anyone there?" The voices on the other side of the raised platform paused. Clearly they had heard me, but would anyone come?

A Fae male suddenly appeared before my cage. I hadn't heard any footsteps; either he could move that silently or had used magic to hide his presence. "Took you long enough to wake up. Let me guess, you need to pee?" he said with a sneer.

I nodded. In the shadows, I couldn't make out much of the male's appearance, only the blond hair. A memory from when I was captured by the prince flashed into my mind. There had been a blond Fae then. "Yes, if you would be so kind as to let me out."

"No," he said coldly.

"No? You would rather I pee on the floor, like an animal?" My voice went an octave higher than normal, revealing that I was not calm as I was becoming aware of the situation I had landed myself in.

He chuckled darkly. "No, you can use the chamber pot."

"But...I don't have one," I protested. A large chamber pot clattered onto the floor in front of me inside the cage. I snapped my mouth shut and glared at him. The male didn't budge.

"I thought you needed to pee," he said after an excruciating amount of time. My bladder was about to take matters into its own hands if I didn't act soon.

I growled low in my throat. "I thought you would allow me the decency of privacy."

He raised an eyebrow. "When did you get the idea that I am decent?" He paused. "If you need to go, then go while I'm standing here."

I bit my tongue hard to keep myself from speaking again and turned my back to him. Using the blanket as a shield as best I could, I lowered myself over the chamber pot and took care of my business. As soon as I stood up, the chamber pot disappeared. I whirled, and the blanket fell to the floor.

Without the warmth of the blanket, I could feel my nipples hardening in response to the cool air in the room. I stared at the Fae, not wanting to make him think I was ashamed of my body by rushing to cover it up. The Fae male smirked and proceeded to inspect me from head to toe, his eyes lingering for a long time on my breasts and the small triangle of hair between my legs. "If you're done staring," I said drily, "can you tell me when I will be able to speak to Prince Tanyth? It appears there is a misunderstanding about what happened with Travaran, and I would like the opportunity to explain myself."

The Fae male rocked back on his heels. "I will relay your request." He disappeared.

I picked up the blanket and wrapped it around myself, then sat down in the corner, leaning back against the bars of the cage. *I wonder how long it'll take to get an answer.*

My eyelids were heavy as I fought off the urge to sleep. *I can't sleep. Not until I have answers.* I blinked when a clatter brought me fully awake and I found myself staring into a female Fae's bright green eyes. She had white hair pulled back severely from her face, and pale, almost translucent skin. Peeking over her shoulders was a large double-headed axe strapped to her back.

"Get up," ordered the Fae female.

I slowly straightened myself to standing with my head and shoulders bent so I wouldn't hit the top bars.

"You're going to come with me," she announced, then inserted a key into a lock that I knew hadn't been there before.

"What's your name?" I asked, wondering if she would even answer me. The male earlier hadn't seemed inclined to give me a name.

"Callyn," she replied shortly, then opened the door and beckoned me forward. As I stepped into the doorway, she held up her hand. "Leave the blanket."

"I don't have anything else," I protested.

She shrugged. "Leave the blanket or I'll take it from you. Your choice."

I dropped the blanket and stepped over it, deciding it wasn't worth the argument. When I was outside of the cage, to my surprise, she handed me a folded piece of fabric. I opened it and discovered it was a tunic. The fabric was coarse, but I pulled it over my head, relieved I would not be subjected to walking the halls naked.

"Now, to ensure you won't do anything stupid." Callyn touched each of my wrists and two heavy metal cuffs appeared, connected by a chain. "Follow me."

I kept my lips pressed together, trying to avoid getting in any more trouble by staying silent. I followed a step behind. I thought we were going to the other end of the room and was surprised when we passed through a door into a dark stone passage. We walked down the passage for a while. There were occasional lamps with Fae light, but no doors that I could see. *Not that they're not there. Clearly the Fae here have magic and use it freely.*

We arrived at a set of doors, and I held my breath as she pushed them open and ushered me inside. I had no idea what to expect would be behind them. *A sitting room?* My jaw dropped, and I quickly covered my mouth, trying to hide my surprise and confusion. It had two smaller sofas meant for one or two people, a dining table for four, and an assortment of decorative furniture.

There was an open door through which I could see a mammoth-sized four-poster bed and another open door that had a full-length mirror and sink. I assumed there was a tub of some sort in there as well.

"Well, what do you think?" Callyn asked after I had ample time to gaze at the rooms.

"Um..." I said uncertainly.

Callyn frowned. "This is your new home."

Eyes wide, I gazed at her. "This is really mine?" I asked, waiting for her to declare it was a trick.

"Yes. As long as you don't give Prince Tanyth a reason to throw you back in the cage," Callyn warned. "Now. I have a small meal for you and then you have time to rest. Either I or someone else will be sent to retrieve you for whatever comes next."

I swallowed, mouth suddenly dry. *Whatever comes next? That sounds ominous.* My gaze fell on the table with a plate of food. My stomach gurgled.

"Eat. Rest," Callyn said, then departed. The door shut, and I heard the distinct *snick* of the lock. *It might be better than the cage, but it's still a cage. I am not free to go where I please.*

A wave of exhaustion washed over me. I grabbed a handful of nuts and a piece of cheese and went into the bedroom. The large four-poster bed was made of dark ebony wood and covered in green blankets. I headed for the wardrobe in the corner and was pleased to find a selection of plain tunics and pants much like I had worn at Jade Wilds. There was also a rose-colored gown and a couple of plain white nightgowns.

I discarded the rough shirt and slipped on one of the nightgowns. I knew I should probably take a bath, but I could barely keep my eyes open long enough to finish the nuts. I really didn't want to fall asleep in the tub. I climbed into the bed, sinking into the mattress. I slid under the covers and was fast asleep.

Twenty-Four

TRISTAN

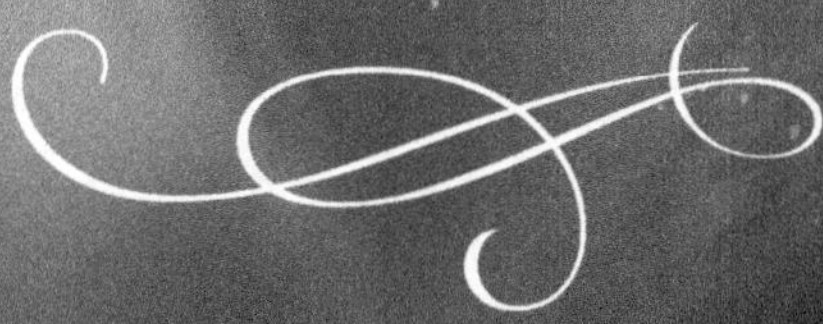

I raised my sword in the air and the crowd around the rim of the arena got even louder. Rough sand stuck to my arms and chest, but I knew brushing it off wouldn't do any good; I'd have to wait for a bath. I sensed motion behind me as the guards retrieved the battered human. When the prince had ordered me to fight tonight, I had expected worthy opponents. Not an unarmed prisoner. The first battle had been quick but satisfying—three Larks who had been captured on the return from Emerald Valley. They had had some sword training, enough to play a game of cat and mouse.

Prince Tanyth gestured and I bowed, then stepped to the platform at the center of the arena. It lowered me into the preparation area, and I rolled my shoulders as I stepped off. *Shower,* I thought, hoping it would help drain the tension. Though the prince might enjoy watching me fight a helpless opponent, I took no pleasure in it, and he knew it. *Maybe this was him expressing his annoyance that I am alive and Travaran is dead.*

Water dripping from the ends of my still-damp hair left a trail of droplets down the hallway. Using the bathhouse had succeeded in cooling my anger, more than I had anticipated. Though the large main pool had been occupied by a large group of female Fae engaged in a lively discussion about preparations for the upcoming party, they thankfully were not inclined to bother me when I chose one of the smaller pools for myself.

I took a deep breath and entered my suite. Though my anger had mostly burned out, I still felt restless. *I wonder what Callyn is doing.* Mind made up, I headed back into the hallway and down to Callyn's room.

I knocked lightly, not entirely sure if she would be in her room or off doing Prince Tanyth's bidding. There was a thump, followed by "Coming!"

My lips twitched in amusement. *I wonder who's in there.* Callyn yanked open the door. Her robe was sliding off of her shoulder and she hadn't quite tied the sash properly.

Under the robe I could see hints of black leather straps crisscrossing her arms, legs, and torso. She was wearing a leather vest that dropped into a sharp V between her breasts and then gave way to the straps underneath them. My eyes followed the path of the straps to where they wound around her waist and legs, but they didn't cover anything—nor did the partially open robe.

"I can come back if you're busy," I teased. An ache started in my groin; clearly my body had a different idea.

Callyn licked her lips and pushed the door slightly farther open. Over her shoulder I could see a female Fae with bright green hair and dark brown skin lying spread-eagle on the bed. I sucked in a sharp breath as need wound through me and my cock got painfully hard. "You could join us."

My eyes widened at the invitation. "Are you sure?"

She laid a hand on my chest and then slid it down to grip my cock, smirking. "I wouldn't offer if I wasn't sure."

"Then yes," I said eagerly and entered the room.

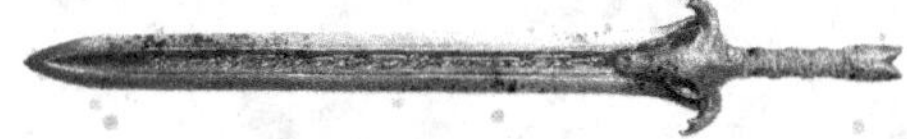

There was a tap on my suite door. "You are being summoned to the throne room," called Fallon. I turned on the light and realized that I had been asleep far longer than I initially expected. *No wonder I'm being summoned. I'm late for morning training.*

I opened the door and poked my face out. "I will be there shortly." I replied.

"Don't take too long. He is unhappy about your antics in the arena and was expecting you to attend him immediately," Fallon said.

I grimaced and then forced my face to smooth back into my mask. "Yes, of course. Let me get dressed."

Shortly, I presented myself to Prince Tanyth. He did not waste any time getting down to business.

"While I was at the battle, one of my scouts found a leon shapeshifter. I want you to find it and bring it back—alive is preferred," Prince Tanyth ordered. I swallowed hard. A leon was a large cat similar to a snow leopard. The wild animal was smaller than a wild snow leopard, though a leon shapeshifter was likely to be close in size to me when I shifted. *This is going to be a challenge.* Bile filed my mouth as I contemplated killing or capturing another shapeshifter, but my hands were tied. With Travaran dead and the prince on edge, now would be the worst time possible to try to negotiate an alternative assignment.

"I will prepare for the hunt," I replied.

"Good," the prince replied.

I walked to the end of the throne room but I heard boot steps. I glanced over my shoulder to find Tanyth directly behind me. "Don't fail me. Or you will be Rethys's next meal."

I blinked once and departed.

Twenty-Five

SERAFINA

Rough hands shook me awake. I groaned and rolled over. "Go away, Fiera," I mumbled.

"I'm not Fiera. Get up," growled Callyn. I opened my eyes all the way and shifted so I could face Callyn.

"Sorry, I must have been dreaming," I apologized.

Callyn shrugged. "It doesn't matter. You need to get up and ready. I have orders for you."

She reached for me again and I glared at her, then sat up and swung my legs over the bed. "If you'll actually give me a moment to get up, I will."

"Everyone who sets foot in Dorcha Palace belongs to Prince Tanyth," Callyn replied. "Your only option is to obey."

"What do you mean that everyone *belongs* to him?" I asked, trying to keep my tone the same as before to mask my growing uncertainty.

"Our survival depends solely on our ability to please him," Callyn replied. "Right now, the task is not for training, it is to prepare you for your formal presentation to the prince."

My brows knit and hot anger ran through my veins, quickly replaced by cold fear. "I've met him already."

172

Callyn must have noticed my fear because she waved her hand at me. "There's no reason to be afraid. This is exactly what it sounds like. There is a gathering in the throne room this afternoon and the prince wants to show you off to his court. We'll get you fed and cleaned up."

"Only a presentation?" I asked, voice shakier than I had hoped.

Callyn nodded. "Yes."

"Do you...do you know what else he is going to do with me?" I asked, stumbling over the words.

Callyn shook her head. "I'm sorry, I don't. The only thing I can tell you is that you are his prisoner and at his mercy. For the time being at least it is obvious that he doesn't intend to kill you." She paused. "Now, let's get some food into you, and then I'll have Verrona come in and help get you dressed for the presentation."

I exhaled, nostrils flaring. Callyn did have a point. If the prince wanted me dead, I'd be dead. *He must have another plan.* I stood up and moved over to the dining table, which was now laden with several platters of meat and vegetables. As I filled my plate, I found myself wondering if the prince had made a ransom demand to King Pharaan. More worry wound through me as I realized I had no idea if the king would consider paying a ransom for me. *I'm his granddaughter,* I reminded myself. *But I'm only half-Fae and have no magic. What use am I to the king of the Fae?*

While I was distracted by my food, Callyn bustled around the room behind me. When I finished and my plate was all but licked clean, I wiped off my hands and stood up.

Directly behind the couch were two stone statues adorned in what I could only assume was meant to be our clothing. I hadn't realized that Callyn was getting dressed with me. *A little odd.* I shrugged it off. *I'm a prisoner and she's treating me okay, so why does it matter?*

The statue on the left was adorned in a dress that seemed to be made of layers of spun gold with a heavily jeweled corset. On the head of the statue was a thin circlet of gold. The second statue had a dress of heavy black silk and a corset with a black-on-black jacquard. Both were beautiful. I could not see why either would be considered a challenge to put on.

"I have help coming for your hair, but we can manage the dresses ourselves," Callyn said. I was about to ask if I would get to choose which dress I was wearing when Callyn moved to the back of the statue with the gold dress. Strands of gold flashed and the dress began to slide from the statue. I grabbed it before it fell to the ground, looking around for somewhere to lay it. *The couch.* I draped the corset on one end and gently put the dress down on the other. I ran my fingers over the fabric and the pieces began to slip off the couch, and I realized there wasn't merely one layer, but three.

"Hmmm," I whispered as I caught the fabric before it landed on the floor. I separated the pieces and studied them, not sure what to do.

"Let me help you," Callyn said. I could hear the whisper of her dress on the floor, I raised my eyes from the couch to Callyn and my jaw dropped in surprise. *She got into it so fast!* The black dress looked much different now that it was on her. The long black lace sleeves trailed down to the end of her wrists with a loop hooking over her middle finger on both hands. The wide scoop neckline showed plenty of skin and just enough of the top of her breasts to tease the males. My eyes traveled down to her waist where the corset ended in a point and the folds of the black silk cascaded down around her feet. As Callyn moved, I realized the skirt was panels and that as she moved, one had glimpses of the entire length of her leg, down to the scandalously high black heels on her feet.

"You're stunning," I said breathlessly.

Callyn twisted her lips. "Thanks, but wait till you see who is attending. Then you'll know I'm nothing."

I narrowed my eyes at Callyn's dismissal of her own beauty but kept my thoughts to myself. Instead, I picked up the end of one of the pieces of my dress. "How do I put this on?"

"Like this," Callyn said with a slight smile. She then lifted the first piece of the dress. As Callyn shook it out, I saw that the first piece was darker gold. She slid it over my head and I peered down at it, it was almost like wearing a sleeveless tunic dress. My jaw tightened when I saw how low the neckline went—almost down to my navel. *There's three layers and a corset, it won't be that bad.* The second layer slid over my head, adding long sleeves with slashes along the top, exposing my bare skin clearly through the gossamer gold. The skirt momentarily billowed around me before settling around my legs. The last layer was dazzling; tiny flecks of what I thought might be actual gold dotted the sheer fabric.

Callyn held up the corset. "Ready?"

I nodded, and she stood in front of me, studying my chest and placing the corset very precisely underneath my breasts. I could feel the boning in the corset pushing my breasts up, but I had been expecting it to cover them, with maybe some flesh showing at the top, like Callyn's. Instead, I had sheer, sparkly gold fabric covering my breasts, and that was it. Callyn stepped around me and began lacing the corset up. I gasped as she pulled it so tight I had trouble taking a full breath.

"Does it have to be this tight?" I asked.

"Yes," Callyn said shortly. I could feel her tying the knot at the back and then she came around me to inspect her handiwork. "I am sure Prince Tanyth will be pleased. Now, your hair..." She gave my damp brown locks a distasteful look.

"Verrona, I know you're here," Callyn called out.

A musical laugh and then a petite Fae female appeared before us. She had a light purple gown of a similar style to Callyn's, and the bodice was decorated with amethysts. Her dark purple hair was done in an intricate braid made of many tiny braids with a strand of small gems woven throughout. "Yes, I am here. I was waiting till you were ready for me. No reason to intrude on your lovely conversation."

Callyn stepped away from me to give Verrona room to conduct her own inspection. "I think we should put her hair up," Verrona said, grabbing a handful of my hair and piling it on top of my head to demonstrate. "What do you think?"

Callyn shrugged. "If you think that will please Prince Tanyth, then do it."

Verrona smiled. "Perfect, I was hoping you would say that." She let go of my hair. It was slightly warm. I opened my eyes wide.

"Haven't you had magic worked on you before, Serafina?" Verrona asked.

I shook my head. "Not on my hair."

Verrona smiled even more. "Then this will be a treat." She waved a hand, and a mirror appeared in front of me as she moved around my back. The mirror let me observe in amazement as all my hair went from being straight to sporting gentle curls. Then my hair began weaving through the air. Occasionally I could feel the poke of a pin being set to hold strands in place. When Verrona was done, soft curls framed my face, and the rest of my hair had been twisted and braided into a coil at the back of my head with select pieces loosely spilling out and tickling the back of my neck. The gold circlet was set on top. Pins of pearls and gold were scattered throughout my hair too.

A loud cough came from behind us, and the mirror disappeared as Verrona spun to face whomever it was. "We need to go," came Fallon's bored voice.

Verrona stayed at my side as the four of us made our way down the corridor. It took me a few moments before I realized this was the way to the throne room. "What exactly is happening for the presentation?" I asked.

Verrona pressed her lips together and shook her head. "You will have to see for yourself." She opened her mouth as though to say more, then closed it, turning her attention to the open doors we were rapidly approaching.

As we stepped through the doors, I gasped. The platform holding the throne had been pushed to the back of the room, near where my cage—which was nowhere to be seen—had been. The walls and columns were draped with black silk. An assortment of couches and lounge chairs were in some of the alcoves, some of which even had privacy drapes that could be drawn. The room was massive, far larger than I had imagined, and it was filled with Fae. Dark colors seemed to be the theme of the presentation, with various shades of dark gray and black being favored by most. *Maybe it's a Fae thing?* I thought, realizing that in my time at Jade Wilds there never had been any sort of celebration or formal party requiring us to dress up, other than my etiquette lessons.

A hush fell across the room as we made our way to Prince Tanyth. I found myself wondering why this felt more like a party—with me as the entertainment—than the presentation I had been told it was. At some point on my path all three of my escorts melted into the crowd. I held my head high, trying to tune out the whispers that erupted around me, keeping my eyes trained on the edge of his throne.

A metallic thud had me snapping my eyes up to the throne. Prince Tanyth, dressed entirely in mourning black, stared intently at me. A blond male Fae stood at his side holding a metal-capped staff, which had made the sound. Tension filled me as I realized it was the male who had given me the chamber pot upon my arrival.

Prince Tanyth gave a slight nod and the blond male began speaking. "Prince Tanyth, may I present to you Serafina Wyantha, half-human." His gaze bored into mine, and I realized he was expecting me to do something.

I dropped low into a curtsey. "Your Highness," I said to Prince Tanyth.

"You look ravishing tonight," the prince replied. His gaze lingered far too long on my breasts. My whole body was tense under his scrutiny. There was a commotion behind me at the doors to the throne room. I fought the desire to turn around and see what it was. *I will know soon enough.*

There was a scraping sound. I winced as it got louder. *Almost like metal on stone.* Prince Tanyth was no longer looking at me, but at whatever was behind me. I turned around so my back was to the prince and I could see whomever was approaching.

There were still some people blocking my view. I was surprised they weren't moving out of the way like everyone else had. A male Fae warrior dragged a cage, maybe even the same one I had been held in upon my arrival, toward the throne. The warrior's slate-gray hair was disheveled with bits of bark and grass peppering his braid. He was wearing a black leather vest that was open. His light gray skin rippled over his muscles as he came closer and I found myself unable to look away. For the first time, I felt an attraction to a Fae male—the wrong Fae male. *Anyone in this court is evil, like Prince Tanyth,* I reminded myself. I took a deep breath and my eyes slid past him to the creature inside the cage. *A leon!* Its tawny fur and the thick mane around its head and neck made it easy to identify. *Where on earth did he find a leon?* At second glance I noticed a glint of metal around its neck. Not only had he succeeded in capturing a live leon, the warrior had been able to put a collar on it. As much as I hated to admit it, I was impressed by the skills required.

The staff thudded on the stone by the throne again and I returned my attention to the prince. The warrior was now next to me with the cage and leon almost within arm's reach.

"Lord Commander Tristan Gilvrye presents to Prince Tanyth a leon shapeshifter!" announced the blond Fae.

Shapeshifter? My hands started to shake slightly and I clutched them together, hoping no one would notice. Disgust filled me that Prince Tanyth would cage a Fae shapeshifter like an animal and that his lord commander would blindly follow such horrible orders. I didn't like the idea of beasts in cages, but at least a beast was not a Fae or human. *But how is the shapeshifter being caged like this any different than how they're treating me?* I bit my lip as I realized that it really wasn't much different, other than the shapeshifter, when shifted, could rely on its natural weapons—tooth and claw.

I dug my nails into my hand. *Focus.* I had been ordered here to be presented to the prince.

The prince's eyes flickered between me and the warrior, then a cold smile formed on his lips. "Lord Commander, if Serafina passes her arena trial, then you will oversee her training."

I watched Tristan out of the corner of my eye and saw surprise quickly masked by anger flash across his face.

"Your Highness, her capture alone proves Serafina has minimal skills. I cannot make a warrior out of nothing," Tristan protested.

Before I could stop myself I blurted, "I *am* a warrior."

Tristan turned toward me, blue eyes bright. He was so tense I could see the pulse in his veins. "You are nothing but a half-human bitch."

I punched him in the chest. As my fist connected, it felt like I had hit a stone wall, not a Fae chest. I winced and shook my hand out. Tristan clenched his fist, and I thought he might retaliate.

Prince Tanyth chuckled darkly and leaned forward, bracing his elbows on his knees. "I'm sure there is plenty you can teach her, Tristan."

About dying? I wondered to myself. I could barely stand to be near him and now I was going to have to train with him for who knew how long. Tristan didn't respond.

We stood in silence, waiting for the prince to say something, when I felt a light touch on my left elbow. I glanced over and saw Callyn had returned. "I'm to escort you back to your room."

"It was only an introduction?" I asked.

Callyn nodded. "Yes. Tristan's arrival has altered the plan, at least as for you." Callyn proceeded to guide me through the crowd and back to my room.

When we reached the door, I turned toward her. "What's next?"

"Your trial will be tomorrow. Make sure you eat again and get some sleep," Callyn said. I nodded and stepped inside my room, shutting the door behind me. I waited until I heard the click of the lock and the sound of Callyn's footsteps retreating before I sat on the edge of the bed.

My lips quivered and I could feel tears threatening to spill over. Two days ago, I was fighting side by side with Fiera and Ghilanna against the Lord of the East, and now I was a captive in the Court of Dusk. *There must be a way to get out, to win my freedom or escape.* I ran a hand over my face, swiping at the tears. *What can I do to convince the prince that he should free me?*

My fingers absently stroked the gold fabric. *If I sleep with him, maybe he'll let me go.* I immediately dismissed that idea. Not only had I committed to waiting to only have sex with my husband, but I also knew nothing about flirting, let alone having sex, and I was certain I would screw things up. *Which leaves proving myself in the arena and with my correct behavior in our interactions.*

If I hadn't been captured, I would have formally graduated as a warrior by now. Which meant by Fae standards I *was* a skilled warrior. I let my hand drop away from the dress, mind made up that I would negotiate with Prince Tanyth for my release if I performed well in the arena.

Twenty-Six

TRISTAN

I held my position in front of the metal cage containing the leon shapeshifter while Callyn escorted Serafina out of the throne room. Anger rolled through me that the prince wanted me to waste time training Serafina, who regardless of what she said was clearly not warrior material.

I could feel Prince Tanyth's eyes on me, but it was several minutes before the prince decided to speak. "Tomorrow you will fight Serafina, and if she proves she has enough skills, then you will train her to ensure that she wins her battles in the arena. If she is successful, then I will release you from your contract."

My jaw dropped open in shock. I snapped it shut, my teeth clicking together. *He's offering me my freedom.* The prince gave me a sharp smile. "I thought that would get your attention. I am not concerned with the methods you use or how many hours a day you require her to train, only with the outcome. All training must happen either within the arena itself or in the training room. There will be guards ensuring that you are following your orders and that she doesn't mistakenly hurt you."

I blinked. *The half-blood, hurt me?* I almost laughed aloud at how ridiculous that sounded. *More likely the guards are to ensure I don't kill her on accident.* "As you wish," I replied with a bow.

Prince Tanyth stood up and walked over to the cage with the leon shapeshifter. "A fine specimen. It should perform well in the arena." I nodded in agreement, not sure if he was even paying attention to me. A teal glow emitted from the prince's hands and settled over the cage, then it vanished. I assumed he had relocated the leon into the dungeon where the other beasts were kept.

The prince strode past me toward his guests. "Now that we have concluded the business matters, let's celebrate!" Glasses of wine appeared in everyone's hands, including my own. The wine sloshed over the edge as I adjusted my grip.

"To the lord commander and his hunting prowess!" The prince raised his glass, saluting me, and the guests followed suit, then everyone took a sip. The musicians started playing and Prince Tanyth moved away from me. I found a server and discarded my empty wine glass. Since the prince had declared me the reason for tonight's celebrations he would likely mind if I left too early.

I made my way over to one of the columns in the shadows and leaned against it. The hunt for the leon shapeshifter had been grueling, and I was tired. I only had to stay long enough to appease the prince and then I could go rest.

Twenty-Seven

SERAFINA

The next morning Callyn barged in before I was ready to be awake. I watched her march around the room through half-closed eyes, starting at the wardrobe, where she pulled out clothing. Deciding that delaying getting ready was not likely to earn any respect from Callyn, I stood up and grabbed the brush off the nightstand, running it through my russet hair. I cringed as I hit tangle after tangle. Slowing my brush strokes, I tried to work them out. When I was almost done Callyn shoved clothes into my arms. The brush clattered onto the stone floor as I tipped sideways to prevent the clothes from falling too.

"Hurry up," Callyn ordered. Eyebrows knitting together, I wondered why she was in such a rush. *She just gave me the clothes!*

Keeping my thoughts to myself, I obediently pulled on the rough, undyed cloth tunic. There were thin shorts for an undergarment and a narrow rope that I presumed was intended as a belt. The tunic fell past my knees. "Do I get pants or a skirt?" I asked, swallowing the bitterness in my throat.

Callyn shook her head. "Sorry, no. This is what you are to wear. No boots either." With a glance, she must have decided I was presentable enough, because she grabbed my arm and half dragged me to the door. Trying to keep my breathing steady, I finally got my feet under me properly, so I was able to keep pace with her as we proceeded down the hallway. Up ahead I saw an intersection. *One, two...*"Three!" *Oh shit, that was out loud!* As we crossed the halfway point, I drove my elbow back into Callyn. She let go of me, and I shot down the hallway as though fired from a cannon.

"Stop!" Callyn's shouts and footsteps were close behind. A cramp started in my thigh. *I didn't stretch.* Frowning, I pushed onward, rounding a corner—and skidded into a dead end.

"Another runner?" It was Prince Tanyth. Fear rolled through me, and I turned around slowly. "I thought you would be smarter than that, Serafina."

Callyn stood next to Prince Tanyth with her sword ready. The prince's teal magic flowed around his hands. Wrapping my arms around myself, I prayed he would not use his magic on me. "I will accompany you to the arena," announced Prince Tanyth.

"Yes, Prince," replied Callyn. She took a pair of shackles off her belt and clamped them onto my wrists, then looped a chain through them and attached it to her belt.

Callyn pushed me in front of her and the prince brought up the rear. Callyn steered me with pressure on my shoulders to indicate where I was to go. We stopped in front of a door at the end of the passageway. It opened without needing to be touched and we went right through. It slammed shut behind us, and I jumped, startled. The prince chuckled darkly.

"Come on, we're almost there," Callyn said. We were on a landing to a staircase that plunged into the darkness. Without waiting for my response, she headed down the stairs. I had no choice but to follow. I expected the staircase to be lit once we began our descent, but there was no light. I found myself going slower than I normally would, afraid I'd miss a step and slide or trip down the rest of the stairs.

As I reached the last step, I walked right into Callyn's back. She whirled and glared at me.

"I will leave the two of you here. Callyn clearly has you under control now," the prince said and then vanished in a puff of teal magic.

Callyn grabbed the chain linking my cuffs and dragged me down the passage. We abruptly turned and went through a doorway. I slammed my shoulder into the wall before I regained my balance from the sharp turn. I wondered why the sudden urgency, when we reached a chamber that was shaped like a sphere. The walls and ceiling were rounded, even the floor. Thankfully Callyn let go of the chain and I was able to regain my balance by walking across the room. There was a bench, which we headed toward.

"Sit. We don't have much time, especially after your escapade upstairs. The competitor before you died too fast," Callyn said, pointing at the bench. I obeyed and sat down, wondering what she meant by "competitor."

"What am I supposed to be doing?" I asked.

"You are going to fight in the arena," she replied. I waited, hoping for a deeper explanation, but Callyn didn't say anything else. *I know how to fight. I haven't spent eleven years training with the Fae for nothing.*

"It's time to go," she announced and then placed her hand under my elbow to guide me to another gate with a guard. The gate opened and Callyn placed her hand on my back, propelling me forward. I took a few shaky steps through the gate, and it clanged shut. Then a light breeze wrapped around me and sent me forward. I tried to dig my heels in but could not regain my balance or stop the magic. At last, I fell onto my face. I made the mistake of keeping my mouth open and it filled with gritty sand. I lifted my head, spitting, trying to get it all out. I was sprawled on what seemed to be an area covered in sand.

Slowly rising to a crouch and gazing up, I discovered high above me were a lot of Fae—though from my place on the ground, they looked like small colorful blobs instead of individual Fae. *I'm in an arena.* Light-colored stone walls rose high above me. I could hear the crowd buzzing in excitement. Occasionally I could make out a few words. I was certain Prince Tanyth was somewhere up there. It wouldn't make sense that he would have me, his prisoner, fight if he wasn't going to be around to enjoy it. I had thought if I was to fight in an arena he would have some sort of special platform, but that did not appear to be the case. *Maybe he's not here.* I shook my head, rejecting that idea. *Why would he have lied earlier? I would imagine he would want to watch the murderer of his son be punished, in whatever this event will be.*

Standing in the middle of the arena was not the best idea. I crept toward one of the walls. Halfway there, a high-pitched whistle sounded, followed by a loud clang. A square began to form in the middle of the arena near where I had been. First, a head of dark pewter-gray hair became visible. Recognition coursed through me. *No way.* The platform raised higher and higher, revealing the rest of the male and confirming that it was indeed the lord commander. In one hand he had a plain sword and in the other a dagger. He wore black leather pants with metal plates sewn into them, but his torso was bare. He was even more fit than I had thought.

A cheer went up in the crowd as the lord commander raised his sword, saluting them.

I could see someone standing up in the crowd, arms raised. "My dear guests! Tonight, we shall watch Lord Commander Tristan Gilvrye, warrior elite, face the half-human Serafina."

I clenched my jaw. Of course the prince would choose to focus on my human half and not my Fae half. To paint me as an unworthy opponent of the "lord commander." *But am I a worthy opponent? I haven't even officially graduated from the Fae training camp.*

Then another whistle sounded, drawing me out of my thoughts. The walls began to move. I hastily leaped forward, not wanting to find out what would happen if I let the wall push me. When the walls ground to a halt, the space that was remaining was about the size of an ordinary practice ring. I found myself only a few paces away from a scowling Tristan. He held the sword and dagger with ease I suspected came from many years of training. Instead of watching his face, I found my gaze wandering to his hands.

A horn blew, and I snapped my eyes up. Tristan launched himself toward me, slashing with his sword and dagger. I ducked and rolled to the side; his sword whizzed over my back. *If I can get the dagger from him...*He came up behind me, interrupting my thoughts, and I was helpless to block the slice he made with the dagger across my arm. I felt the sting and trickle of blood as he danced out of reach. My reaction time was too slow; attempting to track his movements, I found myself getting oddly dizzy. Taking a shallow breath, I ordered myself to focus. I set my feet and let my eyelids slide shut, deciding that I could rely on sound alone until the dizziness went away. As Tristan approached, I could hear his footfalls in the sand and feel the changes in the air as he began swinging a weapon. I ducked, rolled, and twisted out of the way. After a while, I could hear the crowd beginning to rumble. I decided to open my eyes. I chose the wrong moment to do so, because Tristan was spinning toward me, sword and dagger whirling so fast I couldn't see them. He swept past. I gasped in surprise as blood began to blossom across the tunic I was wearing. The tunic that was now mostly shredded. I fell forward on my hands and knees. *The sand!*

Clenching my fist around the sand, I watched through narrow eyes as Tristan halted in front of me. Tension and anger were rolling off him; his piercing blue eyes locked with mine.

"Fight," he hissed.

"I'm trying," I said through gritted teeth, looking for my chance.

"If this is what you call fighting, then the rumors that have been floating around about the great Serafina at Emerald Valley are all lies," he snarled at me. In one fluid motion I stood up and flung the handful of sand in his face.

"Argh!" he bellowed, squeezing his eyes tight and dropping his weapons to rub them. I tried to lift the sword, but it was too heavy, so I snatched the dagger and dove for his legs. Whipping my hand out, I sliced across his left ankle, earning me a growl and a poorly aimed kick.

I dodged easily and circled as he picked up the sword, eyes rimmed in red from the sand. I expected him to rush into the fight again, but instead Tristan began pacing, almost prowling around me, as though he were some sort of predatory cat.

"Tristan, you promised me a fight!" shouted Prince Tanyth. Glancing up, I saw the prince standing at the edge of the rim of the arena, his crown making him seem even taller. I spared only a moment for the prince before returning my attention to Tristan.

"I'd hardly call this a fair fight," I muttered.

Tristan's eyes blazed with anger, and he growled deep in his throat. I took a step back. He swung his arm and tossed his sword; it soared through the air and hit the closed gate with a loud clang. Wary, I held the dagger ready, and Tristan leaped toward me, punching left, then right. I shifted, allowing both to blast past me and making quick, short cuts along his arm.

When Tristan paused to breathe, I began my retaliation. One advantage he had was size, both height and stature, but I knew I could be quicker if I tried. I skipped to the right and then lunged forward, aiming for his right kidney. Fast left punch, right stab, left punch, each one progressively harder. It felt like punching a brick wall, and the dagger wasn't doing much more than scratching the surface either. I took a step back, rocking weight onto my right leg, and swung my left around in a low kick. The heel of my foot connected with the side of his knee. Unfortunately, I had forgotten that his leather pants had metal pieces in them. I grimaced as the metal sliced my bare foot, and the kick did nothing whatsoever to his knee.

I hopped backward a few steps, trying to give myself room to maneuver. My sweat-slicked grip on the dagger was loosening. I willed myself to not drop it. Tristan stuck close, throwing small punches. I blocked a few and others connected. I took a deep breath, wanting to regain the upper hand. I stepped to the left and put all my weight on my left foot, intending to spin and kick with my right. My left leg crumpled; I lost my grip on the dagger and landed on my back in the sand.

Tristan came over to me. I expected him to do something, but was unprepared for the kick he landed on my ribs. The crowd went wild as he kicked me again. I heard the crunch as at least one of my ribs broke. Tears stung my eyes, but I gritted my teeth, refusing to scream. I could barely make out his face as he kicked me over and over.

Twenty-Eight

SERAFINA

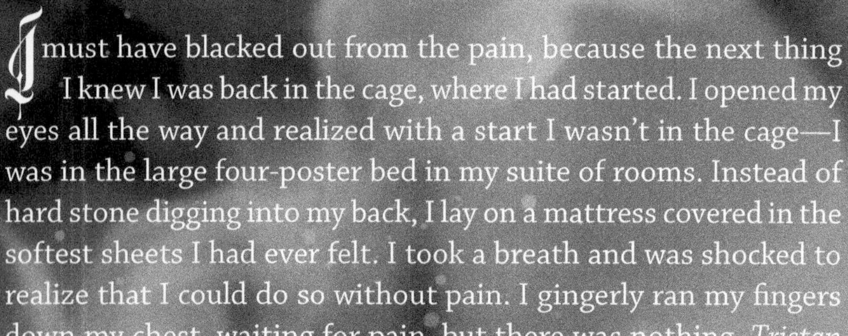

I must have blacked out from the pain, because the next thing I knew I was back in the cage, where I had started. I opened my eyes all the way and realized with a start I wasn't in the cage—I was in the large four-poster bed in my suite of rooms. Instead of hard stone digging into my back, I lay on a mattress covered in the softest sheets I had ever felt. I took a breath and was shocked to realize that I could do so without pain. I gingerly ran my fingers down my chest, waiting for pain, but there was nothing. *Tristan kicked me and then someone healed me. For what purpose?*

I heard muffled voices outside of my room. Worry threading through me, I padded silently over to the door and carefully pressed my ear against the wood.

"The lord commander is unavailable. You will have to over-see her training yourself," came a voice I was almost certain belonged to Prince Tanyth. I shuddered. I did not want to have a repeat arena fight, if you could even call it a fight. *Maybe if they gave me a weapon*. I didn't know enough about Dorcha Palace or Prince Tanyth to begin to guess if he would allow me to have a weapon next time or not.

I heard the key grating in the lock and hastily moved away. A quick glance around the room and I decided to lie on the green couch, hoping it would not look like I had been eavesdropping. I finished draping my arm over the back of the couch when the door opened. I prayed my ruse worked.

Callyn spoke; she was much closer to the couch than I anticipated. Her words were in my ear. "Prince Tanyth was not pleased with your performance in the arena. In Tristan's absence, I have been tasked with ensuring that next time goes differently." Callyn walked around to the front of the couch so she could face me directly.

"Why would it be Tristan's job to train me?" I asked.

"Because he is the lord commander of Dorcha Palace and oversees training of the warriors and those who have been selected to fight in the arena," Callyn explained.

"If I refuse?" I asked boldly, though I was not sure I wanted the answer.

"Did you enjoy the way the arena fight went last night?" she demanded.

"No," I mumbled.

"Remember how that felt every time you think about refusing or making an escape attempt," Callyn said.

Frowning, I got dressed and hastily shoved a meat pie in my mouth before Callyn could rush me out the door. "Ready?" Callyn asked.

I nodded. "Yes."

We walked in silence for a while, then I gave her a sidelong glance. "I want to negotiate with Prince Tanyth for my release."

Callyn's face seemed to get paler. "You are welcome to negotiate with him the next time you are summoned to his presence."

The way she phrased the words made me wonder if she didn't think I should negotiate, or maybe she doesn't think the prince is open to negotiating. I shrugged; it wouldn't hurt to try.

We came to a halt in front of two large wooden doors. Callyn raised her hand, and both doors opened outward, revealing to my surprise an indoor weapons training yard. Callyn led the way inside and when we reached the center the doors closed behind us with a thud that echoed throughout the room. I gazed around at the weapon racks lining the walls.

"Are you going to allow me, a prisoner, to train in here with these weapons?" I asked incredulously.

Callyn stopped walking and turned back toward me. "Yes. Prince Tanyth wants you to fight in the arena and prove you are as good as your reputation from the battlefield."

"Or else what?" I asked, eyebrows arched.

"I don't know what will happen to you. That depends solely on Prince Tanyth." Callyn paused. "I can offer you a bit of advice. He enjoys the spectacle of the arena. Those who perform well are rewarded well."

I blew out my breath and surveyed the weapon racks again, wondering what kind of rewards the prince gave to those who did well in the arena. Maybe asking for my freedom would not be too big of a request. "What weapons did you want to start with?"

Before Callyn could answer, the doors were thrown open hard enough to slam into the wall. I jumped and whirled, hand wrapped around the hilt of the weapon closest to me—an axe. My hand sagged as I tried to compensate for its weight, but I could not prevent the weapon from dragging my hand lower and lower.

Tristan's lip curled in disgust as his eyes roved from my face down to the hand holding the axe. "I thought you said you were a warrior."

"I am!" I growled, blood rushing in my ears. *Where the hell did he come from?*

"Then why, pray tell, did you grab a weapon you can barely keep upright?" Tristan shot back, his eyes sparkling with challenge.

"You startled me," I muttered. Sweat slicked my palms, making it difficult to keep a good grip on the axe. After facing Tristan in the arena weaponless, I did not want to make that mistake again. *If I have a choice.*

"Enemies are unpredictable. You must be able to adapt quickly or suffer the consequences. Now, since that is the weapon you have chosen for today, come here to the middle and we will start," Tristan responded..

Chin at a proud tilt, I walked to the middle, then set my feet in my starting position.

"One, two, three," Tristan instructed. He had a large broadsword that he was holding single-handed. It looked far heavier than my axe, yet he was holding effortlessly.

My first few swings barely got the axe off the ground. I couldn't raise the axe high enough to block, resulting in me giving up ground. *Do not give up.* The last thing I wanted was to prove him right, that I was weak and didn't deserve whatever reputation I had acquired. But the axe was absurdly heavy. *With time it'll get easier.* After I struggled for several minutes like this, Tristan held his hand up. "This is ridiculous."

Exhaling in relief, I rolled my eyes. "I know. But *you* are the one who insisted I use this axe."

"We could swap weapons," he said and offered me his sword hilt-first.

I eyed it and shook my head, certain his broadsword would be just as heavy as the axe. "No thanks. I would like to get a different sword, if you will allow me a chance to select an appropriate weapon."

"Fine, but be fast," Tristan finally said.

Keeping my stride even, I went over to the weapon rack and returned the axe to the empty spot. Then I ran my eyes over the various swords, conducting a quick visual inspection. All the weapons were iron. Judging by the thickness and size of the blades, I selected one that looked like a good match and picked it up. Relief washed through me. While it was slightly heavier than my usual sword, it was a significant improvement from the axe. I gave it a test swing and nodded to myself, then returned to my spot in the middle. *Now I can fight properly.*

Tristan didn't count or ask if I was ready, he just attacked. I spun out of the way from his first strike, but I was ready for the second. Bright orange sparks flew as my blade slid along his. I hopped backward, then darted to the side in a low feint followed by a high strike. Tristan blocked and twisted to the left, his sword chopping down toward my shoulder. Taking advantage of our size differences, I ducked under his arm and sliced at his unprotected hamstring at the last second. I slowed the momentum, so I scratched his leg instead of cutting through the muscle. To my annoyance he didn't even flinch.

Practice continued and I found my rhythm. Gritting my teeth, I sped up, wanting to prove to myself that what happened in the arena had been a fluke. *I was not prepared. It won't happen again.* No matter how fast or slow I went, Tristan met my sword with his.

Sweat dripped off my nose and onto my tunic. I swiped my hand over my face to prevent it from running into my eyes. Tristan took advantage of my distraction and attacked from the side. I barely got my sword up to block in time. At the last moment, he dipped his wrist, and my sword popped out of my hand and sailed through the air. He snagged it with his left and leveled both weapons at me.

"You're dead," Tristan announced.

Cheeks heated in anger, I stood there glowering at him. I knew he was right, which made it even worse. I shouldn't have cleared my eyes when I did, and if this were a real battle, I would be dead. But it was only practice.

"Get some water, then we'll start again," he ordered.

Bristling, I crossed my arms. "I'm fine."

Instead of arguing, Tristan shrugged and noisily drank out of his canteen. I swallowed, my throat suddenly dry. Tristan lifted his canteen and poured it over his head. I had to look away. I *was* thirsty, but there was no way I was going to admit it now.

I wasn't sure how long we had been training for, but I knew it had to be hours. There were more water breaks and even a light snack, and still we trained. Tristan continued to periodically disarm me, and no matter how hard I tried I was not able to gain the advantage. Jaw tight in frustration, I pondered my options. *He never said we had to stick exclusively to swords.*

As Tristan recovered from an intricate high-low combination, I darted in toward him with sharp jabs aimed at his rib cage. Using speed to my advantage, I worked my way around to his right side, then dove into a roll and popped up behind him. *So far so good.* Putting my weight on my right leg, I pulled my left leg in toward me and spun with a kick, aiming for his kidneys. Moments before my foot connected, he gripped my foot in one hand and twisted. Unbalanced, I fell sideways and dropped my sword.

I heard a growl from Tristan as he stalked toward me. I glanced at my sword, then at him, debating if I could get it or not. *I'm going for it.* He lunged, and I dove to the right. My hand wrapped around the hilt and my shoulder slammed into the hard stone floor. I bit my tongue to keep from shrieking at the impact. Tristan's hands gripped my hips, and he flipped me onto my back, pinning me between his legs. *No!* Heat rushed to my face and I raised my sword, but Tristan plucked it out of my hand by the edge of the blade. A thin line of blood beaded on his palm, but he didn't appear to notice.

"Bad choice," he said and threw my sword across the training room, then bent lower over me, pinning my arms over my head.

"No!" I screamed as his breath was hot on my face. I tried to buck him off, rolling my hips, but he stayed firmly in place.

"Dead again," he growled.

I smirked at him, and with one swift motion brought my knee up into his groin. His eyes went wide but to my frustration he did not roll off. *Figures he'd have balls of iron.*

There was a commotion at the door, and I could hear Callyn's voice. "Let me in."

The door hinge squeaked as Callyn stepped in. I tipped my head so I could see her. She seemed annoyed. "Do you have any idea what time it is?"

Tristan stood up, his movements stiff. "Not particularly," he replied.

"Well, it is time for both of you to go to bed," Callyn informed us.

"He wants me to take her to bed?" Tristan said sharply and stood up. I gasped and scooted away from Tristan, fists balled. *I am not going into his bed without a fight.*

Callyn rolled her eyes. "No. You both need to clean up and go to sleep. Tomorrow Serafina is fighting in the arena. You've been here too long as it is. It's almost midnight."

Relief washed through me. I was not going to be raped tonight. *Or ever,* I promised myself.

Tristan's light gray hands held mine pinned to the stone floor of the training room. His thighs gripped my hips firmly. He tipped his head down and lightly brushed his lips against mine, sending sparks all the way to my core. Encouraged by my response, he lightly teased my lips with his tongue, and I parted them eagerly. As he straddled me I began to be aware of pressure building between us and I realized it was his cock. I shifted as much as I could and arched my back, wanting more contact.

The blankets were yanked off and a groan escaped my lips as a rush of icy cold hit me. Shivering, I opened my eyes, and I found myself staring into Tristan's angry face. He looked ready to take a bite out of me. Rubbing my eyes, I tried to wake up enough to sort out where I was and what Tristan might want. Gooseflesh rippled on my skin and I realized that I was naked in bed. A blush crept up my cheeks, deepening as I noticed moisture between my legs, and the dream came slamming back to me. *Tristan kissing me.* I tried to snag the blankets back, but Tristan hissed at me, "What do you think you're doing?"

"Going back to sleep?" I muttered, wanting nothing more than to disappear. *Please don't notice the wetness.* The last thing I needed was the lord commander to ask if I had pleasured myself.

Thankfully he seemed blissfully unaware. "Definitely not. You'll bathe, dress, and then we will lightly train until it is your turn in the arena."

We were in the training room for less than an hour before Tristan deemed it was time and led me to the arena. My thoughts churned. I hated him—of that I was certain. He had beaten me almost to death for no reason. *Then why am I dreaming about kissing him?*

It was a relief to have Tristan behaving as he should, like we are enemies. *We. Are. Enemies.* We walked in silence. I needed to focus on my impending battle, except my thoughts would not obey. I kept throwing sidelong glances at him. *Just because I hate him doesn't mean I can't admire his incredible physique.*

"Do you know what I am going to face today, in the arena?" I asked, no longer able to bear the silence and my thoughts.

Tristan kept walking, and I thought he was going to ignore the question when he suddenly started to talk. "The prince has an assortment of beasts that he often has fight in the arena, including a dragon."

"Dragon?" I squeaked. I'd heard rumors that they still existed, but none had been confirmed.

Tristan chuckled darkly. "Just wait until you must fight Rethys." I worried my lip with my teeth as a sliver of fear worked its way down my spine, and it dawned on me I knew that name. *Rethys*. I had to remember where I had heard it. I was not worried about fighting whatever warriors Prince Tanyth threw at me in the arena, but a dragon? I wasn't sure if I could win, and if I didn't win, would that mean I met my death in Rethys's mighty jaws?

Tristan stopped, and I was too lost in my thoughts to notice. I hit his back hard and lost my balance, falling onto my butt with a thump. "Prick," I snapped before I could stop myself, and the next thing I knew his sword was at my throat.

"Bitch," he growled, pressing the sword tip hard enough to pierce the skin.

"Tristan!" called Prince Tanyth.

Prince Tanyth's eyes went from Tristan to me and back again. "Are you taking good care of my half-blood?" The smile on the prince's face was amused, but the tone was not.

"Yes, Prince," Tristan said woodenly and took a step back.

"Well, you can finish what you started in the arena. Come along," the prince said, leading the way. Before I could stand, I began floating. I tried to put my feet down, but it seemed that Prince Tanyth or Tristan, I wasn't sure who, had decided I could no longer be trusted to walk on my own.

When we halted, we were in the same preparation chamber as before. Prince Tanyth flicked his fingers, and I could move on my own again. "Tristan, you know what to do. Go," Prince Tanyth ordered. Tristan saluted the prince and disappeared through an archway. I could hear voices coming from that direction, but the way the sound echoed on the stone walls, I could not be sure who it was.

I ran a hand through my hair. The prince must have noticed the motion because he smirked. "Let me help you." For a brief moment his fingers glowed with dark teal magic, then it was gone. I blinked, wondering if I had imagined the magic. Then I noticed the changes. My hair cascaded around my shoulders, smooth and untangled, a far cry from the mess my braid had become after training. The rough undyed tunic and pants were replaced with a dark brown sleeveless tunic that brushed my upper thighs. Over the tunic was a short leather breastplate that stopped at my hips, with a leather skirt or fauld that went down to my knees. Completing the ensemble were leather wrist and leg guards, worn but serviceable boots, and a scabbard with an iron sword.

"Much better now," he said. I cringed as he reached over and patted my cheek. *I could stab him now and end this whole ordeal.* I dismissed the idea as quickly as it came to me, my hand swinging loosely at my side. The prince had magic; I would not stand a chance.

"I'll see you soon," he said and then simply vanished.

A guard stepped out of the shadows, his eyes roving, lingering far too long on the fauld. "It is time," he informed me. Jaw taught, I nodded in acknowledgement and stepped forward, making sure there was plenty of space between us. The gate behind him opened, and he beckoned me to follow him. I debated whether I should turn and run. Now, when everyone was distracted by the arena, would be an ideal time. *Look what happened last time—I was trapped in a dead end.* I paused. *No. I need to learn more before I try again. Soon.* Mind made up, I followed the guard until we reached the gate. From here I could see small piles of sand that had been tracked out of the arena by the other competitors.

When the signal came, the guard unlocked the gate and it rolled upward. He waved me through and the gate clanked back into place behind me. Breath eased out of me as I made my way up the tunnel to the arena. *Here we go.* Unlike last time, I was prepared.

Squaring my shoulders, chin high, I approached the arena, my boots sliding on the fine grains before the sand became deep enough to find purchase. My eyes watered at the suddenness of the bright lights illuminating the space. As the spots on my vision began to fade, dread welled up inside of me. There was a series of mossy stone walls in the middle. It reminded me of the practice battles I did back at Jade Wilds, where small groups would go head-to-head in the forest in order to learn how to make use of the features in the landscape, as landmarks to either defend or breach.

I can do this. I gazed around, looking for any hints that there would be others joining me, but I could find none. A bell tolled twice and then I heard before I saw a volley of arrows that was released from the outer wall of the arena. Even though I dodged and wove, the arrows followed me. A burning sensation on my ear had me reaching up with my free hand to find my ear sticky with blood. There was a click and another volley of arrows arced through the air. I tucked into a roll behind one of the short walls, and the arrows thudded into the wall.

I heard a snick and a hiss that caused me to jump as the wall I was leaning against pivoted, revealing an open space beneath it. I shot forward to keep from sliding into the opening and as I did so I heard a loud snarl. A leon leaped out of the hole with a roar, claws flashing. I dove to the side but wasn't fast enough and the claws raked across the back of my right calf. Wincing, I scrambled to my feet and sprinted toward a different wall, but the cat didn't follow. *Be smart.* Once again as I touched the wall, it pivoted too.

I won't make the same mistake. I double-timed it away from the short walls. Expecting the leon to follow, I spun around, sword at the ready, but nothing appeared. *Where did it go?* I took one more step back when I heard a click and the sound of a chain sliding through something. Another opening appeared in the floor, and a leon with a heavy metal collar appeared. *It's the shapeshifter!* I stumbled, almost dropping my sword. The leon leaped forward, claws extended. I dropped to my knee and stabbed upward with my sword. Seconds before the leon landed on me, the sword pierced through its stomach and clean through its spine. The leon shapeshifter died instantly and then fell on top of me.

I panted as I lay in the sand, tugging and pushing at the leon's body, which was at least triple my weight and had effectively trapped me underneath it. *Hurry.* I knew there was at least one other leon in the arena, and pinned, I was an easy target. I closed my eyes and took a deep breath, counting to ten. When I got to ten, I shoved upward and leveraged the leon far enough up that I was able to roll out from under it. The body fell back to the sand with a thump that sent a cloud of dust and sand into the air. I closed my eyes to wait for the air to settle. When I cracked one open, I caught a glimpse of a leon slinking toward me. Its tawny fur blended in with the sand, making it difficult to perceive how far away it was.

Keeping my eyes on the approaching leon, I drifted sideways, wanting to give myself room to maneuver. I was focused on the leon in front of me, when a second leon let out a roar behind me that reverberated throughout the arena and beyond. *Where did that one come from?* I pivoted and rabbited away, vaulting over the dead leon and the open pit from which it had come.

Both leons were clambering after me faster than I had anticipated for such large creatures. The mossy walls were ahead of me, and I was beginning to formulate a plan. *They are fast, but can they jump?* I sent up a prayer and increased my speed heading in between two walls. As I reached them, I used my momentum to bounce between the two walls, steadily gaining height. Finally, I made it to the top of the highest wall. The top was barely wide enough for one of my feet. Fortunately, I had spent time over the years training on narrow objects. I was confident I could stay balanced for long enough to put my plan into motion. The leons split up, answering my question of whether they would scale a wall.

I smiled to myself as one of them veered off around the far side and the other ran right past my wall. Wrapping my hands around the sword hilt, I jumped, landing on top of the leon and plunging my sword into the base of its neck. Jerking my wrist, I tried to remove my sword from the leon, but my sword was stuck. Growling curses under my breath, I fought to free the sword. Muscles bunched, I twisted the hilt as hard as I could.

A roar was the only warning I had as the last leon charged me. I propelled myself sideways using the wall as leverage and went over the top of the charging leon. It skidded to a halt, sending up a sheet of sand. *The perfect cover. Shit.*

Sharp claws pierced my flesh. The low visibility did not hinder the leon. It swiped at my arms and legs three times before I was able to squirm out of the way. Blood seeped out of the wounds and trickled down my skin. Hissing in pain, I tentatively put weight on my left leg.

I gazed around in uncertainty. The leon had disappeared again. A metallic flash caught my attention, and I hobbled over to my sword. This time when I gave it a yank, it slid free easily. With how my shredded leg felt, I doubted I would be able to scale the wall again. Brushing my right shoulder lightly against the wall, I followed it until the end. There was a large gap before the next wall, but instead of crossing it, I decided to move around the end of my wall to the other side.

As I rounded the corner, the leon charged me, rearing up on its hind legs, mouth wide open, ivory fangs flashing as it aimed for my throat. I slashed with my sword, feeling flesh parting under its blade, and danced out of the way. The leon kept coming, snarling and snapping. I backed up, slashing when it got too close, until my back hit a wall. I shrieked in frustration, earning shouts of excitement from the crowd above me. The leon bounded toward me, sending up a cloud of sand each time its heavy front paws hit the ground.

Tears ran freely down my face as my eyes burned. *I will not give up*, I ordered myself. The leon appeared with its mouth almost in my face. I took the sword and shoved it straight up into the leon's jaw. There was a sickening crunch as the blade penetrated through the skull and into its brain. The wall against my back began to move. I swiftly recovered my sword and scooted forward, skirting the dead cat, not wanting to find out if the wall was going to release another leon. I got far enough away from the walls before turning around to see what they were doing. To my surprise the walls were moving up and down and seemed to be rotating as though the whole middle of the arena was on some sort of turntable. *What is going on?*

The movement of the walls stopped abruptly, and they sank back into the floor with a grating sound. A flicker of movement above me drew my attention to the crowd. I immediately recognized Prince Tanyth by his large horned crown, the only feature I could make out from here. The prince began clapping and the crowd quickly followed suit.

I let out my breath. *It's over.* Just as I had seen Tristan do before our battle, I raised my sword in a salute. The screaming got louder. A shimmer surrounded Prince Tanyth and then he appeared in front of me. I dropped my sword and bowed deeply. "Your highness."

"Well done, Serafina," he said.

Encouraged by his praise, I made my request. "I would like to earn my freedom by fighting in your arena."

The prince raised his eyebrows, and his lips twitched. "Why should I give you your freedom?"

"Shouldn't everyone have the chance to be free?" I replied.

Prince Tanyth tapped his chin with his fingers. I hoped he was considering my request and not toying with me. "Very well. If you are successful in your battles, then I will grant you your freedom."

"Truly?" I said in surprise. *He agreed!* Excitement coursed through me; I was able to earn my freedom.

"Yes. Now, why don't you get cleaned up. I will see you later," Prince Tanyth replied, then vanished.

I stared at the spot he vacated in disbelief. *It's always worth asking,* I reminded myself. I walked toward the gate; a weight had been lifted from my shoulders. I only had to win the battles he gave me and then he would set me free.

Twenty-Nine

TRISTAN

I was pressing Serafina lightly against the wall. A moan escaped my lips as she bit my tongue hard enough to draw blood, sending desire roaring through me. I ran my hands down her sides, my thumbs brushing lightly on the edge of her breasts. Serafina deepened the kiss and swished her hips, rubbing against my already aching cock. I wasn't sure how much longer I'd be able to wait.

My eyes snapped open, and I glanced blearily around the room. Tepid water surrounded me; I had fallen asleep in the bathtub. *Why the fuck was I dreaming about the half-blood?* My cock was so hard it hurt, I was too embarrassed to find Callyn and admit to her who I was dreaming about. Using my magic to quickly reheat the water until it was comfortable, I wrapped my hand around my throbbing cock, imagining Callyn riding me, working it until my body spasmed in release.

As pleasure washed over me, it was quickly replaced by anger. Serafina was a prisoner, nothing more. *What is wrong with me?* I dried off and climbed into bed, willing myself to fall into a dreamless sleep.

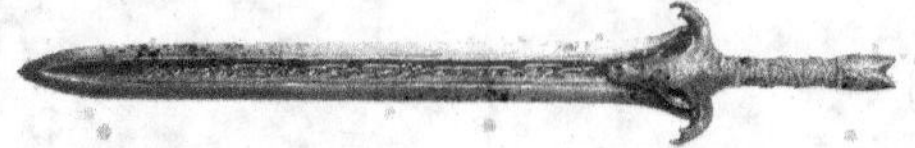

I spent the whole night tossing and turning, unable to dream of anything except Serafina. Her lips, her perky breasts, and how my cock would feel gliding inside of her.

Dressing and eating quickly, I was desperate for a distraction. *Sparring would be ideal, though I doubt anyone else is awake at this hour.*

My muscles were drawn tight as I strode down the hallway to the training room. Hot anger thrummed in my veins as I sent a small burst of gray magic from my hands, sending the doors crashing into the wall.

Bane was staring at me, jaw hanging open. "You okay?"

Growling, I used magic to shut the doors, then faced him. "Do I look okay?"

Bane licked his lips uncertainly. "Anything I can do to help?"

I gave him a sharp smile. "Yes, there is. Spar with me." The words came out as more of a command than I intended.

"Of course," Bane replied.

This better work. Even at the merest thought of Serafina, I felt my cock responding. I forced myself to warm up with stretches. My whole body was taut, and if I didn't stretch, I was likely to tear something. When I felt noticeably looser, I strode over to the weapon rack and removed a double-headed axe, wanting the extra work to help me forget about the dream.

We squared off. Bane sported a short sword and a dagger. My mouth twitched in amusement at his choice. "Ready, one, two, three!" Using a two-handed grip on the haft, I chopped down and at the last moment twisted the blade ninety degrees so I was now aiming for his stomach. Bane blocked, his sword briefly catching on my axe, then jabbed at my unprotected shoulder with his dagger. I felt a brief prick on my arm. *Barely a scratch.*

Bobbing and weaving through a deadly dance, Bane and I chipped away at each other's defenses. Droplets of blood flecked our tunics and arms, and I could feel the trickle of sweat down my back. The longer we sparred, the further away Serafina was in my thoughts. Neither one of us was able to take advantage of the other this morning. I chalked it up to my lack of sleep and whatever had driven Bane to come down so early.

"Let's switch to hand-to-hand," I suggested, taking a step back and lowering the axe.

Bane nodded in agreement, and we returned the weapons to the rack before taking a water break.

It was midday when Serafina finally showed up. Cold anger flared within me at how late she was, ignoring the fact that she was unable to move about freely within the palace. There was a fight planned for tonight and now I had a very small window of time to prepare her. *If she fails I will lose my shot at freedom.*

I straightened my spine and gave her a steely glare. "You're late." Without waiting for her to approach, I snagged a pair of staves out of the weapon rack and dropped one at her feet. "Have you used a staff or a polearm before?" I asked tersely.

"Yes," she replied.

I spun the staff in my hand, impatiently. "Set up." It felt like it took her ages to stand in front of me with her hands in the proper position on the staff.

"One, two, three!" I counted. She tried to catch me off guard and take the first strike, but I blocked her feeble attempt and smacked her hard across the back of her calves. "Amateur," I muttered. She hissed at me and swung again. This time it was a calculated move. I pressed against her staff, throwing all my weight into it and forcing her to back up before she was able to disengage and regroup. *So much for having experience.*

Her speed with the next strike was a surprise. The end of her staff hit my thigh hard. "Ouch," I said automatically. Clenching my jaw, I wondered why I had let the word slip.

"Baby," she mocked.

My eyes narrowed. *Challenge accepted. I'll show her who's the baby.* I spun the staff in my hand and began a combination middle feint, low strike, high strike combination. Intent on executing the correct movements, I failed to see her staff sticking out at an angle. As I lunged forward, I tripped and face-planted. The butt of her staff pressed into the base of my neck.

"Dead," she said.

Before I could respond, the door opened and a familiar chuckle met my ears—Callyn. She started clapping. "Well done, Serafina."

My face heated up in annoyance that my friend would congratulate the prisoner on disarming me—something previously only Callyn *and* Travaran had accomplished. I snarled and flattened my palms against the ground, springing upward. Serafina was distracted by Callyn and had loosened her hold on the staff; it slid out of the way, freeing me. I snaked my arms around Serafina's waist and yanked her to the ground, pinning her on her back beneath me.

We were both breathing heavily. My blood roared through my veins, and I met her eyes, a retort on my lips, but as I stared at her, sparks ignited along my skin. When my cock began to throb in response, I leaped up. *Fuck, what is wrong with me?* I stalked away, my back to Callyn and Serafina. The guards at the door eyed me warily.

I heard murmurs between Serafina and Callyn, but I couldn't make out the exact words. A hand lightly clasped my shoulder and I tensed, ready with an elbow jab.

"Relax, it's me," Callyn said. "The prince wants you to join him in the crowd tonight. Go get cleaned up. I will take care of the rest of Serafina's prep."

I pressed my lips together and nodded. "Thanks." Without another glance in their direction, I left.

Thirty

SERAFINA

Practice with Tristan was disconcerting. I could handle the anger, whether it was hot or cold, but today underneath the anger there had been something else I couldn't put my finger on. *Maybe he got bad news from Prince Tanyth. It's not like I know him, or am planning on ever getting to know him, well enough to be able to read his moods.*

The crazy sparks that had ignited my skin when he pinned me down were just plain weird. I assumed it was his magic reacting oddly to us touching, but I fervently wished that Fiera and Ghilanna were here with me so I could talk to them. Dreaming of kissing a male was uncharted territory for me and they would know how to handle it. Especially when the male wouldn't hesitate to kill me should the opportunity present itself.

I ran a hand over my face. I needed to focus on the present, entering the arena and fighting whatever horrible thing awaited me. Tonight I had a thick leather chest plate and leathers, much like my training gear back at Jade Wilds. I hefted the sword in my hand before striding through the gate and into—*A forest?* I halted in my tracks to stare open-mouthed at the large pine trees dotting the arena. Beneath them was an assortment of green grass and large boulders, similar to parts of the Whispering Thicket I had traveled through to get to Emerald Valley.

I cautiously walked forward, keeping my eyes peeled for whatever was joining me in the arena. I spared a glance at the crowd above me. For the moment they were silent, which I took to mean only one thing: something was coming. Soft at first, then growing louder, I could hear grating stone, but as I looked around the arena, I couldn't identify the source. That was when I realized that the Fae above were shouting and pointing up. I glanced up and saw that the ceiling far, far above me was opening revealing a cloudless sky dotted with stars. *The sky!* Momentarily mesmerized, a screech yanked me back to reality. Eyes to the sky, I watched a dark shape plummet through the hole, and a cheer went up through the crowd. *What the bloody hell is it?* The shape spread what I realized were wings and soared over the top of the arena and then the crowd.

As it banked for another pass I noticed that there was someone on the creature's back. When it flew overhead it got low enough, I was able to study the underside. The wings were covered in deep red feathers, almost the color of wine. The body was also covered in feathers several shades darker than the wings, and the tail ended in a tuft of pure black feathers. It had four legs that were shaped much like those of the leon. I waited for it to come my way again to confirm my suspicions. As it did, I studied the head, like that of a large predatory bird, with a wicked hooked beak and bloodred eyes.

"Griffin," I said softly with a shudder. *Griffins are from the Court of the Sun's territory,* I mused, recalling my Fae geography lessons. Not only was it a griffin, but it also had a rider, which meant they had to have some amount of bonding. Griffins and their riders bonded for life. Griffins were highly intelligent beings and rarely seen in captivity; most preferred death over capture. Which made me wonder to what lengths Prince Tanyth had gone to acquire this bonded pair. A glint of metal around the griffin's hind paw and the rider's neck, gave me a hint of the terrible answer. Like the leon shapeshifter, they had been captured and somehow their magic was being bound by the collar. Compassion swelled in me as I realized they were the same as me: prisoners.

As the griffin circled again, I studied the Fae on its back. The Fae was covered from head to toe in chain mail armor. I fingered the hilt of my sword, debating if I should throw it and try to knock the rider off the griffin. Ultimately, I decided against throwing my sword. *I still need a weapon.* Injured and weaponless was not going to help me stay alive. I knew if I kept my sword, I still had a fair chance of walking out of the arena on my own two feet. I set my feet, anticipating that the griffin would make one more pass and then land, watching for any changes in the griffin's movements indicating the rider had a different plan. As the griffin flew beyond my view, out of the corner of my eye, I saw something whirling through the air. I spun, sword raised as though blocking a strike. The Fae released the object, which I couldn't make any sense of until I felt it wrapping around my neck: the cold, hard metal edges of chain links.

Terror gripped me. *Not again!* I dropped my sword and grabbed the edge of the chain with my fingers, tugging. It was still a little loose. I slipped my fingers under it, trying to get leverage to free myself. The Fae gave a sharp yank and the chain pulled taught, trapping my fingers against my throat.

I heard a snap before it registered that the sound was the bones breaking in my three fingers under the chain. I gasped as the chain put pressure against my windpipe, cutting off my air. The air in my lungs evaporated and the Fae hopped off the griffin and stalked toward me, keeping a firm grip on the chain and the pressure. My vision darkened. *This is the end.*

Abruptly the chain went slack, relieving the pressure on my throat, and I could breathe again. The pine trees came into sharp focus as I inhaled and let my hand with its broken fingers fall limply to my side. *At least I know how to use a sword with either hand*, I consoled myself.

The Fae shoved his helmeted face into mine. "Is that all you've got?" a male voice I couldn't recognize said.

"If you actually fought me instead of cheating, then maybe you would be able to find out," I hissed and crouched down, retrieving my sword from the sand. I wanted to throw sand in his face, but my right hand was in too much pain to try.

Instead of replying, the Fae swept the hand holding the chain up, causing it to uncoil from around my neck and fly into his hand. Not wanting to waste an opportunity I lunged toward him, slashing his right arm. He raised the arm as though it was a shield to block. A loud clang resounded throughout the arena when my sword connected with his chain mail–covered arm. *It's not as strong as plate, though.* He threw the chain at my injured right hand, and it wrapped around my hand and wrist.

I screamed, unable to help myself, as the chain jostled my broken fingers. Chewing on my cheek, I prepared for what came next. He yanked the chain, but I braced against it. I heard more bones snapping, but I refused to give way to the pressure. *I will not give up!* Pulse pounding in my ears, I wrapped the chain around my upper arm, trying to give myself more leverage, and pulled it taut, causing my enemy to stumble forward a few steps. I tossed the chain into the sand. Lightning fast, I rolled and came up behind him, using quick, short slashes across his back and legs. A few missed my original mark and nicked his neck, drawing blood, but the armor was doing its job well. *Too well. Perhaps I can trip him or something.*

The Fae laughed darkly as I continued to shower him in useless strikes. I dodged to the side and tripped over the chain, sending myself sprawling onto my stomach. The sword went flying too and I couldn't see it, let alone reach it. When the cold kiss of his blade caressed my throat, it was almost a relief. "Go on, make the kill," I challenged, and the crowd went wild.

He raised the sword to take the killing blow. I closed my eyes as the sword came down, but the blow never came. I opened my eyes just as the sword vanished. The Fae stood over me, immobile, when the arena simply disappeared.

I blinked, not sure what was going on, and found myself back in my bedroom. I looked around in confusion and confirmed I was alone in my room. I sighed deeply and shed the armor, then climbed onto the bed and curled into a ball. The tears of relief and pain flowed. I wasn't ready to die, not yet, not if I had a choice. I drifted into a restless sleep.

Tristan's hands were wrapped around my throat, strangling me, and then at the last moment he let go and we were kissing.

A sharp pain lanced through my hand and broke me out of the deep sleep I had been in. I screamed and screamed as someone straightened out my broken fingers.

"Serafina, calm down," a harsh voice ordered me. I refused to listen and kept screaming. Part of me was still clinging to the feel of Tristan's lips on mine while my consciousness tried to get in control and wake me up all the way.

"Serafina, you're making it worse. Stop screaming," the voice ordered again. I sucked in a breath and opened my mouth to scream again and found that I could not. Instead I started to cough and thrash around, unable to catch my breath or control my own throat. A few moments later I found I could no longer move of my own free will. I could feel someone continuing to straighten my fingers out, but I was powerless against it. My eyes cracked open to the barest of slits. There was a shadow above me, but without opening my eyes all the way I knew I would not be able to see what was happening. I took a deep breath and exhaled, then opened my eyes wide. Callyn had my arm gripped firmly while a Fae female I didn't know straightened out my fingers. I was on a cot in a room with bare walls and a couple of chairs.

Callyn's lips were pressed together into a thin line. "We are trying to heal you before your bones set incorrectly and we have to re-break them."

I opened my mouth, jaw working, but the words wouldn't come out. I glared at Callyn, assuming she was the one doing the magic and preventing me from speaking.

"I'll let you speak if you promise not to scream," she said.

I gave the barest of nods and found that the pressure around my throat was gone. "What is the point of all this? Fighting, getting injured, and then being healed, only to repeat it again."

Callyn frowned. "You must have misunderstood me. We are only ensuring your bones are set so they can heal properly. Prince Tanyth did *not* give orders for you to receive a full healing." I clenched my teeth to keep the retort that was on the tip of my tongue from being spoken.

I felt a gentle squeeze on my leg before the Fae female attending to my hand lifted her eyes to mine and began speaking. "I will splint your wrist and fingers."

"You seem to want to stir up trouble. The Fae here are doing what they can to survive. Would you criticize them for not wanting to be near you or the conflict you're creating?" Callyn asked tersely.

"Conflict?" I asked in confusion.

Callyn rolled her eyes. "Yes. You won't simply die."

I laughed sharply. "The Fae male with the sword in the arena had ample opportunity to kill me. Honestly, I didn't expect to live after that encounter."

"Prince Tanyth must have promised you something," Callyn replied.

"Is there something wrong with that? Not wanting to give up because the prince made me a promise?" I asked, wondering what had happened to Callyn that she no longer wanted to fight for herself.

Callyn grimaced. "Did he give you exact details on how to win your freedom?"

My eyes widened as I realized what she was implying. "Only that I am successful in my arena battles."

Callyn didn't comment, which made me realize the mistake I quite likely had made in assuming that the prince would be fair, that he would give me my freedom if I won enough battles. *But how many is enough?*

To my surprise, Callyn leaned forward, and her lips brushed lightly against mine before resting near my ear, her breath tickling my neck. "Do not give up hope," she whispered before straightening out and brushing off her tunic, as though touching me had made her dirty.

Silently Callyn stood guard while the healer put my fingers and wrist in the braces meant to help keep the bones straight while they healed. When they were done, I was left alone. I found myself staring at the stone walls. All my injuries began throbbing, but the pain remained at a tolerable level. I wasn't sure what else to do, so I allowed my eyes to slide shut and drifted off.

Thirty-One

TRISTAN

I don't know if Prince Tanyth heard me mention Rethys or if he had already been planning this fight. I sat in a chair next to him, watching the scene in the arena below unfold. I considered myself lucky he hadn't put me down there. I knew that Rethys was one of the prince's most favored possessions. Those who faced him in the arena were typically slated for death.

After the close call with Travaran and I, almost damaging Rethys beyond the ability of magic healing, the prince had become more selective over the battles he put Rethys in.

I gazed into the arena. An assortment of Fae had been chosen for tonight's battle. Half of them had been on a list I had given Tanyth of which of my warriors were still struggling with keeping up with their training and assignments.

I had to write names on the list, or it would be my head on the chopping block. There were times I could push off turning over the list, if we had enough prisoners to fill the slate of arena fights. Creating the list was one of the worst part of my jobs, because I knew I was sentencing people under my command to death.

"I am surprised you didn't put their names on the list months ago," Prince Tanyth said.

I shrugged. "You only permit me to recruit once a year from Embergate."

Prince Tanyth opened his mouth to reply, then snapped it shut as Rethys roared and breathed fire across the arena. I analyzed what techniques the Fae were using and made note of each mistake. One common mistake I had found over the years was the inclination to assume that the beasts used to fight in the arena were stupid. Rethys was highly intelligent, and after witnessing a few of his battles I discovered that he too analyzed his opponents, searching for weaknesses before attacking.

As Fae ran around screaming and on fire in the middle of the arena, Rethys reared up on his hind legs, wings flared, and roared. His eyes caught mine. A dark voice echoed in my head: *I see you.* I wasn't sure if it was a threat or a promise. Then the dragon's gaze flickered to Prince Tanyth.

Out of the corner of my eye I saw a glimmer of fear ripple over Prince Tanyth's face, before it was hidden with malicious glee. I tucked that thought away. *He is afraid of Rethys.* I had no idea how that information would ever be useful, but maybe one day it would be.

The air around the arena shimmered and then the arena became obscured with a dark, glimmering dome indicating the end of tonight's arena entertainment. The prince made no move to leave. I stayed in my seat, waiting for dismissal.

"You may go," the prince whispered.

I gave him a wary glance, and Prince Tanyth's eyes met mine. I was surprised to see tears at the corners of them. The prince rarely let me see this side of him. "Are you sure?"

"Yes. I was just remembering when you and Travaran fought Rethys," Prince Tanyth said softly.

Blowing out my breath, I quietly departed. *This is the first time I've seen him shed tears over Travaran's death.* I wish I knew what it meant.

Wandering the halls, I considered the words Rethys had said. "I see you." *What does he mean? That we're both prisoners of the prince? Or that he knows my secret?* A shiver of fear went down my spine. *I could go ask.* I was halfway down the hallway leading to the dungeon entrance when I heard Callyn calling my name.

Nostrils flaring, I halted and turned around. "Hey."

Callyn slipped her hand into mine and gave me a worried frown. "Is everything okay?"

Licking my lips, I considered what to say. "The prince is mourning his son."

"I see," Callyn replied. "Let's go eat, dinner is waiting in my suite." In companionable silence we strolled down the winding hallways till we reached her suite. It was not too far from my own.

As she undid the magic locking her door, I sniffed the air, my mouth watering as the scent of spiced elk sausage reached my nose. The table was set for three, though as far as I could tell no one else was there.

"Are you expecting someone else?" I asked, selecting a chair and filling my plate.

"Maybe later. That depends on what you want to do," she said, wagging her eyebrows suggestively.

Callyn used her magic to light a small fire and play music softly in the background. My thoughts were still reeling over the death of my men in the arena and then Rethys speaking into my mind; right now just having a conversation sounded more appealing than sex.

After dinner we sat companionably on the sofa in front of the fire. Callyn's bare feet were in my lap and I massaged them as we talked. "Do you know much about dragons?"

"Only a little," Callyn replied.

"Can you tell me what you do know?" I inquired.

She smiled at me. "Of course. They were hunted to extinction over one hundred years ago. Though, the prince has Rethys here, so there is at least one still living. Meaning it's possible others exist. Dragons collect treasure. The art I'm sure you've seen of dragons and these huge heaping hoards of jewels and coins are fairly accurate."

"Do they talk?" I asked.

Callyn giggled. "Talk?"

I sighed. "Yes."

Callyn shook her head. "Not that I know of. I mean, they must communicate with each other somehow, but I have never heard of them talking."

My nostrils fluttered as I gazed into the fire. *If dragons can't talk, how did Rethys speak in my mind? Maybe I asked Callyn the wrong question.*

Callyn's warm fingers trailed up my thigh and brushed my cock lightly. My breathing hitched as she vanished my pants with her magic and ran her nails along my shaft, with just the right amount of pressure for the desired effect. A moan escaped my lips and I flexed my hips, bumping my cock against her hand. "Fuck me," I mumbled, earning a chuckle from Callyn.

"I thought you'd never ask," Callyn replied, sinking in front of me on the floor and taking my cock deep into her mouth. Back arched against the sofa, I tipped my head against the cushions with my eyes closed. Soft lips caressed mine and I opened my eyes.

"Verrona," I whispered in recognition, she leaned down and kissed me again. *Why was I worried about the dragon?* I wondered fleetingly.

My tongue was buried in Verrona's pussy when there was a knock on the door. *Fuck.* I growled, nipping the inside of her thigh with my teeth.

"Don't stop," Verrona gasped, back arching. As much as I wanted to finish, a bigger concern was *who* was at the door.

"I'll get it," Callyn said and slid off the bed, I could hear her pull the robe off a hook and pad toward the door. Ears straining, I waited impatiently for her to open the door.

"Callyn, good evening," Prince Tanyth's voice carried to the bed. I tensed, fear running through me.

"Prince Tanyth, what can I do for you?" Callyn's voice was steady.

"I want to join you," Prince Tanyth replied and stepped farther into the room.

Not good. Quietly I sat up in bed and pulled on my discarded pants and tunic, then walked over the wall and leaned on it casually. Verrona put her lingerie back on and arranged herself on the bed.

My eyes were on the doorway as Prince Tanyth walked in, followed by Callyn. She mouthed *I'm sorry* over the prince's shoulder.

"Why are you here, Tristan?" demanded Prince Tanyth.

Digging my nails into my palm, I replied, "We were just visiting."

"Were you watching them pleasure each other?" the prince asked, his voice ice cold.

I knew I was treading dangerous waters. The prince was never happy when he discovered me fucking, no matter who my partner was. I suspected it was jealousy. "Yes, I was watching them fuck and explaining how things went in the arena since Verrona was not able to watch tonight."

"Come here," the prince ordered, pointing to the spot next to him. Reluctantly I obeyed. "Why are you lying to me?" he snarled and hurled a ball of magic at my chest. I was thrown against the wall, arms pulled taut above me. Heavy iron manacles circled my wrists, and a chain went through them and attached to the wall. My feet dangled above the ground.

220

Prince Tanyth drew a dagger and traced the seam of my pant leg with it, starting at the knee and halting at my cock. "I should cut it off." He paused. "I will be merciful this once, but if I catch you in here again, I will cut your cock off and feed it to you."

Tremors ran through me, a mix of fear and anger. The chains rattled slightly, and I willed myself to be still. Picking a spot on the far wall, I stared at it until the prince returned his attention to Callyn and Verrona. *It could be far worse,* I consoled myself. *He could have just cut it off.*

Refusing to watch, I kept my eyes on the wall past the bed. With the mood the prince was in, I wasn't sure what to expect would happen in the bedroom. The telltale sounds of kissing reached my ears, but that was it. *His anger is directed at me then, not Callyn and Verrona.*

Hardly ten minutes had passed when the prince focused on me again. "Let's go," he said. I opened my mouth to respond, since clearly I couldn't go anywhere chained to the wall, but Prince Tanyth opened a star portal and using his magic pulled us both through it and into my room. He attached my chains to my wall. I could almost touch the floor, if I stretched my foot out.

"There is a timer on the chains. When it ends, they will disappear. Do yourself a favor, don't fuck Callyn again," the prince growled. Then without another word, he vanished.

I glared at the empty space. *His jealousy was over Callyn.* I should have seen this coming; hell I was surprised it hadn't happened sooner. Prince Tanyth wasn't jealous about the sex; the core of the problem was my decades-long friendship with Callyn. But you couldn't force a friendship, you had to earn it.

Exhaling, I opted to try meditating, not sure I could fall asleep while strung up in chains.

Thirty-Two

SERAFINA

Previous injuries could not have prepared me for the excru-ciating pain of healing from most of the bones in my right hand being broken. Dreams of Tristan haunted my sleep and unending pain chased me in my waking hours. Because I was unable to enter the deep sleep state needed to heal, the process was taking far longer than normal.

Food showed up like clockwork, but otherwise I had no visitors. *Not that I could have a conversation through the pain.* Mercifully I was left alone in my rooms, though part of me won-dered if no one knew how slowly I was healing.

Throughout the day I would exercise, hoping wearing myself out from physical exertion would cause the dreams to go away. I ran through various stretches, curls, push-ups—mostly one-armed as my right hand and wrist were still too painful to put weight on. So far it wasn't working; I continued to dream of the intense kissing sessions with Tristan.

After eating dinner, hardly able to keep my eyes open, I wrapped myself up in blankets and fell asleep on the couch.

I was in a tent. At first, I didn't recognize anything, but then the rough edges solidified, and I recognized it as Commander Meriel's tent. The commander was sitting at her table in one of the plush blue chairs. Steam rose from a silver teapot. The other chair held King Pharaan. I stumbled backward in surprise. Why am I dreaming of Commander Meriel and King Pharaan?

When I finally got over my shock enough to scoot closer to them, I could understand their words.

"Any news?" King Pharaan asked.

Commander Meriel shook her head. "No. After she was captured during your ride to the mine, she just disappeared. I do have a theory though."

"Which is?" *pressed the king.*

"You're not going to like it," *Meriel said.*

The king shrugged. "My granddaughter disappeared without a trace, and could possibly be the answer to our prayers—the lost Fae queen. These are not ordinary times. Tell me what you suspect."

Meriel pressed her lips together into a thin white line, then glanced in my direction. Her eyes met mine. This is a dream, it's not real, and she can't see me, *I told myself.*

"Years ago, I was romantically involved with Prince Tanyth, before he was a prince," *she began.*

The king waved his hand. "Yes, I know that, and I also know that you ended it after he almost killed you."

Meriel gasped. "No one knows about that."

The king arched a single eyebrow at her. "There is a reason I am King. Go on."

Meriel coughed and continued. "Over the time we were involved I learned that he felt the prophecy about the lost queen was true. He also let it slip at one point that if he ever came across the lost queen, he would kill her."

The king drummed his fingers on the table. "I would need proof before I could accuse Prince Tanyth of kidnapping her. Without it, no one would support my claim, and we would be fighting him alone."

He hesitated. "I don't know if I'm strong enough to do that, or how much power he wields now."

Meriel nodded. "Yes. But you have wanted to go after him for years. This is our chance."

The king shook his head. "I can't risk it without the support of the other courts."

"What if I'm right and we're wasting precious time we don't have?" Meriel demanded.

"Serafina is not a helpless human child. She is trained and has proven herself, both at Jade Wilds and at Emerald Valley. You must have faith she can survive until help arrives," King Pharaan said.

Meriel spoke again. "I was far older than she is when I became entangled with Tanyth, and I barely survived. I understand that you are speaking not exclusively as her grandfather but as king of the Fae. I implore you to consider how every hour and every day that passes, we risk not only that she might die, but that she will be pushed past the breaking point."

King Pharaan opened his mouth to speak, but I could no longer make out the words. The tent began to fade, and in its place for a moment I saw the snow leopard.

I woke up with a start, drenched in sweat. The couch was beneath me. I tapped the base of the lamp and the Fae light filled the room with a soft glow. All of the lamps in my room had been magicked so I could tap them to turn them on, confirming I was in my suite at Dorcha Palace. *Was that a dream or something else?* I understood dreaming about Tristan given our constant close proximity, but a dream of Commander Meriel didn't make any sense. *Or it's the commander's seer magic at work. She never really explained how that kind of Fae magic functioned beyond her being able to see the past and future.*

I was working on a set of curls when I heard the lock click on the door behind me. I ignored it and finished my set, then rose to face the door, eyes widening when I saw Tristan there, wearing his training gear.

"What are you doing?" he growled.

"Exercising," I replied indifferently.

"You look like shit," he said in a muted voice.

Detecting a hint of concern in his tone, I scoffed. "If I could actually sleep, maybe I would look better."

"Why aren't you sleeping?" he asked, eying me and then my bed, though he stayed by the door.

Licking my suddenly dry lips, I responded, "Bad dreams."

Tristan gave me a sympathetic look as though he knew what that was like. I had not been expecting him to sympathize with me over anything. My eyes wandered over his face, taking in the dark circles under his eyes and the hollowness of his cheeks, then settling on his full, soft lips. Mine parted and I could feel my heart starting to race. I even took several steps toward him before I stopped myself, blushing deeply. *I was going to kiss him!*

"Well, tired or no, you are required to attend a banquet tonight. Let's go," Tristan said. Instead of waiting for me to respond, he started to walk away.

My thoughts drifted to the dreams of him strangling me. Fury boiling in my veins, I lunged for Tristan's unprotected back. Fists curled, I drove my right hand into his right kidney, followed in quick succession with my left. I winced in pain as the punch strained the barely healed fingers and wrist.

At the second punch I threw, Tristan spun around, and before I knew what was happening, he drove his fists into my gut right-left-right. I gasped and then puked, spraying both of us with the vile contents of my stomach. My stomach was still heaving as I fell to my knees, but I wasn't sure if there was anything left in it to come out. *I should have run instead.* I focused on trying to slow my breathing and regain control of my body.

"You..." Tristan snarled, then grabbed a chunk of my hair and lifted me to my feet by it. Tears stung my eyes as he twisted his hand in my hair hard. I prayed they would not fall; I didn't want to give him satisfaction. Nor was I willing to beg for forgiveness.

Tristan dragged me by my hair out of my room and into a huge bathhouse a few doors down. Laughter echoed in the room with a high arched ceiling. The damp from the stone clung to my feet, and I shivered, noticing other Fae were in here. *Maybe I will meet someone who can help me escape.* It didn't take long before the Fae who had been occupying the bathhouse noticed us and a hush fell across the room.

Grip tight on my hair, Tristan opened his mouth and bellowed, "Everyone get out!" None of the Fae hesitated; they grabbed their belongings and towels and vanished, and within a few minutes we had the room entirely to ourselves. I wasn't sure that this was a good thing.

Tristan's grip didn't change until the room was clear. Then his fingers relaxed, releasing my hair. He took a few steps back, nostrils flared, breaths sharp.

Facing him, my back to the pool, I opened my mouth to speak, when he threw his arms out, startling me, I took a half step backward, my heel sliding on the edge of the pool. Before I could regain my balance I toppled into the water with a huge splash. I opened my mouth, which was the wrong thing to do, and it filled with hot spring water. I started choking, arms flailing, momentarily forgetting what I should be doing. One of my feet scraped the bottom of the pool. *I can stand up!* I thrust with both legs and shoved myself upward. My head broke the surface, and I stood there gasping and spitting out water. *He could have helped.*

Tristan stood at the edge of the pool, arms crossed. "You need to wash. No one wants to be around a stinking half-blood."

Glowering at him, I yanked the soaking nightgown over my head and threw it at his chest. Unfortunately, I missed my mark. Face heating, I grabbed one of the jars and opened it, pouring some of the soap into my hand. Swimming farther out into the pool, I scrubbed my hair. *Tristan isn't wrong, I do stink.* The soap lathered nicely, and I must admit it was a relief to be able to get clean.

I ducked under the water to rinse myself off, and when I resurfaced, Tristan was no longer standing at the edge of the pool. I could hear splashing in another pool and presumed he was bathing too. *Thank goodness he's staying away.* I sank into the water so only my head was above it, savoring the heat and letting my thoughts drift.

Maybe it's time I demand that the prince agree to a number of battles I win. Encourage him to give me a final goal. No one has come looking for me, not my friends, my commander, or even my own family—King Pharaan. The Fae at Dorcha Palace are clearly terrified of Tanyth or completely under his control. Tonight at the banquet I will make my demand. I paused for a moment. *Whatever it takes, I will do, no matter what.*

Another part of my mind decided to chime in then. *What if he makes other demands, beyond fighting?* A shudder rippled through me as an image of being chained to the wall and whipped until my back was in shreds. *Or worse, what if he demands I sleep with him?* I didn't know if that was something he did or not. I prayed I would not find out.

I became aware of the slight slap of feet on the wet stone, and I turned toward it. Tristan was standing at the edge of the pool with only a towel around his waist. Water glistened on his chest and all I could do was stare; his body was incredible. I snarled in my thoughts, *He is the enemy.* And yet I had been having dreams of him where he most definitely was not my enemy. I gasped as I felt a tendril of desire working its way down my body, I bit my cheek, drawing blood. *I cannot lose sight of my objective.*

Unfortunately, Tristan must have noticed because he gave me a wicked smile and then yanked the towel off his hips, revealing how well-endowed he really was. But what bothered me was that his cock was starting to get hard. *Does the idea of fucking a female he hates have that much appeal?* I blushed and looked away.

"Verrona should be here shortly to take you to the room to get dressed," he said. I was hoping he'd pick up the towel again, but he left it discarded at his feet. "Your towel and robe are there." He pointed by the stairs where a folded towel and robe awaited me.

I swam toward the stairs closest to the towel and robe and emerged, hastily snagging the towel off the ground and wrapping it around myself. I glanced over my shoulder and saw Tristan watching with intense burning in his blue eyes. Deciding that Tristan was not my concern for the moment, I used the towel to dry off and then slid the robe on and dried my hair.

A throat cleared delicately behind me, and I turned around. Verrona was standing there, and Tristan was nowhere to be seen. I plastered a smile on my face and moved toward her. "You look much better than the last time I saw you," Verrona said by way of greeting.

I arched an eyebrow. The last time I recalled seeing her was the party she had dressed me for when we first met. Nothing had been wrong with me then. "I helped get you cleaned up after your last arena battle," she said by way of explanation. My mouth formed an O; she must have seen me when I was unconscious.

"Let's get back to your room so I can start working on you. You'll be pleased to know your gown does not require you to wear a corset," Verrona informed me as we began our trek back to my room. She then proceeded to tell me about the banquet tonight and who would be there. The way she spoke made me feel as though many important Fae would be present, but I was unfamiliar with the names she was saying. I couldn't decide if that was because I had never heard of them before or if they were using different names. *I will find out soon enough.*

I shivered; the hallway was not very warm, and my hair was still damp from the bath. When we walked through the doors into my room, I was surprised that the temperature was much warmer than the hallway. Verrona must have noticed my reaction. "I decided you'd probably be happier if I warmed up the room. I don't know why Prince Tanyth insists on keeping the palace so cold all the time. Your dress is over there." She waved a hand at the statue by the large mirrors that hadn't been here before.

I stepped around her toward the dress of deep emerald-green velvet. The top had velvet gathered at each shoulder and adorned with large diamond brooches. There were delicate gold chains draping over the arms, but no sleeves. The neckline plunged into a deep V from the neck to the navel and the rest of the gown was cascading folds of emerald velvet in a luxurious skirt. *Verrona was right, there is no corset*...I thought without any amusement. I continued my examination and discovered the back of the dress down to barely above my hips was almost nonexistent.

I ran a tentative hand over the fabric. It was very soft. "It's lovely," I said to Verrona.

"I thought you'd like it," she replied. "Now let's take care of your hair first and then get you in the dress. This one you can pull on from the bottom up, so we don't have to worry about ruining your hair or face."

I stayed silent. Verrona was clearly the master here. When the dress was on and Verrona decreed me presentable, she directed me to the mirror. I peered into it and did not recognize the female peering back. I was a little taken aback by how much skin it showed and where the deliberate lines of the dress led your eye. I could only hope that showing some skin would convince the prince to give me a specific number of battles to win to be free and would not have the opposite effect, making him want me to stay longer.

"It's time to go," Verrona announced. She linked her arm in mine, and we proceeded through numerous hallways until we reached the throne room. She led me directly to Prince Tanyth. He was wearing all black again. I thought it made him look even more terrifying than normal, but I schooled my face into a bland expression. As I curtsied, a hush fell over the room. I felt a blush creep up my cheeks.

"Serafina," Prince Tanyth said silkily. He came down from his throne and took my hand in his, raising me from the curtsey and placing a light kiss on my knuckles. "You look ravishing."

"Thank you, Prince Tanyth," I replied softly, peering up at him under my eyelashes.

He gave me a slight smile before directing his attention to someone behind me. I felt the brush of a leg against the edge of my skirt before I could see who it belonged to. When I saw it was Tristan, I could not hide my cringe, especially after what had happened the last time we were together. "Kiss her," Prince Tanyth ordered.

I gasped in shock. Tristan gave me a cold smile. "As you wish." He stepped in front of me and set his hands lightly on my waist. I wasn't sure if it was to keep me from running or how he liked to position himself for a kiss.

I tipped my chin up, lower lip trembling with nerves, and Tristan bent down, his lips lightly brushing mine before he pulled back. They were softer than I had expected.

Prince Tanyth growled. "I don't know what that was, but it wasn't a real kiss."

Tristan didn't react to the prince's comment; instead, he kissed me again. His mouth was velvety soft and the feeling of sparks running down my body from my lips to my core intensified the longer we kissed.

The prince coughed. "See, you do remember how to kiss."

Tristan let go of me and stepped away as though I were burning him like a hot coal. I was surprised at the change in his behavior. I may not know much about kissing, but it certainly hadn't felt like he didn't want to kiss me.

To my surprise, Tristan made a sharp ninety degree turn and departed.

"Serafina, you must go after Tristan and the two of you will dance," Prince Tanyth ordered. I sighed and grated my teeth together. I had no choice but to obey. *Kissing Tristan had been better than I expected, but that didn't change that we had both been following orders.* I frowned. *Should I really be considering kissing a Fae of my own free will who under orders severely beat me?* Goosebumps rose on my arms as I remembered how Tristan had kicked me over and over the first time we were in the arena together. Willing myself to focus on Tanyth's order to find Tristan and dance with him, I peered around the room, trying to figure out where Tristan had gone. The bystanders who had hastily parted as he had passed through had bunched back together during my conversation with Tanyth. Now I found myself surrounded by many Fae who all looked very similar in the dim light.

Suddenly, Callyn was by my side, hand lightly on my elbow. "You are playing a dangerous game," she whispered.

I gave her a confused look. "I'm not playing."

Callyn gave me a sharp glance. "Then your understanding of the situation is far less than I thought."

My eyes widened; I still had no idea what Callyn was talking about. "We kissed as ordered," I muttered.

"It looked like more than just a kiss," Callyn hissed.

"It was my first kiss," I protested. "Besides, he almost killed me the first time we fought in the arena. What reason would I have to do anything with Tristan other than following an explicit order?" A shiver of fear went down my spine, even as the words fell from my lips.

Callyn stopped our progress through the throng of Fae and yanked me around to face her. I twisted my fingers in my dress. Callyn's grip on my arm was tight and she shook her head. "I understand that this might be new to you. But your life is not the only one at stake. Everyone here is alive because the prince wishes it so. If you become too much of a nuisance or break too many rules, then he will order your torture or death. Were you aware that the prince caught Tristan having sex and chained him to the wall overnight as punishment?"

My mouth dropped open, and my heart stuttered in my chest. *Punished for having sex?* Callyn continued, "This court is *not* a game, it's real, the danger is *real*. So now you will find Tristan and dance with him. When you're given orders to kiss, you will kiss. If you're given the order to fuck, you will fuck. You do not have to like it, or enjoy it, but you will *obey*."

I gasped as her words hit me hard, like punches to my gut. I had obeyed; Tristan was the one who had been ordered to try again. *Why am I getting blamed for his mistake?* Anger and a million other things ran through my mind, including that I had given up my chance to ask the prince about my battles. *I will have another chance.* Callyn's words were also a wakeup call, a harsh reminder that everyone in this court was only here because Prince Tanyth wished it so. No one could come or go without his approval. *We're all slaves.* My lips quivered as emotions coursed through me. I finally nodded and Callyn resumed guiding me through the throne room.

It took a while, but we finally found Tristan leaning against the wall, arms folded and glaring at anyone who looked his way. He looked like the cold and brutal warrior he was. I started to shake slightly as nerves gripped me. *I will obey,* I reminded myself.

Callyn smacked my arm. "If you can face him in the arena, you certainly can handle dancing with him here." She gave me a gentle push toward Tristan. I took a few steps forward; he still hadn't noticed me. *Or he has but is hoping I will leave him alone.* I gave a delicate cough, then took another step forward. I did not want to surprise him and find out what weapons he might have to stab me with.

I held out my hand and curtsied. "Lord Commander, may I have a dance?" I spoke softly, meeting his eyes.

"No," he said coldly and turned away.

I straightened and reached out, touching his shoulder with my hand, then yanking it back sharply as a jolt of energy went through me. Quicker than I could see he grabbed my wrist, spinning me around, then pulling me in, causing my back to collide with his chest. I squirmed; everywhere we touched little sparks erupted. I could feel his breath hot on my neck. "What part of no don't you understand?" he growled into my ear.

"Prince Tanyth ordered us to dance," I said, keeping my breathing slow, refusing to react to his anger or to the way his chest felt against my back. His breath tickled the nape of my neck and I wondered what his lips would feel like there.

He let go of my wrist and ran his hand down my breast to my hip and back up. My core began to throb in response to his touch. A trail of sparks ran across my skin and my lips parted involuntarily. He grabbed my waist and spun me around so we were facing each other. A sharp comment was on the tip of my tongue, but he didn't give me a chance to voice it. He kissed me. He started aggressively, but when I didn't resist, his lips softened slightly. I melted into him. *Tristan chose to kiss me.* My heart fluttered in my chest as I tried to process what the kiss meant.

He pulled back, his eyes darkened with what I thought may be desire, a contrast to the cold smile on his face. "Let's go dance for the prince." He tugged on my hand, and before I could reply, led me on to the dance floor. My mind churned at what his touch was doing to me. *Maybe I'm imagining it since I haven't been able to sleep.*

Eyes bored into my back as we wound our way through the crowd before finding an open space to dance. Tristan slid us effortlessly into the middle of the number. After a few moments I recognized the song. The steps were simple and repetitive. Relief washed over me; I could ease into dancing with him. Tristan's hand on the small of my back was cool to the touch. His other hand held mine with light pressure to guide us through the steps, but nothing more. The sparks I had felt earlier were mercifully absent.

Three dances in and I was enjoying myself. Tristan, however, kept his expression cold and distant. As though dancing were merely another order. *Which is exactly what it is,* I reminded myself.

When the song changed again, about half the Fae dispersed. It took me a second to realize why. The song was different—the tempo was stronger, aggressive. Tristan's steps changed, and he pulled me sharply toward him. Our bodies collided and sparks erupted, so intense I tilted my chin down to make sure they weren't visible. Then he twirled me away from him. As I spun, I could see his expression had changed; it was no longer cold. *Does he feel the sparks too?* The dance continued. He would twirl me away and then bring me back, his steps confident, arrogant, wholly male, and *possessive.* Every time I spun away, I found myself praying he would pull me back. I wanted—no, I *needed* to feel him against my skin. Distracted, I stepped on his toe, earning me a snarl of warning.

"Sorry," I whispered, cautiously meeting his eyes as we whirled around the dance floor, our bodies pressed tightly together. His gaze was intense, fiery and no longer cold or angry. All I could think of was Tristan, as though it were just the two of us on the dance floor. He swept me into his arms and his kiss scorched my lips, demanding. A throbbing at my core began and when he tipped his head back for a breath, I barely stopped myself from pulling his face back down to mine. The kiss was full of passion and need—a far cry from how the evening had begun.

The music faded, and the orchestra ceased playing altogether. Tristan looked over my shoulder and I felt his body go rigid. I swallowed, my throat suddenly dry; there was only one reason he would react like this. Tristan's hands fell away from me, and he took a step back.

Hands clapped behind me in a slow pattern. "Well, well, well," came Prince Tanyth's voice from behind me. The prince halted in front of us. "I guess you decided to follow orders after all.

That was remarkable," he said, gaze roving from my face to my breasts. My cheeks burned and my skin began to crawl as his eyes lingered far longer than was polite before he met my eyes.

The space beside me was much colder than it had been moments before. Out of the corner of my eye I could see Tristan retreating off the dance floor while the prince crept closer. He took his hand in mine and waved to the orchestra. The music started up again, and he set his hand on my waist, pulling me against him. I remained silent and fought the desire to pull away. *I must obey.* Deep down I knew if I bailed on this dance, there would be consequences. No one else joined us on the dance floor. The prince kept us pressed close together. "You are mine," he said in a menacing voice. My legs shook, but I didn't respond. I continued dancing, wishing this were over. He tipped his head down and nuzzled my neck—then, he struck.

His teeth sank into my neck, and I gasped in surprise, struggling against his strong grip on my arms. "Let me go!" I shrieked. The prince ignored me, holding me firmly in place and licking the bite. Bile rose in my throat. In one swift motion I yanked my knee up into his groin. Prince Tanyth's iron grip released and I sprinted across the dance floor, slamming hard into something. *Please be Tristan. Please be Tristan.*

Shaking, I peered up, and to my dismay it wasn't Tristan I had run into, but Bane. *Uh-oh.* Bane's laugh carried across the throne room. He clamped his hands around my arm and twisted it behind my back so I couldn't knee him in the groin too.

Prince Tanyth's stride was more of a prowl than a walk as he approached us. Blood dribbled down his chin. *My blood*, I thought in revulsion. With Bane holding my arms behind my back, I was unable to do anything as the prince clamped his mouth on mine, prying my lips open with his tongue before thrusting it in my mouth. I could taste the coppery tang of my blood. His hands ran down my back and pulled me even tighter. I could feel his cock hardening against my dress. Despair filled me as I realized the prince could do what he wanted. *This is his court, his rules. I don't have a choice.*

I closed my eyes and let him have his way. I imagined it was Tristan kissing me again. When the music stopped again, I opened my eyes and the throne room was empty save the two of us.

"Thank you for the dance, Serafina. Good night." The prince gave me a chaste kiss on the cheek and vanished. I felt a tug around my middle and then suddenly I was in the middle of my bedroom. *He used magic on me.*

I yawned and then yawned again, unable to stop. I slowly undressed, barely able to make my fingers work to escape from the gown. It slid to the floor, and I stepped out of it and climbed onto the bed. My eyelids were so heavy I couldn't remember if I pulled the covers up before sleep consumed me.

Tristan twirled me around the dance floor. My heart pounded in time with the music and every time our bodies collided, I wanted to stay there forever in his arms. The music continued and so did our dance. His eyes were dark with desire and a quick glance at his pants confirmed that he was aroused too. As I spun into his arms again, I wrapped my arms around him, pressing our bodies tightly together. His cock bumped between my thighs, and I gasped as I felt dampness there.

"Maybe we should find somewhere more private," he suggested with a wicked grin, then kissed me.

Thirty-Three

TRISTAN

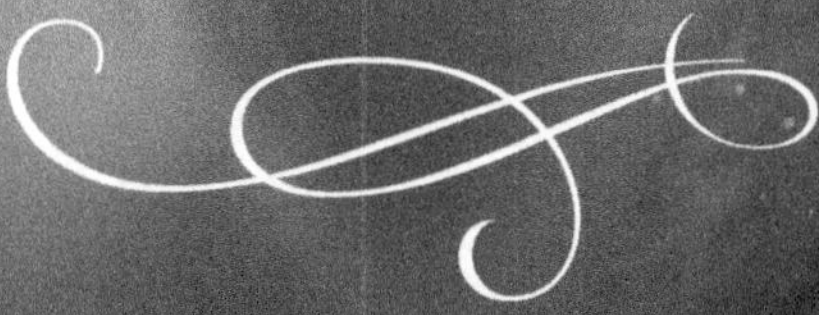

I burst through the doors to my bedroom. Dancing with Serafina had been a mistake, even if it was an order. My heart thundered in my chest. Deep down I knew Prince Tanyth was manipulating us. The order to kiss, then dance. He had to have heard about me dragging her to the bathhouse. *Maybe he wants to see how far I'll take my anger without his express orders to punish her.* I was certain Prince Tanyth had a plan for her, but I hadn't been looped in yet.

I squeezed my eyes shut, and I swore I could feel her in my arms again—and the little electric currents that seemed to run between us whenever we touched. I growled under my breath. *What is wrong with me? Serafina is off-limits. There can be nothing between us.*

Running my hands through my hair, I decided the lack of sleep from my dreams was clearly getting to me. *If I can get a good night's sleep I will be able to think straight again.*

My gaze drifted over to the fireplace mantle, where there were several crystal decanters of various Fae drinks. Decision made, I poured myself a glass of almost-clear Fae wine and took a long sip. It burned my throat on the way down, but even with one sip, warmth spread from my belly to my limbs and the tension drained away. By the time the glass was empty I could barely stay upright. The room spun and my eyes were heavy. With wobbling steps that took me sideways as often as straight, I eventually reached the bed and collapsed on top of it.

I was shapeshifted into a snow leopard and walking through a forest. Ahead of me, Serafina sat on a blanket in the emerald-green dress from the dance. As I approached, a skitter of sparks rippled along my fur. They didn't hurt, but as I closed the distance between myself and Serafina, they did increase, as did my growing need to have some sort of contact.

When I was close, she tentatively stretched out her hand. I gently bumped her fingers with my head, hard enough that she would know I was real, but not enough to hurt her. She trailed her fingers through my fur, I started purring. The energy between us was so intense I thought Serafina was glowing from it. Her fingers worked their way down my spine, and I took a step closer, my furry legs brushing hers. One more step and I'd be in her lap. When she wrapped her arms around me, I lost my hold on the shift and returned to my Fae form. Mere seconds later I felt my cock jerk and my whole body spasmed as a massive orgasm rolled through me.

A loud knock sounded on my door. I rolled over and fell out of the bed, hitting the nightstand with my arm and sending it crashing onto its side. The knocking got even louder. "Hang on!" I shouted, using my magic to project my voice while I tried to untangle myself from the sheets without knocking anything else over.

Finally, I got free. I walked over to the door and yanked it open. Prince Tanyth shoved past me, sending Fae light around the room so we weren't in total darkness.

"Is something wrong?" I asked, yawning. I had no idea what time it was, only that I had been dreaming of Serafina and now I was awake.

Tanyth gave me a long look, his eyes traveling from the top of my head down to my feet. "What were you doing?" he asked me.

Cold seeping up from the stone into my bare feet was doing wonders to wake me up. The haze of the dream was rapidly being replaced by annoyance. *I haven't done anything wrong. I obeyed his orders to kiss and dance with Serafina and then expressly returned to my room.* "Sleeping," I gritted out.

"You didn't use a star portal to send someone away and pretend you knocked something over?" he demanded.

Anger flooded me. Muscles coiling, I growled, "I am not lying to you. I was asleep. Go check the bed if you don't believe me. I've been in my room since I danced with her."

Prince Tanyth bared his teeth at me, then conducted a thorough inspection of the bed. I ground my teeth together, waiting for his response.

"Fine. You were here, sleeping naked, alone. I wanted to talk to you," the prince replied.

"Okay..." I said, wishing he would get to the point.

Tanyth waved his hand and a table and two chairs appeared along with a pair of glasses and a carafe of wine. I sighed and used magic to call in a black silk robe. *I should have known he wanted to have a conversation.*

The prince filled both glasses and offered me one. Only once I had drunk about half of my wine did he start talking. "You know the prophecy?"

Don't piss him off. "The Fae have a lot of prophecies, so you will have to be more specific," I reminded him in a neutral tone.

"I mean the lost Fae queen prophecy," Prince Tanyth replied.

"I know the story in the book *Bedtime Tails*," I responded, wondering where he was going with this.

Tanyth drummed his fingers on the table and drained his glass. "Well, I think it is true, or at least has the potential to be true. I am pretty sure that Serafina is the lost Fae queen."

I jerked my hand in surprise, hitting the glass and sending it sailing over the edge of the table. I flicked my fingers just in time, creating a cushion of dark gray magic. I floated the glass back onto the table.

"How did you come to that conclusion?" I asked. *This is not good.*

Prince Tanyth drummed his fingers impatiently on the table. "She has met the first two criteria. 'First, she will prove her battle prowess. Look closely or you might be blinded, for when the Fae queen returns, not all will know her, yet everyone will follow her.'"

I considered my words carefully. *If the prince truly believes she is the lost Fae queen, then her life is in peril.* After my most recent dream it was clear to me that something was developing between Serafina and I, and I wasn't entirely sure what. *And I could be next on his list.* "What do you intend to do?"

Tanyth licked his lips and gave me a wicked grin. "Turn her into my mate," he replied.

My eyes widened; the prince knew as well as I did that Fae had no control over choosing our own mates. We could only hope that someone we had an affinity for would be the individual we bonded with. The whole process was not entirely understood—other than the part where no one has ever successfully controlled it. I was not going to correct him though. I thought about the sparks and energy between Serafina and me. *What if* that's *the mating bond?* I bit the inside of my cheek, drawing blood, before I could shout my discovery.

I swallowed hard, my throat dry, at the implications of the prince's plan if Serafina was indeed supposed to be my mate. "I see. When are you intending to turn her into your mate?" I asked, wondering if I could somehow prepare her for the event.

240

"Tomorrow, when she wins her next battle, I will propose," he replied, pouring us another glass.

In one gulp I drained my entire glass of wine, then twirled the empty glass in my fingers. "Now that I know what your plans are for tomorrow, did you have any specific orders for me?"

"Yes, that is the other reason I came. There is a disturbance near the border we share with the Lord of the West, and I want you to investigate and ensure that none of the humans have entered my territory. Take a few squads or none, I'll leave the decision up to you. Make sure that you can handle whatever is going on. I don't want to send you out twice," Tanyth said.

"Understood," I replied firmly.

Tanyth stood up and I followed suit. "You shall depart at dawn." The table, chairs and wine disappeared and Tanyth vanished a moment later.

I sat down on the edge of the bed, thinking hard. *Is he sending me away because there is a problem or because he thinks I will interfere with his plan to propose to Serafina?* I shook my head. It didn't matter; I could not refuse the orders he had given me. Tomorrow I would depart for the border with a squad.

Thirty-Four

SERAFINA

I woke up with a start. The sheets were wrapped around me. *Another dream about Tristan.* Thankfully I wasn't drenched in sweat this time.

My bladder began to protest being ignored, so I climbed out of bed and headed to the bathroom. Fae lights glowed in the living area, so I wasn't left stumbling around in the dark. After going to the bathroom, I started to head back to the bedroom when I noticed the dining table had food on it. Snagging a tunic and pants out of the wardrobe, I got dressed, my stomach gurgling in protest, and I sniffed the air. The tantalizing smell of sausage and fresh bread drew me to the table. I loaded up a plate and sat down, digging in. I figured with the appearance of a breakfast spread that it had to be morning.

As I was polishing off my plate, a knock came at the door. "Come in!" I shouted. Usually when I was in a room and someone wanted me, they barged in. It was strange that someone was knocking.

Callyn came in. She had armor on and a sword strapped to her side. I sat up straighter. "What's going on?"

"Nothing you need to worry about," she said dismissively.

"What am I doing today?" I asked, hopeful for some information.

"You have another fight in the arena," Callyn replied.

"Against Tristan?" I asked nervously.

Callyn gave me a sharp look, and I gulped. *Stupid!*

"No. I don't know the details. Only that once you are done eating I am to escort you to get prepared," Callyn said.

I motioned to my plate. "I'm done eating. Should I get dressed?" I asked, realizing I was still in my nightgown and had never taken a bath last night.

Callyn debated the question. "Yes, you can get cleaned up and dressed here. The only thing not in this room is your weapon."

I nodded. "Then I will get ready." When Callyn didn't object, I stood up and proceeded to bathe and dress.

When I returned to her, I was wearing a light brown tunic, dark brown pants, and soft black boots. My russet hair was in a tidy braid down my back.

Callyn inspected me. "Good. Let's go."

We walked in silence to the same prep room I had used previously before my arena fights. There was a single sword on the rack and nothing else in the room. "The sword is for you."

"Where is the guard?" I asked, wary that no one else was around.

"He will arrive when I depart," Callyn said.

"You're not staying?" I asked.

Callyn shook her head, hand resting on her sword. "No, I am needed elsewhere."

I wanted to ask her where to find out what was going on. Why was I fighting in the arena when she was needed elsewhere, armed as though she was going to fight in the arena? *Or fight somewhere else?*

Lost in my own thoughts, I didn't notice Callyn had left until I heard the thud of the door shutting behind me. Silence filled the room.

I wasn't sure how long I waited before a guard showed up. When it was clear it was going to be a while until I was sent into the arena, I sat down and tried meditating. It must have worked because I jumped when the keys hit the gate.

"Let's go," he barked.

I stood up and snagged the sword off the rack, then walked over to the now open gate. He locked it behind us, then gestured that I should lead the way. When we got to the end of the tunnel the next gate was unlocked and already open.

"Go on," he said impatiently.

I took a deep breath, squared my shoulders, and headed into the arena at a brisk walk. Every time I had fought in the arena it had been set up differently. I had no expectations for what awaited me today. The sand that had previously covered the ground was gone. In its place were stone blocks. I could see some grates, which I presumed were holding cells, like where the leons had emerged from. I didn't know what it meant that they were not hidden today.

There were several walls ahead, set up in a maze-like formation. I could see empty shackles on the one closest to me. Then I heard it. Whimpering and the rattle of chains. I continued farther into the arena, creeping closer to the walls, ready to strike with the sword if anyone came my way. As I approached the walls, I could see there wasn't merely one set of shackles, there were many—and some had rotting body parts still attached.

There was a grinding noise and more walls began rising around me. I took off running, not waiting to see if something other than walls was going to pop out of the ground if I stayed in one place. I went past the first wall and then rounded the corner and almost ran into a sobbing, naked human suspended from the second. From the size and obvious body parts, I was confident it was a human woman, not a Fae.

"Let me help you," I said and reached up for the cuff around her foot.

"He will kill you," the woman sobbed.

"Who will kill me?" I asked, confused. I ran my fingers over the cuff, looking for a keyhole or latch.

"Don't waste your time on me," the woman said. I ignored her and continued messing with the cuff. I finally found a hole, and I shoved the tip of the sword into it, twisting it, trying to get it loose. My focus was only on the cuff.

A sword hit the wall beside me, narrowly missing my face. I yanked my sword free of the cuff and spun around, blocking the next strike. I recognized this male—Bane. He glared angrily at me.

"You don't have to do this, Bane," I pleaded. I had no illusions he would listen, but it would never hurt to try.

Instead of replying, he swung again. There was no finesse in his moves. He seemed to have one purpose: to take me out. On his next swing I ducked and came up behind him. Sweeping my sword in a backhanded arc with a high feint, I successfully sliced the back of his unprotected hamstrings. He fell to his knees, swearing, and I darted away. I knew I should finish it, but I couldn't make myself take the kill. Not yet. *If he comes for me again, I will,* I promised myself.

I dodged to the left and followed the next wall. I heard more clanking of chains before I could see the next prisoner attached to the wall. As the prisoner came into view I recoiled in horror. The last one had been a human female, but other than being dirty and chained, there wasn't anything wrong. This was a naked human male who was riddled with oozing open wounds. I sniffed the air and realized they were festering. "Sir," I called softly as I forced my feet to approach him. What I really wanted to do was puke up my breakfast. He reeked. I knew then that it wouldn't be worth the risk to save him, because he was not going to survive much longer. Yet part of me hesitated. I couldn't bear to see someone suffering like that.

I heard a whirring and ducked just in time as a flail whirled over my head and slammed into the wall. Chunks of stone went flying. I rolled across the floor to give myself enough space to get up. I leaped to my feet and brought my sword up, blocking the flail. The chain wrapped around my sword. My assailant grinned. All I could see were teeth. The rest of the Fae, for I presumed it was Fae on height alone, was encased entirely in plate armor. I gave my sword a tug, but the blade was still wrapped in the chain. Still grinning, my assailant pulled hard, and I stumbled forward. The Fae yanked again, and I tried bracing against it, but I still was forced to give up more ground. I clenched my teeth. I didn't want to lose my sword, but if the chain didn't loosen, I was going to have to. In a last ditch attempt, I took half a step forward, and to my relief, the chain loosened. I slid the sword out and swung hard, aiming for the wrists.

My assailant shuffled out of the way and swung the flail. I was not fast enough and the spiked ball hit me in the low back. I gasped at the sharp pain, grateful the spikes had rounded tips, otherwise I would likely be dead. I knew the flail allowed for a greater reach but was not ideal in close combat. *I need to get closer, without getting wound up in the chain.*

After a cursory visual sweep of the arena, I sprinted toward the wall to the side of my assailant. I kept myself balanced and ran straight up it. When I reached the ideal point, I did a backflip and swept down with my sword, striking at the narrow gap between the helmet and the shoulder armor. Speed worked in my favor and my sword sliced deep into the Fae's neck. As I landed on my feet I yanked my sword out. Blood sprayed everywhere as the assailant collapsed.

I picked up the flail, deciding it could come in handy, and walked away from the body. So far, I had come across two prisoners and two enemies. I knew there had to be more to it. The prince was not going to have me defeat two who had been relatively easy.

Something hit the back of my head and I crumpled, blacking out.

I was in a forest that looked vaguely familiar. Two cloaked figures were ahead of me. I approached slowly, not wanting to alert them to my presence. They did not turn toward me when I was only a few feet away, which is when I realized this was another dream. With their hoods up I could not quite make out their faces, but when they began speaking, I knew who it was—Commander Meriel and Prince Almar.

"Prince Tanyth refuses to give me an audience," Prince Almar said. I could hear the anger in his voice.

"Then he must *have her," Meriel replied.*

"We cannot go to war over one girl, not without proof she is even still alive," Prince Almar said.

"If Solana were here..." Meriel started.

Prince Almar hissed at her. "Solana is dead. How dare you bring her up."

"Because Serafina is her daughter. I don't understand why you are so reluctant to admit what Serafina represents. The king has ordered us to find Serafina no matter the cost," Meriel replied.

I woke up chained to one of the walls in the maze within the arena. My head was pounding and I could feel a lump forming where I'd been struck. Thankfully whoever had chained me had chosen a location where I could still stand on my own two feet— only my hands were cuffed. My tunic and pants were torn, but I couldn't remember anything after being hit, other than the dream. Ignoring my headache, I twisted, trying to get a look at the chains. I was surprised to see the chain was quite long and went through a loop anchored into the wall.

Silence stretched across the arena, I backed as far away from the wall as I could and was able to get two strides in before leaping up and grabbing the rough edge of one of the blocks making up the wall. Climbing, I used the tips of my fingers and toes to get purchase on the stone, until I was able to grasp the top with my entire hand and pull myself up. It gave me a good view but did not solve the problem of being chained to it. I sat down, straddling the wall, and began testing each link of the chain, hoping one of them would be weak enough to break. I was about to give up when I found one that had a little bit of rust on it. There was a pointy corner on one of the stone blocks up here. I maneuvered closer to it and stuck the chain over the point and sawed back and forth. Over the noise of the chain, I thought I heard something else.

Sure, enough I could hear an object scraping along the wall not too far away. I resumed breaking the chain, and the rusty link popped off. I gave the chain a tug and started looping it around my arm to pull it up, grateful I could move about freely. With the chain rolled up, I jogged across the top of the wall. Just before I reached the end, the wall I was on began rotating and the wall I had been aiming for sank into the ground. I braced my legs, arms spread wide, balancing precariously and praying I wouldn't fall off. When the wall ceased moving, I was facing a giant. The top of his head was at the level of my feet on top of the wall. He had a huge lumpy face with a metal cap on his head, a large club with jagged spikes on the end of it, and a chain mail vest on. His huge hairy feet were bare. It took the giant a moment to realize I was in front of him. When he did, he roared, and I got a view of his two big teeth and a blast of his putrid breath.

I knew I had to jump off the wall. I had no room to maneuver, and up there he had a clear view of my every move. I darted to the right and he swung his club, making it whoosh through the air. I vaulted over the top of the club but misjudged how close I was to the edge of the wall and tumbled off.

The giant swung again, chopping down as though to smash me. I ducked, and the club slammed into the ground, sending vibrations across the arena floor. As I gripped the chain, an idea came to me. I ran straight at the giant, and as he slashed the club again, I rolled underneath his leg, wrapping the chain around it as I went. He twisted, trying to find me, and I ran to the front and through his legs again, making a second loop with the chain. The club sailed over my head, and the giant rocked back on his heels, then slammed the club down. I yanked hard on the chain, pulling it tight using all of my weight. The giant lost his footing and fell backward, landing hard on his back.

I heard a loud crack as his head hit the ground, I was surprised to see that he dropped his club. He lay motionless. *He must be knocked out.*

Releasing the chain, I ran over to the discarded club and tried to pick it up, but it would not budge. Unwilling to give up, I examined the spikes, wiggling a few to see if they were loose. No luck. I was about to try another spike when suddenly I was being pulled. *The chain!* I realized my mistake. The giant had not been knocked out—he was getting up, and now he had ahold of the chain, which was still attached to me.

Instead of letting the giant continue to reel me in, I sprinted for him and ran right up and over him. I wrapped the chain around his neck as I sailed past his shoulders. He twisted and reached behind him, trying to grab me as I pulled the chain tight around his throat, swinging a few feet off the ground.

I don't know how long I swung there, but finally he gave one last gurgling gasp and fell over dead.

The walls began to slide back into the ground, and I could hear one set of hands clapping. Which didn't make sense—there was a whole crowd watching. Then Prince Tanyth strode through the gate, still doing the slow clap.

"Very, very good my dear Serafina. I am quite impressed, especially after you let yourself get captured so easily. I had begun to doubt your abilities. Now, I will reward you," Prince Tanyth announced.

I gazed at him warily and stayed silent.

"Don't you want to know what your reward is?" he asked. I thought I heard annoyance in his voice but was not entirely sure.

"Of course, my prince," I replied automatically, insides churning at the possibility he'd award my freedom.

He smiled, but it did not reach his eyes. "Good girl." He stood directly in front of me and took my left hand in his, and then there was a ring in his right hand. I gasped as I realized his intentions.

"Serafina, I want you to be my wife," he said and started to slide the ring onto my finger.

"No!" I shouted and darted away before he could strike me for my defiance.

Prince Tanyth's voice sounded in my ears, though I was almost to the arena exit and far away from him. "You deserve an award worthy of your success in the arena. What better than marrying a Fae prince and becoming co-ruler of the Court of Dusk?"

My jaw tightened, determination and anger filling me. The prince had lied about earning my freedom and I was done playing his games.

Mustering all the strength I had left, I sprinted through the gate, catching the guard by surprise. I burst into the hallway and raced for the stairs. Arms pumping, I bounded up the steps two and three at a time. The door at the top was open. I rushed through and kept going, throwing a glance over my shoulder. I slammed into something hard. Heart hammering in my chest, I drew a ragged breath as arms encircled me.

I peered up and was surprised to see Callyn. "Let me go!" I pleaded.

Sadness filled Callyn's eyes. "I can't. The best I can do is deflect his anger."

I sagged as the adrenaline that had kept me going drained away. "Okay," I replied softly. Callyn escorted me back to my room. Just as she shut the door behind me, I heard the prince's angry shouts down the hallway.

Busying myself with running a bath, I did my best to tune out the sounds outside my door—the prince punishing Callyn.

Will he punish me, too, to prove he is in charge? Or is Callyn's sacrifice enough to appease him? As I climbed into the bath, I ran over his words in my mind. My reward, *to be his wife!* I doubted he wanted me as a co-ruler; I had seen enough during my time at Dorcha Palace to know that the prince was the only ruler here.

Thirty-Five

TRISTAN

I reviewed my orders to investigate the disturbance on the border that Tanyth's lands shared with the Lord of the West. This was the first time since Travaran's death that Tanyth was allowing me to leave the palace. Not that I had had a problem with staying. I had some new recruits who were in sore need of proper training. Tanyth had never told me which camp they had come from, but it was obvious their standards for allowing Fae to graduate was far below the ones Embergate had held. A matter I was correcting with the help of my second-in-command, Elashor.

I made my way to the barracks. I knew which squad I wanted to take with me, so it was a matter of informing them, giving them a moment to gather their gear, and departing. We would run to the border. If I pushed them to their limits, we could make it by the end of the day and observe whoever was there with the cover of night.

Mind set, I opened the door, startling a few of them. "We have orders," I announced. Instantly they were on the alert, tugging their tunics into place as though the prince might come in here too. "Silver squad, we're going to the border to investigate the Lord of the West's movements. Depending on exactly who we discover, I have the authority to make any necessary decisions."

Laeroth raised his hand. I inclined my head in acknowledgement, and he spoke. "Which route are we going and how long do you expect us to be gone for?"

"We will be running and taking the most direct route from Lochan Sgàile until we reach the border or find the Lord of the West's people," I explained. "As for how long we will be gone, maybe two or three days. We will be running, so only pack what you can carry and without hindering your speed."

"No star portal?" he asked. I shook my head. Laeroth spoke again. "Weapons?"

"You choose. This isn't a training exercise. We could end up fighting Larks or it could simply be a negotiation. Whatever you are most comfortable with. However, you are required to bring at least one weapon; you cannot rely exclusively on your magic," I explained. "I will be back in five minutes. Be ready or it could mean trouble with the prince."

When no one else deigned to speak, I left, heading for the training area where I was sure I would find Elashor and Bane.

I pulled open the double doors. Elashor had a sword and Bane had an axe, and they were fighting with their left arms tied behind their backs. My lips twitched in amusement, and I cleared my throat. They ignored me. I counted to thirty, and when it was clear that they were not going to stop on my account, I raised my hands and sent streams of dark gray shadow magic at them.

Immobilized, Elashor and Bane glared at me in annoyance.

"I need to give you orders now, not wait all day for you to finish your match," I explained, then released my magic. "You can always finish when I leave."

"Then are you going to tell us?" Bane demanded.

"I am leaving with silver squad. Don't fuck up anything while I'm gone," I said, meeting first Elashor's eyes, then Bane's.

It became obvious quite quickly that I needed to make silver squad, probably all of the squads, run more often. I was in front, setting the pace, and not one of them could keep up. It was pitiful. At our first rest stop I examined each of them and realized that if I tried to drive them to run faster than they were capable of, it would only slow us down in the long run.

As they sat panting and guzzling water from their canteens, I began speaking. "Running like this should not be as challenging as it is. Clearly, we need to spend more time building your stamina when we return to Dorcha Palace. The last thing I need is for you to fall apart during a prolonged battle. When we return, you will spend an hour every morning running laps, until all of you can run a full day in there, without tiring."

"The arena?" Valor said color draining from his face.

I sighed. "Yes. You're aware that we cannot train out here in the forest as I would like. I can put in the request, but the odds of the prince agreeing are slim to none. The arena is the only place we have that much space without interfering with anyone else's duties." I fully intended to make the request to exercise outside the palace, but I knew that Tanyth would never agree. If we went outside, he would not have total control of our actions—a harsh reminder of the nature of our contracts with him. No one else said anything. Not that I expected them to. Of course, there would be a significant amount of danger running in the arena. If Tanyth was in a good mood, then the squads would be left alone to their exercise. If Tanyth was angry or feeling *playful*, they might find that they would not only have to run, but fight.

"Let's keep going," I announced. As one, the squad stood and put away their canteens. I took off at a jog.

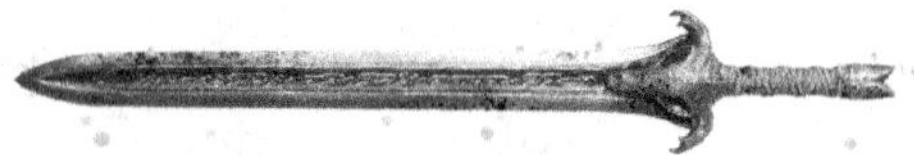

It was late and I could tell the squad was tired, but I wanted to evaluate the Larks before we went to sleep.

"What are we doing, Lord Commander?" asked Valor. I turned and looked at him and the rest of the males. They were all waiting for my orders.

"*Quietly*, set up camp. No fire. I know you have dried meat and whatnot, so once you've set up your bedrolls, go ahead and eat. I'll be back as quickly as I can," I said.

Valor's eyes were wide in surprise. "You don't want us to scout instead?"

I shook my head. I knew that any scouting they did would likely draw attention; they were tired and prone to mistakes. If we were going to have to fight, I preferred to do so when the squad was capable of fighting. It was possible I could single-handedly defeat the humans, but that would also rely on the squad not hindering me. "No, this is the best course of action. I will devise a plan when I return."

I walked away, using my magic to help me melt into the trees and near invisibility—a task made much easier with only the barest hint of moonlight and the cover of the forest. As I moved through the trees, I considered my options. *If the humans have any way of detecting magic, then they would notice my presence even if I shield myself with shadow magic. But if I were to shift, that would be another matter entirely.* I knew when a Fae shapeshifted, they were almost impossible to detect, because for some reason the magic that seemed to leak from our Fae bodies was contained in our animal shape. Since my objective was only to gather information, I decided that shifting would be my best option, as long as I did so well out of range of any of the silver squad. It would also give me an outlet for the tension that had been riding me since dancing with Serafina and the dream I'd had that she could be my mate.

I stopped moving and listened to the forest for several minutes. I could not hear any of my warriors, which meant they were following their orders. Ahead, I could see the barest flicker of a small fire. *Just enough to cook food on*, I thought. *Though still unwise if they were concerned about being noticed.*

I closed my eyes and took a deep breath, focusing on the snow leopard. I felt my magic flowing through me, and one moment I was in my Fae form, and the next I was a snow leopard. I had to ignore the urge to run and jump and play. Finally, after years, I was able to shift, even if it was only for a short time. *Focus*, I reminded myself. I padded silently through the forest, keeping my ears tuned for anything that might be approaching while I eased my way closer to the fire. I eventually found a tree that looked promising.

With a leap, I quickly climbed the trunk and onto the first branch. It gave me the height I needed to see who was around the fire. There were about ten Larks. They had horses tied to stakes at one side of the fire and a neat row of tents on the other. It seemed like they were telling jokes or something. I laid my head on my paws and waited.

A man with a beard stood up and began putting away his plate and utensils. Soon the others followed suit. When they were done, he doused the fire.

"The plan for tomorrow, can you remind me one more time?" a younger man said to the bearded one.

The bearded one grimaced. "Fine, but please remember it this time. We will rise early tomorrow and begin panning the river. This is where King Hanover said we would find the object. The sooner we can find it, the quicker we can get back on our side of the border."

I flexed my claws, digging into the tree. *A magic object?*

The younger man nodded. "Dawn. Got it. I'll see you in the morning, then."

I kept my attention focused on the bearded man who I thought could be the leader of this group. When it became clear that nothing else of interest was going to happen, I backed out of the tree and faded into the forest.

A branch snapped behind me and I spun, claws out. A red-haired Fae female glared at me, sword raised. Lips curled in a silent snarl, anger and a small tendril of fear wound through me. There was a good chance my squad would find out I could shapeshift if I couldn't handle this female quietly.

I kept my eyes on her as she took a half step forward and I shifted back to Fae form, broadsword out. I lightly tapped her sword with mine.

"I don't want to fight," she said. I raised my eyebrow; her sword and actions told a different tale. "I'm Fiera. I know you came from the Court of Dusk."

My eyes widened and I wondered how she knew that. I belatedly realized that my armor had the court emblem on it. "What do you want?" I asked, keeping my voice low. The last thing I needed was to draw the attention of either the humans or my squad.

"Your prince captured my friend Serafina and I want to know where she's being held," Fiera said.

Her bold demand took me by surprise. Most Fae were afraid of warriors from the Court of Dusk. *Not this one, it seems.* "Dorcha Palace. It's impenetrable."

"I'll find a way," she said confidently.

I envied her confidence and prayed for her sake that she didn't get caught. Slowly, I sheathed my sword. "Go, before the others hear you."

Fiera started to turn away, then stopped and pivoted toward me. "Your secret is safe with me." I bowed my head in acknowledgement. For reasons unknown to me, I felt that I could trust Fiera, even though I'd never met her before. *If she betrays me, then we'll both suffer.*

Clenching my fists, I watched Fiera fade into the woods, hoping for both our sakes that she wasn't caught. She was trespassing on Prince Tanyth's territory, and anyone from his court who came across her was required to take her into custody and escort her to the palace.

Valor noticed my approach first and had his sword drawn before anyone had moved. I let my magic dissolve and became fully visible.

"Tristan, you've returned," Valor said, and I wasn't sure if it was a greeting to me or a warning to the others.

"Yes. There are ten Larks, and at dawn they are searching the river for some sort of object. They did not specify which part of the river, but my assumption is that it is the part closest to where their camp is. I was not able to glean any information about the nature of the object they seek," I explained.

"Are we going to prevent them from searching the river?" Valor asked.

"No. Prince Tanyth is going to want whatever the object is. Therefore, it makes more sense for us to let the Larks do the work to find it and then apprehend them," I replied.

"Very well, so we will observe until they find the object. I will make sure everyone knows we are to be ready at dawn," Valor said.

I nodded. It meant we would only get a handful of hours of sleep, but some would be better than none. I felt energized after shifting and I knew sleeping was going to be almost impossible, but I had to try.

I found my pack, undid my bedroll, and stretched out on top of it. I closed my eyes and took a deep breath, counting to ten.

I must have fallen asleep because when I woke up, I had been dreaming of Prince Tanyth telling me he was going to somehow force the mating bond to work between him and Serafina. I bit my lip. *I don't care about Serafina*, I reminded myself. *She murdered my best friend and deserves anything Prince Tanyth devises to torture her. Doesn't she?* I growled low under my breath at my treacherous thoughts.

Valor must have heard me, for I could hear him whispering to the others that it was time to get up. I stood up and stretched, then put away my bedroll and strapped my sword on. The males were lining up. I glanced at the sky. From under the trees it was difficult to see the sun rising, but it was obvious the sky was going from dark gray to pale pearl gray; it was time to go.

"We will retrieve our gear later. No need to hinder ourselves," I informed them. "We shall head straight for the river. Make sure you focus on not being able to be seen or heard as you move. If we find their location, we will loosely circle them and then wait until they find the object."

They all bowed their heads in acknowledgment. I gave them the signal with my hand to move out and we took off at a jog, moving silently through the forest.

I was not personally familiar with this part of Tanyth's territory, but I had studied the map before we left. The river curved and, if the map was to be believed, had a wide section very nearby before it narrowed again. *A good place for an object to get stuck in the shallows*, I surmised.

We quickly reached the river. I sent half the squad across, jumping at a narrow spot. I watched as they fanned out and faded into the trees. The rest of them faded out on this side. I could hear the Larks even though I couldn't see them yet. I followed the sounds of their splashing until I was close enough to observe but hidden from sight.

All ten Larks were in the water with pans. It looked quite comical how they would scoop up some gravel and then lift it up and swirl it around, hunting for the object. Some of them were chest-deep in the water and had to submerge all the way to get a new scoop of gravel. I watched for a while and then closed my eyes. If they found what they were looking for, I could expect them to make quite a commotion, especially since they were oblivious to the twenty Fae surrounding them.

With my eyes still closed, I took a deep breath and listened, filtering through the sounds the Larks were making until I found the sounds of the forest. It was then that I felt an odd humming coming from the water. When the humming got louder, my eyes snapped open.

The bearded man thrust his hand into the air, and I could see what looked to be a metal dagger glinting in his grasp. "Found it!" he shouted—then all hell broke loose.

Arrows were fired from across the river. I could see flashes of magic coming from my side. The bearded man's hand was still thrust into the air, and as an arrow was about to impale his head, a huge blast of bright-green magic erupted out of his hand. Everyone flew backward, Fae and human; even the bearded man was thrown backward into the river.

"Fuck!" I growled and then launched myself toward the river. I had a sneaking suspicion the object *was* a magic object, and some of them could be quite nasty if not handled properly. I drew my sword and cut down any humans in my way. I didn't have time to play nicely. I needed to get my hands on it before the human idiot destroyed us all.

Splashing through the water, I ran as fast as I could. By now the bearded man realized I was coming for him. I could see a flicker of movement as the Fae on the other side of the river noticed I was going for the object and were tightening their positions.

With one last stride, I was within sword reach of the bearded man. "Give me the dagger," I snarled.

The bearded man narrowed his eyes but didn't move. He wasn't intimidated. "No," he said firmly.

I lashed out with my sword, sweeping it across his neck. His head went sailing into the air and a wave of bright-green magic slammed through me, launching me into the air and forcing me to drop my sword. As I struggled to right myself so I would land on my feet, a thought flickered through my mind about the prophecy Travaran had once said Prince Tanyth believed in, and the dagger it spoke about—Dragonfang. My midair maneuver barely worked as I hit the edge of the riverbank and started sliding. Arms out, I was able to regain my balance. I was certain the second blast had been directed at me. Sometimes magic objects would bond to people, which would enhance the individual's magic abilities if they had any—and usually gave the magic object the ability to defend itself. It appeared Dragonfang had decided to bond to the man, even in the few moments that he held the dagger. My choice to behead the human had resulted in the dagger retaliating.

I heard a splash and watched Naevys, one of my newer warriors in silver squad, dive into the water to retrieve the dagger. There was a green flash under the water and then his body floated to the surface, gently tugged by the slow current of the river. I sighed. *Stupid, foolish male.* Before anyone else could repeat the mistake, I had to get the dagger. I called a pair of thick leather gloves to my hands and then ran a few steps and jumped into the river. I dove under the surface and quickly found the dagger. With the leather gloves on I would be protected from its magic, which I assumed required skin contact. I pulled the dagger free of the rocks that were holding it in place and surfaced.

While I retrieved the dagger, the rest of my squad dealt with the humans. Three of the humans were kneeling on the sandy bank, hands tied behind their backs; the rest of them were dead. I strode out of the water and examined the dagger.

It was bright silver, and the hilt was in the shape of a dragon with two green gems for eyes. The detail on the hilt was exquisite; you could see each tiny scale in perfect detail. The blade itself was short. All these features confirmed it was indeed Dragonfang. I tucked it carefully into my belt and then brought my attention back to our prisoners.

"Tell me who sent you," I demanded coldly, locking eyes with each of them in turn. *Will they say nothing, or tell the truth?* The first two had faces of stone, but the third was shaking like a leaf, though he didn't reply.

I motioned for Valor. "Take these two over there." I waved in the direction of our camp. "Don't let them escape."

Valor nodded, and with the help of the other squad members, led the two prisoners away. I focused on the Lark who was shaking. When the other Larks left, he started shaking even harder, his face drained of all color. "Who sent you?" I said, stepping closer.

"King Hanover Atwood, Lord of the West," the man replied. I was surprised that his shaking didn't impair his ability to speak.

"Did you know when you were sent that you were looking for Dragonfang?" I asked.

"Dddd...rag...gon...fffff...ang?" he replied in a high-pitched stutter. "Nnnn...nnno."

"Are you sure? I heard your leader say that you were hunting for an object in the river," I pressed.

"I...I...don't know. I just—just cook for them," the man said, his stutter finally starting to resolve.

I sighed, wondering if I would be able to get more information out of the other two prisoners. I guess I would have to find out. *Or I could bring them back with me and let Tanyth interrogate them.* Taking them back would be a death sentence. If they were Fae it might be worth the risk of letting them somehow escape. Larks, on the other hand, were not worth facing the prince's wrath for.

I made a motion to Valor, who had returned once he had settled the prisoners. "We are going to take their horses and bring the prisoners back with us. If we place them on the horses, then we can travel at our normal speed."

"Won't they try to run away?" Valor asked.

I shook my head. "Not if I tie them to the horses so they are not in control of the horse, merely attached to it."

Valor didn't reply. He took hold of the prisoner's arm and led the way back to our camp.

We kept up a continuous jog the entire way back to Dorcha Palace. The three prisoners were tied over the horses and spaced out so they could not talk to one another. The return was the easy part; everyone knew where we were going, and it gave me the opportunity to figure out what I was going to do.

I could feel Dragonfang humming, though I wasn't entirely sure that anyone else could hear or feel it. I didn't know enough about this dagger to know if being able to hear it was a good or bad sign. What I did know was that Prince Tanyth had been hunting for Dragonfang for years and would be pleased that I had found it. I was also concerned because it meant that if the Fae story was indeed a prophecy, the prince would only need the *Grimoire* to complete the set.

Become one with flesh
Summon the dragon with his fang
Bloodsong sang with glee
The one who can tame the three
Can maim all foes against thee

While I didn't believe the prophecy was real, I had to consider what the consequences would be if it *were* real, and what it would mean if Prince Tanyth had control over the three objects. The prince would have far more power than he had currently and could quite possibly overthrow King Pharaan without much effort. After years at the Court of Dusk, I was not sure that I wanted Prince Tanyth to force all Fae to live as I had been living—a prisoner with the illusion of control over my own life.

I sighed. I knew I didn't have a choice. The entire squad was aware I had Dragonfang, and unless I intended to overthrow Tanyth solo upon our arrival, the only option was to turn it over. If I didn't, he would question my motives for keeping the dagger for myself.

Thirty-Six

SERAFINA

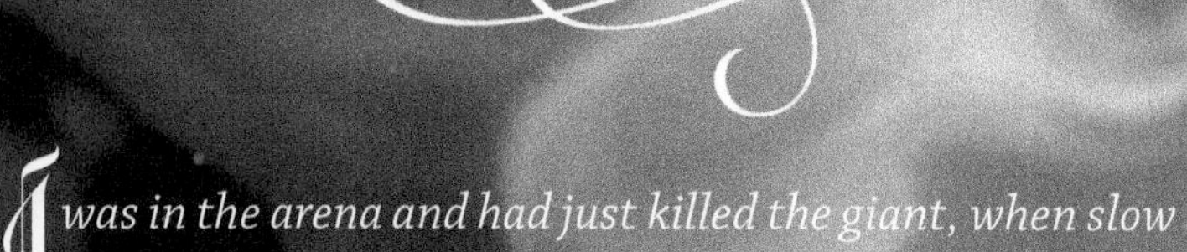

I was in the arena and had just killed the giant, when slow applause began behind me. Prince Tanyth approached. "Dearest Serafina, will you do me the honor of marrying me?"

I shook my head. "Never!" My fingers were still tightly gripping the chain I had strangled the giant with.

Prince Tanyth snarled and snapped his fingers. Tristan appeared at his side on his knees, bound in chains, with a heavy silver collar around his neck like the one that had bound the leon shifter. The prince held a sword to Tristan's neck with one hand and in his other hand he held a ring. "If you refuse to marry me, then I will kill him."

I gasped and stumbled forward, all color draining from my face. I could feel the tug of something between Tristan and I, and the thought of him being dead felt like I'd be killing part of myself.

"Ah, you do care for him. How sweet," spat Prince Tanyth, digging his sword into Tristan's flesh so that a trickle of blood began dripping down his neck. "Now choose!"

I glanced at Tristan. He shook his head. Telling me to refuse? I took a step forward and snatched the ring out of the prince's hand, then slid it onto my finger. "I will marry you, as long as you don't kill him."

Prince Tanyth nodded, and the sword vanished. "I promise I will not kill him." He then stepped forward and yanked me into his arms, kissing me.

I sat up in bed, sweating. I touched my left hand, confirming that there was no ring on my finger. I ran a hand over my face, trying to slow my breathing. "Just a dream," I muttered. I lay back on the pillows and closed my eyes again, praying for no dreams so I could sleep in peace for once.

I was in the arena and had just killed the giant, when slow applause began behind me. I whirled, fists up, when I saw it was Tristan. "What are you doing here?"

"I love you," Tristan replied, closing the gap between us. As soon as we touched, energy snaked around our bodies. I threw my arms around him, not wanting to let go. "I love you," I whispered into his ear. He kissed me deeply, and I found myself wanting more. I didn't want to kiss him, I wanted him inside of me. I wanted to marry him.

I woke up to a quiet knock on my door, followed by the sound of it opening. "Good morning!" Callyn called.

I rubbed my eyes. I had slept, but the dreams alternated between Prince Tanyth demanding I marry him and Tristan declaring his love for me. I did not feel nearly as rested as I had hoped. *Maybe I should ask for a sleeping draught tonight.*

"What's on the agenda for today?" I spoke.

"Training, and then there is a party to announce your engagement," Callyn replied, eying me.

Fallon met us halfway down the hallway to the training room. "Change of plans. Prince Tanyth has ordered Serafina to attend him in the throne room prior to beginning practice."

I frowned. *Now what?*

Callyn halted in front of the doors to the throne room. The guards opened them. "Go on," she said.

I threw my shoulders back and held my head high as I walked into the throne room. Guards were stationed at each column, but there were no guests, only Prince Tanyth sitting on his throne.

He wore his large antlered crown, as well as that gray fur cape with large paws on the shoulders. *Just like when he captured me.*

When I got to the end of the aisleway I dropped into a deep curtsey. "Your Highness."

"My dearest Serafina. My wedding present to you arrived earlier than I expected and I couldn't keep it a secret any longer," the prince announced.

I glanced at him warily. *Wedding present?*

The side entrance to the throne room opened and Bane brought in a captive who was wearing a hood and struggling against his hold. Eying the captive, I determined it most definitely was not Tristan, and relief washed through me. The Fae was lighter boned than he was.

Bane halted between me and Prince Tanyth and shoved his captive to its knees, then yanked off the hood.

I rocked back on my heels as though I had been slapped, my body frozen with fear. Fiera glared defiantly at Bane from her place on the ground. Her face was covered in dirt and her hair was disheveled, but she otherwise seemed unharmed. A strangled sob escaped my lips as I dropped to the floor, hugging my friend. *No!* my mind was screaming. I would not wish this existence on anyone. For days I had been hoping someone would rescue me, and look where that had gotten me—my best friend was now a captive too.

Suddenly arms wrapped around me and pulled me off of Fiera. I struggled, but the iron grip refused to let up. Bane smirked at me and shoved the hood back on Fiera, then dragged her back the way they came. Even after they were gone, I was still being held.

"What do you think of your present, dearest?" Prince Tanyth asked sweetly.

Struggling against my captor, I wrestled myself free and launched myself at the prince. Right hand curled in a fist, I threw a punch at his jaw and he caught my hand in his. His grip was tight and unyielding. I swung my left hand toward his stomach and he blocked it with his arm, then squeezed my right hand tightly. I hissed in pain.

Prince Tanyth chuckled. "What do you think you're doing? You can't win."

I spit in his face. He let go of my hand and slapped me hard enough to send me reeling backward. The prince leaped, fists pummeling my chest and abdomen, careful to only hit places that could be covered. Before I could react, arms wrapped around mine, pinning them behind my back. My energy drained quickly as the beating continued and I sagged, pain lancing through me. My legs were close to giving out. Finally, the prince backed off.

"You will thank me for your gift," the prince hissed.

Woodenly, I replied, "Thank you for my gift."

The prince made a motion with a hand and my arms were released. I collapsed onto the ground and curled into a ball. It wasn't long before rough hands tugged on my arm.

"Get up," Fallon said.

"No," I replied. Everything hurt and I was struggling to process that my best friend was now a prisoner too.

Fallon shook my arm. "Serafina, we need to go to the training room." His voice was low. Putting my hands flat on the floor, I pushed myself up. Taking my time to adjust to the new pain in my body from the beating. I wanted to protest that they expected me to train after the way I had been treated, but I was too worn out to care.

The beating followed by training with Callyn was overwhelming. Even though we focused primarily on hand-to-hand combat and strengthening exercises, I frequently felt lightheaded and off-balance.

To my relief Callyn refrained from commenting on my performance; she merely stated the purpose of the techniques—"To build stamina." Though I could not decide what type of stamina she was referring to. Cringing, I realized perhaps it was bedroom and not battle stamina. Apprehension rolled through me. If I agreed to marry the prince, then I would belong to him, body and soul.

"If I agree to the prince's proposal, what does that mean?" I asked Callyn.

Callyn gave me a nod of approval. "Good question. As ruler of a court, he is required to have a formal wedding. The proposal and engagement serve as the announcement of your intentions, and then once the wedding happens, you would be his wife."

"So, it's not binding until the wedding?" I inquired.

Callyn gave me a sharp look. "It is not *official* until the wedding. The Court of Dusk has a requirement that there be a witness during the consummation of the marriage."

I let out my breath slowly. *I have some time.*

Not wanting to dwell on the wedding, I changed subjects. "I want to see Fiera."

Callyn shook her head. "You are not permitted to see her."

My throat tightened and my fingernails bit into my palms. "I see," I ground out.

"I will escort you to your room so you can bathe," Callyn said. I nodded, not wanting to speak for fear I would start crying, which would gain me nothing.

Back at my room, I took a long, scorching-hot bath. My mind was made up. I would find Fiera and then accept the proposal. Unfortunately, as I emerged from the bath, there was a soft tap on the door and then it opened. I sighed deeply. *I'll have to create another opportunity to search for Fiera.* The footsteps stopped near the open door to the bathroom. I wrapped myself in a robe and started to dry my hair.

"I am here to ensure you get ready for the party tonight," Callyn announced. "Verrona is coming shortly with your gown."

Verrona walked into the room. She had a basket on her back and a dress draped over her arm. "Tonight, we are keeping it simple. A black silk gown with gold accents."

Verrona set down her basket and held the dress out for me to look at it. It had long billowing sleeves of sheer black silk. The bodice and skirt were made of solid black silk, and there were fine threads of gold woven on the borders. I was surprised at how modest the dress was compared to some of the ones I had worn in the past, but I wasn't going to complain. Not showing off every inch of my body to all bystanders was a welcome change.

I removed the robe and discarded the towel I was using to dry my hair. Verrona said nothing, simply held out the dress, and I stepped into it, pulling it up and sliding my arms into the sleeves. She stepped behind me and began to lace the corset. Thankfully she laced it slowly, allowing me time to adjust my breathing as it pulled against my bruised ribcage.

When she was done with the dress, Verrona used her magic to dry and style my hair. For tonight, she did several small braids that were then woven together for a larger braid, with half of my hair remaining loose. She gave me a thick gold torque, and I placed it around my neck. I cringed at the feeling. I knew it was a lovely necklace, but it felt more like a slave collar than anything.

"Beautiful," Verrona said and stepped in front of me, inspecting her work.

Callyn nodded in agreement. "Now let's go, we don't want to keep the prince waiting."

"Thank you," I said to Verrona and followed Callyn out. She led me on a familiar path to the throne room where most of the parties were held. I could feel my hands shaking slightly and I realized I was nervous.

Callyn guided me over to where Tanyth waited and then left us alone. Though we weren't really alone—there were Fae courtiers throughout the throne room. Several were just a few feet away, but they were all absorbed in their own conversations. I curtsied and met Tanyth's eyes.

"Good evening, Serafina. You look delightful tonight." His voice wound around me.

My lips parted, but long moments passed while I tried to find my words. His gaze lingered at the torque before I found myself gazing into his dark green eyes. I took a step forward. "I accept."

Prince Tanyth's eyebrows flicked upward. "The proposal?"

I nod. "Yes, I agree to marry you."

Prince Tanyth took a step toward me and leaned forward, but then his eyes flickered to someone behind me. He gave me a light kiss on the cheek, barely touching the skin. "Excuse me, wife," he said softly, then moved past me. A tremor of excitement rippled through me. *Prince Tanyth is distracted. I can leave and find Fiera.*

Thirty-Seven

TRISTAN

The entrance to Dorcha Palace was lit with strings of Fae lights and dark-colored ribbons. *A party*. The last thing I wanted to do was attend a party, but it *was* the perfect opportunity to present Dragonfang. The prince loved theatrical formal presentations because they ensured that everyone in his court knew he was the one who held power.

I avoided the most direct route to my rooms. Covered in dirt from the journey, I had no wish to draw unnecessary negative attention to myself. Confident the prince would agree with my decision, I quickly bathed and dressed. With the dagger wrapped in a black cloth and tucked into my belt, I departed for the party.

There were whispers circulating about what Serafina was wearing. I made my way through the crowd until I could see Tanyth. He was standing close to Serafina. I took a few steps forward and Tanyth caught my eye, then said, "Excuse me, wife." My eyes widened in surprise that he would use that moniker with her. *Unless his plan worked and they're now married*. It seemed too fast; I had been gone less than two days. *Maybe he just proposed*.

Unwilling to let the prince distract me from my task, I waited till he was close enough, then removed the dagger from my belt and held it in my open palms, bowing deeply. The cloth slipped as I had intended, revealing the dagger, which was now glowing a very faint green. "May I present to you, my prince, Dragonfang."

A vicious smile broke out on Tanyth's face and he greedily snatched the dagger from my hands. There was a flash of bright green and then the dagger's magic vanished. Nothing detrimental happened, so I assumed the dagger had accepted Tanyth as its new owner. "You have done well, Tristan. Where did you find it?"

I straightened up and met his eyes. "The humans, who were the Lord of the West's men as you suspected. They found it in the river, and I retrieved it for you. I brought three prisoners for you to interrogate should you wish."

Tanyth rotated the dagger back and forth in his hand. Over his shoulder I could see Serafina as she waited by the throne. "I will interrogate the prisoners tomorrow," Tanyth said absently. "You can go."

I bowed again and flowed into the crowd. I wasn't entirely sure what to do. I knew Callyn was here somewhere, but after the dream I'd had of Serafina while on the outing and Tanyth's *wife* comment, I couldn't decide if I wanted to be alone or with company. I wandered around till I found the food table and filled up a plate. There was an opening along one wall; I claimed it for my own and leaned against it while eating and observing. A few Fae were dancing, but most were talking in small clusters. Occasionally I heard someone mention my name and Dragonfang. I wasn't surprised the news had traveled around the room quickly. It always did, whether it was good or bad.

Plate empty, I vanished it, then turned to move deeper into the room and bumped into someone hard. "Excuse me," I growled angrily, then gulped. It wasn't the Fae's fault I wasn't watching where I was going.

"Sorry," Serafina replied.

Emotions running high, I wrapped my hands around her arm and pulled her back to the wall. "Where are you going?" I demanded, bracing my arms on both sides of her face.

"To get food. Is that a crime?" she said lightly, though she didn't make a move to escape. My heart pounded in my chest. *What am I doing?* I snarled to myself. *She is his wife, and if he's watching...*

This close, her scent wound its way through me, cinnamon and orange. I inhaled and felt my cock responding. The feeling of sparks where our skin brushed was intensifying. I growled and leaned close, which only made matters worse for me. Temper rising, I blurted the words without thinking them through. "So, you're his wife now. Was he kind to you your first time, or did he force himself on you?" I snapped my jaw shut, shoved myself off the wall, and walked away. My breathing was ragged, and a mix of anger, fear, and desire warred within me. I headed for the door and burst through it.

What is wrong with me? I could hear the growls still coming from my throat as the emotions welled up—fear, anger, and longing. *Serafina's off-limits. They're engaged, possibly married already.*

Instead of going to my room, I went down to the training area. When I got there, I stripped down to my underwear and began going through hand-to-hand combat exercises.

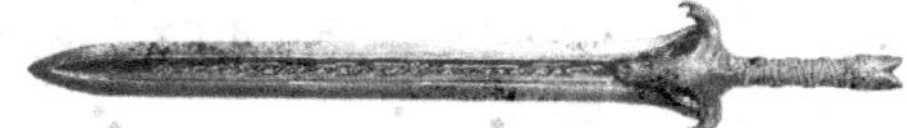

A few hours later the door opened. I whirled, bristling at the intrusion. I had come here knowing that everyone was either at the party or asleep and I wouldn't be disturbed.

"You left so quickly," Prince Tanyth said in a disappointed tone. "Did you not like my party?"

I blinked, unsure of what to say.

"I see. Well, I missed you, and so did Callyn," Prince Tanyth said.

"I needed to practice. When I was out with silver squad I realized how I have not kept up on my hand-to-hand combat training and decided, why not start right now?" I said the words in a rush.

"You don't look as though you need to practice," Tanyth replied. "Since you're so eager to practice, why don't you show me where the prisoners are, and you can aid in the interrogation?"

I nodded and used my magic to call in more appropriate clothing. Black leather pants and a leather vest that was open in the front, my sword belt with a longsword and dagger around my waist, and the special boots with a hidden dagger tip.

Tanyth didn't comment on my new attire. He led the way to the level below us where the prisoners were being kept in the dungeon. I kept my anger at the prince in the forefront of my mind, knowing it was the only way I would survive the interrogation. He let me choose which prisoner to start with, so I chose one who had refused to give up any information. *Please be quick to break,* I prayed.

I yanked him to his feet and Tanyth opened the door for me, then slammed it shut as the other two prisoners made a dash for the opening. We went across to a moderate-sized room that had an assortment of tools inside. There were two chairs, a table, and a stretcher, as well as many other useful items. I shoved the prisoner into the chair that was only a frame where the seat goes without a hard surface to sit on.

Tanyth smirked in approval and selected a weapon—an iron ball on the end of a chain attached to a stick. It took all of my control to not cringe and cover my cock with my hands. The prisoner, poor soul, looked at the weapon in confusion. Tanyth handed me the weapon and I gave it an experimental swing. The iron ball whirred through the air.

Tanyth leaned against a table, eyes boring into the prisoner. "Did you know that the object you sought was a magic object?"

The prisoner pinched his lips tightly together. Tanyth gave me a nod. Envisioning it was the prince and not the prisoner sitting in the chair, I spun the handle twice, and on the third rotation brought it up under the chair. It connected perfectly, and the prisoner howled in pain. Blood dripped under the chair.

"I will repeat the question. Did you know the object you sought was magic?" Tanyth said, bored.

The prisoner shook his head. Tanyth gave me a nod. I began to spin again. As I adjusted my arm to swing under the chair, the prisoner shouted, "Wait!"

With a sharp flick of my wrist, I halted the iron ball just a hair before it connected.

"Well? Are you going to answer the question, or should I have my lord commander hit you again? I have heard it's possible to perform without testicles, though I have not known anyone to survive long enough to try it out," Tanyth said coldly.

I schooled my face into cold fury, though I wanted to curl up in the corner and protect my cock and testicles from such treatment. I also knew why Tanyth took this approach first; it almost always worked, both on males and females. Swift and excruciating, they would talk.

The prisoner gulped. Tears streamed down his face, but he was not sobbing. "The Lord of the West hinted it could be magic and that if it was there would be a great reward for bringing it back."

"And?" pressed Tanyth.

The prisoner shook his head. "I don't know any more."

Tanyth flicked his fingers at me and before the prisoner knew what was happening, I whirled the handle and smashed the iron ball into him. "Again," said Tanyth.

I obeyed, striking and striking. The blood that had started as a dribble was now gushing. Finally, Tanyth raised his hand to halt me. "Take him away and get the next prisoner."

I untied the prisoner and dragged him out of the room. Instead of returning him to his comrades, I stuck him in a different cell.

I knew the odds of him surviving for much longer were slim. He was bleeding too heavily. Taking a shaky breath, I squared my shoulders and locked away my emotions, then shut the gate to his cell and locked it. I retrieved the other prisoner who had refused to speak. He began to struggle as we approached the tool room. Keeping my grip firm, I shoved him inside.

"Feisty," commented Tanyth. I couldn't tell if he was excited about that or not.

"Do you want him on the chair too?" I asked, eying the blood-splattered chair.

Tanyth shook his head. "No. Strap him to the table." *Uh-oh.* I clenched my teeth. *Do not react.* With the chair, I knew exactly what was going to happen to the prisoner. The use of the table left far too many possibilities to dwell on.

I yanked the man onto the table and began strapping him in. When all the buckles were secured, there was a flash of magic as Tanyth locked the prisoner in place.

"Which tool do you want me to use?" I inquired, licking my dry lips.

Tanyth shook his head. "I will do it this time." I noticed he had Dragonfang in his hands and was twisting it so the lamp-light caught it. The dagger's green jeweled eyes almost seemed as though they were watching me. I shivered slightly. *It's just a weapon, it can't watch me,* I told myself, before stepping back to the wall and leaning against it.

Tanyth stepped forward. Instead of asking the prisoner a question, he took the tip of Dragonfang and dragged it lightly in a straight line across the man's collarbone. As soon as the dagger pierced his skin, he began screaming. A thin line of blood welled up and then disappeared. I was confused. *Where is the blood going?*

"Now that you know how Dragonfang feels, you will answer my question," Tanyth said, pressing the dagger into the prisoner's ribcage but refraining from piercing the skin.

"Did the Lord of the West warn you that you would be traveling into my territory to find the object?" Tanyth asked.

"Yes," replied the prisoner. "But he said it didn't matter. That we had nothing to worry about."

I choked back a laugh. Foolish human king, to say that his people could cross into a Fae court's territory without permission and without there being any consequences.

"Did he give you instructions for what to do if you did come into contact with Fae?"

"Yes, he said to kill any Fae we saw," the prisoner replied.

Tanyth dug the dagger between his ribs. Blood began to drip, and then I saw the dagger glow green and dark shadows appeared on the blade. *It's absorbing the blood,* I realized in horror.

The prisoner began sobbing. I knew that the wounds Tanyth had given him, while painful, likely would heal without issue given enough time.

"Is there any other information you have to share?" Tanyth queried. The prisoner began mumbling. "Speak up!" growled Tanyth.

"The Lord of the West thought there might also be a vein of iron that far out of his lands, and he wanted us to investigate the possibility of mining. We did not find any evidence of iron or any other metal for that matter. Just the dagger. Though someone swears they saw a cat in a tree. I think it was sleep-deprived fantasies." The prisoner closed his eyes, likely resigning himself to the fate of being killed on the table with Dragonfang. My whole body tensed. *Someone saw me in the tree.*

Tanyth gave me a sharp glance that I couldn't decipher. With a flick of his fingers, the magic undid the straps and freed the prisoner. I stepped closer and wrapped my hand firmly around his upper arm, pulling him off the table to stand.

"Put him in with the other one we damaged," Tanyth said. "There will be arena fights tomorrow evening and I want all three of them in there."

I nodded and half-dragged, half-guided the prisoner to the cell with the other one I had tortured. I half expected him to be dead when I got there, but no—he was muttering and sobbing, clearly alive, though likely wishing he were dead.

When all three prisoners were secure again, I returned to Tanyth, wondering if he was going back to the party or would expect me to, or if I could retire for what was left of the night.

"Come, let's walk back to your room," Tanyth said. Side by side we walked up the stairs and down the hallway. The prince finally spoke as we were a few strides from my room. "What did you make of the prisoner mentioning seeing a cat in a tree?"

I froze, then curled my lip and growled. "It was likely only one of the small forest cats. They often prowl at night."

"Did you see a cat in a tree when you were scouting?" Tanyth asked.

I bared my teeth at him. "No. I did not see a cat in a tree. I was also not looking for a cat in a tree. I was trying to determine what the Larks' purpose was."

Tanyth pressed his lips together. I couldn't tell if he bought my lie or not. "Good night, Tristan," the prince finally said.

I bowed. "Good night, my prince." I waited until Tanyth disappeared down the hall to enter my suite, exhaling in relief that he had, at least for now, believed me.

Thirty-Eight

SERAFINA

I was fast asleep when I heard a sound near the bathroom. I reached under the pillow for a dagger and my hand came up empty. I frowned, not sure who would be trying to sneak into my room in the middle of the night. *Tanyth?* But I quickly dismissed that idea, because the prince had no reason to sneak around, not in his own palace, or with his future wife.

I quietly swung my legs out of the bed and stood up, fists curled, ready to attack whoever was in my room. Small balls of Fae light were sent around the room, revealing—Tristan.

I took a step backward and the back of my knee hit the bed. I sat down hard on the edge. He was the last Fae I had expected to sneak into my room, especially after how angry he had been earlier.

"What do you want, Tristan?" I asked, keeping my voice low enough that no one in the hallway would hear.

"You," he said and took a few steps forward. The closer he got, the more I could feel the sparks growing between us. There was even a strange tug at my center. I stood up, and my feet moved me closer to Tristan, even though that had not been my intention.

"What is going on?" I asked, confused. We were now mere arm's-length apart. What I really wanted was for him to touch me.

He took the last step and kissed me. When our lips met, the intensity of the kiss almost drove me to my knees. Panting, I pulled back. "What is going on?" I asked again.

Tristan gave me a light kiss. "Do you feel the sparks? The tugging?" I nodded, not entirely surprised he felt it too. "That is what a Fae mating bond feels like."

My lips parted in surprise. "I'm not Fae."

"You're half. It's possible you can experience one," Tristan said.

"What do we do about it?" I asked. The idea that Tristan and I were mates was a surprise, but not an unpleasant one. Things between us had changed so much since my arrival.

He shook his head. "It's not something we can change. Over time, it will strengthen." Then he kissed me. I melted against him, the ache inside of me increasing. I ran my hands down his back, wanting more. He cupped my butt and picked me up. I wrapped my legs around him, his cock pressing into my apex. I moaned when he gave a slight thrust of his hips and it bumped my clit, pleasure rolling through me. Tristan carried me back to the bed and gently laid me down on my back. My night shirt was scrunched up under me, and I was naked from the waist down.

Tristan's gaze lingered, and I squirmed. He chuckled and leaned over, giving me a deep kiss, then he plunged his fingers into my folds. I spasmed as a wave of intense pleasure went through me. His fingers stroked and teased. I moaned as his fingers pulled out, but they were quickly replaced by his tongue. As soon as his tongue began thrusting I exploded in pleasure, shudders rocking me.

Tristan lay beside me on the bed with a satisfied smile on his face. I kissed him. "What about you?" I started to let my hand drift to his cock, but he caught it before I could touch him.

"I want nothing more than to be inside of you right now, Serafina. But we cannot be caught," Tristan said.

I twisted my hand, trying to free it from his grip. "We won't. I need all of you inside of me," I whispered.

There was a sharp knocking on the door. Tristan sprang up. "See!" he hissed.

Hide! I mouthed. He shook his head and simply disappeared. I stared at the space he had just occupied in confusion. Then I glanced down at myself and the bed. I hastily rearranged myself and yanked the covers up to my chin, hoping whoever it was would believe that they had woken me up.

The door opened and Callyn entered. "The prince wants to see you immediately in the throne room."

I blinked in surprise. "Now?"

"Yes. Hurry up and get dressed," Callyn said, moving over to my wardrobe and quickly selecting a tunic and pants and shoving them in my arms.

"What is it about?" I asked as I pulled the undergarments on, followed by the black pants and gray tunic.

Callyn sighed. "I have no idea. You will have to see when you get there."

I brushed my hair and put it in a quick braid. Callyn hadn't given me a fancy dress, so perhaps it was early morning training he wanted me to do. *With Tristan.* My cheeks heated up as I remembered what his tongue had felt like.

"Are you ready?" Callyn asked, frowning, but she did not ask me any questions. *Does she know?* I wondered.

"Yes, I'm ready." I walked toward the door. We trekked in silence to the throne room. I ran different scenarios through my head, but the one that made the most sense was that the prince wanted me to do extra training or something along those lines.

Callyn and I were about to turn the corner that would put us in front of the throne room doors when Tristan appeared. Pressing my lips together, I tried to keep my cool.

"Change of plans," Tristan announced, keeping his voice quiet. "We're going to train."

Callyn nodded in acceptance. "Okay, I'll see you around." As Callyn disappeared from sight, I blew out my breath in a rush.

Tristan tugged on my hand. "Come on, we don't have much time."

Confusion flooded me. "Time for what?"

Tristan held a finger to his mouth and led the way deeper into the palace. After a while I realized that the hallway was sloping downward. Initially I thought he was going to take me somewhere to finish what we'd started before Callyn showed up; now, though, I had no idea what he was doing.

Eventually we reached a thick wood door. He placed his hand on it and there was a flash of gray magic, followed by a click of the lock. The door opened and we stepped inside. There was a rustling of fabric in the corner, but there was hardly any light. A quiet thud indicated Tristan had shut the door. The room lit up—with magic, I surmised—and revealed Fiera huddling in the corner.

I threw myself at her. "Fiera!" I sobbed.

Dirty arms wrapped around me and we clung to each other. *No wonder Tristan wouldn't tell me where we were going.*

"Are you okay?" Fiera whispered in my ear.

"I'm managing," I whispered back. "There's so much I need to ask you. Tristan and I…"

"We're out of time," hissed Tristan, his hand clamped on my shoulder.

"I need more!" I said louder than I intended, causing Tristan to dig his fingers sharply into my skin.

"Be safe," said Fiera, then she pushed me with all of her strength.

I tilted backward, colliding with Tristan's legs, and he hauled me up and led me to the door. I expected to go through it but instead he stood there with his ear against the wood. My hands trembled with nerves. *What if we get caught?*

The door flew open. Tristan stumbled through it—and into Verrona.

"What are you doing with the prisoner, Tristan?" gasped Verrona.

"Verrona, please," Tristan pleaded, something I had never thought I'd hear him do.

Verrona shot a glance down the hallway and motioned for us to step out. "I won't tell anyone. But if I'm questioned I am not going to lie. Now, go wherever you're supposed to be before someone else finds you."

Hanging on Verrona's arm was a basket of food. "Thank you," I told her, and Tristan whisked me down the hallway toward the training room.

Bane was standing in front of the doors blocking our way. "Lord Commander, you are needed elsewhere."

My heart skipped a beat and I could feel Tristan bristling beside me.

"Where, precisely?" demanded Tristan.

"The guard in the dungeons is sick today and the prince wants you to take his post," Bane replied.

"I see," Tristan replied, his voice sounding strained, but I wasn't sure why. *Surely he has been in the dungeons before, where the beasts are?*

Tristan abruptly turned and went back the way we had come. I leveled my gaze at Bane. He pushed open the door. "After you."

I won't let Bane frighten me. Straightening my spine, chin held high, I walked inside. The door thudded shut behind me. Before I could get my bearings, a teal hand gripped my arm. "Serafina."

Fear coursed through me. Before I could respond, Prince Tanyth stepped in front of me, eyes filled with cold anger. "I learned of your visit to Fiera."

Fingers digging into my palms, I stayed silent, knowing there was no response I could make that would solve the predicament I was now in.

"You were not given permission to visit her. Each time you disobey me, your friend will lose a limb. How do you think she'd fare against Rethys without any arms?" he asked coldly.

His threat jolted me into action. "You wouldn't."

"Are you going to gamble with Fiera's arm or leg that I'm lying? Will she ever forgive you when I tell her she lost her arms because you, her *friend*," he said with a sneer, "weren't able to be an obedient wife?"

I worried my cheek with my teeth. He was right and likely wasn't bluffing. Fiera meant nothing to the prince, but everything to me. As I considered my words, the prince caught me off guard when he closed the gap between us and kissed me. I recoiled, but his iron grip kept me from pulling away as he forced his lips onto mine.

Finally, he stopped kissing me. "Bane is going to handle your training today."

I cringed, but with the threat of Fiera losing a limb hanging over me, I remained motionless until the prince left.

Thirty-Nine

TRISTAN

Tension rolled through me as I made my way down to the dungeon where the beasts were. The assignment was ridiculous given no one needed to be down there full-time. I stayed down there for an hour, thoroughly inspecting all of the cages and the food preparation room. Losing myself in the work was far more challenging, with constant hisses, caws, and roars reminding me of what would happen if my shapeshifting secret got out.

The only thing to console me was that Fiera had not told Serafina—yet. Which meant she was keeping her promise. *Can I protect both of them?* I ran a hand over my face. I was worried that if I didn't protect Fiera, Serafina would never forgive me, but there was a much higher risk that the prince would discover how close Sera and I had become. Even now I had no way of knowing who had been waiting for her in the training room.

Inspection completed, I headed for the entrance to the arena where the silver squad and other warriors in my command were waiting for our first running session, as I had promised would happen when we returned. "To begin with, we will keep our gear minimal. I want you to focus on building your stamina without the extra weight of armor and weapons. Once you have accomplished that, then we will work on adding more weight. I don't know when you lot lost your stamina, but I fully intend to rectify the problem," I explained.

In a double column, with me at the head, we took off at a jog up the ramp and through the gate that led into the arena. There was a layer of sand a few inches thick, but otherwise it was empty. "We shall run around the perimeter." When my feet hit the sand, I sped up. Everyone had already warmed up, so I didn't need to worry about taking it slow. I also knew if I took off at full speed I would win the race, but the purpose of this session wasn't to prove who was fastest.

When we were about halfway through, Tanyth showed up and immediately beckoned for me to come talk to him. I motioned for my men to keep going and met Tanyth in the middle. The arena was large enough that no one would overhear us unless we wanted them to. Fury rolled off Tanyth. I stopped when I was about a sword-length away and waited.

"Serafina is marrying me," Tanyth snarled. Dragonfang was in his belt and was beginning to glow in reaction to the prince's heightened emotional state.

I was confused by Tanyth's announcement, given he had told me the news last night. *Unless he knows about what I did with Serafina?* There was no way he could though; we were quiet.

"No one but me is allowed to touch her," Tanyth replied.

"Do you want to take over her weapons training then?" I offered, hoping to appease him.

"No," growled Prince Tanyth. "But if there is any hint that you're doing more than training, I will make sure you are no longer capable of feeling sexual pleasure ever again." Tanyth fingered the dagger. "I am also concerned that as much as you have claimed to have been hunting shapeshifters for me all these years, you have been lying. That you haven't done everything in your power to eradicate them."

I gave him a bored look. *I can only hunt if I get the order. He won't give me the freedom to leave.* "Yet when was the last time you let me go on a real hunt? I haven't been anywhere near Glass Oasis in over a decade. Who knows what magic the youngsters have developed in that time."

"I will consider sending you out to hunt, then, but there are other matters that are more important. Such as your next arena battle and the matter of the newest prisoner," Tanyth said.

"As you wish," I replied with a curt nod. "What are your plans for the prisoner?"

"She will be fighting tonight. If she survives, then you can add her to your schedule for training tomorrow," Tanyth replied. *Maybe he hopes to keep Sera in line if she has more access to Fiera.*

"Is that all?" I gazed at what my males were doing. Half of them were walking, the other half were doing some weird-looking jog, but none were running. "I need to finish up the session." Tanyth nodded in approval.

Sprinting away, I cut off the group along the wall. They immediately got into formation. *Likely because Prince Tanyth is watching.* "Whatever you were just doing does not count as running." Deciding to add some drama for the prince's sake, I called a whip into my hand and with a snap of my wrist, flung it into the air and cracked it. They all jumped. "Now RUN, or I will use this on you!" They took off, and I cracked it behind them as motivation, trying to not laugh.

Session complete, they were all drenched in sweat, not a dry speck of skin or clothing on any of them. I shook my head. "Get cleaned up and then go to your posts. I will see you in the morning."

Callyn found me as I was finishing final preparations for my fight in the arena holding area. She frowned at me. "You're not going last, Serafina is." Which meant I wasn't the grand finale as I usually was. It boded well for Serafina, but likely was a bad omen for what I could expect in the arena.

"Other than my position in tonight's entertainment, do you know anything else that would be useful?" I asked Callyn. Sometimes she was able to glean useful bits of gossip as she did her duties on the opposite side of the palace. *Maybe she knows about what happened after I left Sera at the training room.*

She shook her head. "Not tonight. He was vicious, but not talkative. Please be careful."

Trying to mask my disappointment, I forced a smile. "I promise I will do my best," I said. We both knew all too well it may not be possible to be careful.

Callyn stepped close and kissed me lightly on the cheek.

"Callyn," called Fallon from the hallway. She gave me a slight wave and departed.

I was wearing a hard leather breastplate and thick leather pants with extra strips of leather sewn in. My sword was in my hand, but I had not been permitted to wear a sword belt nor any heavier armor.

I heard footsteps but didn't turn to see who it was. I had a good guess.

Tanyth came up right behind me. I could feel his legs brushing mine. Tensing, I wasn't sure what he was going to do, only that it likely wasn't going to be good.

Tanyth ran his hand along the waist of my pants and slid his hand underneath them, grabbing my cock. He began stroking it. Hot anger ran through me but, try as I might to shut off my body's response, I could not stop myself from responding to the prince's ministrations. With Prince Tanyth's hand on my cock, I was afraid to do anything other than allow him to touch me. Just as it felt like I was about to get my release, a sharp object pierced my lower back. Tanyth's hand withdrew but the pain did not as he twisted the blade. If the wall had not been in front of me, I would have collapsed.

The blade pulsed as it was withdrawn, casting an eerie green glow across the stone. *Dragonfang.* Tanyth's breath was hot in my ear. "Consider that your only warning." Then he was gone. Tears streamed down my face. I could feel blood seeping out of the wound and down my back.

I slowly straightened. *This is his game,* I reminded myself. *I must not let him win. I must go out there and stay alive.* I swayed on my feet and was shocked to find a firm hand gripping me.

"Pull yourself together," Bane said. After his recent aloofness toward me, I was surprised that Bane was even here. I nodded and ran a hand over my face, wiping away the tears of pain. I closed my eyes and let the feeling of calm fall over me before opening them again. He handed me my sword, and I took it. Bane did not let go of me until the very last minute.

I stepped into the arena and a cheer went up in the stands. They began calling my name. "Tristan! Tristan!" I walked into the middle of the arena and painfully raised my sword. I knew from the height of the stands that likely no one could see the blood dripping out from under my armor, and if they could, no one would care.

I heard the metal door opening behind me, but pain slowed my reaction time. By the time I was facing the gate, the tiger was almost on me. I positioned my sword, bracing it with both hands so as the tiger leaped, I was able to stab upward and impale it. What I didn't account for was the weight of the cat. It fell on top of me. We landed with a huge cloud of sand, and I was trapped. *Stupid mistake.* I pushed and tugged, but Dragonfang must have done more than stab me, because I had no strength at all.

A chain snicked, and another door opened. The crowd had grown silent. I was pinned and unable to free myself and another tiger, or something else, was heading my way. I closed my eyes. There was no reason to watch; I knew there was only one outcome.

The weight of the tiger disappeared. I opened my eyes, confused. One of the human prisoners I'd captured when I recovered Dragonfang—the one who had not been tortured—was looking at me, wide-eyed. I stared at him in disbelief, but I did not have time to ask him any questions. I could hear a chain moving. I snagged my sword out of the sand and held it ready.

Luvon, the Fae male who had been slowest in the run this morning, was charging toward us with a flail in each hand. I set my feet and waited. *Sword against two flails.* Moments before Luvon was within reach, the prisoner launched himself at Luvon.

Luvon twisted and as the prisoner passed him, he spun his right-hand flail and jerked it down sharply. It hit the prisoner on the head, and he fell dead, freeing the flail. Luvon grinned at me. I kept my face blank, counting the number of spins he was doing with each flail. From our training sessions I knew that Luvon followed a very specific count, though it would change depending on his mood. If I could figure out what it was, then maybe I would stand a chance.

It's three-two, I decided, and I stepped into his reach as he paused between swings. I swept my sword to the left in an upper-cut. But Luvon wasn't following a three-two count. The right flail hit me on the leg and I fell forward as it swept underneath me.

"Get up," Luvon growled.

I didn't want to get up. Pain rolled through me and I had no strength. I wanted to let him end me here and now. *What about Serafina?* I tried to shake off that thought but couldn't. I found myself worrying about what Tanyth would do to Serafina if I died. Using my sword, I pulled myself up.

Luvon danced forward, swinging the flails hard but never getting quite close enough for them to hit me. I took a step to the right and Luvon mirrored me; I took one back and he stepped forward. Taking a deep breath. I threw myself forward, and instead of striking with the sword, I kicked with my right foot and connected with his left wrist. I heard it snap and the flail fell to the ground, his wrist dangling uselessly from the end of his arm.

Luvon howled in pain and anger. I bared my teeth at him and began circling. My steps were slow. I could feel the snow leopard wanting to take over, to shift, to heal me, but I fought it and won—barely. I knew the same move would not work a second time. Luvon may not run very fast, but he was a quick study when it came to taking measure of an opponent. He slashed a sharp diagonal with the flail. Using the opening as his arm extended and spun, my sword sliced through the leather armor protecting his ribcage.

The flail whistled by my head, and I could feel a trickle of blood and a sting where it sliced my ear. I swept my sword in front of me, trying to keep Luvon back far enough to keep him from hitting me again. Eyes locked on Luvon, I didn't see the dead prisoner in front of me, and I tripped. Thankfully I remembered to tuck into a roll, but I was not prepared for what rolling would do to the wound in my back. I almost bit through my tongue as pain seared through me. Unable to complete the roll, I found myself flat on my back in the arena. Luvon's face loomed above me. I watched as he raised the flail and began the swing that would end my life. At the last moment, I mustered the strength to yank my sword up and got lucky. Luvon had positioned himself so that as I thrust upward with my sword, he fell upon it with the momentum of his strike.

The flail swung loosely over my head. I let my sword lower to the ground and blacked out.

I had the sensation of being carried, but I wasn't entirely sure. Until the movement stopped.

Serafina spoke. "Is he dead?" she asked. I could hear the fear in her voice.

"Not quite," said Callyn, though I wasn't sure if Callyn was carrying me or someone else.

The next thing I knew I felt Serafina's lips brush mine before I blacked out again.

Forty

SERAFINA

I was in the bathhouse when Callyn found me, washing my hair for the third time because I was quite certain it was still covered in blood and guts from my arena fight.

"You are either naïve or ignorant, I haven't decided which," Callyn informed me before she discarded her robe and joined me in the pool.

My throat was suddenly dry. "I'm neither," I replied, trying to focus on cleaning my hair.

Callyn chuckled darkly. "You kissed Tristan in front of a lot of Fae who will report it to Tanyth, your betrothed. You are playing with something far more dangerous than fire, making a move like that, especially now that he also has your friend."

I frowned. The kiss had been something I did in the moment. I honestly hadn't considered the consequences, only the fear that if Tristan was going to die I needed one last kiss. "I should not have kissed him," I admitted. *Is Fiera going to lose her arm because I kissed Tristan?*

Callyn put her hand on my shoulder, and I met her gaze with my own. "Be prepared for the consequences."

"And is he…going to stay exclusive?" I asked.

Callyn laughed. "You must have him confused with another prince to voice that question. Tanyth fucks anyone, anytime, anywhere he pleases. While I expect the mating bond, should you be blessed to have one, will encourage him to seek your arms the most, as will the desire to produce an heir, I doubt you will satiate his needs. For one, you don't have a cock."

I stared at Callyn, confused. "Are you implying if I had a cock, it would be different? I thought he favored females…"

Callyn dunked her head under the water, and when she resurfaced, she replied, "No. I was merely implying that you offer him one kind of satisfaction, and there are times where he seeks other things." Then she added softly, "As do I." She continued in a normal voice, "If I were you, I would focus on your duties as betrothed and then wife, and make sure your body and soul are exclusively his."

Mulling over Callyn's words, I rinsed my hair again. Callyn had admitted that she liked both male and female partners, as did the prince. There was also the other warning that even an innocent kiss would be enough to bring the prince's anger down on me.

I took a deep breath. Callyn was being rather open; now would be a good time to ask her my questions. "You mentioned the mating bond…how does it work?"

Callyn nodded as though she was expecting the question. "Occasionally it will start with dreams or a feeling between the pair, which typically increases with physical contact. Sex is required for the pairing to be completed."

I twisted the ends of my hair in my fingers. I was pretty sure I was mated to Tristan, but I was betrothed to Prince Tanyth. *How am I going to get out of this situation?* I gave her a tired smile. "Good to know." I hesitated as the next question formed; I wasn't even sure it was relevant. "Can shapeshifters have mating bonds?"

Callyn stopped lowering herself into the pool and stared at me. "All Fae can have mating bonds, regardless of the type of magic they possess." She lowered herself the rest of the way into the water. I waited, wondering if she was going to add anything else. "Have you been having dreams of shapeshifters?"

"Sort of..." I licked my lips, considering my next words as I glanced around, confirming we were alone. "I have dreams of Tristan."

Callyn gasped and surged closer to me. "Keep your voice down!" she hissed. "Did you pay attention to nothing I said earlier!" Our bodies brushed, she was so close to me. I thought Callyn was going to reprimand me again, but she didn't. She leaned close to embrace me, her lips near my ear. "Is Tristan your mate?"

"Maybe," I said softly. Everything that Callyn had said and Tristan had told me made me believe it was likely true. Tristan and I were mates—or would be if we ever had a chance to have sex and finish the bonding process.

"No one else can find out," Callyn said. I nodded in understanding.

The stakes were climbing even higher without an exit in sight. My hands started shaking. The water around us was vibrating and making small splashing sounds as I shook. Just as I discovered someone who would love me for me, it could all be crushed because I had allowed myself to be captured by the evil prince of the Court of Dusk.

Callyn's mouth was moving but I could not hear her words. I stared at her blankly, and she slapped me. "Snap out of it. I realize what you learned might change a lot of things for you personally. But one thing it doesn't change is that you belong to Tanyth. We are *all* his. It doesn't matter what pretty titles he gives you or what contracts myself, Tristan, and the other warriors have signed; the truth is still there. You can fight and lose, or you can play along, and maybe, someday, things will get better for you," Callyn said passionately.

"How long have you been here?" I blurted out, trying to let her words and warning flow through me and break through my psychological pain.

"Fifty years," Callyn said.

My jaw dropped open as I realized how she likely knew all too well what would happen if I ignored the advice she was offering me freely, because she had seen it, *lived it*, for fifty years.

"How...how do I do it? How do I survive something like this?" I hoped she would give me some magical answer.

"You lock away your emotions. Fae are good at that; humans, I'm not sure. But try. Until now, you have been following this path to be his wife. Do not give him a reason to doubt your commitment," Callyn said.

I grimaced at the thought of letting Tanyth kiss me again, but deep down I knew she was right. I had to do this, especially with Tristan's and Fiera's lives on the line. "What about Tristan?"

Callyn shrugged. "He knows how to handle himself and is very aware of the consequences for his actions."

After bathing, I dressed in a plain tunic and skirt, then accompanied an unfamiliar Fae female to a private dining room that I had never been in before. I sat at the table and waited. I had a feeling I was waiting for Tanyth. By the time he showed up I was debating if I should eat something to appease my hunger or wait.

I stood up and curtsied deeply, smiling at him. *My husband.* Thinking those words left a bad taste in my mouth, but I made sure my expression did not change.

"Serafina," he said and came over to me. He tipped his head down and kissed me lightly. It took a moment before I registered that he was holding a dagger with an intricate hilt to my heart. "Why did you kiss Tristan today?"

I took a deep breath and felt the dagger press harder into my chest. "I thought he was dead," I said honestly. I had no idea if he had been dead or alive when I had made the hasty choice.

The pressure of the dagger disappeared. Tanyth gave me another kiss, this time far more intense, before he sat down in the chair next to mine. "A mistake. I will give you one mistake, but do not kiss him—or anyone else for that matter—again. If you do, Fiera will pay the price."

I nodded and stared at my plate. The prince put food on it and indicated I should eat. Every bite tasted like ash. I consumed less than half of what he gave me. I knew throwing up on him would be a mistake and hoped he would not require me to finish the meal.

"Now that we've eaten, I want you to come with me," the prince said. He stood and offered me his hand. I took it, trying not to cringe as I did so. *Stay strong for Fiera and Tristan*, I reminded myself.

Prince Tanyth led me down the hall. I was certain we were going to the training room. I had been there enough times by now that I thought I could likely make it without an escort. *Not that I can get anywhere useful without an escort to escape.* I heard weapons clashing, muffled by the heavy wooden doors.

The guards opened the doors under the prince's command, and we went inside.

I stifled my gasp with my hand. Bane and Fiera were sparring with axes, and there were small cuts up and down Fiera's arms and legs—though on closer look they were healing almost as fast as she was getting them. I tore my eyes from my friend and realized that Bane had similar cuts. *An even match?* This was not what I had expected the prince to want to show me.

"Come, let's sit on the bench so we can observe," he said and gestured to the bench on the far wall. Prince Tanyth sat next to me so that our shoulders were touching. I stifled the need to scoot away from him.

Once we were sitting, Bane sped up his attacks and Fiera couldn't quite keep up. Bane pushed her onto the defensive while he struck with his axe over and over. Each time it connected with Fiera's unprotected arms, it would slice, deeper than when we first walked in. Soon Fiera was covered in rivulets of blood from over a dozen wounds.

Bane spun in a feint and Fiera fell for it. He twisted to the left and dragged his axe across her back. Fiera fell to her knees and Bane held his axe to her throat. I gasped as he pressed the blade till it cut her.

I stood and shouted, "Stop!" Bane didn't even look my way. "Stop!" I took a step toward Bane and a hand curled around my arm.

"You don't give orders around here," Prince Tanyth chided.

I glared at him. "You said if I behaved you wouldn't kill her."

Prince Tanyth chuckled. "And who is the one holding the blade?"

I growled, "He takes orders from you."

"He also has his own free will that he may act upon. I gave you a choice, too, if you wanted to accept my proposal, which you did," the prince replied.

I turned to fully face him, and his hand loosened slightly. "What do you want?"

"For you to be my wife. The wedding is in three days," he said.

I bit my lip, not sure how to respond. I had already said yes; I wasn't sure what more he wanted me to do. "I'm looking forward to it," I said in a monotone voice.

Forty-One

TRISTAN

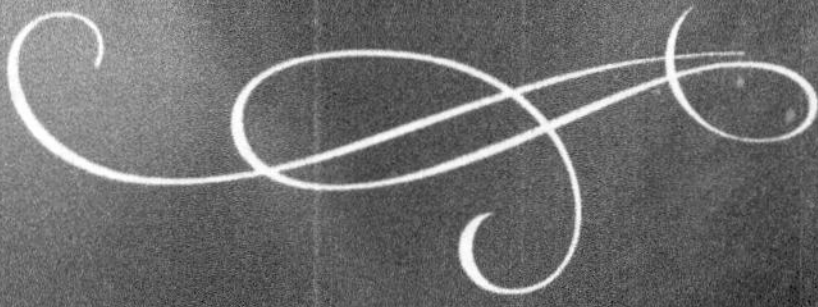

I was stuck in bed for two days. Even my quick Fae healing abilities were no match for the magic in Dragonfang. No one had come by to check on me, not Callyn, Fallon, or even the prince, though I knew if Tanyth had visited I may not have survived the encounter. I think I slept a lot. When I was asleep, I had dreams of being hunted as a snow leopard in a dark forest, or I was looking for Serafina and couldn't find her.

As I sat up, I determined that today I would get out of bed. I swung my legs over the edge of the bed and cautiously set my feet down on the floor. I stood, and to my delight my lower body was cooperating and supporting my upper body. I took a few steps. The stab wound in my back was sending occasional sharp pain, like someone driving a nail into the wound, but otherwise I thought I was okay. As I walked across the room to the dining table and magicked myself some food, I decided the dreams didn't matter. *I am alive and I can catch up on what is happening here when I leave this room.*

While I ate, my thoughts drifted back to everything that happened before I entered the arena and in the arena. Tanyth had stabbed me because he had gotten wind of how intimate some of the moments of our training session had become. Thoughts of Serafina flickered through my mind, and I bit into an apple angrily. *I need to control my emotions or I will endanger us even more.*

Meal finished, I went through a series of stretches, followed by light exercises. Normally I would head to the training yard to do these, but I wanted to be certain about the state of my wound and physical prowess before I saw anyone. As I settled into my routine, I found I was able to tune out the pain from the dagger wound. I picked up my sword and continued.

There was a light tap on my door. "Come in!" I yelled and kept working on the series of combinations that would end my session.

"You're alive," Callyn said tartly.

I threw her a look over my shoulder and ended my combination with a spin. "Of course I'm alive."

"I had my doubts," she said.

I raised my eyebrows. "It wasn't that bad."

She clicked her tongue in disagreement. "You can think what you want. I saw how you looked when they brought you out of the arena. We both know how dangerous Dragonfang is, and then you had to get stabbed with it."

I growled. "It's not like I said, 'Hey Tanyth, can you please stab me with Dragonfang?'"

Callyn rolled her eyes. "I am sure you didn't say that. It is not my business, but you are treading on very dangerous ground. The two days you were recovering have been a challenge, to say the least."

I opened my mouth to ask what she meant, but Callyn shook her head and changed the topic. "I was sent here to relay an order. It has come to the prince's attention that there is another disturbance at the edge of Lochan Sgàile and Whispering Thicket. It's not near the human territory line though, so he unsure whether it is Fae or more humans attempting to be sneaky."

"Who am I to take?" I asked. The order did come as a surprise, though Tanyth had said he would send me out to hunt shape-shifters soon.

"Just you," Callyn said.

"Just me?" I replied, unsure that I had heard her correctly.

She nodded. "Yes. He did mention something about speed and that you are fast, and your squads are slow. So perhaps that is why he wants you to go solo. You are to leave immediately. See to whatever you need to and then go."

I blew out my breath. This was a strange new development, but I was not going to question Tanyth. I would go and find out whatever I could about this new intruder and return quickly. He was correct about one thing, I could move way faster than those in my command, though I hoped to rectify that soon.

"Is there anything else you wanted to share?" I pressed. I was hoping she would tell me about Serafina, but furious at myself for hoping she would.

Callyn locked gazes with me and took a step closer, then another. Her lips brushed against mine lightly and she began to talk in barely a whisper. "The wedding is in one day. Don't be late." I kissed her.

She pulled away, setting her hand on my chest. "If you want to make it back in time, hurry."

Rooted in place, I watched as she departed. I ran my hand over my face and tried to come up with a list of items I would need. "The edge of Lochan Sgàile and Whispering Thicket" was vague given that the two shared a border for several miles within the Court of Dusk's territory, but I figured I could start at one end and go to the other. Running full speed the entire way, solo, I could make it in a few hours. I wanted to blend in with the forest, so I chose a long-sleeve tunic that was a mix of browns and greens and brown pants. I chose a scabbard that went across my back so it would not hinder my movement as much but still be accessible. It also left my hands completely free for any magical attack I might need to initiate. My soft brown boots were light-weight, and I had paid to have magic worked into the leather that enhanced my ability to move silently and undetected. I stuck a few pieces of dried meat in a pouch around my neck and then deemed myself ready.

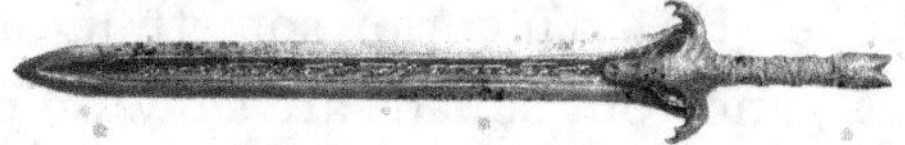

I was about to step outside of the palace when a runner came with a note that told me it was likely there were two or three Fae and the location had been narrowed down further to by the creek.

Once I made it outside, I took off. Without a companion I could move at my own speed, which was fast. The breeze was refreshing as I sped across the hills, around the occasional patch of forest.

When I was close to my destination I shifted and immediately started purring. It was one of the snow leopard instincts that I had trouble suppressing at times, the need to purr during intense emotions. I was able to keep it quiet, but I knew if some-one were to lay their hand on me, they would feel the vibrations. I shook myself and slunk into the trees.

I could smell the wood smoke from a small fire long before I could see it, just as I could tell by scent alone there were two Fae, a male and a female. I approached cautiously, even resorting to a slow creep to get close enough to hear what they were talking about.

The female Fae was speaking. "I am confident Prince Tanyth will agree to see me." Her voice seemed familiar, but I couldn't place it. *Maybe from Glass Oasis?*

The male laughed harshly. "I am confident that if you get an audience with him, he will kill you, not talk to you." I blinked; they spoke as though they knew Prince Tanyth well. The haughty demeanor of the male made me think he must be highly ranked within one of the other courts. *I wonder who they are.* As I debated what to do, they stopped talking.

"Who is there?" the Fae female called.

I snarled, unable to suppress it in time. The female stood up and walked toward my position. Too close for me to be confident that the magic that was supposed to be hiding me was working.

"It's me, Commander Meriel," she said in a low voice. Her hands were out in front of her so I could see she did not have any weapons. "Did Prince Tanyth send you?"

I snarled again. I really didn't want to talk to her when I was shifted. I could mind-to-mind, but I wasn't sure if anyone knew I could do that, and I most certainly didn't want to give them more leverage with Prince Tanyth than what I had already given them—that I could shift into a snow leopard.

Keeping my eyes open, I let my magic flow through me and shifted. I had my hand on my sword hilt when I finished the shift, a warning.

"You came to Glass Oasis when I started having trouble with my father," I said in recognition.

"Yes," she replied.

"You said you would protect me, and yet I got sent to Embergate, and now..." I let my words trail off. I wasn't sure I could trust her given her promise all those years ago and what had happened.

"I'm sorry," Commander Meriel replied. The Fae male stepped forward. "This is Prince Almar, from the Court of the Moon."

I inclined my head. Prince Tanyth had spoken of the Court of the Moon as being the closest to King Pharaan and most likely to support the king. I straightened my shoulders and turned my face into that of a bored, cold Fae male. "Why are you here?"

"We are looking for Serafina Wyantha. She disappeared near the emerald mine and I thought, given the tension that is often between King Pharaan and Prince Tanyth, that maybe she somehow ended up at the Court of Dusk. I was hoping to get an audience," Commander Meriel explained.

I forced myself not to react, but it was a challenge. *The Court of the Moon is looking for Serafina.* A sliver of fear worked its way through me. Prince Tanyth did not like other courts looking into his business. Every time it happened, he got violent. Not only toward those trespassing on his land, but also to those in his court.

"I don't know who that is," I replied, deciding it would be safer for everyone if I denied knowing Serafina.

"Are you sure?" Meriel pressed.

My lip curled, anger flaring. "Yes."

"Tristan, talk to me." Meriel's voice invaded my mind. I shuddered.

"Serafina is not in Prince Tanyth's court," I replied aloud.

"Tristan! She is your mate," Meriel said.

I gasped, wondering how she was able to tell that Serafina was my mate when the bond hadn't even finished forming. "How do you know that?" Prince Almar watched our exchange silently.

Meriel spoke aloud. "When the bond is exceptionally strong, it can be felt by others."

I growled. "*He* could know." I started to turn away. I didn't have time to waste with Commander Meriel; I needed to get back to Serafina. I had been an idiot to leave her alone or to believe that we could keep what was between us hidden from the prince. I paused. They had come here looking for Serafina; I could at least do them the courtesy of warning them. "You must leave immediately. I was sent to investigate the disturbance and eliminate it if necessary. If you linger I cannot guarantee your safety," I said, returning to words that I knew well—a warning to trespassers.

"Is that a threat?" demanded Prince Almar.

I shrugged. "Take it as you will. You seem knowledgeable about Prince Tanyth. If you feel comfortable experimenting, then be my guest and stay longer." Without giving them time to say anything else I headed back in the direction I came from, melting into the trees. Before I was out of earshot, I heard Prince Almar start talking. The distance muted some of their words, but most were clear enough.

"We need to leave," said Prince Almar.

"Prince Tanyth has her, I'm sure of it," Meriel said.

"Have you lost your mind? Tristan said he doesn't know the name," Prince Almar demanded.

"Yes, he did say that, and did you see how he reacted when I said I could feel the mate bond on him? Honestly, I was surprised Prince Tanyth sent Tristan. I had heard rumors Tristan was in the court, but as you know, no one ever comes out alive. Which makes it impossible to gather information," Meriel replied.

I had lingered too long already; I needed to get back as fast as I could. While I ran, the thought nagging me was that Commander Meriel was a seer; there had to be a reason why she was interested in Serafina, and why it would matter if she could feel a mating bond on me. *Are they connected?*

My thoughts drifted to *Bedtime Tails*, supposedly based on Fae prophecies, but no one I knew had ever seen a prophecy come true. *But the prince is interested in preventing the lost Fae queen prophecy from happening and also believes in the one about the three artifacts.* I stumbled over a rock and almost didn't get my feet under me in time. I shrugged it off and kept going. *What if the stories are real?* I visualized the book in my hands and recalled the lost Fae queen story:

When tension rises and war with the humans has come, the
lost Fae queen will return.
First, she will prove her battle prowess.
Look closely or you might be blinded, for when the Fae queen
returns, not all will know her, yet everyone will follow her.

Be warned, the Fae queen must stay pure until the Great Cat
finds her and their souls unite.
With their souls bound, the heir will be found.
The Fae queen's magic will return, and together they will
defend the Fae from the end of time.
Time is of the essence, or the Fae will fall to the darkness.

I took a deep breath, running the words over in my mind. *If I am the Great Cat and my mate is Serafina, then it* could *be possible that Serafina is the lost Fae queen.* I could feel my hands starting to shake at the enormity of this. I ran harder than I had ever run before. *I need to get to her before it's too late.* As I took a deep breath, another thought reared its head. *What can I do to save her? To save us? I am bound by a blood contract and she is a prisoner.* I halted abruptly, taking deep breaths. Returning without a plan, no matter how fast I made it back, was not going to help gain freedom for anyone.

I closed my eyes and shifted, then scoured the forest with my mind for Commander Meriel. *"Serafina is at Dorcha Palace,"* I said into her mind, hoping I hadn't traveled too far for her to hear me.

"I see," came the tart reply.

"I need your help. Serafina is supposed to marry Prince Tanyth tomorrow."

Commander Meriel didn't reply right away. I had to assume she was conferring with Prince Almar. *"Prince Almar will ask for an audience and then I can help you escape."*

I frowned. *"If you were wanting to negotiate for a magical object it might work, but I doubt he would agree otherwise. Unless you already received an invitation to the wedding?"*

Meriel's reply was quick. *"As ruler of a court, if Prince Tanyth is following protocol, then Prince Almar should have and is permitted one guest. The perfect excuse to be in Dorcha Palace."*

I wasn't sure it was the best plan, but it was all we had time to come up with. *"Don't be late,"* I replied and then took off at a dead run. *Maybe it will work.*

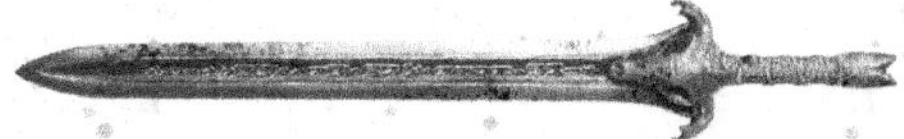

Upon my return to Dorcha Palace I caught wind of rumors about the wedding preparations. Who possible guests were and what the decorations would be. I wanted to find Serafina but knew I couldn't go straight to her room without raising suspicions.

Bane caught me in the hallway before I reached my room. "There is a pre-wedding party tonight. Since you've returned, Prince Tanyth is ordering you to attend."

"Thank you for letting me know," I replied. Bane gave me a curt nod and departed.

I took my time cleaning up and getting dressed. I didn't want to give the prince any indication something was amiss.

I peered in the mirror. I wore black silk pants and a matching open black silk jacket. My dark gray hair fell loosely down to my bare chest, hiding the well-muscled torso. My skin was paler than it should have been; the years I had spent at Embergate it had been dark brownish gray, but here, with so much time underground, it was pasty with a grayish tinge. *Unhealthy.* Yet everything else about me was the epitome of a Fae male in his prime. My eyes were deep blue. I was grateful I hadn't inherited my father's eyes, which changed with his mood. It would have made it far more challenging to have a place in the Court of Dusk if my eyes were able to give away my true feelings.

Satisfied with my appearance, I headed to the party. *Be smart,* I ordered myself. Shoulders back, head held high, I entered the throne room. A quick glance at the throne confirmed the prince was not there. I wasn't sure if that was because he hadn't arrived yet or was mingling. There was no obvious antler crown walking around.

Snagging a glass of wine off the buffet table, I wandered deeper into the crowd of guests, making note of who was there. I caught a flash of red hair and blinked in surprise when I saw Serafina's friend Fiera being escorted by Bane. *What is Bane up to?* I shook my head—I could not get distracted by Bane.

A tugging feeling at my core had me following a winding path till I arrived at a couch.

Serafina was lying on a couch and looked tired. "Hey," I said quietly.

She glanced up at me, her eyes barely flickering in recognition, before she stared at the column behind me. "Go away."

I clenched my fist, nails biting into my palm. "I can't do that."

"So, you suddenly care?" she growled, venom in her voice.

"I never stopped," I said softly. I sat next to her on the couch; as my arm brushed hers, sparks erupted within me. I sucked a breath in through my teeth as need wound through my body.

Serafina slid her hand onto my leg. I wanted to put her hand on my cock, but there were too many witnesses. *My leg will have to do for now.* I racked my mind for a way to get us both out of here without it being in chains. Her fingers trailed up my thigh and my breathing hitched. I set my hand on hers to prevent her from going any further. "Not here," I whispered.

An idea occurred to me. I stood up. "I'll be right back." I quickly snatched two glasses of wine from the table and returned. "Please drink this." I handed her the wine, and she took three sips before setting it down. The awkward silence grew between us.

Precisely three minutes after I had offered her the wine, she gave me a look of terror and then leaned over and started puking. Everyone nearby scattered. I moved so I was behind her and held her hair out of her face while she braced her hands on her thighs and kept throwing up.

When she finally stopped, she was gasping.

"Do you think you can stand up?" I asked.

She nodded, seeming afraid to speak. Ignoring the puke on her and the floor, I wrapped my arm around her shoulder, tucking her close, and led her out of the throne room, toward her room.

When we got inside, I shut the door behind me. I wanted to touch her, needed that connection like the air I breathed, but I had no idea what had happened while I was gone. I didn't want to push Serafina if she didn't feel the same way.

Serafina took a step toward me and reached out with her hand, then threw up, splattering me from head to toe in puke. I wiped my hand over my eyes before opening them and wrinkled my nose. It smelled awful.

"Sorry," she mumbled, before bending over and heaving again.

I gently lifted her hair out of the way even though it was already filthy. When she stopped and stood up, she gave me a half smile and wiped the back of her hand along her mouth. "Not exactly how I was hoping our reunion would go."

I raised my eyebrow. "Will you tell me what you were hoping for?"

In one stride she was in my arms, clinging for dear life. I wrapped my arms around her and tipped my head down, lightly brushing her lips with mine.

"You smell," she said, wrinkling her nose and peering up at me.

I chuckled. "Only because you puked on me. I think a bath is in order."

"Are you going to stay?" Her voice was a little shaky. I wasn't sure if it was from being sick or something else. "I am not allowed to be alone with any males."

Her comment led me to believe she was afraid; she wasn't alone in her fear of discovery. But the bond was strung tight between us and I wasn't sure I could walk away again. "Until you're in bed, yes," I replied. I made the mistake of glancing at the bed and was met with a vision of her riding my cock hard.

I blinked and bit my tongue trying to focus on the first task—getting clean.

Instead of waiting for her response, I briskly walked over to the tub and turned the water on to hot and filled it. I used my magic to speed up the water, so it was only a few moments before the tub was ready. I glanced over at Serafina and saw her staring at me, trying not to smile.

"What?" I asked.

"You're covered in puke from head to toe, and…" She burst out laughing as a piece rolled off my head and hit me square in the nose.

I rolled my eyes. "You don't look much better."

Our eyes met and her lips parted slightly, I took a half step forward, and she threw up all over me. I began cursing. I must have given her the wrong amount of the drug that would induce vomiting, not calculating for her being a half-blood.

"You should get in the bath. It will help," I said as I wiped chunks of puke off my chest.

The sink ran and I presumed she was rinsing out her mouth, then I heard a splash and glanced up. She had discarded her dress and climbed into the tub. I glanced down at my jacket and pants; I desperately wanted a bath too. But now Serafina was in the bath. *I could leave; I should leave. What if we're caught?*

The mate bond continued to tug on me. I wanted to get in the tub, but caution was winning. I tugged the jacket off and Serafina's eyes caught mine. "You need a bath too," she said and crooked her finger at me.

My eyebrows shot straight up. *She's inviting me into her tub? Maybe the bond is doing the same thing to her too.*

"Don't be shy," she said and motioned again for me to come.

I frowned; this was not a smart thing to do. For so many reasons. But she was genuinely asking me to come join her. It wasn't a calculated request or an order. *I should refuse.* Yet I found my feet walking closer to the tub.

"Very well, I will join you," I finally said as my legs hit the edge of the tub. I closed my eyes and let my magic flow through the room. If I was going to throw caution to the wind, I could at least take some precautions. The magic I was releasing would mask the real sounds we were making and replace them with sounds of Serafina occasionally puking. I also added a lock to the door, so that someone could not unlock it, even with a key, and surprise us. I was not intending to make tonight a repeat of being stabbed with Dragonfang.

Serafina seemed oblivious to the fact that I had done magic. I slid my pants off and climbed into the tub, pieces of puke sliding off and floating around the water. I scooped them up with my hand and flung them out of the tub, causing Serafina to giggle.

"What?" I asked.

"You just flung those onto the floor. Someone will step on them," she said and giggled.

I shrugged. "Someone will clean the floor."

I closed my eyes, to block her out more than anything. The tub could have easily fit another Fae, so it wasn't that she was touching me, simply that she was there, and naked. No matter how badly I wanted her, I did not want to force anything. I would wait, no matter how long it took until she was ready. As soon as I stepped into the tub, I had become instantly aware of her, in a way I'd never been aware of another female. I reached out with my mind, brushing against hers, but there was nothing. She truly had no magic—even though I could feel the bond between us, I could not touch her mind. *Maybe it needs to finish forming for that to happen.*

I felt her movements in the water before she touched me. She started on my leg, her fingers featherlight, as she explored the hard muscles of my lower and upper leg. It took me a moment to realize it was curiosity driving her. Her light touch sent hot desire right through my core. I bit my tongue hard to stifle the moan as my cock hardened to the point it was painful.

"What's wrong?" Serafina asked innocently.

I opened my eyes, meeting hers, and for once was unsure of how to respond. *If I'm honest, will I scare her away?* I wondered, knowing if she only looked down or moved her hand slightly, she would know without me saying anything.

"Are you feeling better?" I asked, deciding distracting myself would be better.

Serafina gave me a wan smile. "Yes. I don't think there's anything left in my stomach." She kept her eyes on mine but shifted her body so that she was straddling my lower legs, the inside of her thighs grazing the top of mine. I offered her a slight smile, willing my body to cooperate and not ruin things between us. She ran her hand over my chest, exploring the defined muscles. I held my breath, but her hand never went quite low enough.

"Are you okay?" she asked, giving me a worried frown.

"Mmmhmmm," I mumbled. I don't think she believed me.

Her eyes dropped and her gaze went straight down. "Oh!" she gasped and rocked back, peering at my cock, her hand raised as though she might touch me. *Please touch me*, I prayed. Instead, her hand was frozen midair.

"Turn around," I said softly.

"What?" she asked, confused.

"Let me help you wash your hair," I replied and grabbed one of the jars with soap, pouring some in my hand.

Her eyes flicked to my face and then back down to my cock, before she scooted off of me and turned around. I stretched my legs along her sides and began massaging her scalp with my fingers, working the soap in. A low moan escaped from her and I almost jabbed her in the back with my cock as my body reacted. I closed my eyes to regain control and continued massaging her head, working my way down to her neck and shoulders. Her muscles began loosening under my ministrations.

I took a shallow bowl and filled it with water, rinsing her hair out. When the soap was gone, I continued my massage, except this time I lowered my mouth to her shoulder, trailing light kisses.

A whimper escaped her lips. "I need you," she whispered, tilting her head so she could see me.

"You have me," I said softly, kissing her velvet lips. They parted and allowed my tongue entrance, welcoming me. I could feel the magic of the mating bond tightening around us. When she paused for a breath, her eyes were dark with desire. "I *need* you, Tristan, like a fish needs water to survive."

I nipped her lips. "I need you too. You are part of me, Serafina." I took her hand and placed it on my heart. She turned so she was facing me. With her left hand on my heart, she let her right settle lightly on my cock, hesitant. I bit back a groan as her feather touch almost sent me over the edge.

"Let me pleasure you like you did for me," she said sincerely.

I shook my head. "Thank you, my love, for that, but right now, what I want the most is to bury my cock inside of your folds as far as I can go. If you want me to."

Serafina nodded. "Yes." I swept her into my arms and used my magic to dry us off, then I carried her to the bed. I set her down on the bed and nudged her legs open with my knee before settling between her legs.

I dipped down and caught her mouth with mine before trailing kisses down her neck to her breasts. I ran my tongue around one nipple, then the other, and then grazed them with my teeth. She tensed beneath me. I kissed her again and as I thrust my tongue in her mouth, I did the same with my fingers into her folds. "You're so wet for me, Sera," I said softly against her lips.

I withdrew my fingers and wrapped them around my cock, slowly guiding myself in, fighting the urge to go fast. I wanted her to have time to adjust to my thickness. As I sank my full length into her, she whimpered. I immediately stopped and pulled out. "Am I hurting you?"

Serafina nipped my lip with her teeth. "Put it back!" she hissed. I chuckled and obliged the demand.

Forty-Two

SERAFINA

The bed was soft beneath my back as Tristan slid his cock inside of me. My toes curled as pleasure rolled through me, and he reached over and flicked my nipple with his fingers. The energy between us was more intense than it had ever been before. True to his word, Tristan was gentle. The pressure was strange to me, but the pleasure was so intense, I didn't mind. I just wanted more. "More," I mumbled, earning me a nip from Tristan.

"Greedy," he said. Then sped up his thrusts. It felt like he might drive himself all the way through me, he was so huge. But he didn't; somehow we fit together like we had been made for each other. *Maybe we have if we're mates*, I thought.

One more thrust and pleasure exploded through me. I covered my mouth with my hands to stifle my scream. "Serafina," Tristan moaned as he went with me. Then, he gently lowered himself over me, though I was certain he was still bearing most of his own weight.

"*Tristan*," I said, though strangely I couldn't hear the words with my ears.

"*Serafina,*" he replied. Then I realized we were talking mind-to-mind. He pushed up, so we were gazing at each other. "Do you feel it?"

I nodded. "You mean the bond?"

"Yes," he replied. I realized I could feel more than I had. Desire, love, and fear wound through me. It took a moment to realize it was Tristan's emotions I was feeling and not my own. Until then I had forgotten we had a reason to be afraid. *Tanyth.* I squirmed underneath Tristan and he rolled over, freeing me.

"What have we done?" I whispered, horror filling me.

Tristan kissed my forehead. "Only what had already been started. The bond was forming before he ever proposed to you."

"But I'm going to be his wife!" I hissed, eyes wide as I realized what that meant and the implications of what Tristan and I had just done.

"Hush," he said and pulled me to his chest, running his hands through my hair. "*Commander Meriel has a plan,*" he told me mind-to-mind.

He held a finger to my lips when I started to speak. "*She is coming as a wedding guest.*"

I nodded in understanding. *A rescue is planned. I can survive for another day.*

"I must go," Tristan said sadly. He caressed my cheek and sat up. "Everyone believes you're sick. Let's keep it that way."

He stood up and called in a fresh set of clothes for himself, then another for me. It was a tunic and pants, the same as what I had been wearing for training. Suitable clothes if I was still feeling unwell. He focused on the bed and the sheets remade themselves, as though nothing had happened.

"I will see you soon," Tristan said.

"I love you," I replied, eyes misting. *He has to go; we cannot win our freedom if he doesn't leave.*

"I love you," he said and then walked to the door. The magic that had been around the room disappeared, then he opened the door. Over his shoulder I could see Prince Tanyth was in the hallway, hand raised to knock. Tristan glanced back into the room, a disgusted look on his face. "She keeps throwing up. I've done what I can and tried to get her to clean up, but it's a war zone in there."

I covered my mouth to stifle my laughter; the last thing I needed was for the prince to hear me and discover what had *really* happened.

Prince Tanyth spoke. "Call for the healer to attend to her." The door shut, and I was alone.

Not for long. The Fae healer showed up within minutes of Tristan's departure.

The Fae healer checked me over in silence. "How do you feel now?"

I shrugged. "I feel fine. I haven't puked since I got into the bathtub."

"Likely too much drink for your human self," the healer declared.

I kept myself from reacting to his statement. I was half-Fae, but clearly the healer didn't feel like acknowledging that. "Yes, that's what I thought."

"Get a good night of rest and you shall be fine," the healer ordered, then departed.

Once my door shut, I breathed a sigh of relief and then threw myself on the bed. The party had been a strange one. Tanyth had been volatile tonight, but thankfully had allowed me to find my own entertainment. Then Tristan had appeared, and I'd gotten sick, and then we'd...I blushed deeply. *Had sex.* I forced myself to say the words in my mind.

For as long as I could remember, I wanted to wait to have sex till I was married, but we hadn't waited. *If I had, it would have been with Prince Tanyth not Tristan.* I didn't find myself at odds with my decision, but I had never thought a Fae mating bond was something I would experience. The way Fiera and Ghilanna had spoken about them, it was as good as being married. Though Fae still went through the formalities of a wedding even if the bond happened before the wedding.

I yawned, then climbed into bed and pulled the covers up. The healer was right—sleep was exactly what I needed.

I was standing in the forest facing a steaming pool. A hot spring? I took my time picking my way around rocks and tree roots before my feet touched the water. It was deliciously hot. I waded in and let myself under the water.

When I returned to the surface, Tristan was there, his feet touching the edge of the pool. I reached my hand out to him, and he came toward me, taking my hand in his. His other hand wrapped around my back, pulling our bodies close. I leaned my head on his chest and took a deep breath. His fingers began gently combing my hair, then moved to rubbing my earlobe. A soft moan escaped from my lips, and he kissed me then. I felt the barest tingle of something, and then it was gone. He moved his hips against mine and I nipped at his lips, wanting more.

Using his knee, he nudged my legs open slightly and then guided himself inside of me. My pleasure built quickly. He picked me up, wrapping my legs around his waist, changing the angle of his cock and driving even deeper than before into me. One thrust and I was spasming as the orgasm blasted through me. I leaned against his arms and was surprised when the pressure inside of me was building again. Tristan nuzzled my neck and bit me lightly, sending us both spiraling in pleasure so intense it felt like I was going to black out. As I draped myself over his shoulders, I heard a sound in the forest. I sleepily looked up and then the feeling of Tristan changed. I glanced down and saw I was holding a rotting corpse. I started to scream.

I woke up screaming. I was completely drenched in sweat; the sheets were soaked. I thrashed, trying to escape from the wet sheets and the feeling of a corpse touching me.

My door burst open and Fallon came inside, sword raised. Fae light lit up the room. I fell to the floor, free of the sheets, gasping.

"Where is the intruder!" shouted Fallon.

I got myself into a kneeling position, hands braced on my thighs, and peered up at him. "There is no intruder. It was a nightmare."

Fallon explored the entire suite, yanking open cabinets and thrusting his sword inside. Eventually he seemed to be satisfied. I was telling the truth; it was a bad dream. "Are you okay now? Or should I call for someone to stay with you the rest of the night?"

I shook my head. I was afraid that if he called for *someone* it would be Tanyth. When who I really wanted was Tristan.

Fallon nodded and bowed, then left, taking the Fae light with him. My room was once again shrouded in darkness. I reached over and tapped the base of the lamp on the nightstand, illuminating the room with a soft glow.

I found myself wondering if it was a coincidence that Tanyth had threatened both Fiera and Tristan, then I took a bath with Tristan, followed by dreaming of having sex with him in a hot spring and him turning into a corpse. *What does it mean, though?* Walking to the dresser, I found a fresh long tunic and exchanged my damp sweaty one for the clean, dry one.

I rubbed my forehead, trying to make sense of the dream. *We're bonded, so it must be a dream of my fear that he will die.* A fear that I knew was grounded in facts.

And what of the wedding? What if the rescue doesn't work out and I become Prince Tanyth's wife? Despair filled me, and though I told myself I needed to have hope, I kept replaying images of Tanyth's cruelty. The first fight, where he had forced me into the arena without armor or a weapon. Exhaustion and fear from each encounter I had with him, not knowing what he would punish me with next. And then he captured Fiera. What would happen to my friend if I was rescued, and she was still here? What about when I'm his wife? Would Fiera ever be safe, or would she always be held to guarantee my cooperation?

A gasp escaped my lips. *Would he do the same thing with Tristan?* I couldn't decide what would be worse—the thought of living without Tristan if he were to die, or having him here in the palace, but out of reach.

I choked back a sob and curled into a tight ball, consumed by hopelessness and wishing it was all over.

The bed shifted, and a weight settled behind me. Warm arms wrapped around me, pulling me close as Tristan soothed me through the bond. *"I'm here, always."* I snuggled against him, a feeling of safety and love cocooning me. I fell asleep, and for the first time since I arrived at Dorcha Palace, I slept without dreams.

Forty-Three

TRISTAN

Dawn approached and fear clung to me as I arrived back in my suite. I hoped Serafina would forgive me when she woke up in bed alone, but the entire time I had held her I had been terrified that Prince Tanyth would discover us.

I was confident that the mating bond was now fully in place. We could talk mind-to-mind and feel each other's emotions, which was what had sent me running for her when I had felt her overwhelming despair. Thankfully she had been in bed and not trying to take her life, but I had never felt that much loss coming from one person before.

I was tired but afraid if I let myself sleep now I would miss whatever was going to happen today. Wedding day. I snarled and my fangs began to elongate. *It should be my wedding day to Serafina, not Prince Tanyth's. But the future can still change. Commander Meriel is coming.* It would do us no good if I allowed myself to give up hope.

Ready for my morning practice session with the silver squad, I was lost in my thoughts about what drills we would run today, and wondering what kind of preparations a bride went through. As I walked out of my suite. I plowed right into Serafina, knocking her into Callyn. I had to jump sideways to keep from falling on top of them.

"Watch it!" growled Callyn.

Serafina caught my eye for a second and blushed deeply before ducking her head and accepting Callyn's hand up.

I schooled myself into cold aloofness and went in the opposite direction. It was the longer route to the training room, but it would ensure that I didn't run into Serafina again. If she was going to blush like that every time, I laid eyes on her, then we would quickly have a major problem on our hands. The best solution was to steer clear of her as long as possible.

Forty-Four

SERAFINA

I am a fool, I repeated over and over to myself as Callyn guided me somewhere. I hadn't been paying attention when she told me what our destination was. Our path led us through hallways that I swear were heading deeper down into the ground. She halted at a large metal door and opened it with a set of keys. When we were inside, she tugged it shut and I heard the lock click into place.

"Today, you are feeding the beasts that fight in the arena," Callyn explained.

What an odd task for my wedding day, I thought and wrinkled my nose as the stench in this corridor crashed into me. It smelled like rotting meat.

There was a small room that was quite cold. Inside was a table with a couple of knives and some huge hanging slabs of meat. "You will be cutting the meat that is necessary for each animal and then feeding them. I will remain here to make sure you don't do anything stupid with knives. However, if you accidentally lose a limb while feeding, then that is your problem, not mine."

I pinched my lips together. "Can I cut any piece of meat or does each beast have a preference?"

Callyn rattled off a list of beasts and meat preferences. I crossed my fingers, hoping I wasn't expected to remember the list with one recital. I focused instead on the first four beasts and their meat preferences and set to work with the knives. There was a line of metal pails that I presumed were for meat. As I made my cuts, I deposited each order into a bucket. When I had the first four done, I turned to look at Callyn. "Can I feed the first four?"

She nodded. "As you wish."

I picked up the four buckets and followed her down the hallway. I could hear shrieks, growls, and other animal sounds. When the first four were fed we repeated the process.

I found my rhythm cutting the preferred meats for each beast, noting that like Fae and humans, even individuals in the same species had personal preferences—one tiger liked elk hearts and pig heads, while the others preferred deer haunches.

Tristan invaded my thoughts. The mating bond that had formed between us. His hands as they massaged my scalp, his arms as they wrapped around me in comfort, and the feel of him inside of me. I felt my desire stirring and an unbidden image of Tristan on the bed with me straddling him soaked my underwear.

Tristan's voice drifted to me. *"You're making it challenging to focus on training."* It felt muffled.

I lifted my arm to brush a piece of hair out of my eyes and to hide my smirk from Callyn. As I continued slicing up the meat, I conjured an image of him lying on the bed and my hand stroking his cock. The knife slipped as I swore I felt his fingers bury themselves in me. I moved my fingers out of the way barely in time to avoid cutting through them. Searing pain shot through my thumb and I looked down, realizing I hadn't been quite fast enough. Blood was streaming out of a large gash on my thumb.

"You should pay attention to what you're doing," Callyn said sagely from her chair by the door.

I frowned. "Do you have anything I can bandage this with?"

Callyn tossed a rag to me; I narrowly caught it before it hit the slab of meat. I wiped my hands on my pants and then tore strips from the rag and wrapped my thumb tight enough to stop the bleeding.

"Are you okay?" came Tristan's worried voice.

"Fine. You're right, this is dangerous. I have a knife," I said and then closed my mind to him and sawed through an elk carcass, ignoring the ache that was spreading through my arms.

I was butchering meat for hours and my whole body was sore from the unfamiliar work required of today's task. We didn't stop for lunch or a water or bathroom break. Callyn hadn't offered, and I chose to not ask. When we fed the last beast on the list, Callyn locked the door to the room with the meat and the knives and then we headed back up the sloped hallway.

I glanced down at myself and shuddered in revulsion. I was covered in blood, bits of guts, fat, and other things. My hair felt sticky too. "I hope you will let me bathe. When is the wedding anyhow?"

Callyn chuckled. "Of course. Bath and then food. We have time. The wedding is late." The response didn't answer my question other than informing me we did not need to rush.

When I was clean, fed, and dressed and covered in a black silk robe, Callyn escorted me toward the throne room, but instead of going straight to the double doors, we turned left and paused in front of an open door on the left side of this narrower hallway. "This is where I leave you," Callyn said, and then gave me a curt nod and retreated down the hallway.

I entered the room and discovered it was some sort of library. *An odd place to get ready for a wedding,* I mused. As I walked farther inside, I saw a statue like the previous ones that had displayed other gowns I had worn. This one had a white dress. I bent over, inspecting the dress. The fabric was heavy, weighed down by embroidery and beading. *And diamonds*, I realized. A strange use of a precious gem, I thought, but what did I know about Fae weddings? I had never attended one.

Verrona appeared shortly after Callyn left and helped me to dress.

"Eat. Callyn will come for you when it is time," Verrona announced and then departed.

I walked over to the table and peered at the food, but after spending most of the day cutting up raw meat, and the wedding binding me to Prince Tanyth rapidly approaching, I had no appetite.

A scratching sound had me reaching for a dagger I did not have. I curled my fists and faced the bookcase where the sound was coming from. The bookcase began to open. I bit my lip and held my fists steady. A head of dark gray hair emerged first, and then unfolded to reveal Tristan. I exhaled in relief.

Forty-Five

TRISTAN

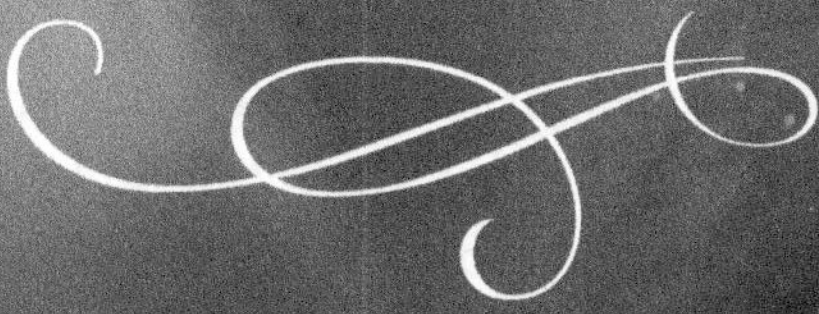

I left the bookcase door slightly ajar and stared openly at Serafina. Words failed me. Her russet hair had been braided into a crown with the rest curled, and small pearls were threaded on a nearly invisible wire through her locks. Her shoulders were bare, with the neckline drawing the eye toward her ample breasts. Appreciation for her breasts was quickly replaced by anger that anyone but me would be enjoying the view. The sweeping skirt had in my opinion far too much fabric to wrestle with.

Serafina closed the gap between us and kissed me. I rocked back on my heel, not expecting her to make the first move first. I pulled her close. *"I love you,"* I said to her mind as we kissed.

"Claim me," she said. Confusion filled me; I wasn't sure what she was talking about.

Her hand slid down my pants and cupped my cock. *"Claim me,"* she repeated, and I understood. I fumbled with the waist of her dress and she shook her head, then gathered the folds of the dress in her hands and pulled it up.

I rolled my eyes. Of course it had to be a complicated dress. *"Are you sure?"*

Serafina nodded. I pulled her to me, wishing I could get rid of the dress, but worried if I made it vanish with magic I would never get it back on her properly and the prince would know.

I kissed her, desperate. Neither one of us knew that the rescue would work, and at the back of my mind there was a flicker of doubt. This really could be the last time I held her in my arms. One hand I kept on her waist and the other I ran up her thigh, delighting in her reaction, as I lightly ran my thumb over her clit. I plunged two fingers into her, swirling and teasing, and she moaned against my lips. I slowly lowered myself to my knees in front of her.

The moment my knees hit the floor I heard something outside and froze. Footsteps passed by the door and kept going. I let out a shaky breath. *Too close.* I stood up and took her hand in mine, leading her to the table. With her dress I thought this might be the best option. I lifted her up onto it, and as she moved her dress out of the way and spread her legs, seeing her wet folds threatened to undo me.

I swiftly undid the ties on my pants and freed my cock, then stepped between her legs. My cock bumped the apex of her thighs and a moan escaped me as the tip of my cock became slick with her. Serafina put her hands on my hips and tugged. I thrust into her. Deeper than I had intended, but she didn't protest.

I started slow, but her nails dug harder into me and I took the hint and increased my speed. I was surprised when she leaned back on the table, tilting her hips, allowing me to plunge further than before. The effect was electrifying as she sent me deeper and deeper. I felt her folds tightening and her heartbeat sped up. I didn't stop as the pressure built in both of us. I quickened my strokes, relishing how well our bodies fit together. One more thrust and I sent her over the edge, following immediately in her wake. Kissing my mate as our bodies spasmed together, the bond thrumming between us.

"I love you," I said.

"I love you," she whispered as the doors burst open..

A rough hand grabbed me and a snarl ripped from my throat. I backed away from Serafina, not wanting to hurt her, and threw an elbow to the Fae behind me. He let out a loud *oof* but refused to let go.

I had a split second to make the right decision. Praying Serafina would not panic, I shifted into snow leopard and let out a loud snarl that reverberated throughout the whole building, not just the room.

"It's about time," said Prince Tanyth from the doorway. He launched himself at me, sword flashing. *He knew!*

"*Run!*" I called through the bond.

I dashed, striking for his legs with my claws. I connected, but not as deeply as I had intended. Once I had been just as deadly as a snow leopard as I was in my Fae form, but it had been years, and I was regretting my choice to shift. Even though I knew I was no match for Prince Tanyth as a weaponless Fae.

I felt the sword slice through my hind leg. I roared and lunged toward Tanyth, but my leg gave out, unable to bear my weight. For the first time in many years, I found myself praying. Praying that Serafina would get herself out before Prince Tanyth got his hands on her.

I hobbled toward Tanyth on three legs, hoping I could get close enough to do some damage with my claws. But the prince kept dancing out of the way, laughing at me. "Not so tough now, are you, Tristan?"

I lunged, my jaws wide, and clamped on Tanyth's leg. I snapped my jaws together and gave a satisfied growl as I felt his bone shatter.

I heard a scream and then there was a brief moment of pain, and everything went black.

Forty-Six

SERAFINA

It only takes a moment to change your life, I thought as Bane dragged me down the hallway. I fought every step of the way, punching, biting, kicking, but no matter how many times I connected, Bane refused to let go. *A Fae on a mission.*

Minutes ago, I was confident that Tristan's rescue plan would work. How wrong I had been. A shudder went through me as I replayed Tristan biting the prince, and then a silver collar, like the one on the leon shapeshifter, had clamped around the snow leopard's neck.

Bane shoved me into a room. I fell onto my hands and knees and hit the hard stone floor. I pulled my legs tight to my chest and rocked back and forth. Bane's heavy breathing was interrupted only by the dripping of water, like a faucet had been left on.

"You stupid bitch. I don't know what you did to Tristan to corrupt him, but ever since you showed up he hasn't been the same," Bane snarled furiously.

I stared at the wall, refusing to meet his gaze.

"You are getting married—today," he said. My eyes widened and my stomach clenched. "Did you really think the prince would cancel the wedding after he found Tristan fucking you?"

Keeping my eyes on the wall, I bit my cheek, drawing blood. Nothing I said would help my situation. "*Tristan!*" I called through the bond. I could still feel him in my mind, though he was unconscious and unresponsive to my call.

Bane stood for a long time before the healer came. I was surprised Prince Tanyth had sent for the healer, because I wasn't hurt. Lifting my head slightly, I saw the healer had a steaming pot of what appeared to be tea in his hands. "Leave," ordered the healer. Bane slammed the door shut behind him. The whole room shook from how hard he shut the door.

"Now, Serafina, come here and I will get you cleaned up for your wedding." The healer waved his hand and yellow magic flowed from his fingers. A set of two chairs and a small table appeared.

I reluctantly stood and walked over to the chair closest to me. I balanced on the edge.

"Drink this," the healer said and handed me a cup of tea.

Cringing at the horrible smell, I set the cup down on the table. "No thanks."

The healer tsked. "It will help you feel better. Drink. That's an order."

Anger washed over me. *I don't want his tea to feel better, I want to know where my mate is.* I took the cup and with a flick of my wrist tossed its contents in the healer's face.

Yellow magic flowed around me, pinning my arms to my sides. Try as I might, I could not move. The healer refilled the cup and floated it over to me. The cup pressed on my closed mouth, but I refused to obey the silent command.

"As you wish," the healer said coldly. Suddenly, my nose felt as though someone was pinching it tightly shut. Unprepared, I had not taken a deep breath, and the little air I had in my lungs was gone. I gasped and my lips parted, sucking in air. The healer took advantage, and using his magic, the teacup poured the nasty tea into my mouth. I gagged as the tea went down but could not make my body obey and throw up. It was the most disgusting tea I had ever had; it tasted like pee. *There's no way something this bad is going to help me.*

I closed my eyes and let my chin fall on my chest. There was a weird buzzing sensation over my skin and then it was gone.

A teal hand on my arm brought me back to my senses. Everything felt slower than normal. I wanted to jerk my arm back away from the prince, but it wasn't moving nearly as fast as I wanted. "What do you want?" I croaked, my throat dry.

"You, my love," Prince Tanyth said, and caressed my cheek with his hand. I felt myself leaning into it. *No! No!* my mind screamed, but I couldn't stop the action. He dipped his head down and captured my lips with his. When he thrust his tongue in my mouth, I bit down, and coppery blood flooded my mouth. His grip on my face was strong, preventing me from pulling away. As he kept me in place, I kissed him back, leaning into it even.

Eventually Prince Tanyth withdrew his mouth from mine and glanced over at the healer, whom I had forgotten was in the room. "The tea alone is not enough. Bring me the pot so I can enhance it. The last thing I need is for her to spoil my plans."

The healer brought the teapot over to the prince and Tanyth set his hand on it. Teal magic, so dark it was almost black, spilled out of his hand and surrounded the pot. I stared at him, not comprehending what he was doing with his magic but wishing he would kiss me again. *Or even better, if Tristan kissed me.* Tears welled in my eyes as the collar going around Tristan's neck flashed through my thoughts. "Where is Tristan?" I demanded.

Prince Tanyth ignored my question, pouring a fresh cup of tea and holding it to my lips. "Drink and I will answer your questions."

Obediently I parted my lips and let him pour the tea down my throat. I swallowed, my nose wrinkled in distaste. "That tea is awful."

He set the cup down on the table and glanced at me. "I'll be back shortly." I nodded and sat down in the chair. *Where is Tristan?* I wondered. *Wait, who is Tristan?* My vision was clouding. I closed my eyes, not wanting to get dizzy.

The creak of the hinge had me opening my eyes as a blond-haired Fae entered the room. He seemed familiar; I searched my mind for his name. "Fallon," I said with a smile.

He frowned at me and tugged someone out from behind him. A Fae female with bright red hair; her hands were bound in front of her and she had scrapes on her arms and cheek. "Serafina!" the redhead gasped, and threw herself toward me.

I shot out of the chair, knocking it over, and backed up till I was pressed against the wall. My whole body was shaking. "Stay away from me." *Why would a prisoner behave like we know each other?*

The redhead thankfully stayed back, tears streaming down her face. *Why is she crying?* "It's me, Fiera, your best friend," Fiera said.

I shook my head. "I've never met you before."

Fallon opened his mouth to say something when the door was pushed open the rest of the way and Prince Tanyth strolled in. "Out now. Fallon, I will deal with this transgression later. Bane will make sure Fiera gets back to her cell."

My back pressed into the cold damp stone wall; I kept my eyes on the prince, hoping he would explain why the prisoner had come in here. With a flick of his fingers, the door shut. "Serafina, I am sorry you had unwanted visitors. I don't know what Bane was thinking allowing them to come in and disturb you like that."

I peered around, not wanting to meet his eyes. "Who were they?"

"Don't waste your time worrying about it. I missed you." He closed the distance between us, stopping an arm's length away.

My chest tightened and I stepped forward, throwing my arms around his neck. Tremors ran through me. The prince wrapped his arms around me and began humming. "You're safe. No one will get you."

"Promise?" I mumbled against his shoulder.

He leaned back, studying my face. "I promise you will always be safe with me." The words felt familiar, but who else would have made such a promise to me other than Tanyth?

Prince Tanyth kissed me lightly, and I melted into him. Tendrils of desire spread throughout my body and I deepened the kiss. He ran his hands down my sides and I desperately wished I could get out of this annoying dress. I must have made a noise for he tipped his head back slightly. "Eager, my love?"

I nod fervently. "Yes. I am yours and you are mine."

He nipped my nose. "Nothing pleases me more than to hear those words come from your lips. However, we must wait until after the wedding."

I sighed in disappointment. "But didn't we already have sex?"

The prince's eyes darkened and he took a step back. "Let's get you some more tea, then we can talk about the wedding."

"Okay," I agreed.

The healer came into the room smiling and poured me a fresh cup of tea. Prince Tanyth offered me the cup. "There's a good girl."

I took a sip and smiled. It was delicious. "How good of you to remember my favorite tea blend."

"Of course, my love," he replied. "I have a few more matters to attend to and then we shall head to the wedding."

Wrapping my legs around the unicorn, I relished the black velvety fur touching my skin. My fingers were wound in the silver mane, and we galloped through the vibrant grass field toward a huge green hill. There was a commotion outside, bringing me out of my

334

daydream. Prince Tanyth walked in. He was wearing all white, a stark contrast to his usual dark garb. "Hello, my dearest," he said with a sad smile. "I am sorry to inform you, but the wedding is going to have to be postponed. Your family and I have more to negotiate, and they feel it best if you return to Jade Wilds while the discussions happen."

Staring down at my empty hands, tears trickled down my cheeks. *Postpone our wedding? But I love him.* "I don't want to postpone it. Aren't I allowed a say in the matter?"

Prince Tanyth gently patted my hand. "I am sure your family will take your desires into consideration. But given it would be a marriage uniting two Fae courts, it is not a simple matter."

I swiped at the tears on my face. "Then why did you lead me to believe that we were going to get married tonight?"

"Because King Pharaan's representatives just showed up and I am required to allow enough time for negotiations if the request is made," he replied smoothly.

I ran a finger over my wedding dress. His response confirmed my suspicion that King Pharaan was only interested in using me as a pawn to strengthen his position as king of the Fae. The words he had spoken when we were together in Emerald Valley about wanting me to make my own choice clearly had not been true, otherwise a negotiation would be unnecessary.

I blew out my breath and immediately regretted it as a sharp throbbing began in my forehead. *Hopefully this insane headache will go away as quickly as it showed up.*

"Are you okay?" the healer and Prince Tanyth asked simultaneously.

"No, I have a headache," I replied.

Prince Tanyth poured a cup of tea for me. "The tea will help." I took the cup. A feeling of déjà vu hit me hard, but I couldn't recall ever taking a cup of tea from anyone in this room. I obediently drank and the headache immediately began to subside.

"Thanks, that is better," I said gratefully. "You said someone is here to take me to King Pharaan?"

"Yes, I will take you to them," Prince Tanyth said. He helped me stand and linked his arm through mine. "I'm sure once everything is sorted out you will return soon."

Accepting his response, I let the prince escort me to my awaiting family.

Forty-Seven

TRISTAN

Stretching, I was startled when my paws hit hard metal bars. *Why am I still shifted?* My eyes snapped open and I stood up, whacking my head on the bars above me. I thought about my Fae form and nothing happened. That's when I remembered: Prince Tanyth had put a collar around my neck. The very same type of collar I had used to imprison other shapeshifters for him that made it impossible to shift.

I lay down and rested my head on my paws. My memories of what happened in the library were fuzzy. Since I had never worn one of these collars before I had no way to know if that was from the collar or something the prince had done to me. I remembered making love to Serafina in the library and getting creative due to the wedding dress. The enormous amount of love I felt for her and the strengthening mating bond between us. I paused and hunted within me for the mating bond. It took me a while to find it, because I expected it to be bright and pulsing, as it had been since it had reached full strength. Instead, it was dull. I gave the bond a mental tug. From what I knew about mating bonds, Serafina should be able to feel it. I waited and nothing happened. *It's still there, it's not gone, she must be alive,* I consoled myself. *But why is it so dull?* I didn't know, only that it could not be a good reason.

Snarling, I vividly recalled the feel of crushing Prince Tanyth's leg in my jaws, then the collar being snapped in place. Yet after that nothing, until now.

The rescue Commander Meriel had promised had not been timed well enough because I was in a cage somewhere in Tanyth's palace and Serafina was...*I don't know where.* Heart racing, I considered the possibilities for where she was, terror growing as I realized I could not save her unless I could get free first.

Closing my eyes, hoping it would help settle my emotions, I drifted into a restless doze. The telltale sound of stone grating on stone had me alert instantly. Unwilling to let my visitor know I was alert, I opened one eye the barest of slits. Prince Tanyth walked in with a smug expression.

"How do you like your new accommodations?" Prince Tanyth asked. "Oh, right, you can't answer me. I've been wondering how long it would take you to make the mistake and shift."

I stayed still, refusing to react.

"Serafina is safe, if you're wondering. Or safe enough. I have returned her to her family until we can renegotiate the terms of our wedding." He paused, I assumed to give me a chance to react.

I blinked at him a few times and that was all I allowed myself.

"You will be fighting in the arena shortly. I think it is fitting that your first opponent is Callyn," Prince Tanyth informed me, then left.

I closed my eyes. Serafina had been returned to her family. *Is that why I can't feel her? Because she is simply too far away? Or did he tamper with us?* Then I realized that the prince hadn't specified which family she had returned to—the Fae or the humans.

Forty-Eight

SERAFINA

I woke up with a wicked headache as I looked around, trying to figure out where I was. The last thing I was certain I remembered was Prince Tanyth escorting me down the hallway at Dorcha Palace to my family. Then we went through a star portal and the details became less clear after that.

The tent I was in seemed familiar. Shifting in the bed caused the fur blankets to slide off and expose my arm, which was covered in a white long sleeve. I pushed the blankets farther and saw I was in a long tunic or nightgown. Out of the corner of my eye I saw the desk, the very desk that had been in my tent at Jade Wilds. *Negotiations for my wedding are happening at Jade Wilds?* Uncertainty filled me. My grandfather, King Pharaan, lived in a palace near Emerald Valley, which was two days' ride from here. Jade Wilds was part of the Court of the Moon's territory. *Why would Prince Almar be involved? He's not my family.*

My gaze settled on the desk, which had a mirror with a carved wood frame. My silver hairbrush was sitting in front of the mirror. There was a folded note with my name on it as well. My eyes flicked around the room, identifying other things familiar to me. Confirming this was indeed the tent I had lived in for eleven years at Jade Wilds.

Reaching my arms over my head, I stretched, then stood up. *Lying in bed won't get my questions answered or resolve the head-ache.* I slid the nightgown off and walked over to the full-length mirror, staring at myself. Something caught my eye in the mirror on my collar bone, under my hair. I lifted my hair and saw there was what looked like a bite mark from a large animal. I ran a finger over it and the mark completely vanished. *What the hell?*

I blinked and looked at myself again in the mirror, noting the circles under my eyes and the paleness of my skin, but there were no other strange marks or scars. I moved over to the chest of clean clothes, and as I hovered my hand over the light green tunic, I noticed a slight tremor as a feeling of loss shot through me. Bracing my arms on the chest, I stared at dark gray pants, willing myself to calm down. *I haven't lost anyone and I know exactly where I am. Everything will be better with some food.*

Dressed, I opened the note. It was brief and to the point. Commander Meriel wanted to talk to me over breakfast this morning. Meaning I didn't need to be ready to train right away. I assumed it had to do with the wedding negotiations with Prince Tanyth.

I strode across the camp, relishing the feel of the early morning sun on my face, even though it was already warm and likely to get unbearable later. *Maybe I can get Fiera and Ghilanna to go swimming with me.* Breakfast was always buffet-style to accommodate for different training schedules. The kitchen would refresh the food every hour or so from dawn till lunch time.

I filled a bowl with porridge and selected a biscuit, then sat down. No one else was around. I half expected Ghilanna to meet me here and was eager for her company. Halfway through my bowl of porridge, Commander Meriel came over. She gave me a strange look, then smiled and sat across from me. "How do you feel?"

"I have a terrible headache," I replied and the pounding in my temples increased.

"I might be able to give you something for it," Meriel said. "Ghilanna will be here soon. She was thrilled to hear you are back from Dorcha Palace."

"Where has she been? And what about Fiera?" I asked. I could not remember where my friends had said they were going.

"Ghilanna was visiting the Court of the Moon and deciding if she wanted to take a long-term position there. Fiera is out on a hunt and isn't due back for another week," Commander Meriel said.

Mulling over her response, I took a few more bites of my porridge, wondering why it felt like the answers were not quite right, but I couldn't come up with a good reason the commander would lie to me.

A flicker of magic and a steaming cup of tea appeared on the table. "This will help with the headache." The magic and the tea-cup felt familiar. I shrugged it off, though; this was not the first time the commander had given me a cup of tea.

I gave her a smile of appreciation and took a sip. It had a slightly bitter taste with a large amount of mint. *At least it doesn't taste like pee.* I almost spit it out as I chuckled, wondering where the hell that idea came from. Finally, I managed to squeak out. "Thank you."

Commander Meriel nodded, seemingly oblivious to my actions. "Now, when Ghilanna arrives, I want you to start working on some specialized training. I was thinking it would be beneficial if you work on your stealth techniques."

"Stealth?" I asked.

"Yes. If you wanted to sneak up on someone and apprehend them without causing a scene. Swords are great, but sometimes a small dagger or knocking someone unconscious is more appropriate," Meriel explained.

I twitched my lips in amusement. "You want me to learn how to be a thief?"

Meriel chuckled. "I guess you can look at it that way. Whatever helps you acquire the skills faster."

Forty-Nine

TRISTAN

The prince had lied. My first arena battle was not with Callyn, it was with several of the Fae in the squad I trained with. Whether or not they had been informed I was anything other than a mere snow leopard, I won't ever know. Regret filled me after each kill I made; only the thought of Serafina kept me going. Killing Fae in the arena did not seem to help my standing with the prince either. I was sedated and returned to the cage each night.

I lost track of time. Sometimes they would throw me pieces of meat. Usually it was rotting, but I knew I had to eat it no matter how much it made my stomach hurt. If I didn't keep up my strength, I would never make it out and find Serafina. Part of me wanted to give up. I had found my mate, and then she had been ripped from me before we had had a chance to do anything.

I ran through all our encounters the past weeks and realized how many mistakes I had made. Yet, Sera had still fallen in love with me. I didn't deserve a female as good as Serafina was.

I drifted off into a restless sleep.

I was at Jade Wilds, the training camp of the Court of the Moon. In front of the tent where Prince Tanyth had met Serafina the first time was Commander Meriel and Prince Almar. They were having a heated discussion.

I stepped closer. Neither of them seemed to notice my presence, confirming that it was indeed a dream.

Prince Almar spoke softly. "Something is wrong with her."

Meriel sighed. "I think Prince Tanyth did something. Tristan said it would be a rescue attempt, and yet when we got there for the wedding, Prince Tanyth said he was willing to hand her over."

"You felt the mating bond forming on Tristan. Shouldn't it be on Serafina too?" Prince Almar asked.

"In theory yes, though since she only half-Fae, perhaps it is not as easy to detect on her," Meriel replied.

"At least we have her, and she is safe," Prince Almar said.

Meriel tapped her fingers on her cheek in thought. "Yes, she is safe with us. Hopefully I can talk to her and discover what happened while she was at Dorcha Palace."

The dream faded and blackness enveloped me.

I woke up to find that they had moved me. I was in one of the cages underneath the arena. I could hear the crowd overhead but tuned it out, focusing on the weird dream about Meriel, Prince Almar, and Serafina. *Maybe it was an actual vision of what was happening. I don't really know how the mate bond works, so perhaps that's what it was.* If there was any way it had been real and not my imagination, then I now had more information to work with. Serafina was alive but had been tampered with by Tanyth, and she was going to Jade Wilds. Which meant I knew where to find her—if I ever got out of here.

Prince Tanyth unlocked my cage and stood to the side. I stared at him from the back, unwilling to move.

The prince's eyes narrowed. "Are you sure now is the best time to have a contest of wills?"

I hesitated. I wanted to turn my back to him, and if this had been before I had known I was mated to Serafina, then that's exactly what I would have done. Except now, it was not only me who would suffer, it was my mate. While I knew I would not hesitate to do anything necessary to protect her, I also knew that deliberately pissing off Tanyth would only temporarily sate my anger and do nothing to help me escape.

Avoiding his gaze, I exited the cage. One advantage of being stuck as a snow leopard was not being expected to speak. The cell we were in was not very large, but I selected a spot to sit that was as far away from the prince as I could manage. I could hear the crowd above, so I assumed he was here to tell me something relevant to the impending fight. The prince enjoyed toying with his prey. I hoped for once he would get on with it quickly, so I could fight in the arena and then return to the cage.

Prince Tanyth took a step toward me. The hair on my back rippled; I wasn't sure if he noticed or not. "As before, you must kill your opponent. Or try," The prince said with a smirk.

I remained unmoving. The prince looked me up and down and then simply disappeared. When I was sure he was gone, I flexed my claws, and a few moments later a guard showed up at the door to the cell. "It's time," the guard said, keeping his voice neutral. I recognized him but couldn't remember his name, not that it really mattered. I wasn't going to speak to him mind-to-mind—it would not accomplish anything. I knew if I wanted to escape it would have to be between fights, not during one. There were too many Fae around during the fights.

I followed the guard. He kept glancing over his shoulder at me and I could smell the fear radiating from him. We finally reached the platform that would lift me into the arena. As I brushed past the guard, I could feel him shaking. *Maybe I should try to escape* now. *This nitwit is about to pee his pants, he's not capable of stopping me.* I closed my eyes to block out the guard. I had to focus. I had no idea who or what would face me in the arena, and I needed to do everything in my power to make it out alive.

I heard the chains cranking before the platform began moving. As it slowly creeped upward, white grains of sand began to fall around me. Before the platform came to a halt I leaped out into the arena, paws met with soft white sand. I peered around, scanning for any hint of what might be coming, ears straining for sound. There were four walls about six feet tall in a circle around me, but there were gaps between them that were the width of each wall. It created a barrier for my opponent or myself to hide behind. I eyed the top of the wall, wondering if I could jump onto it, but without knowing how wide it was at the top, I didn't feel that would be a wise decision.

I chose a wall and crouched, prepared to leap on my foe. A gate materialized in the arena wall not too far from my position and rolled open. I backed up, hoping that the warrior on the other side had not noticed where I was.

Immediately after the gate opened, my opponent charged toward me, wearing a mix of darkened plate and chain mail. I ducked around the wall, listening for the telltale clink of the chain links to indicate what the Fae's next move would be.

A sharp tug on my tail had me spinning, claws out, teeth snapping. A cruel laugh echoed from underneath Fae's helmet. That, coupled with the tail tug, I knew it was Callyn. *Shit.* Now it wasn't only my life on the line, but the only Fae I'd ever been close to. *I cannot lose Callyn too.* I decided at that moment that I would do anything I could to ensure Callyn's victory—her life was worth more than mine. Prince Tanyth would be appeased, and Callyn would be safe.

I bunched my haunches and leaped. Callyn ducked as I sailed over her and jabbed upward into my unprotected belly with the hilt of her sword. She missed and I landed with a thud and sprinted to the nearest wall. As I skidded around it, I came face-to-face with a dirty human wielding an axe.

I snarled and darted forward, weaving. The human almost dropped the axe, and I pounced, raking my claws across his unprotected chest, then clamping down on his throat. The crowd roared above me.

I shook my head, sending droplets of blood flying, and peered around the other side of the wall. I caught a glint of metal and thought it was likely Callyn. I creeped forward, though my effort to go unnoticed was undermined by the crowd's shrieks of "Behind you!"

Callyn spun, and we charged toward each other. I swiped at her legs with my claws, but they slid off the plate mail. I felt the burn of her sword as it grazed my back. I recovered quickly and raced back toward her. There was a gap in the plate at her waist and at the back of her legs.

When I was a few strides away, the sand between us started to move, an opening appeared, and a group of three confident humans rose on a platform.

I leaped onto the nearest one before they had made it entirely into the arena. He toppled sideways while the other two tried to skewer me on their swords. I jumped off the platform and retreated. I needed to catch my breath.

Unfortunately, I didn't get the break I wanted. A human female with short hair and a leather vest ran toward me, skillfully swinging an axe. I dodged her first strike and maneuvered behind her, swiping at her unprotected legs.

The human stumbled but did not fall, even as blood leaked heavily from her wounds. Her eyes met mine. "Die, you Fae filth," she hissed, though the words carried, as though they were being magicked so the audience could hear.

*One...two...three...*I leaped for her throat and missed. My claws got caught in her leather armor. I twisted, trying to disengage, when I felt stinging on my forehead. I snarled and brought my hind feet up, claws out, and pumped. I thudded into the sand, free of the human. She took a few wobbly steps and collapsed. I was confused. *Maybe from the head wound*? Then I saw a sword withdraw from the human's back.

I blinked. *Callyn*. I took a deep breath and forced myself to get up. The wounds were not enough to kill me, only to be an annoyance.

We circled each other. I made note of the smears of blood on her armor, her missing helmet, and small scratches on her hands. A low growl started in my throat. Callyn took a step toward me and then we ran toward each other. I twisted out of the way at the last moment, and her sword slammed into the sand and sent up a cloud of dust. I spun and sprinted with everything I had left, hoping to knock her over. She was in my path and then suddenly she wasn't. A sharp pain went through my left hind leg, and I snarled and hissed as my momentum carried me across the sand, sending up a cloud of dust in my wake. Blood dripped into my eyes from the cut on my forehead, and I could feel blood leaking from the deep wound on my left hind leg. I tried to rise, but a wave of dizziness washed over me, and I flopped into the sand. I knew Callyn was coming and would finish me off, as was her right.

A tall shadow fell over me and the cold metal of the sword caressed my throat. As the sword drew a line, there was a sharp stab of pain, followed by a gush of blood, and then nothing.

Fifty

SERAFINA

Philanna and I spent a week working on stealth techniques. By the end of the week, I felt confident I could sneak up on any humans I encountered and maybe about fifty percent of the Fae. The headaches unfortunately had not resolved, though they did not get any worse.

Meriel had mentioned last night that she had another matter to discuss. I was expecting it to be a new training technique since I had adequately mastered stealth. Once again, I headed to the table set up for breakfast.

I filled a bowl with eggs, sausage, and potatoes, then sat down. Meriel came over as I stuck my first bite in my mouth.

"Good morning," Meriel said in greeting. I gave her a nod and started chewing my food.

"Your grandfather has requested you return to court," Meriel said.

I dropped my fork, which fell straight into my eggs and scattered them everywhere, on me and all over the table. "My grandfather?" *It's about time. I thought I was going to see King Pharaan right after I returned.*

"Yes, King Leonard. It appears your uncle has met an untimely death and now you are the sole surviving heir. The king's health has been declining the past couple of years. His message was urgent and not a request; it was an order. You will return and take your place as heir of Gaskal and future Lady of the South," Meriel announced.

I stared at her, dumbfounded. Not only was she talking about a different king, but what she said was impossible. *Me, heir?* Struggling to process her words, questions and memories wound through me. I distinctly remembered being told I would be returned to my family. *I assumed I would be returning to my Fae family, but perhaps that was my mistake. I have a human family too.* Sadness washed over me. *They're dead.* Or at least my parents were. The king of Gaskal had never done anything to warrant me calling him family.

"This wasn't supposed to happen," I muttered.

"Life doesn't always follow the path we expect," said Meriel sympathetically.

My thoughts whirred around my head as I struggled to comprehend what she had told me. "I don't know anything about how to be an heir."

Meriel gave me a sad smile. "Yes you do. What do you think all your training these past twelve years has been for?"

"My *human* grandfather would never allow a Fae warrior to become queen of Gaskal. The other human kings will never acknowledge a female in the role of Lord of the South," I said, frustration bubbling up. King Leonard had hated my mother and held no love for me.

Meriel sighed. "Serafina. First off, you are only half-Fae. In this situation your physical traits that favor your human half are in your favor. When someone looks at you, the first thing that comes to mind is human. The monthly etiquette lessons and tests, those have been to prepare you for spending time in a human court."

350

My anger rose. "You knew this would happen!"

"No, I did not. What I did know is that one day you might wish to visit your father's family and that you would be more comfortable if you had a grasp of their culture. It would allow you to be less foreign to them," Meriel explained.

I didn't want to believe her—I wanted to blame her for the predicament I was in. "Do I have a choice?" I asked.

"No. When your mother brought you here, she knew this possibility existed, but hoped for your sake it would never come to pass," Meriel replied.

"Why?" I asked, trying to keep a sob from escaping. I felt so alone.

"Because it is a lonely road you walk, as a link between two species. Becoming heir and eventually the queen of Gaskal is not going to ease your burden, it will only add to it," Meriel explained.

"Can Ghilanna come with me?" I asked with hope in my voice. Maybe if my friend could come, then it wouldn't feel like I was getting exiled.

Meriel shook her head. "No, she cannot. She is not human and the king anticipated you might ask to bring companions and said it was not to be permitted. He is confident when you arrive you will find new friends among the courtiers."

Tears began to trickle down my cheek. *Alone, again.* The news rocked me to my very core. I was being ordered to the place my mother had rescued me from, back to the people who were certain to hate me now that I was expected to one day rule. I angrily wiped the tears from my face. "When do I leave?" I finally asked.

"You leave tomorrow. Don't bother packing. I have a trunk of items you are permitted to take and you will get an entirely new wardrobe when you arrive at the palace," Meriel said.

Why does this feel familiar? I bit my lip as a sharp pain formed behind my eyes. *Perhaps if I go to Gaskal I will get rid of the headaches.*

I ate my food in silence and then put my dishes in the dirty dish bin and went back to my tent. There was nothing I could do about it. I was leaving for Gaskal tomorrow.

Fifty-One

TRISTAN

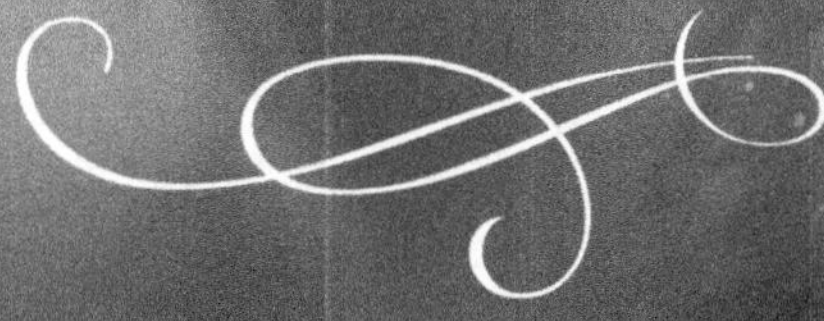

When I woke up, my leg and head were throbbing, and I didn't recognize where I was. The walls and ceiling were made of light gray stone, but there were no windows and at first I was sure I was still at Prince Tanyth's court. A door slowly opened and to my surprise Callyn walked through. She had a bandage on her arm, but otherwise was the picture of health.

"You're…" I gasped as I realized the words came out of my mouth. I glanced down and my eyes got huge as it sank in that I no longer had a collar around my neck and that I was in my Fae form.

"Hi," Callyn said and cautiously walked into the room.

"Where are we?" I asked, a thread of fear worked its way through me. The collar was gone, and I was in an unfamiliar room with Callyn. *Is this some trick*?

"We are…well, I really shouldn't tell you. But we are safe, that is all you need to know for now," Callyn replied.

"How?" I asked incredulously.

"Magic. I made it look like you were dead, and since *he* has no use for you dead, he disposed of your body as he does with other beasts," Callyn replied, keeping her voice soft. She sat at the edge of the bed and tentatively set a hand on my sheet-covered leg.

"We're free," I said, eyes wide, not sure I was ready to believe it.

Callyn nodded. "Yes, we're free. The prince released me from my contract when I killed you."

I stared at her. We were both clearly still wounded, but somehow, she had managed to get us both free. This female, whom I loved like a sister, and had put through hell and more to please the prince, had saved me. And yet I had a feeling that escaping Prince Tanyth couldn't have been that easy. Someday, sometime, the other shoe would drop.

"I don't know where Serafina is, if that is your next question. I can only manage one task at a time right now, and making sure we are both healthy is my top priority. Once we are both well, then I promise we will find her. No matter what it takes," Callyn said.

I closed my eyes, emotions roiling close to the surface. "You should hate me," I finally said in the barest of whispers.

Callyn's fingers grabbed my chin lightly and I opened my eyes. "You were only trying to survive, as was I. Were there times where I hated you? Yes. But *I do not hate you*, Tristan. Honestly, I don't know if I would have survived as long as I did if you hadn't been there."

I pulled my hand out from underneath the sheet and squeezed her hand lightly. "As long as things are okay between us."

Callyn nodded, and I swore I could see the glisten of tears in her eyes, but I kept that knowledge to myself.

"Are you hungry?" she asked. My stomach gurgled loudly, and we both burst out laughing. "I'll take that as a yes."

I gave her a small smile. "How long was I unconscious for?"

The smile fell from her face. "Three days. You would mumble things. 'Embergate' was one of the words you repeated a few times. I knew you were still alive when you did that. But I was not expecting you to need that long to heal."

My lips twitched. "I was dreaming about the end of my training at Embergate and some memories when I first took command of Prince Tanyth's warriors."

"Interesting," Callyn murmured, then stood up. "C'mon, let's get some food. I think if you can talk to me for this long you should be able to manage going into the other room and sitting at the table to eat."

I could feel pain radiating down my leg and was not nearly as confident as Callyn was that I could walk. But I decided that if she felt it was worth trying, I might as well. Besides, it would be useful to know if I could walk in case we needed to leave in a hurry. Callyn did not seem concerned that Prince Tanyth could find us here or would even come looking, but I was not nearly as optimistic.

I woke up to voices in the other room. I recognized Callyn's immediately, but it took a few minutes before I could identify the male.

"We need to see King Pharaan, it's urgent," Callyn insisted.

"He has greater concerns than granting either of you an audience," Prince Almar replied.

"The king is not worried about his granddaughter?" she demanded.

"You mean Serafina? He knows exactly where she is and that she is safe," Prince Almar said harshly.

Relief washed through me. Even if Prince Almar wasn't willing to share details, knowing that Serafina was safe was enough for me. The door shut and then I could hear Callyn's footsteps as she approached my room.

"Did you hear that?" she asked.

I nodded. "Enough to know Serafina is safe."

Callyn grimaced. "Safe, yes, but by whose standards? I would feel better about the whole thing if we could talk to King Pharaan, but you are in no shape to make a more formal request and per the royal family, I have no status."

I was not sure where she thought I had acquired any sort of status. Maybe there was some information she had that I was not yet aware of. "Now what?"

"You need to finish healing. Then we will go to Jade Wilds, which is where I have determined Serafina is, and see for ourselves how she is doing," Callyn said firmly.

"Sounds like a good plan," I replied, yawning.

"Rest, my friend. I will wake you if anything changes," Callyn said and gave my shoulder a squeeze.

Fifty-Two

SERAFINA

The morning of my departure, Aurae, the Fae assigned to help me, had come into my tent first thing and woken me up. Meriel had said nothing about departing early. I had nightmares about running down the hall of the palace in Gaskal, screaming. Something had been chasing me, but whenever I turned around there was nothing there.

Most of my belongings were still in the tent, which spoke volumes about how little I was truly allowed to take with me. Aurae was holding a garment wrapped in gold paper. I sat up in bed and beckoned her to open it. She revealed an ivory dress with an overlayer of gold lace, I also spied a petticoat and corset below the bulk of the dress.

"Meriel wants me to help you get dressed. There will be a light breakfast for you in the carriage and lunch at the palace," Aurae explained.

I tossed off the covers and stood up. Aurae gasped when she realized I was completely naked. I didn't care what she thought. The headache Meriel had promised to help me with was still raging, causing the control I had on my temper to fray at an alarming rate. "Are you going to help me get dressed or stare at me?" I snapped.

Aurae lowered her eyes and laid the dress out on the bed. She handed me the petticoat first. This one was wider than anything I'd worn before. I glanced over at my weapon rack, wondering if I could get away with strapping daggers to my legs. *When she leaves, I will,* I decided.

It took the two of us about thirty minutes to get me into the dress and my hair up. I had not been expecting to wear a crown; it felt strange to have weight on my head that was not an armored helmet. The myriads of pins in my hair to keep it in place only added to my headache.

Aurae walked around me, checking for anything she missed. She was about to start a third circuit when I put my hand up. "It's fine. You have done your job. Now, please, I would like a few moments to myself." She nodded and then departed.

I blew out my breath in relief and hustled over to the rack. The ridiculous shoes they had picked out for me would make it almost impossible to hide a dagger at my ankles, but I could wear the thigh sheaths. It took me far longer than I had expected to get them on. The skirts kept shifting and getting in the way of the buckles.

I finished and stood up, straightening my dress and making sure I hadn't messed anything up in the mirror before heading outside.

A large gold carriage was parked in the training area. The way the sun made it sparkle, I was confident it was real gold. Four matched white horses were harnessed to it. The driver and attendants were wearing hunter green, cream, and gold livery of the king of Gaskal.

Everyone nearby stopped talking when I emerged. Most of them bowed or curtsied too. It felt wrong. I studied each of their faces, wondering what they thought of my transformation. After the battle at Emerald Valley, I had earned everyone's respect, so that finally after all these years I was equal to the other Fae warriors. Yet here I was, parading around like a human and departing to begin my journey as heir and future queen of Gaskal.

I was disappointed that Meriel had not come to say goodbye, but I was being ushered into the carriage and not allowed to delay my departure. I sighed in resignation and climbed in. The door snicked shut behind me.

As Aurae had promised, there was a tray with an assortment of pastries for me to snack on. I ignored it and kept my gaze focused on Jade Wilds.

I am to be queen of Gaskal, my grandfather hates Fae, and I am never going to be allowed to come back here again. The friends I made, the respect I have earned, it has all been for nothing.

As the carriage picked up speed, we entered a thicker section of the forest, and I could have sworn I saw a large white cat following us. But when I blinked it was gone, leaving me with a headache from hell. I shut my eyes and drifted off to sleep, dreaming of deep blue eyes.

Epilogue

TRISTAN

I pulled the hood up tighter around my face, not that I had anything to worry about—no one here could see through the magic glamor, even if they caught a glimpse of my face in the shadow of the hood. I was sitting at a table at Wayside Inn.

My plan to seek aid from King Pharaan was a bust. I had thought he of all the Fae would have been most invested in rescuing her, but I had clearly been mistaken. *Or no one believed me.* I briefly closed my eyes, unwilling to admit that the reason for my failure hadn't been because King Pharaan didn't believe in the lost Fae queen, but because without Serafina at my side, I failed to prove she was my mate.

Now I was surrounded by humans, at an inn in Gaskal, searching for a way to prove that she was my mate and the lost Fae queen. Even though I knew she was in the palace, the mating bond had not changed; it remained dull, and she was unresponsive to my attempts at contacting her through it. I prayed that if I could get close enough to Serafina, it would become vibrant again.

There was a thump. My eyes snapped open and I had a dagger at the newcomer's throat before I recognized Callyn.

Her gaze fierce, Callyn announced, "I have a plan to get to Serafina."

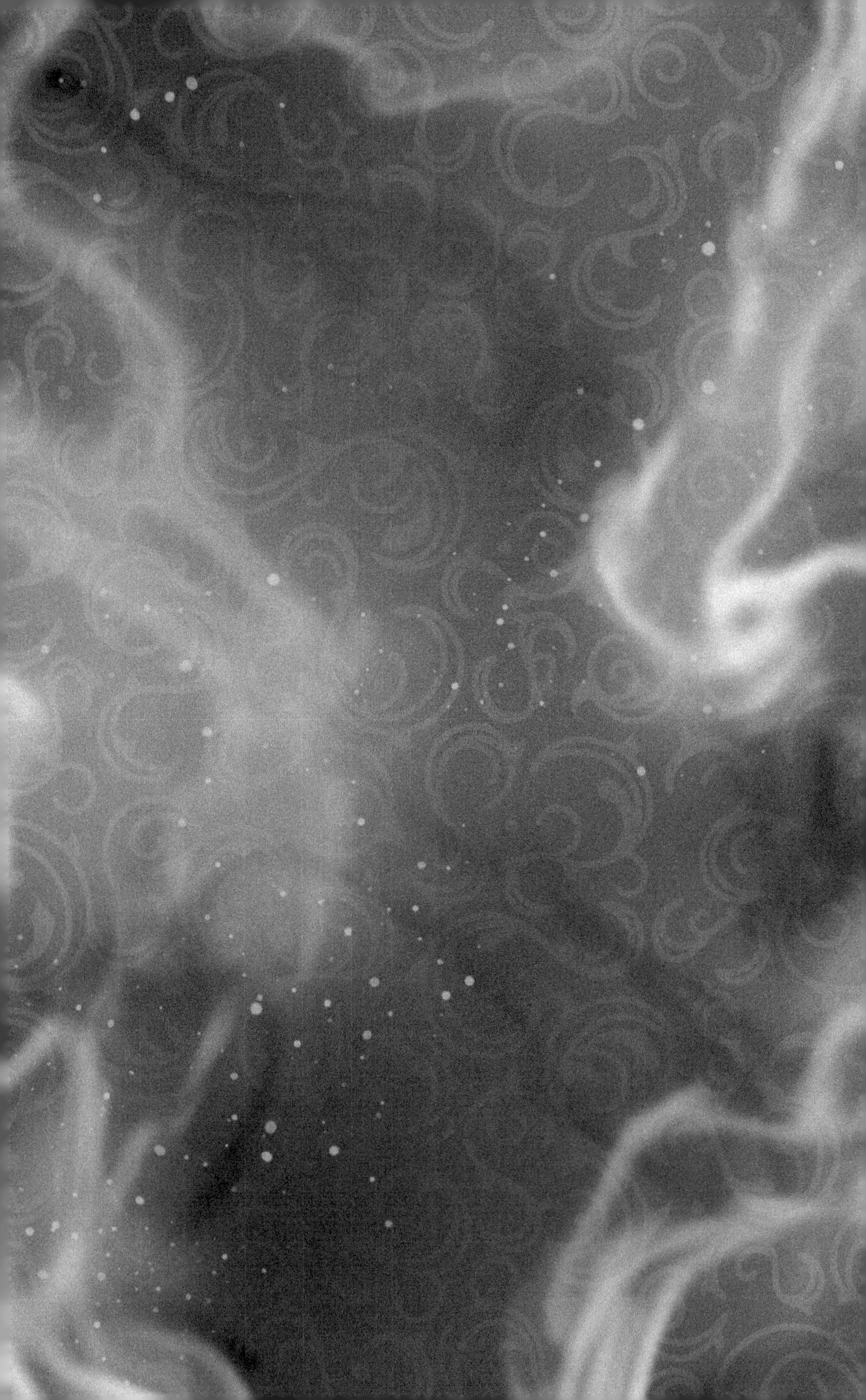

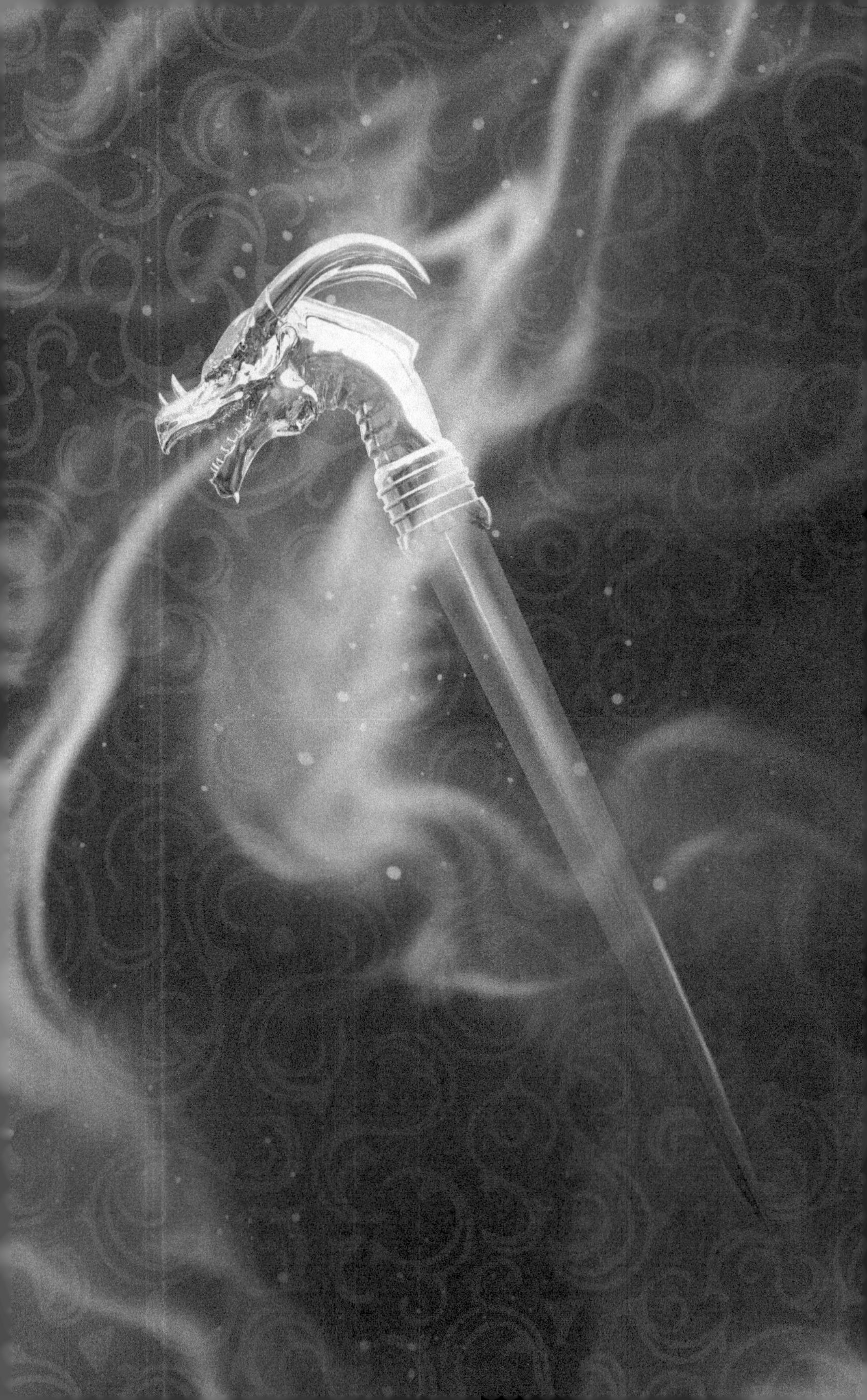

ABOUT THE AUTHOR

E.R. Jensen was born and raised in Los Angeles, California. She has lived in Oregon and Idaho, and currently resides in Atlanta, GA with her husband and three sons.

When not writing E.R. can be found enjoying her horses, traveling, and spending time with her family.

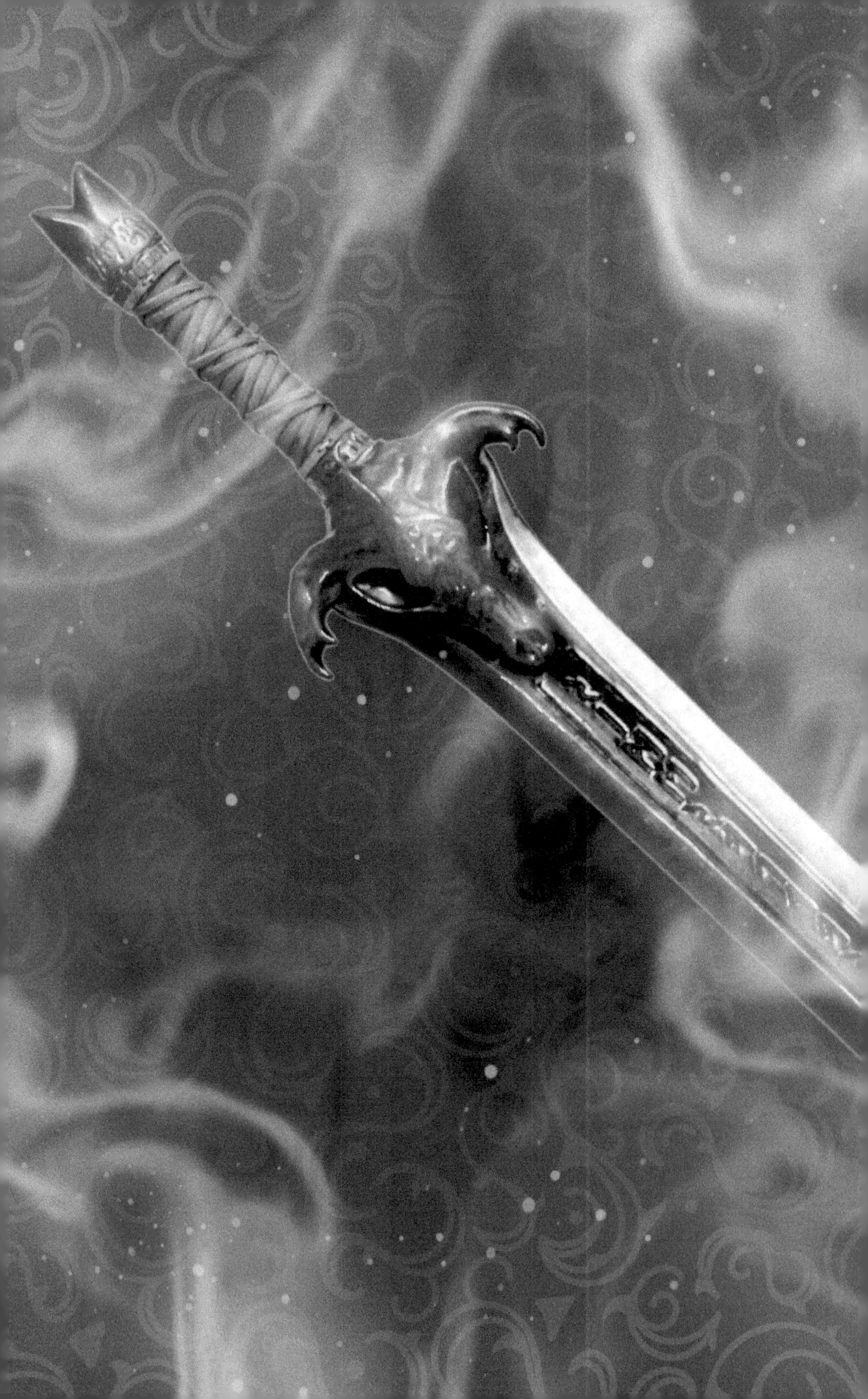

ACKNOWLEDGEMENTS

Diving into a new genre wouldn't have been possible without my amazing team. Therena C. I appreciate our new friendship and your willingness to advise as I navigate the challenges I'm facing. Melissa thank you to for bringing my vision to life in the design of the book. Madison thank you for giving me the push I needed to develop Tristan into the character he was meant to become.

COMING SOON

Heir of Blood
Lost Fae Queen Book Two